REMEMBERERS

C. EDWARD BALDWIN

Ink & Stone
PUBLISHING

REMEMBERERS

Ink & Stone Publishing

ISBN-13: 978-0692356760
ISBN-10: 0692356752

Cover Design by Clarissa Yeo
Yocla Designs
www.yocladesigns.com

Ink & Stone
PUBLISHING
The Carolinas * Georgia * Virginia

This is for Matheral & Natasha

Rememberers

"Ignorance is not bliss; it's dangerous." - Josh Levy

By C. Edward Baldwin

Ink & Stone
PUBLISHING

REMEMBERERS

CHAPTER ONE

Thursday, August 20

A shadow of a person's head stretched across the length of the basketball court, ending just north of the free throw line at Father Frank McCarthy's feet. McCarthy dribbled the ball on the edge of the shadow head two times before shooting and ultimately swishing the free throw. It was his tenth make in a row—his own version of being *in the zone.* He retrieved the ball and this time went to the near side corner of the court. He didn't look back at the gate. If shadow head wanted to talk, McCarthy thought, he'd only to open the door to the half gate and come on in. Eying the goal, he launched a high arching shot toward the basket. It found its mark perfectly.

The basketball court was half the size of a regulation one and was squeezed into the back parking lot of Our Lady of Faith Catholic Church. A few dozen parking spaces had been sacrificed for its creation, but none of the parishioners, at least not publicly, begrudged their six-foot-eight priest a little recreation area to partake in his favorite sport. Rumor was that McCarthy, a former center on his college basketball team, had had a decent shot at playing professionally somewhere in the world if not for his higher calling.

Swish! Shot number twelve, this one from the top of the key, dropped effortlessly through the basket.

"Looks like you're pretty good," a deep baritone said from behind him.

Without looking in the direction of the shadow head, the obvious owner of the deep voice, McCarthy went back to the free throw line, dribbling the ball. "I'm fair, I suppose. Care for a little one on one?"

The door gate creaked open, and McCarthy heard dress shoes clack across the cement. "I'm afraid I'm not properly attired."

Shot number thirteen also found its mark. "Maybe next time then," McCarthy said. After retrieving the ball, he turned to face his visitor. Though not as tall as the priest, the stranger had above average height nonetheless. McCarthy guessed his height to be around six-three. He wore a dark brown suit with a blue tie loosened at the collar. He was young, thirtyish perhaps, with a good mop of brown hair. Judging by his dress, demeanor, and the briefcase clutched in his left hand, McCarthy guessed a government man.

Confirming the priest's mental assessment, the stranger extended his right hand. "Special Agent Dennard Bennett."

The agent's grip was strong. "Special Agent? What's with the briefcase? I don't see many of those."

"I carry one on occasion," Bennett said.

"You're FBI?" McCarthy asked.

"Immigration and Customs Enforcement," Bennett said.

"ICE," McCarthy said. "Well, what brings you to my neck of the woods?"

"Phillip Beamer."

McCarthy's eyebrows furrowed as if trying to place the name. "Phillip Beamer? Is he an illegal immigrant?"

"No, he *was* a US citizen."

"Should I know him?"

"I don't know," Bennett said. "I was hoping you could tell me."

"Why don't you just ask him?"

"I can't. He's dead."

2

McCarthy put the basketball down and nodded toward a bench near the gate. A small tree stretched over the gate, partially covering the bench, and offered a welcome respite from the late summer sun. The two men walked over to the bench. Bennett sat down at one end of it while McCarthy reached into a cooler that had been placed at its other end. He pulled out two plastic bottles of water, handed one to Bennett, and sat down beside him. "Dead? I don't understand."

Bennett put the briefcase down by his feet. He twisted the cap off the bottle of water, and took a long swig. "Man, that's good and cold." He wiped his mouth with the back of his hand. "Beamer was murdered."

"Murdered? Well, he couldn't have been a member of my parish," McCarthy said. "I would've heard about a murder."

"The murder wasn't committed here in Philadelphia. It happened in South Carolina."

"South Carolina? Then what brings you here?"

Bennett placed the water bottle at his feet and then picked up the briefcase, laying it across his lap. He opened it, producing a sandwich-sized plastic bag. He opened the bag carefully and pulled out a slip of paper, handing it to McCarthy.

Taking the piece of paper, McCarthy placed his water bottle down on the ground. He read the words out loud. "I am the Alpha and the Omega, the First and the Last, the Beginning and the End." He looked at Bennett as if to say, "And?"

"Do you know anything about it?" Bennett asked.

"It's Revelation 22:13."

"Anything else?"

"Like what?"

"What does it mean?"

McCarthy looked at him curiously. "What does my take on this passage have to do with the death in South Carolina?"

"There wasn't just the death in South Carolina. There were two others. One in London, and another in Cairo. The verse was found near each victim."

"You're saying the three murders are connected?" McCarthy asked.

"It appears so."

"That's a rather large geographical area for a serial killer, don't you think?"

"I don't think we're dealing with a serial killer."

McCarthy's eyebrows pinched upward. "Oh, then what are you dealing with?"

"I don't know. But that's why I'm here."

"Here? Why here? What could I possibly know about this?"

Bennett reached back into the plastic bag and this time pulled out a business card. He handed the card to McCarthy. "Look at this."

McCarthy took the card from him and handed back the slip of paper. He looked at the card; a corner of his mouth lifted slightly. It was one of his.

Father Frank McCarthy

Our Lady of Faith Catholic Church

19 S. 14th Street, Philadelphia, PA 19107

215 555 2332

FatherMcC@ymail.com

McCarthy shrugged his shoulders indifferently. "I pass these out all over."

"Flip it over," Bennett said.

McCarthy turned the card over. In red scribbly penmanship were the words:

McCarthy Knows.

Bennett watched McCarthy carefully as the priest read the words without emotion. "The card was found among Beamer's belongings. You have any idea how he would have gotten it?"

McCarthy handed the card back to Bennett. "I don't know. It's like I said before. I pass these out all over the place. It's just another way to spread the gospel." He smiled uneasily.

Bennett put the card back into the plastic bag alongside the slip of paper, and then put the plastic bag back into the briefcase. Next, he took out a picture and held it up for McCarthy to see. "Do you recognize him?"

McCarthy studied the picture levitating in front of him and then slowly shook his head. "I'm afraid I don't. Is that Beamer?"

"It is."

McCarthy cleared a little phlegm from his throat and looked away from the picture. "Does he have any family in the area?"

"We haven't been able to locate any next of kin. So far, you're the only lead."

"Lead? Well, that's quite unfortunate. It makes me sorry that I can't be of more help."

"What is it that you know, Father?" Bennett asked. He placed the picture back inside the briefcase.

McCarthy bit his lower lip, shaking his head negatively. "Nothing of this, I'm afraid."

"Have you received any phone calls or emails from Phillip Beamer?"

"Doubtful. I get a ton of email. But the name doesn't ring a bell. I'll certainly go through my email this evening and let you know if the name shows up."

"Mind if I check your computer?"

McCarthy chuckled reflexively before realizing that the agent's request had been a serious one. McCarthy shook his head slowly. "I'm sorry, but I do. You must understand that many of my emails are from members of my congregation. Most of the emails are of very personal and private natures. I don't think the authors would like any eyes outside of mine viewing them." He retrieved his water bottle from near his foot and drained it. Afterwards, he tossed the empty bottle into the open-top metal trash barrel a couple of feet from the bench. "I wish I could be of more help. I really do. But I have no idea why a Phillip Beamer would have my business card with those words written on the back. And I certainly have no idea how three people a world apart from each other would reference the same biblical quote. I suspect it's probably all mere coincidence."

"That's a helluva coincidence, wouldn't you say?"

"Maybe. But then again, maybe this sort of thing isn't so unusual after all."

"Meaning?" Bennett said.

"We're a lot more connected due to the internet these days. It's possible that the individuals were linked in that way and were no closer than so called Facebook friends."

Bennett took another swallow of water. "I guess anything's possible. But there's something else you should know, Father."

McCarthy tilted his head. "And that's..."

"All three victims had been suspected in the plotting of terrorist acts. Plots in Cairo and London were thwarted last year. A plot in South Carolina was averted just last week. Three foiled plots, three dead terrorism suspects."

"You're certain these victims were involved in the planned attacks?" McCarthy asked.

"Investigations are still ongoing," Bennett said. "But I will say in relation to Beamer that evidence of a planned attack on a federal building was found on his computer hard drive. He was killed before the attack could be carried out."

"Maybe that too was a coincidence. Maybe his death didn't have anything to do with terrorist intentions."

Bennett chuckled this time. "You're a big fan of coincidences. Humor me for a moment and assume, for argument's sake, that all three deaths were related and all three murders were committed by the same individual or group. Why quote that Biblical verse? Why place your business card with the cryptic message 'McCarthy Knows' on the body of the last victim?"

"I don't know," McCarthy said with an air of irritation. "I suppose it's another mystery of life. Forgive me if this sounds somewhat callous, but if three people are dead who were planning to murder hundreds, if not thousands, of innocent people, then would that not be a good thing?"

"Killing someone is not necessarily a good thing, Father."

"I believe some capital punishment advocates would disagree," McCarthy said solemnly.

Bennett placed his briefcase back down onto the bench and then stood up, carrying the water bottle to the trash barrel. He stared down into it for a second before dropping the bottle inside it. He turned back toward McCarthy. "We can't have people conducting their own terrorist investigations, certainly not to the extent of sentencing people and then ultimately executing them. We need to find out who's behind these killings and how they're getting their information. Now personally, I don't really care how these vigilantes are finding out about terrorists, be it psychics, fortune cookies, or freaking images found in a jar of mayonnaise. What I do care about is people taking the law into their own hands. They should hand over whatever information they have to the authorities."

"And once this information is in the hand of the authorities?"

Bennett returned to his spot on the bench. "We'll analyze it for relevance and proceed accordingly."

McCarthy stood up. The sun had shifted positions and now his shadow was cast over Bennett, engulfing the agent in a blanket of darkness. "It seems Mr. Bennett that someone has elected to cut out the middle man. But I will be of little to no use in helping you find this someone. I don't know anything about any terror attacks or dead terrorists. I'm a Catholic priest. I know about the Trinity. If you come to Mass on Sunday, I'll be more than willing to share with you all that I know on that particular subject."

Bennett peered up at the priest. "You sure there's nothing else you wish to tell me, Father?"

"I'm afraid not," McCarthy said. "And now, if you'll excuse me, I have a few more minutes of recreation time."

Bennett looked casually over at the court. "Sure, Father. But there's one other thing." He reopened the briefcase and this time pulled out a couple of 5X7 photos, handing them to McCarthy.

The priest took the pictures, looking at them reluctantly. They were crime scene photos. His mouth opened immediately.

"Beamer's head was nearly decapitated," Bennett said. "A sick bastard did that. Most of those stab wounds you see there were done postmortem. And the words, 'McCarthy Knows,' on the back of your business card were written in the victim's blood." He paused as if intending to drive the ominous point home. "If you know something, Father..."

McCarthy cut the detective off, pushing the photos back into his hands. "I don't," he said simply, and turned, walking quickly back onto the court.

Bennett called after him. "If you don't mind, I'd like to sit here a while. My flight doesn't leave for a couple of hours."

"Stay as long as you want," McCarthy said. He retrieved his basketball and went back to the free throw line. Looking mournfully back at Bennett, he opened his mouth to say something, but then smacked his lips shut without saying another word.

At 10:05 p.m. that same evening, McCarthy finally received a return call from Bishop Richard Boland. Boland was the Catholic Church's ranking stateside representative in the Alliance of Initiates (A.I.). A.I. was a subgroup of the United Religions Organization (URO), which had been modeled after the United Nations and had a single goal of uniting all the world's religions into one global organization. When the call came in, McCarthy was sitting alone in his office with his feet propped up on his desk, his gaze rotating from his desktop phone to the framed, vintage Larry Bird poster displayed prominently in the center of his office wall. He'd placed the call over five hours ago, getting Boland's voicemail. Unsurprisingly to McCarthy, his initial concern after the ICE agent's visit had not been about whether he himself was being deemed a suspect in a capital murder case, but rather what his negligible connection to Beamer's murder would mean for URO and its offspring, A.I. Was this but the first shoe to drop in the possible unraveling of one of history's longest held and best kept secrets? As he'd waited for Boland's return call, he'd realized that his initial concern may have been a bit superfluous.

For 99.5 percent of mankind's present and past, A.I. wasn't even a figment of the imagination. It simply did not exist. Even amongst the initiated, the organization's history and origin was shrouded in as much mystery as the combined histories and origins of the Bible, Koran, Torah, and the tenets of Buddhism and Hinduism. Although its mother group, the URO, had its coming out party in the year 2000 (five years after announcing its intent to form a religions organization patterned after the United Nations), there would be no such coming out party for A.I. The organization still believed, as the URO had for many years, that the world was still not yet ready for certain truths. It was the very reason for URO's self-concealment throughout its history. The organization, despite its fairly recent announcement, had actually been in existence well before the birth of the United Nations. In fact, some of the senior members of URO routinely bragged amongst themselves that the UN was actually based off of it rather than the other way around.

For years, neither URO nor A.I. kept written records. The only people who knew of the existence of either were its members. And these were individuals who'd been gleaned from the rolls of the world's varied religions and were used to keeping secrets. But after its year 2000 public outing, URO made a fair amount of information about itself available on the internet. Outside of race and nationality, religion remained the most dangerous bastion of separation amongst people. Worldwide, more people were still being killed in the name of religion than for any other reason. URO's self-disclosure was its effort to start the tides of change. But A.I., for the foreseeable future, would remain as it'd always been—nonexistent.

The full criterion for acceptance into A.I. was a closely guarded secret, kept by a small handful of its elders who only passed it on orally to longstanding members of A.I. who'd been chosen in a manner more rigorous and selective than the initial selection process to get into URO. However, the first step was a relatively cut and dried one—acceptance into URO. Afterwards, potentials for A.I. were observed and tapped for membership by a sitting A.I. member who'd confirmed the individual's enlightenment and could verify the individual's correct decoding of the allegorically hidden messages in the individual's chosen religion's documented history, e.g. the Bible, or Torah. And subsequently, but perhaps more importantly, the individual's categorical acceptance of the truths thus revealed.

After a quick exchange of greetings and niceties, Boland said, "Your voicemail sounded tense."

"I was visited by an ICE agent today."

"With regard to?" Boland asked.

"Phillip Beamer."

"Phillip Beamer," Boland repeated sourly. "What brought an ICE agent to Philadelphia concerning a death in South Carolina?" The bishop was formerly of Philadelphia but now lived in an oratory in Rock Hill, South Carolina. He'd ordained McCarthy twenty years ago, bringing him into A.I. ten years later. Although McCarthy would never admit it publicly or privately, he trusted Boland more than he did the Pope.

"My business card was found on Beamer's body."

A bit of spit had obviously risen up in Boland's mouth; McCarthy could hear him swallowing it back down. "Your card? He's getting clever."

"Well, that's one way of putting it," McCarthy said.

"And you have another?"

"Desperate. Conniving. But I feel he's up to something else."

"Such as..."

McCarthy leaned back in his chair, rubbing his chin. "I don't pretend to know more about Rememberers than what A.I. has shown me. I know that they have the ability to remember past life cycles. I know that we're able to use that ability to document major disasters and tragedies, including terrorist attacks that have occurred in the previous life-cycle. And by doing so, A.I. has been able to prevent some of those tragedies from occurring in our current cycle, and thereby saving countless lives. I know that not all tragedies are created equal. For reasons known only to A.I., some have still been allowed to happen. I don't question the reason for the discrepancy as I've never questioned A.I. Mainly because I know that there are still some truths that I'm still not privy to. And I imagine that A.I.'s reasoning for the discrepancy is based on those truths. But I still maintain that the altering of history or the future is dangerous. I feel he is going to show us how."

"I see," Boland said.

"Our rogue Rememberer doesn't care about reasoning. I believe his intent is to create chaos. If we don't find him soon, he will accomplish whatever he's seeking to do. And whatever that is can't be good for mankind."

"We mustn't panic."

"He's taunting us," McCarthy said strongly. "The Bible verse, the card, the mutilations."

Boland groaned noticeably. "Mutilations?"

"Yes, apparently he visited Beamer after our man left. What he did to the body is unspeakable. I think it's his way of letting us know that he's no longer content with us beating him to the punch. He's an egotistical maniac. And he's sending us a message that he's about to up the game."

"What message?"

"On the back of the card, he scribbled 'McCarthy Knows' in blood. That was for us."

McCarthy knows?" Boland repeated.

"The agent wanted to know if I knew what it meant."

"This agent, does he suspect you're somehow involved?"

"It's hard to say. But he didn't fly all the way up here just to say hello. I imagine the authorities had nothing before and now finding my card on Beamer's body gives them something. Between the card and the cryptic message, the rogue is accomplishing exactly what he wanted to."

"And that's?"

"Putting the authorities on our trail will get us off his. At the very least, it'll slow us down. I believe it's also his way of letting us know that he's upping the ante."

"Upping it to what?" Boland asked, his tone indicating he hadn't fully accepted that proposition. "Doing his own terrorism?

McCarthy stared absently at the Larry Bird poster and didn't immediately answer. "That's a possibility. He knows what we know. We know what he knows. He could have warned Beamer that we knew about him. He could have gotten him to change plans, to blow up something at another time and place. But he decided not to. Instead, he allowed Beamer to be killed, and then he goes behind us and mutilates the body, placing my business card on it. Why?"

"I admit it's curiously sadistic. But, he's a madman. The ability has affected him. There's much we still don't understand about it. Perhaps seeing tragedy even before it actually happens has warped him somehow."

"I think there's more to it than that," McCarthy said. "He's up to something. I know it."

"What does our man say about this theory of yours?"

"I haven't discussed it with him," McCarthy said flatly. "I called you first. You should advise A.I."

"I will. But you should fill him in."

McCarthy took a deep breath. "He's closer to you."

"In proximity only," Boland paused. "He's your mentee."

"Yes, I know."

"Hmm," Boland said. "I sense your reluctance to talk with him."

McCarthy took a deep breath. "I have another thought. Only I'm not sure how to say it."

"You simply say it," Boland said.

"I think we should pull him off of this."

"Pull him off?"

"Yes," McCarthy said slowly, measuring his words. "He hasn't been the same since London. He's different."

"How is he different?" Boland asked.

"It's hard to explain. But even still, maybe the way we're using Rememberers wasn't God's intent for the ability in the first place. Maybe it's like you said—affecting. Maybe it's a disease to be eradicated with the rogue being the first to be infected, with the others soon to follow. We're giving Rememberers too much power. We're eliminating people based on their information. We're allowing them to play God. We're allowing *him* to play God. It's dangerous."

"You worry too much," Boland said.

"Someone has to," McCarthy retorted.

"It doesn't have to be you," Boland said glibly. "A.I. is much stronger than you think. And they're impressed with him. Taking him off this is not an option."

McCarthy stiffened, bracing himself for the impact of his next statement. "I'm not saying just take him off this. I think he should be removed from A.I. altogether. Put him back with the other two on the URO level."

Boland literally shouted. "Are you mad? Need I remind you that he's your submit in the first place, a very unique find I might add. A.I. was most thrilled with your submission. We once again have a bona fide Rememberer within our ranks. Do you understand the significance? It's due to a Rememberer that A.I. even exists in the first place."

"I'm aware of the history," McCarthy said irritably.

"Then you're aware of how important the remembering ability is to A.I."

"He'll still be a part of URO, just like the others. We'll still have access to his ability."

"It's not the same," Boland countered.

"A.I. is bigger than one being," McCarthy said. He was down to clichés now, not a good sign, but he pressed on anyway. "He's too unpredictable, as ironic as that may sound. I believe he could be more dangerous than the rogue."

"I disagree. He's young, brash, and maybe even a little cocky. But he's not dangerous. Youthful vigor is no threat. It only needs to be tamed. You should rein him in, not stifle him."

McCarthy rubbed his forehead with one hand while gripping the receiver harder with the other. "Rein him in without stifling him? You know his history. He could have a little of his father in him. How am I to rein that in?"

"Oh my, mentee, have you not learned anything in all our years together? The apple doesn't necessarily fall close to the tree. Don't let jealousy guide you."

McCarthy was silent for a moment. This was classic Boland, quick to sucker punch. But McCarthy wasn't biting. "My only concern is for the Church."

Boland feigned ignorance. "And what concern is this?"

"If the feds were to dig and were somehow able to unearth our association with A.I., we could quite possibly have a monumental crisis on our hands, making the sex abuse scandal look like jaywalking."

Boland laughed faintly. "I never imagined you to be melodramatic. But let me soothe your concerns. Although A.I.'s beliefs may be somewhat unconventional and hard for the average person to grasp, they will eventually be known and accepted by all. Truth is truth. But in the unlikely event that the feds were to dig up a connection between A.I. and the Church, and the Church deemed the world still not ready to accept truth, then I, you, and a very small minority in the Church's hierarchy as a result of those findings would fall on our swords. The Church would quickly disavow any knowledge of A.I. as well as dissociate itself from the activities of obviously roguish members of its clergy. The Church would ultimately survive and would no doubt emerge as strong as ever. Remember, it's been historically adept at handling scandals of all sorts. Besides, it's like you'd said before—some decisions are made based on certain truths that you're not privy to."

McCarthy went silent again. Then, after a few moments, he said, "You're right. He's young. I'll rein him in."

"Good," Boland said. "But don't stifle him."

"Wouldn't dream of it," McCarthy said.

CHAPTER TWO

Monday, August 24

Detective Jeremy Stint looked absently at the clock on the wall of his office. He was vaguely aware that it was 7:30 p.m. But his mind wasn't on the time. He was thinking about Phillip Beamer's murder. The murder, which had been committed in the first week of August, had been the first murder in Buckleton in nearly a decade. Murders in Buckleton were as rare as a truth-telling politician. The town was located in a sweet spot in South Carolina about halfway between Charlotte and Columbia. It was off the beaten path for drug runners, therefore drug traffickers and the peripheral trouble usually accompanying them tended to avoid it. It was a town made up mostly of the elderly and middle agers with small children. Young people, considering it the boondocks, high-tailed it out of town as soon as their parents and the law allowed, never looking back, which was just fine by Stint. He'd spent twenty years working homicides in Richmond, Virginia, where murders had seemed to occur as often as hands got dirty. The cities could have their mass population's largess of crime. He'd take the slow pace of Buckleton any day of the week.

The rarity of murders in Buckleton made the occurrence of one more horrifying for the town's citizenry, especially since with Buckleton being a small town, the victim was usually known by all. Strangers were as rare as murders in Buckleton, which made Phillip Beamer's death doubly concerning. No one in town had known the man. It was as if he'd dropped into the town out of the clear blue sky.

Stint reread his notes on the Beamer case. The victim's landlord, Mabel Jones, had nearly tripped over the victim's body on the morning of August 6. It was five o'clock in the morning and Mabel was leaving the house on her way to her second business. She was the proprietress of Belle's Cafe. Beamer had been left on her front porch, stabbed to death. Mabel had been up since four and hadn't heard Beamer leave the house. She thought he was in his room, which was on the house's second floor along with the rooms of her three other borders, all of whom had been sound asleep, hearing nothing.

"I tell you that man was as quiet as a church mouse," she'd said to Stint during her first interview at the station. "He'd barely make a sound. I hardly knew he was there. Unlike those other three who clunk around like show horses."

She'd rented a room to Beamer just two weeks earlier. He'd passed her background check and had excellent credit. He'd told her he was a freelance writer and was working on his first novel.

Mabel sipped from the cup Stint had brought her. Drops of coffee trembled down the cup's sides, lightly dotting the table around it. "He said he needed a quiet place to work. And you know there's no quieter place than Buckleton. Even the wind tiptoes around here. I had no reason to doubt him. Everything had checked out. He was so nice and he paid me six months in advance." When she finished, she looked weakly at Stint as if seeking his forgiveness.

Stint remained stone-faced, but he didn't begrudge the woman's making of a buck, nor did he fault her for harboring a bad apple. Background and credit checks were the staples of the industry and were often a landlord's best and only defense against weirdoes and deadbeats. But they weren't foolproof. Heck, even reference-checking didn't always expose poisonous fruit. There was simply no surefire way for landlords or employers to keep a potential Ted Bundy or Jonathan the Bum from entering their places of business or humble abodes. It was impossible to know everything about everyone. Sometimes personal baggage moved in silent lockstep with applicants. "Did he have any visitors?" Stint had asked her.

"Nary a one," Mabel said. "Like I said, I hardly knew he was there. He was as quiet as a church mouse."

Church mouse, Stint thought somberly. It had been a morbidly fitting analogy. Beamer's head had been nearly decapitated, as if his neck had been snapped off by a human-sized mouse trap. Crime of passion perhaps, he thought.

There was a light rap on the doorframe to his office.

Stint looked up and saw the ICE agent standing in his doorway, holding a briefcase. After the Beamer murder, the agent had shown up at his office unexpectedly. Stint had no idea what Beamer's death had to do with national security. But then again, he didn't know what the death had to do with anything. "Agent Bennett, come on in."

Bennett stepped into the office and closed the door behind him. Stint offered him the client seat in front of his desk. After an exchange of pleasantries, Bennett sat down in the offered seat and laid his briefcase across his lap. He opened it, pulling out the plastic bags containing the business card and crime scene photos. He handed the items to Stint. "I appreciate you letting me borrow these."

Stint laid them on his desk. "No problem, just professional courtesy. I'll put them in our storage safe. Would you like to share with me why you needed them?"

"Let's just say I wanted to gauge the reaction of a little birdie."

"A suspect?"

Bennett bit his lip. "It's hard to say."

Stint waited a moment to see if the agent was going to add to the short statement. When it was clear that he wasn't, he said, "We don't get much violent crime here. You can imagine the stir this one has caused. If there's anything you could share to help me solve this thing..."

"You're not going to solve it," Bennett said.

"How's that?" Stint asked, his dander rising. "I know we're a smalltime outfit, but there's no cause to..."

"That's not what I mean," Bennett interjected. "You're not going to solve it because the murder had nothing to do with Buckleton."

"Well, even a random act of violence happening in my jurisdiction is still my responsibility," Stint said.

"This wasn't a random act of violence."

Stint snatched up the plastic bags and stood up. He walked over to a floor safe tucked into the back corner of his office. He turned the combination lock and popped open the door. He paused and turned to face Bennett, holding the plastic bags up in the air. "Don't you think one professional courtesy deserves another?"

There was a brief pause, and then Bennett said, "Is this place secure?"

Stint just looked at him. Buckleton had a two man police force. Stint was the police chief and lead detective—well, only detective. The other member of the force, Raymond Johns, was home, probably just about ready to tuck his five-year-old son into bed.

"Okay," Bennett said, obviously catching the detective's drift. He nodded for Stint to return to his chair. The police chief placed the plastic bags inside the safe, closed the door, and readjusted the combination lock. After he returned to his chair, Bennett said, "Phillip Beamer was also known as Abu Dawood. He was an American citizen with ties to Al Qaeda."

"He was a terrorist?" Stint asked.

"He was a sleeper cell, planning a terrorist attack against America. He and a group of his cohorts were going to blow up the Strom Thurmond Federal Building in Columbia. We'd been tracking his email communications for a number of years. We'd known about Beamer or Dawood since 2001."

"Who took him out? Was it us?"

"By us, you mean the US government?"

Stint nodded.

"No," Bennett said. "There were no plans to take Dawood/Beamer out. We would have prevented the attack, but he was worth more to us alive than dead."

"Then who?"

Bennett's face drew in as he slowly shook his head. "We don't know."

"But you have a theory," Stint said.

Bennett looked at him curiously for a moment as if trying to gauge his aptitude for hearing the absurd. "Yeah, I do. It's a wild one, maybe even too wild to mention."

"I've been in law enforcement over twenty years. I've just about heard them all."

"A psychic," Bennett said in a matter of fact tone.

"A psychic?" Stint repeated.

"I think someone knew what Dawood/Beamer was planning to do, and then either they or someone they directed killed him before he could carry it out."

"Huh," Stint said. He was skeptical, but not dismissive. He'd known stranger things, like the man who'd thought his dog had commanded him to kill. "What about his cohorts?"

"What about them?" Bennett asked.

"Were any of them killed, too?"

"No," Bennett said. "We have a couple of the ones Dawood/Beamer communicated with via email in custody. But they, too, were sleeper cells and hadn't actually met him."

"Why would someone kill only this Dawood/Beamer character?"

"Because he was the leader. Killing him ended the planned terrorist threat. Dawood had been the lead domino. The other cells were to follow his instructions like trained seals. They knew none of the particulars of the assignment, only their specific roles in it."

"Okay," Stint said. "Let's say a psychic was involved. You have a vigilante on your hands that killed a known terrorist who was planning a horrific act of terrorism against the US. End justifies the means, right?"

"You don't really believe that, do you?" Bennett asked.

He didn't. Vigilantism was just another form of law breaking. To allow it would jeopardize the rule of law in society, ultimately leading to chaos. Not to mention the very real possibility that a vigilante could kill the wrong person. Stint didn't say any of this, but he didn't need to. He could tell Bennett recognized a slip of the tongue when he heard one. "So why do you think he was killed here in Buckleton?"

"Because he was here. His death wasn't connected to the town in any other way."

I guess that's good to know, Stint thought. The last thing Buckleton needed or wanted was someone targeting its citizens. "What's your next step?"

Bennett poked the inside of his jaw with his tongue and looked away. "There isn't a next step. Right now, we wait."

"What should I do about my investigation?"

"Unless you're a glutton for the punishment of an unsolved murder, I'd table it. Beamer's killer is most likely a world away from Buckleton."

*   *   *

Monday, October 5

Kallie Hunt slowly opened her eyes and held her breath. Lying on her back, she looked expectedly up at the ceiling. She was in her bedroom at the house she shared with three other college students. She waited another minute before turning her head toward the alarm clock on the nightstand. It was 6:57 a.m., three minutes before the alarm was set to go off. She turned back toward the ceiling again. After another minute passed, a feeling of relief washed over her and she finally exhaled. There was nothing unusually familiar about this morning. There was no déjà vu sensation. For the fourth time in as many days, she awoke without the sense of redundant weirdness that had engulfed her for nearly two straight weeks. It appeared she was back to her old normal self again. Yes, that was the word, normal. For whatever it was worth and for whatever it meant. She was beginning to feel normal and not as if she was the star of a real life twilight zone episode, where she'd known everything that would happen to her right down to the slightest nuance. But thankfully this morning, there was none of that. Normalcy was such a great concept.

She smiled, sat up in bed, and stretched. Normalcy, even of the perceived variety, never felt so good. Now, what do normal girls think about? She asked herself playfully. "Boys," she answered immediately, her smile widening. But a smart normal girl, she chided herself, particularly one who didn't have any boys in her life right now anyway, would be wise to think about the history exam she'd be taking in just a little over an hour from now.

As soon as her feet touched the floor, the alarm went off at its appointed time. She tapped the side of her fist against it, silencing it. She scuttled to the bathroom, thanking the heavens that it was clear. It was one of the benefits of scheduling eight o'clock classes. Usually none of her housemates rose before ten.

The shower was quick, but revitalizing. Once finished, she stepped out and went to the sink. Standing in front of the mirror, she brushed her teeth and washed her face. The girls at Bengate College would no doubt seethe with anger-juiced jealousy if they knew that her total bathroom time was less than ten minutes. Only a third of which was spent looking at her reflection in the mirror, just long enough to make sure she had no toothpaste crust at the corners of her mouth or any nestling eye buggers. She didn't wear makeup, and the only thing that ever touched her lips was lip balm during the winter months. She was a natural beauty with a perfectly symmetrical face, big bluish-green eyes, and smooth olive-brown skin. Though her long brown hair was malleable and easily accepted most styles, she would often, as she did this morning, simply twist it into a ponytail. Her grandmother often said she'd inherited the best physical characteristics of three races. Her mother had been African-American and Native American and her father, whom she'd spoken to exactly three days her entire life, was Dutch-Irish.

After finishing up in the bathroom, she returned to her bedroom where she laid blue jeans and a short-sleeved red blouse on the bed. Though it was October, the weather felt closer to summer than fall. Temperatures were expected to be in the high seventies for at least another week. Fall months were tricky like that in North Carolina. Before the end of the month, her daily ensemble would most likely include thick sweaters and corduroy pants. After getting dressed, she snatched up her cell phone from the nightstand and headed to the kitchen to devour her typical morning feast of cheese toast chased with a big glass of orange juice.

Outside, the morning newspaper dangled perilously off a hedge. Stepping onto the morning-dewed lawn, she caught the newspaper just before it fell to the ground. Evidently, the newspaper guy had an aversion to porches and driveways. Just once, she'd like to retrieve the paper with only a simple kneel-down on the way to her car. What nineteen-year-old reads the paper religiously anyway, her housemate Maggie's voice rang in her head. "Tsk," she answered in reply. Her mother had gotten her started reading the newspaper when she was eight years old. It was now an ingrained habit and hard to kill off.

Her cell phone chimed as soon as she opened the door of the Civic. After throwing her book bag and the newspaper onto the passenger seat, she checked the caller ID screen. It was her grandmother. She tapped the accept icon. "Good morning, grandmother," she said with as much cheeriness as she could muster.

"Well, you sound better this morning," her grandmother said.

"I'm fine, grandmother, honest."

"I didn't ask," her grandmother said.

Kallie nestled the cell phone between her ear and shoulder as she resurrected the engine and slowly backed the car out of the driveway. "It's why you called, isn't it? You want to know if I experienced it again. You want to know if your only grandchild, in fact, your only living relative, is still on the precipice of a nervous breakdown."

"Stop that kind of talk, child. I don't think you're having a nervous breakdown. I think you're stressed about being behind in school and I think you're still grieving."

"It's been a year, grandmother," Kallie said.

"Some people do not get over the death of loved ones in only a year's time, especially their mother's death."

"I'm handling it."

"I know you're handing it," her grandmother said. "But maybe you should have sat out another semester. Maybe started back in the spring. Especially since..." her voice trailed off.

"I know tomorrow makes it exactly a year since mom died. But that would have been the case whether I was here at college or home with you."

"It's at times like these that I wished Janie had more children. Perhaps if you didn't have to go through this alone."

"I'm not alone, grandmother. I have you."

"I know you do, sweetheart. But Janie was my daughter and I miss her terribly. But you," she paused, "losing your mother at your age..." Her voice trailed off again as if she couldn't bear the thought.

"I'm nineteen. I'm not exactly a baby."

"I know you're not. Still, if you had an older sister or something!"

"Honestly, grandmother. I'm fine and I don't think that having a sister would've have made the situation any better."

"Maybe, maybe not, but she could have better understood those déjà vu sensations you've been having."

"I don't know if she could've helped with that either, unless she were a therapist or shrink," Kallie said. She wished now that she'd never mentioned the sensations to her grandmother because the old woman was going to worry herself silly about them. But the sensations had been unsettling. Kallie had experienced the first one about three weeks ago. For the two weeks after that, she'd had at least one a day, mostly in the mornings. And then late last week, they'd stopped as suddenly as they'd appeared. During the sensations' onslaught, she'd researched déjà vu on the internet and found some interesting facts about it on the Wikipedia website.

Déjà vu meant "already seen" in French. It was a phenomenon of having the strong sensation that an event or experience currently experienced had been experienced in the past, whether it had actually been or not. When she'd been in elementary school, Kallie used to get the sensations every now and then, but they'd never lasted longer than thirty seconds and there was never anything freaky or unnerving about them. In fact, through her research, limited as it was, she learned that children between the ages of seven and nine were the most likely to experience the sensations which seldom lasted as long as a minute. Of course, Kallie wasn't nine and her recent sensations had generally lasted longer than thirty seconds. But yesterday had marked the fourth straight day she hadn't felt any sensations. And with this morning's nonoccurrence, she was optimistic that she was well on her way to a full week of normality. Maybe whatever had caused the sensations previously had now resolved itself.

"It's not natural to have those types of sensations as much as you've had them."

"Maybe not," Kallie said, bringing the Civic to a stop at the end of a long line of cars waiting at a traffic light. Since over half its population was associated with its namesake college in some form or fashion, morning rush hour in Bengate mainly consisted of a herd of cars dashing in the same direction toward the campus. "But I'm fine now," Kallie continued. "I haven't had any sensations for almost a week."

"That's good news. But maybe you ought to still speak with somebody."

"You mean a shrink?"

"Stop calling them that," her grandmother said. "Anyway, I meant you should speak to your pastor."

"I don't think that's necessary, grandmother. My pastor's a very busy man."

"No pastor is too busy for a member of his flock, which reminds me… You've never told me the name of your pastor or the name of the church you joined."

There's a good reason for that, Kallie thought. In the next moment, the car in front of her suddenly slammed on its brakes, almost causing Kallie's Honda to rear end it. Luckily, she was able to slam on the Honda's brakes just in time, avoiding a collision, but not from uttering the expletive that her grandmother clearly heard.

"What did you say child?" her grandmother asked.

Kallie, straining her eyes ahead to see what had caused the car in front of her to stop like that, didn't immediately answer. She saw the squirrel scampering across the street and into the parking lot of a church. *A freaking squirrel,* Kallie thought. She looked ahead and met the eyes of the other driver in the car's rear view mirror. The driver, a red-haired woman, simply shrugged her shoulders and drove on.

"Kallie," her grandmother said.

"Oh, I'm sorry," she said, turning back to the squirrel that'd now darted up the side of the monument that announced the name of the white-brick church.

New Vibe Community Church

Pastor Johnny Swag

Sunday services 10 a.m. & 6 p.m.

Bible study Wednesdays, Noon & 7:15 p.m.

"I said my pastor's name is Swag, Reverend Johnny Swag," Kallie said.

"Swag, huh? It sounded like something else. Reverend Johnny Swag. It doesn't sound like a preacher's name."

"Well, it is. He's the pastor of New Vibe Community Church."

"New Vibe? Is that a Baptist church?"

"What difference does it make, grandmother? You wanted me to go to church and I'm going to one."

"I don't want you joining a cult."

"A cult? Honestly, grandmother! You're too much," Kallie said. "My church is not a cult. Besides, I'm not weak-minded enough to ever step foot inside a cult. Okay?"

There was a long pause, as if her grandmother was really considering the possibility. "Well, all right," she said finally. "I want you to call him."

"Call who?"

"This Reverend Johnny Swag. Tell him about these sensations you're having."

It was easier to humor the old lady than to argue that preachers weren't doctors or psychologists or psychiatrists. Johnny Swag would be no more able to tell her about her sensations than that squirrel scampering across the street would. "Yes ma'am, I will. But I have to go now. May I call you later?"

"You know you can call me anytime, dear."

Kallie parked in the student parking section and hurried to class, trying to forget the lie she'd just told her grandmother. Kallie didn't like lying to her, but her grandmother thought going to church was a cure all. The truth was, Kallie hadn't stepped foot inside a church since she'd left her grandmother's house. It wasn't that she'd lost faith in God. She still had as much or as little as she'd ever had. But God and religion just weren't a priority right now. Besides, Kallie honestly felt better, and she was confident that the déjà vu and whatever had caused it were now gone. She hated she'd told her grandmother about it in the first place, needlessly worrying her.

Five minutes before the start of class, she took a seat at the front of the room. She started to reach into her book bag for her notes but decided against it, instead zipping the bag back up and placing it down by her feet. If she didn't know the material by now, a five minute cram session wasn't going to tilt the scales one way or the other.

At exactly eight o'clock, Professor Sampson sauntered into the class with a wide Cheshire cat grin on his face, as if he harbored the world's biggest secret. He carried a briefcase in one hand and a stack of exam papers nestled in his other. A short, plump man with a hairline that had retreated to the areas just above his ears and the nape of his neck, he reminded Kallie of a fat small-town mayor from an old black and white television show. "I gather that we're ready for our little exam today," he said, eliciting a collective muffled groan from the class. Apparently satisfied with that response, Sampson dropped his briefcase down beside his desk and then moved in front of Kallie's desk where he thrust a siphoned off portion of the exam stack at her. "Take one and pass the others back."

As Kallie reached for the stack, she saw some movement out the corner of her eye. Thinking it was her classmate's pencil rolling off his desk; she instinctively leaned over and placed her hand on the floor to catch it before it hit the floor. But when she did so, she immediately realized that the pencil had yet begun to move. The realization temporarily froze her in place, which kept her hand on the floor when the pencil finally began its descent five seconds later, landing securely in her palm.

Observing her mistimed, yet successful pencil rescue, the professor's eyes widened. "Woman's intuition?" he asked, lightheartedly.

Kallie didn't answer. With her pencil-clasped hand still on the floor, she looked anxiously down her row of desks. None of the students seemed to be paying her the least bit of attention. Chances were they hadn't even seen what she'd done. Yet, she felt as if all eyes in the class were on her. Slowly, she sat up and handed her classmate his pencil. *Of all days, Seth Winters would choose today to sit beside her.* She avoided his brown eyes, focusing instead on his lips, which didn't help at all. His lips were moist and curved. She felt weak and silly. He mouthed something, but Kallie couldn't make it out. She felt as if she'd been sucked into a soundless vacuum. She looked around once more and suddenly felt a tightening in her chest. She snatched up her book bag and bolted out of the room, nearly knocking over a tall cactus plant standing soldier-like near the door.

CHAPTER THREE

He was now known as Gerald Principe. And as Gerald Principe, he loved making the 3 a.m. rounds patrolling the halls of the United Corporate Bank Center building, known to the Charlotte locals as the UCB Center. A gentle quiet permeated throughout the place during those wee hours of the day, despite the fact that there was always a fair amount of foot traffic in the halls, thanks to the interconnectedness of the world's financial markets. As the bank's corporate headquarters, the UCB Center stayed open on some level twenty-four hours a day, every day of the year.

Although the bank never completely shut down, it did on occasion slow down, at least in spirit, creating what Principe considered controlled calm. It was more noticeable during the December holiday season when even some of the bank's top brass sported the occasional festive mood for at least a couple of hours during Christmas week. At other times of the year, the calmness wasn't as easily detectable. In the finance industry, hustle and bustle was the accepted norm. No one ever wanted to be accused of doing anything less than a hundred miles an hour at all times. Employees entered the building at all hours of the day and night, always seeming to be in a hurry. Lunches were often speed-eaten as if jobs were disappearing during hourly absences. Still, pockets of calm existed, unnoticed by most eyes, and observable only to someone tuned to the pulse of the building and its people and who was uniquely versed in the detection of the subtleties of the human spirit.

Principe had such ability, though he hadn't formally studied psychology. In fact, he hadn't even gone to college.

He'd entered the military right after high school, quickly claiming his birthright by becoming a munitions specialist. Principe's family (he no longer used the family's actual surname, not even in thought), who had migrated to the States from Italy after the Great War, thought highly of his great-grandfather who'd been an expert in blowing up bridges during the war. The skill and appreciation for blowing up things had come to Principe naturally, but so had his ability to read people, to see through the steeliest of facades. One of the things that he'd quickly learned shortly after taking the security officer's job at the UBC Center was that the twenty-four hour a day hustle and bustle was often a mirage.

It wasn't that the bank's employees were being intentionally deceitful. It was that they were people. Humans weren't the robots that they tried so hard purporting themselves to be. Humans eventually get tired. Sure, there were some with unbelievable stamina and who were able to last much longer than others. But all get tired eventually and need rest. Most humans are conditioned to getting that rest in the morning hours, with 3 a.m. being the optimal time. Likewise, most people, particularly those with 8 to 5 jobs, felt midday was the perfect time to refuel with food. As a result, according to Principe's unscientifically proven theory, most brains literally wanted to eat and sleep at the same traditionally appointed times, despite what their bodies were required to do or were doing.

Principe didn't need education to know this. One of his unique gifts was detecting minor changes in people's states of being. And despite the hard, determined looks of people at three in the morning and their speed-rushing of meals at lunchtime, Principe could detect a brain's rebellion as it unconsciously kicked in to what he referred to as its calming mechanism. At three in the morning, people worked at slower paces than they would have even five hours later. It was as if they were school children placed in the hands of the proverbial substitute teacher for the day. Whenever he caught the gaze of a fellow third-shifter, it was as if they shared a secret.

Reaching the end of a long corridor, he paused and turned around. He was on the fiftieth floor. His eyes roved, looking for anything different or out of place. Of course he found nothing. Everything was as it should be. The sameness he'd expected. UCB Center's security was top notch. There were video monitors, seen and unseen, placed strategically throughout the hulking nine hundred feet high, seventy floor building—the tallest in the state of North Carolina. Entrance into the hallways of the building required a magnetic ID pass card. If an unauthorized person or persons had succeeded in getting onto the floors, either the boots on the ground or the eyes in the control room would quickly ferret him or them out. There'd literally be nowhere to hide. In addition, like Principe, all the security officers had either a military or law enforcement background, with expert training in the use of all types of weaponry and hand-to-hand combat techniques. Principle himself had a particular expertise in the use of explosives. It would be virtually impossible for any unauthorized person or persons to penetrate the building or to avoid capture if they were somehow able to enter. The bank had spared no expense in securing its protection from enemies foreign and domestic, seen and unseen.

Except for one thing, Principe thought ominously as he exited the corridor onto a stairwell. United Corporate Bank Center had unknowingly entrusted a wolf to help watch over its sheep. He descended the steps, the sound of his footfalls echoing off the walls. When he reached the lower landing, he backed underneath the ascending stairs and leaned against the wall out of the monitoring camera's view. He brought his hands up to his head, rubbing his temples. Lately, his visions had become too acute and the accompanying headaches were almost unbearable, making him wonder if he'd make it to Thursday, October 29. But he knew he had to somehow or another. That date marked the last of the demon-moons.

There wouldn't be another one of its magnitude for at least a quarter of a century.

The day would also mark the eightieth anniversary of the stock market crash of '29, a fortuitous coincidence. Principe was not into celebrating such ominous dates in American history. But he knew that after the execution of the largest home-brewed terrorist act since the Oklahoma City federal building bombing, investigators would look for some significance for that particular date. Even amateur sleuths would claim that it was no coincidence that a terrorist act against a bank would occur on that date. And of course, in addition to the unleashing of horrific forces, the likes of which the world had yet to witness, there would be the killing of a would-be president who was scheduled for a visit to the building on that very day. The death of the highly popular freshman senator would be an added bonus—a change in an already determined history. *Oh, it was simply too perfect.* He could suffer through the monstrous headaches a while longer.

After the fated events of that day, his matriculation into malevolence would be complete and the headaches would be over. There was comfort in that realization. His calling was a blessing. Sometimes he wished he also had the capability of fast-forwarding to that special day. It was virtually impossible to live in the moment when a more fantastic moment was just on the horizon. But that was just ego talking, he chided himself. Ego bred impatience. Ego birthed foolishness. It was ego that had him tagging bodies in Cairo and London, and recently in South Carolina. But thumbing his nose at A.I. had been a short-lived pleasure. He would no longer make such egotistical mistakes. There was a grander prize on the horizon. One he would wait patiently for. For now, he would graciously accept every moment of his existence, even now in his weaker state. For it would make that glorious future day and the life to come all the more gratifying. He pushed those thoughts away, refocusing on the task at hand. Gathering himself, he continued downward to the forty-eighth floor. When he reached it, he exited the stairwell and tapped the button of the radio on his shoulder. "Officer Principe, East Corridor's clear."

"Ten-four, Gerald."

"I'm going to take a potty break," Principe said into his radio mic.

"Okay. I'll see you in control in thirty."

"Roger that, Mike." It was another of the benefits of working the third shift. When talking amongst themselves at this hour, his fellow security officers usually eased off the formalities.

The restrooms were the only areas in the building where there were no cameras, although there were hidden cameras at the entrances to the restrooms, letting the control room monitor the restrooms' comings and goings, but not the doings inside. After verifying he was alone in the restroom, Principe went to the last stall. This one housed the toilet for the handicap. It was a high-sitting affair. Principe liked using it because it made him feel as if he sat upon a throne. However, he didn't need to use it now for that purpose. Instead, he climbed atop it and pushed aside the ceiling tile. He craned his neck into the darkness of the top deck and saw the bomb's numerical face. It was still intact and counting down, just like the others. The countdown was merely a failsafe he'd created to ensure that he wouldn't activate the bombs before the twenty-ninth. It was merely a prophylactic measure for his unpredictable ego. After the numbers reached triple zeroes, he'd only to press a couple of numbers on his cell phone to create the explosions that would forever change humanity's course.

CHAPTER FOUR

After she'd childishly run out of Professor Sampson's class earlier that morning, the professor had been nice enough to allow Kallie back into his classroom to take the history exam. Now, a couple of hours later, she stood outside his office, her hand poised pre-knock over the doorframe. The door was slightly ajar. Though she couldn't see the professor from where she stood, she could hear papers shuffling and the stilted creakiness of a weighted office chair.

Though she really didn't have anything more to add to the apology she'd already given and risked further embarrassment, she felt she owed him an additional explanation for her earlier behavior. Of course, she really didn't have a viable excuse for her actions, at least not one she could accurately articulate. How could she explain having been spooked by an eerie déjà vu sensation at the exact moment of her first interaction with *Seth Winters*? And besides, the professor was probably too busy to hear lame explanations anyway, particularly any involving her possible mental breakdown and nonexistent love life. She dropped her hand down by her side and started to turn away.

"My door is always open, as you can see," the professor called from inside his office. "You've come this far, you may as well trek the last mile."

She pushed the door forward and walked into his office. Her nose was immediately appeased by a pleasant flowery odor immersed in the air, which amazingly put her at ease. The professor was partially hidden behind a huge desk populated by several plants and neat mountains of books and stacks of papers.

"Ah, Ms. Hunt," he said when she'd stepped beyond the cover of the door, his head peeking over a virtual miniature forest. "I'm afraid I hadn't enough time to grade the exams."

"It's not that," she said. Her voice was soft and hesitant. "I just wanted to explain about earlier."

He parted the blend of academia and foliage on his desktop down the middle and indicated the chair in front of his desk. "An explanation is unnecessary; but please, come have a seat." He was wearing a pair of telephone headphones.

Kallie sat down in the offered chair. She opened her mouth to start the explanation she'd yet to completely flesh out in her mind, but was stopped by the professor's raised hand. "Just one moment please," he said. He turned to his right and began tapping on a laptop that was atop a side extension of his desk. On the extension to the professor's left side were a small, neat stack of papers and a cup of pens and pencils. Kallie smiled inwardly. Sitting behind his u-shaped, greenery-topped wood desk, wearing headphones, and tapping away on his laptop, the professor looked like a jolly little spaceship operator.

After a few moments, he faced her again. "Sorry about that. But if I didn't complete my train of thought that letter wouldn't have gotten finished anytime soon. Now, you were about to say…"

During the brief respite, she'd decided to start with another apology. "I want to apologize again for running out of your class this morning."

The professor smiled warmly. "As I'd told you before, there's no need to apologize." He paused and shifted awkwardly in his seat. He looked off to the side for a moment as if struggling to recall the first few words of a previously rehearsed speech. When he faced her again, he spoke deliberately. "My mother is ninety years old and my dad is ninety-three. I'm fifty-three years old and I can't begin to imagine what it's like to lose a parent, let alone, to lose one at your age. I can only offer my heartfelt sympathy."

"You know about my mother?" Kallie asked.

"I remembered she died from cancer. You were in my class last year when you dropped out of school to go home to care for her. After class this morning, I took the liberty of looking up the date she died and I know that tomorrow will mark a year since her death. It's understandable what you're going through." He paused again, treading lightly. "We do have grief counselors on campus. Maybe you should talk to someone."

Kallie nodded noncommittally although she was pleasantly surprised at the fact that he remembered she'd lost her mother and seemed genuinely concerned. For a period of five seconds, she weighed it as a benefit of attending a small private college versus a large public university. The professors evidently took the time to know their students. "Thank you, professor. But..."

He leaned forward in his chair. "That wasn't what was bothering you? Forgive me for being presumptuous."

"No, it's not that. I mean, I don't consider you presumptuous. I appreciate your caring. It's just..." she hesitated, unsure of what she was trying, wanted, or even was willing to say.

Despite the unplanned student-teacher conference, Sampson regarded her with kind, patient eyes. "What's the matter?"

It took her another full minute, but then the words began to flow easily. With tears streaming down her face, she told him about the déjà vu sensations she'd experienced during the past few weeks and how she'd thought until the pencil-dropping incident this morning that they'd ended. She'd like to think it all was just related to grief, but she honestly believed she'd handled her mother's death well. She missed her mom, but she'd arrived at a tacit appreciation of the perils of living. Death, sickness, and heartbreak, among other

things, always loitered nearby, and eventually each would
have its say and day with everybody who walks the earth,
and the appointments wouldn't necessarily be time oriented.
No particular age group had a monopoly on bad stuff
happening. If you had a fluid understanding of that, then you
could enjoy and appreciate the other moments of your life
when the perils were kept at bay. "No," she reiterated, "my
sensations aren't related to grief." She paused again, this time
making it the terminus point. She didn't know what else to
say. She was only certain that the sensations weren't related
to grief. But just what exactly they were related to was a
frightening mystery to her.

When it became obvious that she wasn't going to say
anything more, Professor Sampson leaned back in his chair
and looked off to the side. His face was contemplative. She
stared at him, wishing she could read his thoughts. He'd been
kind and patient with her up to this point. Maybe it was in his
job description to do so or maybe it was part of his natural
personality. Maybe one or both of those things were true or
perhaps neither was. In any event, this wasn't his problem. It
was hers. She didn't want to impose on his kindness whether
it'd been initiated by his employer or his own human nature.
His 'what's the matter' was likely a recalibrated 'how are you
doing,' where no one wanted to hear a list of grievances. A
simple 'doing well,' whether true or not, was the expected
and desired response. After a few moments, those concerns
shuffled back into her mind's recess when he asked, "What
kind of cancer did your mother have?"

Kallie closed her eyes for a quick moment. "Brain
cancer."

"I see. And you feel your déjà vu sensations are somehow
related to the disease?"

"Well, couldn't they be?" Kallie asked.

"It's possible, I guess," Professor Sampson said. "Of
course, I'm not a doctor. However, I do know that cancer is
not necessarily hereditable. Yes, you may be at a higher risk

than others. But it's not a given that you'll develop cancer because your mother had it."

"I know. I guess I should see a doctor about the déjà vu. But..." She dropped her head and didn't finish her sentence. It made perfect, logical sense to visit a doctor. But the perils of living didn't prescribe logical sense.

"Kallie," Professor Sampson said.

She looked up.

"I have a colleague of mine who is a specialist in the area of human memory. In fact, I believe she's currently doing a study on déjà vu. I recall her saying that the sensation is most likely related to some kind of memory failure."

"So you don't think my sensations are related to cancer?"

"Right now, I'm afraid I can't say one way or the other. But from what I understand, déjà vu is sometimes related to failed recollections of things you've experienced in the past. Of course, I'm not the expert. Why don't you go see my colleague? If this is not something related to her area, then you're only out one day on your trek to your doctor. But you'll be up one fascinating individual. Her name is Dr. Karen Frost."

*　　*　　*

Professor Frost's lab and office were located on the bottom floor of the science building. Frost headed the Department of Psychology's Neuroscience Program. According to Sampson, Frost was a contrarian who'd requested to be in the science building because a lot of scientists continually made snide remarks about psychology being akin to junk medicine whose theories couldn't stand the rigors of scientific testing.

Kallie stood at the door to the lab and read the small sign that hung over it.

Psychology is not descriptive science, it's simply psychology

She had no idea what it meant, but she assumed it was probably a missive intended for the scientists in the building.

The lab looked like the campus' other classrooms, except that desks were replaced by rows of tables fronted by caster-fitted chairs. Atop the tables were computers with seventeen-inch monitors connected by thick black cables to space-age looking goggles. A lone man sat at one of the tables. He was wearing a set of the goggles and typing on a keyboard. Kallie walked over to him and looked over his shoulder.

Obviously feeling her presence, he held up one finger. "Just a sec." Staring intently at the computer screen, he moved his head from side to side and up and down. As he did so, the onscreen camera zoomed about the room. It was virtual reality. It looked like the living room of a house. There was a computerized image of a couch and loveseat. He rolled the mouse on the keypad, moving from the living room, down a hall, and eventually into a kitchen. He paused on an image of a refrigerator. He tapped the keyboard, morphing the virtual house into a virtual forest. Again, he moved his head around and rolled the mouse. His virtual-self was obviously exploring the area. Computerized images of trees and overgrown plants showed onscreen. After a few moments, he paused again, this time in front of a tree. Then he clicked a couple of keystrokes, returning to the kitchen. A few moments later, he removed the goggles and swung around, facing Kallie. "How can I help you?"

Kallie had been transfixed by the onscreen images and it took her several seconds to reorient. After a quick shake of her head, she said, "I'm looking for Professor Frost."

"She left about an hour ago," the man said.

"Is she gone for the rest of the day?"

"Ordinarily," he said. He nodded at a cell phone on a neighboring tabletop. "She'll be back, but I'm afraid she's not going to be in a good mood. She's very time-conscious. She probably hadn't factored into her schedule having to come back here to retrieve that."

Kallie shrugged her shoulders. "Mind if I wait for her?"

"Suit yourself." He turned back to the monitor, putting the goggles back on.

"Are you playing a game?" Kallie asked, looking at the computer screen.

"No, this is part of our research. We use this to help recreate déjà vu sensations in our test subjects. The onscreen images are replicates of real life images, of real life places. When you put on these goggles, you're immersed into another time and place. We expose our test subjects to the scenes on the computer screen, and afterwards, we'll hypnotize them, making them forget that they'd ever seen the scenes. Later, we'll take them to a real world recreation of a particular scene. Using this technique, we've found that we've been able to recreate déjà vu-like sensations in many of the subjects."

"Why would you want to create déjà vu?" Kallie asked.

"So that we can study the sensation. Since it's so fleeting when it occurs naturally, we haven't been able to interview someone who's right in the middle of one or even right at the end of one. When we do talk to them, they can remember very little about the sensation, mostly only about how weird they'd felt during it." He took off the goggles and lifted them up to her. "Want to try?"

She took the goggles and sat down at the computer. She looked at the goggles for a moment before slowly putting them on. They fit like the ones she used for swimming.

"Looking around works the same way in virtual reality as it does in reality. You simply move your head. But to walk or move around, you need to use the mouse," he told her.

She nodded her head and instantly saw what he meant. The effect was negligible, no different from if she'd nodded her head in real life. Nothing in the room itself moved. But moving her head enabled her to look around the room.

Before, when she'd stood over him, the images in the room had looked computerized, appearing to grow larger and smaller as he moved his head. But with the goggles on, everything took on a realistic quality. She was in an actual house! Still in the kitchen and standing by the refrigerator, she continued looking around. There was a stove, above which was a microwave oven. The countertops were granite and there was a butcher's table in the middle of the room. Weirdly, it was a kitchen not too dissimilar from one she'd often fantasized about having in her own home one day. Anxious to see more of the house, she rolled the mouse, moving her virtual-self out of the kitchen and over to a set of stairs.

The first room she entered upstairs was a nursery. The room was done in lovely shades of blue. A crib with a light blue quilt hanging over its railing was catty-cornered against the back walls. Next to it was a rocking chair with an oversized stuffed teddy bear sporting a huge welcoming grin sitting in it. Kallie moved to the center of the room, standing there for a few moments. In an odd way, she felt as if she was peeking into a version of her future. Closing her eyes, she could almost picture her future husband. She couldn't make out any of his facial features, but she sensed love for her in his heart. She smiled as she imagined him putting the crib together in anticipation of their first born. After another moment, she slowly inhaled and reopened her eyes, looking around the room nostalgically, although it wasn't decorated exactly the way she'd have done it. Instead of blue, she'd probably paint the walls in pastel pinks if they were having a girl or deep reds if they were having a boy. She'd hang red-framed pictures of smiling and happy animals on the walls. I'm being silly, she thought; marriage and family are years away, if ever. She'd first have to find a man. She moved the mouse again, walking her virtual-self out of the room.

The next room was the master suite. A king-sized four-poster bed stood boldly in the center of the room. As her virtual-self approached it, her real-self, for whatever reason, felt anger start to boil within. Totally immersed in the virtual room, she looked off to the side of the bed and saw his and hers walk-in closets. She turned her head to the other side and saw a dresser that was almost as long as the wall itself. She spotted a framed picture atop the dresser. From where she was standing, she could tell it was a picture of a family— a husband, wife, and three children. But she couldn't make out any of their faces. Moving the mouse, she walked over to it and picked it up. Her real-self was holding her hands up to her face. In the picture, all the members of the family remained faceless, except that of the man. She stared long and hard at his face. It was the face of her father. Her real-self squeezed her fists together as her virtual-self squeezed the framed picture, breaking the glass before slamming the frame down on the dresser top. Meanwhile, her real-self pounded the desktop, rattling the mouse, almost knocking it to the floor. Angrily, she removed the goggles, violently shifting herself back to the present.

The man gingerly took the goggles from her trembling grasp. His voice was strained. "What's wrong? What happened?"

Before she could answer, a tense female voice called out from the doorway of the lab. "What in the dickens is going on in here?"

CHAPTER FIVE

Dr. Karen Frost's cramped, windowless office was located in the back of the lab as if it had been created as an afterthought. It was hardly larger than a prison cell. But Frost, like a budget conscious warden, had made efficient use of its limited space. It contained a small bookshelf, filing cabinet, and a desk sandwiched between two similar-style chairs. The room's off-white walls were bare save a framed picture of Frost, her husband, and two children. There was no evidence anywhere in the room of Frost's academic or professional successes. No framed degrees, certificates, or pictures of Frost shaking hands with anyone of supposed importance.

At four-feet-eleven inches tall, Frost was a petite woman in physical dimensions only. She had a commanding presence and she spoke in a thorough but efficient manner, as if she'd only allotted a certain amount of time for talking. After entering her lab and seeing Kallie at the end of what appeared to have been a mini mental breakdown, she escorted the teen to her office and soon had her relaxed and extremely open to divulging every detail of her life.

"We used to think that memory was like putting groceries away," Frost said. "You put your bread in the pantry. Your salt and spices in one cabinet, rice and pastas in another. Later, when you needed something, you knew exactly where to retrieve it. Conventional thinking was that memory operated in much the same way with the brain storing an event into memory and later recalling that memory if and when it's needed."

"Memory recollection," Kallie offered.

"Exactly," Frost said. "However, in the 1970s, a Canadian cognitive psychologist named Endel Tulving discovered that memory retrieval wasn't quite that simplistic. He found that there were actually two kinds of memories, episodic and semantic. A semantic memory is recalling facts like knowing the capital of North Carolina is Raleigh. But your episodic memory would recall your actual trip to Raleigh. You may even recall how the food smelled at a bakery you visited there or even how loud the trains were. You mentally relive the experience. That is the process of remembering. Being able to recall a fact and to remember an event are actually two separate abilities, which subsequently means that there is a distinct difference between recognition and recall."

Kallie furrowed her brow. "I don't understand."

"Okay," Frost said. She appeared to relish the opportunity to explain. "Have you ever been to a zoo?"

"Yes," Kallie said.

"What kinds of animals are usually found at a zoo?"

Kallie paused for a moment, recalling her last visit to the zoo. It had been a second grade field trip. "Monkeys, gorillas, elephants, giraffes."

Frost smiled. "What you just utilized was semantic memory. And if I'm guessing correctly, you were recalling a specific time you went to the zoo?"

Kallie nodded her head. "It was my second grade field trip."

Frost settled back in her chair. "Tell me about the trip."

"I don't remember much about it," Kallie said. "Other than a gorilla picking his nose and flicking a booger at us."

"Close your eyes," Frost said gently.

Kallie closed her eyes.

"Now describe for me the zoo experience. Do you remember the size of any of the animals or how they smelled?"

Kallie paused, searching her memory. "The elephants," she said finally. "I remember how huge they were." After another moment, her nose twitched. "And the stench." In her mind, she could see the huge pile of crap. One of the elephants had defecated. "A wind had caught the smell just as we approached, pushing that foul odor toward us. I remember us giggling and running away to see the alligators."

"You can open your eyes now," Frost said confidently. "That is episodic memory. You didn't simply rattle off facts. You relived it. You recalled sights, sounds, smells."

"I guess I did." She hesitated. "But where does déjà vu fit in all of this?"

"We believe déjà vu is a false memory."

"False memory?" Kallie repeated.

"Yes, a false memory is a recollection of something that hadn't actually happened." Frost's mood suddenly darkened. "Perhaps the most vivid and recent examples of false memory occurred in the nineties during what I can admit now was a bleak period in the field of psychology." Her face twitched slightly as she added, "And yet another reason for scientists to disrespect the field."

There existed a contentious relationship between scientists and psychologists, with the former critical of the latter's supposedly lackadaisical attitude toward scientific testing and an unwillingness to submit psychological theories to rigorous testing before unleashing them onto the public as truisms and proven facts, often, according to some scientists, to disastrous results. To emphasize this point, scientists often cited a few inglorious moments from psychology's past. The creation and advancement of eugenics, a practice rooted in the belief that desirable genetic traits were hereditary. This scientifically unproven and untested belief led to many atrocious acts, including the castrations and/or sterilization of men who had so called undesirable genes, the abortions of otherwise healthy fetuses, and forced pregnancies. And then there was the lobotomy craze of the 1950s, when psychology had somehow convinced the populace that snipping off a bit of the brain could cure all types of mental illnesses. Countless people were irreparably harmed by a procedure that could accurately be described as psychological horse manure.

But in the nineties, psychology had supposedly reached a new low, not necessarily because of the commission of deadlier procedures or even an increased number of victims, although a significant number of lives were affected and thus were also irreparably harmed. No, the main issue with psychology's nineties' 'repressed memory recovery' crusade was that it had occurred in the nineties. It was a time when one would have thought that both psychology and the public authority would have learned from the lessons of the past and would not have based so much of society's legal and public policy on what was basically unscientifically proven hogwash. Yet, everyone from lawyers, to school teachers, to wives, and to juries accepted wholeheartedly any psychologist's declaration that he'd recovered evidence of child abuse or sexual molestation or some other vile act buried deep within the recesses of the victim's mind, sometimes decades after the alleged incident. Marriages broke up. Families were ruined. And people went to prison, and least of all, psychology suffered yet another black eye, all because the public had once again accepted another of its untested theories as scientific gospel.

"Is that why you have that sign over the lab entrance about psychology not being descriptive science but rather simply psychology?" Kallie asked.

"Yes," Frost said. "I'm a scientist as well as a psychologist. I know that may seem like a misnomer. But it's really not. Every scientist is a psychologist. But every psychologist is not a scientist. The imagination of a psychologist is what gives scientists all those wonderful theories to test in the first place. But, unlike a scientist, a psychologist is not willing to disavow something simply because he can't prove it."

"Okay," Kallie said, detecting a bit of bitterness in the professor's voice. "But the example you just cited was a false memory supposedly planted by someone else. That's different from déjà vu, right?"

"Technically, but the concept's the same. In déjà vu, you have a recollection of something that you can't connect to anything because there's nothing there to connect it to. It doesn't exist. In the repressed memory craze of the nineties, psychologists planted recollections in people and then insisted that the attaching memories were repressed when, in fact, they hadn't actually existed in the first place."

This was all interesting, Kallie thought. But she didn't know what it had to do with her. Why had she felt anger when she'd been in the virtual reality bedroom? Why had she seen her father's face on the picture frame?

"Anyway," Frost said, eerily sharing Kallie's thought. "Let's go back to your experience in the virtual reality scene. You're sure you've never seen a similar room or been inside your father's house?"

"Yes ma'am," Kallie answered softly. When they'd first retreated to Frost's office, Kallie told Frost that there'd been nothing familiar about that room. She'd never seen it before or been in one like it. But all of a sudden, she'd felt herself getting angry just standing in the room. Then she'd spotted the picture on the dresser drawer. She'd spoken with her father exactly three times in her lifetime and had not once been in his home. According to her mother, her parents were once high school sweethearts who had broken up shortly after Kallie's birth. Kallie hadn't spent much time thinking about her father during the years. She hadn't suspected that she'd had any pent up frustration toward him.

"Let's go back to that picture frame," Frost said.

"Okay."

Frost regarded her solemnly. "There was no picture frame. The picture hadn't been digitally created. It'd existed only in your mind. The virtual scene had only included a bed and dresser." Josh Levy, who'd allowed Kallie on the computer, to Frost's chagrin, had told Frost that he'd seen Kallie's virtual-self walk over to the dresser and pick up air, in conjunction with what her real-self had been doing at that exact moment.

"Am I going crazy?" Kallie asked.

"I don't think so," Frost said. "I don't have answers now. But I would like to schedule you for a MRI scan so that we can run some tests."

"Why a MRI scan?" Kallie asked, feeling uneasy.

"There's no need for alarm," Frost said. "We run MRI scans on all our test subjects. We study the images and use them for comparison purposes amongst the subjects."

Kallie felt her throat tightening. "Should I be concerned?"

"No more than you already are."

"Have you ever found something serious in the scans—I mean amongst the test subjects?"

"Truthfully, we found a tumor once. It was small and the young man had apparently been living with it for a while without any problems. We advised him to set an appointment with his doctor. It ended up being no major deal and he went back to living with it. Simply having a brain tumor is not necessarily cause for concern, unless it's malignant."

Kallie nodded. "My mother had brain cancer." She swallowed hard. "Do you think it could be cancer?"

"I'd hate to answer that question before running the scans. I'm sorry to hear about your mother. But only about five percent of brain tumors are related to hereditary factors. So I wouldn't immediately jump to that conclusion. Besides, your sensations may not have anything to do with a tumor. We'll just have to run the scan. Besides, there are other possibilities."

"Like what?" Kallie asked.

"It could be simple memory malfunction. Some issue with the cells in the temporal lobe area. The temporal lobe region is the area of the brain responsible for memory retention and storing new memories. Epileptic seizures also occur in this region." Seeing Kallie shift uneasily in her chair, Frost quickly added, "But I wouldn't go worrying about having epilepsy now either. Let's just run the scans before conceiving all the possible dire outcomes. I can schedule a MRI scan for as early as this Friday."

Kallie bit her lip, but couldn't suppress her growing concerns. "If the sensations aren't related to epilepsy or tumors, why would I start getting frequent déjà vu all of a sudden? I mean, why now?"

Frost considered the question for a moment before answering. "If we take those known possibilities off the table, then the question becomes a little challenging to answer. Despite the fact that déjà vu has been around about as long as written history with St. Augustine having made references to it in 400 A.D., scientists are yet to have a full or consensus understanding of it. New types of it have even surfaced in recent years, including one named déjà vecu. This condition afflicts a person with the belief that he's already lived through most of his life at least once previously. The cause of the déjà vu condition remains under dispute, with such wildly different opinions such as it being related to reincarnations, to it being evidence of past lives, or to it being a misfiring of memory cells. I consider myself a psychologist by heart and practice, but a scientist by nature. The nature of déjà vu itself is hard to quantify, much less its cause or meaning. The scientist in me wants scientific proof of something before declaring it so. And Friday's MRI would go a long way in ruling out disease or epilepsy as a cause for your sensations. Ruling out reincarnations or past lives would be next to impossible. But, unlike most scientists, I'm not foolish enough to deny the existence or possibility of something because I'm unable to prove it. But I would be the first to admit that while the 'what' of déjà vu can often be a shapeless figure hard to fully grasp and ever-changing, the 'why' of it could prove even more elusive. But again, I'm hesitant to speculate at this point. Let's run the scan first."

Josh Levy was waiting for Kallie when she left Dr. Frost's office. He wanted to formally introduce himself to her and also apologize to her for putting her in the virtual reality world in the first place. "It was a dumb thing to do," he said. "We usually run the subjects through tests before we get to that stage."

"But, you made an exception for me," Kallie said light-heartedly.

Josh smiled sheepishly. "I guess I was showing off. I usually don't do that."

"Blinded by my beauty?" she said in a sarcastic tease.

Josh laughed. "I guess you could say that."

"Well, in that case, I accept your apology."

She found Josh cute in an offhand sort of way. He had small brown eyes and stringy darkish hair that draped over his forehead. He was twenty-nine years old but acted younger somehow. It wasn't due to immaturity. She really couldn't say what it was. He was obviously intelligent. He'd told her that he was in the psychology graduate program after having earned B.A degrees in religious studies and psychology. The more she thought about it, she realized it was probably because he reminded her of Shaggy from Scooby-Doo. Josh was very laidback and she found him easy to talk to. They conversed for a while, as if they'd known each other forever. When Kallie became conscious of the lateness of the day and started to reluctantly leave, four gabbing students suddenly walked into the lab, playfully bickering with each other like siblings.

Josh explained to her that there were only five students in Dr. Frost's graduate program, mainly because the criteria to get into it were brutal. In addition to having at least a 3.6 grade point average and near perfect GRE scores, Frost required participants in the program to have advanced themselves in another discipline as well as in psychology. The four gabbing students were the other ones in Frost's program.

A few moments later, after everyone had settled down, Josh introduced them to Kallie. "I already told you that I double-majored in psychology and religious studies. Cedric Leggett over there," he pointed to a skinny, bespectacled kid sitting at one of the desks, "psychology and biochemistry." Cedric smiled awkwardly at Kallie and then looked away. "Veronica Ross," Josh continued, nodding to the only female in the group. She was pretty with a wide toothy smile. "Psychology and criminal justice. Evan Carmon, psychology and business. He's also working on his MBA now." Evan was sitting at a desk with his back to her. He threw up an index finger and then put on the goggles and began pecking away at the keyboard.

"Evan's actually a math whiz," Veronica offered. "He only majored in business because of his incessant quest for riches."

"A man's got to eat," Evan said in an unapologetic tone. He continued staring intently at the computer monitor. Kallie could see that he was wearing a white collared shirt with suspenders. Even from the back, he looked the part of a young Wall Street exec.

"Does it have to be caviar?" Veronica asked.

"Don't see why it shouldn't be," Evan smirked.

Josh cleared his throat. "And finally, and leastly I might add," he said laughing and pointing to a cornrowed kid sitting near the back of the room, "that's Marcus Leazer. He double-majored in psychology and biology. I think he's going to be the first Negro doctor in his part of the state."

"That's very funny coming from a recovering Jewish crackhead," Marcus said. He threw a balled up piece of paper in Josh's direction. Josh caught it and tossed it into the trashcan.

Seeing Kallie's shocked face, Veronica said, "Don't mind those two. They're closer than brothers. Now that you know our super powers," Veronica added jokingly, "what are your special skills?"

"If you mean what I am majoring in," Kallie said, "I haven't decided yet. I'm taking a psychology class now. I enjoy it. But, I'm not sure if I want to major in it."

Cedric said, "Psychology is the basis..."

"Of everything," Dr. Frost interjected as she walked out of her office. "You guys don't spend too much time sitting around gabbing. Your project is not going to complete itself. The heavens have bestowed upon you, a gift." She nodded toward Kallie.

"Yeah," Marcus said. "And what's her claim to fame."

"She's one in 700,000 for starters," Josh said.

CHAPTER SIX

Externally, Our Lady of Faith continued about its business in its usual orderly fashion. Mass, confession, and Bible study were held at their regularly appointed hours. There were the normal visits to the sick and shut-ins and the Church seamlessly continued with its various charity pursuits. Its doors remained open and its priest was mostly available. In fact, as was typical for this time of year, there'd been one wedding and two funerals in the nearly eight and a half weeks since Phillip Beamer had been brutally murdered on the front porch of a boarding house in South Carolina. However, none of Our Lady of Faith's parishioners knew of any particular connection between that horrific event and their own consecrated grounds. Then again, none of them knew that their own priest, one Father McCarthy, had been questioned about the murder by an immigration agent, not two weeks after Beamer's body had been nearly stumbled over by his landlady, the sweet, but ruthlessly hardworking, Mabel Jones. But to be fair, no one knew about that particular interrogation, except McCarthy, Bishop Boland, the questioning agent himself, and perhaps one or two other interested souls within ICE. The information had been purposely kept out of the media, and well, if even the media hadn't gotten wind of it...

The church didn't hold mass on Mondays, and McCarthy generally used the day for a little R&R, which typically for him involved a basketball in some way, shape, or form. He stood at the top of the key on the church-provided basketball court, gazing wearily at the goal. He'd bricked seven straight shots. He stepped back about a couple of feet and pound-dribbled the ball. Still eying the goal, he rotated the ball with his fingertips and launched another jump shot. *Clack!* The ball caromed off the backboard, barely glazing the rim. He feebly reached for it as it bounced past him, missing it by a hair. It continued rolling toward the bench, eventually going under it and thudding softly against the back wooden fence, rolling back a bit before coming to a dead stop under the bench. McCarthy sighed before walking over to the bench. He plopped himself down on it without even bothering to retrieve that malevolent round piece of rubber residing beneath him.

Sitting on the bench, McCarthy thought about the agent's initial and so far only visit to see him. McCarthy had thought for sure he'd soon see Dennard Bennett again. He'd halfway expected to be harassed regularly until he admitted knowing something in relation to Beamer's murder. But there'd been no further contact with the agent whatsoever. Of course, there was no way McCarthy could know what was going on behind the scenes, or what other paths Beamer's murder investigation had opened, or even if Bennett was simply playing possum, preparing to strike with a search warrant or subpoena at any moment, perhaps delivered for effect during mass or confession. All such possibilities had nested at the back of his mind since that day in mid-August. Thankfully, none of it had come to pass. He hated not being able to work fully with any branch of law enforcement or government agency. But it was beyond his control. The nature of his knowledge and the scope of his responsibilities had set the boundaries of cooperation.

You could not negotiate with evil. And make no mistake, terrorists were pure evil and thus were subject to elimination without delay, debate, or due process. Rememberers had enabled A.I. to execute the necessary task of the elimination of terrorists without fear of mistake. Rememberers' documentation of future events was beyond dispute. But law

enforcement and government agencies would be hard pressed
to understand. They were not conditioned to operate on faith.
They operated by sight and evidence of things seen. There'd
be questions and needless discussions. Subsequently,
terrorists would go free and evil would live on, free to
continue destroying anything and everything.

But in the grand scheme of things, McCarthy wouldn't
have it any other way. The government needed its self-
imposed boundaries. There was danger in a free-flowing
government, knowing what McCarthy himself knew, and
then executing countrymen and foreigners alike with neither
trial nor second thought. McCarthy had been charged with a
great duty. One in which the all-knowing Father had
advocated for him many years before.

McCarthy was twenty-two when he'd first met Father
Richard Boland, nearly thirty-five years ago. He'd just
graduated from Carroll College where he'd led the Fighting
Saints to four straight conference championships. After his
college eligibility ran out, there'd been talk of a NBA free
agent deal, maybe even a late second round draft selection.
"Worse comes to worse," Billy Felton, a sports agent with the
Lockett and Lorde sports agency had said, "you can play
overseas. Off the top of my head, I can name a half dozen
European teams that would pay top dollar for your services.
I'm talking hundreds of thousands of dollars. And with that
Christian bit, you could possibly add a few endorsement
deals to the pot."

"That's just the thing," McCarthy had said. "It's not a bit.
God's calling me. I'm not playing professional ball. I'm going
to serve Him."

"You can do both," Felton pleaded.

"No," McCarthy had said evenly. "I can't." He didn't feel
the need to go into the whole shebang about the dangers of
trying to serve two masters. He simply turned away from
Billy Felton and walked away. And with that, he'd also
turned his back on the opportunity to be paid royally for what

he truly enjoyed doing. His friends that weren't calling him stupid were saying he was making a noble sacrifice and would get his reward in Heaven. But even they'd had it wrong. He didn't feel as if he was making a sacrifice and he wasn't doing it to receive some grand reward in the afterlife. As far as he was concerned, God had already given him his reward by creating him, and then when He'd had no reason to do so, had immeasurably increased it by giving His only begotten son. A sacrifice? Man, there was nothing McCarthy felt he could ever do to repay God for what He'd already given him. McCarthy knew he could never adequately explain how he felt to his friends, so he hadn't bothered trying. But with Father Boland, McCarthy hadn't needed to explain his actions. Father Boland, the college chaplain, had instinctively understood.

"This basketball opportunity you speak of," Boland had said. "It's like candy. Very sweet candy that tickles your taste buds. You're like a child with it. You'd be like the proverbial child in the candy store, gluttonously happy, devouring every sweet morsel. But no matter how much you'd eat, you wouldn't be able to get full, and eventually you'd probably even get sick. God, you realize, is like a full course meal. Even a small portion of Him can feel fulfilling. Yet, the next day, you'd be hungry again. And, you'd eat another portion, and again feel full. Until the next day when you'd start the whole process over again. Serving God, you realize, is like that. And that's what you want. It's what you seek."

McCarthy felt the tears streaming down his face before he'd realized he was crying. Boland had nailed it. His simple analogy had so nailed what McCarthy had felt. God was the very sustenance of his life. A sacrifice? Not by a long shot. It had been he who'd needed God, needed to serve him. It was not the other way around.

Boland had gently placed his arms on McCarthy's shoulders, looking into the young man's eyes. With the back of his hand, he wiped McCarthy's tears away. "I can see that your desire to serve the Lord is genuine."

On the strength of a strong recommendation from Boland, McCarthy enrolled in the Seminary. After graduation, he applied and was accepted to the diocesan priesthood formation program in Scranton where Boland had recently been installed as the ninth Bishop.

In Scranton, the new bishop saw that the initial faith and confidence he'd bestowed in the young priest candidate had been well deserved. McCarthy had an insatiable thirst and appetite for God's written word. He ritualistically studied his Bible and prayed to the Father for guidance and understanding. McCarthy's devotion to his studies prompted Boland, despite his own demanding and hectic schedule, to devote a fair number of hours a week to Bible study with McCarthy. He was impressed with the younger's growing insight into the Bible's true meaning. On one such studying occasion while the two of them sat at a table in Boland's office, McCarthy leaned back in his chair. "I always suspected that the Bible shouldn't be taken exactly literally. I mean, no one lives over a thousand years now, if they ever did. But now I'm seeing something else. I believe there're messages hidden in it. I feel God is talking to us in some secret code."

Boland, who'd had his head buried in his personal Bible, looked up at McCarthy. "What sort of messages?"

"Here in Genesis," McCarthy said, fumbling back to the front of his Bible. "It says that God created the world in six days, resting on the seventh. For years I thought that literally meant that on Monday, he created something. Tuesday he created something else, on and on to the end of the week, until finally coming to rest on Sunday."

"And now you no longer believe that?" Boland said with a quizzical glint in his eyes.

"No, I don't. A twenty-four hour day is a man-made concept, based on the rotation of the earth on its axis. Just as a year is a manmade concept based on the earth's trip around the sun. God created man, Earth, and Sun. The very instruments man used to develop his concept of time. It becomes plainly obvious that God's concept of time would be much different from that of man."

"Go on," Boland encouraged.

"So taken literally, the Bible is not completely accurate. But if you look beyond the words or rather deep within them, it makes a lot more sense." He looked back down at his Bible, turning a few more pages. "Like here, it describes the fall of man as occurring when Adam accepted the fruit from the Tree of Knowledge of Good and Evil from Eve." He looked up again at Boland. "The core of the story is true. But I think we get so wrapped up in trees and fruit that we've missed the whole point. I mean, there are people who have literally spent their lifetimes looking for the Garden of Eden. But they fail to see the significance of how the first woman's alignment with Satan led to her disobedience, or even how Adam's love for Eve led to his own downfall."

"You're saying such a Garden never existed?" Boland asked.

"What I'm saying is that the Garden shouldn't be the focal point of the story. The principals of the story are what's most important—man, woman, and Satan. I believe the focus should be on them, specifically the original meeting between woman and Satan, and then on the following one between woman and man before man ate of the fruit. I believe it's the only way to really understand the fall of man."

Impressed, Boland smiled broadly. "I believe you're ready."

"Ready for what?" McCarthy asked.

Boland didn't immediately answer. Instead, he stared deep into McCarthy's eyes for the longest time. McCarthy felt as if the bishop's eyes pierced holes through his own pupils, right through to his soul, to the very core of his being, his spirit. Finally, Boland spoke. "Years ago, before you entered

Seminary, I thought you'd be capable one day of knowing absolute truth. Tonight I'm certain of that. You're ready for a truth that precious few souls throughout history have been privy to."

Boland's short spiel led to McCarthy's acceptance into URO and eventually his initiation into the Alliance where he would learn about time-cycles and eternal return. By looking into his eyes, Boland had deemed McCarthy worthy of receiving such knowledge and fully capable of handling the responsibility that came with it. Boland used the words many fathers and mentors often said to young gifted charges. "With great knowledge and privilege comes even greater responsibility." Those would be the same words McCarthy would use in speaking with his young North Carolina mentee over thirty-five years later. Back in August, Boland had told him to rein the young man in without stifling him. The directive, though spoken rather easily by Boland, had at the time seemed a daunting task to McCarthy. How do you rein in, but not stifle, a cocky, young knucklehead? It seemed rather oxymoronic.

But surprisingly, the task had been a fairly easy one to complete. The reason? His mentee hadn't actually been the cocky knucklehead McCarthy had believed him to be. The young mentee was agreeable, and at the end of their conversation, he'd even vowed to be more considerate of the goals and wellbeing of A.I. Their conversation had gone so well that it was decided they should have at least one a week. It would be a fairly simple way to ensure that A.I., McCarthy, and the young preacher/Rememberer were all on the same page. The ritualistic phone call would occur on Mondays, which added the benefit of allowing the two of them to discuss their Sunday sermons.

Reaching under the bench to grab the basketball, McCarthy realized that the calls had become the highlight of his Mondays.

*   *   *

South Park Mall was sparsely populated on Monday evening. It was nearly four weeks before Halloween, and almost eight weeks before Black Friday, the official start of the holiday season shopping frenzy. After that date, the mall would be crushed daily until Christmas with a deluge of anxious, excited shoppers looking for the perfect gifts for loved ones. But this evening's light foot traffic, a calming before the retail storm, was exactly what Gerald Principe had desired.

He sat on the edge of the table-high granite wall encasing the fountain and watched a woman push a stroller toward Neiman Marcus. For a few weeks now, he'd been coming to the mall after his security shift ended, preferring the milling about of strangers to the quietness of his dark apartment where an onslaught of images, visions, and his thoughts constantly pushed against his skull. Without benefit of distractions, he was finding it increasingly difficult to separate the 'here and now' from the 'as yet to be.' A loud television or blasting radio proved ineffectual, as did his computer; all such technological things had become merely irritants. People, especially in small doses, usually did the trick. After the woman and stroller left his line of sight, his thoughts returned to Phillip Beamer.

He hadn't personally met Beamer, having come across the now dearly departed in a chat room. On some level, Principe regretted Beamer had to sacrifice his life for the cause, especially since a man of Beamer's murderous capabilities could have proven useful in so many different ways. The would-be terrorist's monstrous desire to blow up a federal building, thus killing hundreds, had been a noble desire indeed. But in the grand scheme of things, it was only small potatoes and, alas, Beamer had but one life to give. The erstwhile terrorist had not the capability or knowledge to open the gateway for the others. And therefore, despite being a kindred destructive spirit, Beamer's death had been necessary for the true cause. With his remembering ability, Principe could have warned Beamer of his impending demise. Instead, Principe allowed the federal building which had been successfully destroyed in the previous life-cycle, to be saved this go around and the architect of its planned destruction to be killed. He'd given a scented bone to the increasingly bothersome A.I.

As a group of giggling teenage girls flocked past him, he wondered if his ruse had been successful in putting the authorities on the scent of the Alliance of Initiates, thus impeding A.I.'s efforts to find him. A.I. was particularly troublesome, as it no doubt had elicited the help of one who shared Principe's unique "remembering" ability. He didn't know the exact number of others like him, but A.I. would only need the one anyway. And it had been him, Principe was certain, who'd given A.I. the names and locations of the other gate-openers. Only with the help of a Rememberer could A.I. have successfully foiled his two previous attempts. But Rememberers could be fooled, Principe thought.

Suddenly his stomach growled and he realized that he hadn't eaten dinner. As he walked toward the escalators leading to the food court, he felt an uncannily welcomed uncertainty about his future for the first time since his remembering ability had first manifested itself. Perhaps Beamer's sacrificial death had borne fruit after all. Another time-cycle perhaps? It was an intriguing possibility.

CHAPTER SEVEN

Kallie headed back to the boarding house as darkness and rain fell. Through the Honda's rain-pecked windshield, streetlights twinkled dimly like fallen angels as she drove by. She hadn't expected the visit to Dr. Frost's lab to turn out as well as it had. To be honest, she hadn't known what to expect. All she'd wanted and needed were answers about her déjà vu sensations, which was why she'd walked over to the lab immediately after Professor Sampson had suggested it.

The good thing was she learned that although daily déjà vu sensations were rare and troubling to her, they weren't exactly unique and were most likely related somehow to memory issues, issues that, once identified, could possibly be sorted out, enabling her to resume a normal life, one that wouldn't feel as if it was a rerun. Josh said there were a couple of cited cases for the condition. It affected about one person in 700,000. He'd added, "It might even be more than that, since some people may be living with the condition and not saying anything about it for fear of being considered mentally ill."

Living with it! Josh's words echoed in her head as she turned the Honda onto her street. Living with it meant not dying from it. She could fully embrace now the realization that a fear of dying had been what had mostly bothered her about the sensations. She'd thought she was dying. She'd thought the déjà vu sensations had been an indication of cancer or some other brain disease, especially since her mother had died from brain cancer. Kallie had thought that the disease was something that she herself could one day inherit. In hindsight, she supposed that she could have gotten a MRI earlier to alleviate her concerns. She could have found out sooner if she'd had cancer or a tumor. But then again, she acknowledged, there'd been a measure of hope in not actually knowing. Rational thinking or not, the not knowing of something bad seemed equal to the whisper's chance of finding out something good. But her conversation with Dr. Frost had changed her outlook, convincing her that getting her brain scanned was not only a good thing but a necessary one. Frost had said that the test was the first step in trying to determine what was causing her sensations, which could be a number of things and not necessarily anything life threatening. It had been the 'not necessarily life threatening' part that had most convinced her. Now she wasn't afraid to have her brain scanned. In fact, she welcomed it, despite the fact that the tests could still reveal something sinister like a tumor. At least now she understood that there were other possibilities as well, potentially fixable possibilities. Friday could not get here soon enough!

She approached her driveway and saw that her parking space was occupied by a gray, late model Volvo. "Just perfect," she said as she found a place to park at the curb. Evidently, one of her housemates had a suitor who'd had the unmitigated gall to roll up in here like he owned the joint.

She entered the house and started to make a mad dash upstairs to her room. She didn't want to see the offending culprit who'd parked in her spot. She already didn't get along with two of her housemates. Having to curse out one of their boyfriends sure as heck wasn't going to lead to a sharing of warm fuzzy feelings.

She'd gotten halfway up the stairs when Maggie called out to her. Kallie stopped and turned. Maggie came out of the living room. *Maggie with a boyfriend?* she thought. Maggie was the only housemate she got along with and actually liked. She was a pretty girl, though a bit chunky in places where girls never wanted to be chunky, particularly those who entertained thoughts of movie dates and park walking with members of the opposite sex. Maggie had once told Kallie she was at Bengate to get an education, not a husband. And as if to punctuate the declaration, Maggie dressed in the frumpiest clothes she could find, which didn't at all compliment her body dimensions. To make matters worse, she didn't wear makeup and rarely did anything about her hair, often choosing to let it flop about her face. Maggie had taken to Kallie because she'd thought she'd found a kindred spirit in the 'take me as I am species.' The difference was, as Maggie herself admitted; Kallie's 'as I am' had come in a much better package than Maggie's had. Still, Maggie was a confident woman who was very comfortable in her own stretch-marked skin.

"You have a visitor," Maggie informed her.

"Me?" Kallie asked as she slowly descended the stairs.

"Yes, you," Maggie said. "It was bound to happen sooner or later. You can't look like that without expecting someone to notice eventually."

"Ha, ha. Very funny. Who is he? What's his name?"

Maggie scooted past her and headed up the stairs. "Why don't you go into the living room and see. Apparently, he's loaded. That's his car in your parking spot."

As soon as Kallie entered the living room, she heard Maggie bursting with laughter upstairs. She looked over at the figure sitting on the loveseat. Seeing her, he stood up. Kallie's eyes widened. Her visitor was a minister.

Reverend Johnny Swag was the twenty-five year old charismatic preacher of New Vibe Community Church. He was strikingly handsome with piercing blue eyes and a square jaw line cleft-dimpled ever so slightly. He was dressed conservatively in a black suit, complete with a white clerical collar. He smiled hesitantly, extending his hand. "I assume you're Kallie."

Cautiously, Kallie shook his hand. His grip was firm. His hand felt cold. "Yes, I am."

"I know what you're thinking," Swag said. "Why am I dressed like some sort of Puritan preacher? Trust me, there's a logical reason for it. I know if I dressed this way all the time, I wouldn't get near the number of young people to join my church. But the truth is, if I don't dress like this some of the time, I'm going to lose some of my elderly. So you might say this is a kind of compromise. I mostly wear this suit on Mondays when I visit some of our sick and shut-ins. There's something about a black-suited preacher that's comforting to many of our seniors. They feel the suit is a reverence to God, and therefore He might look more kindly on my prayers for them."

Kallie nodded and motioned for him to return to his place on the loveseat. She sat in the flower-printed recliner. She wondered why he was here.

As if reading her mind, he said, "I received a call from an Octavia Hunt this morning..."

Oh, Kallie thought. She might have guessed. She visualized her grandmother hurriedly looking up Swag and New Vibe as soon as she'd hung up with Kallie this morning. Oh that woman, Kallie steamed.

Swag continued. "She told me her granddaughter was a member of my church and she asked me if I knew that her granddaughter wasn't feeling well. And if I didn't, then shame on me for not checking on the wellbeing of a member of my flock. Of course, I tell her that although New Vibe is not a mega church, I do have a right good-sized congregation. It's not entirely possible for me to know when someone at the church is sick unless someone calls and tells me. She said, 'I am calling.'" Swag chuckled. "So, I thanked her for the call and that's why I'm here. Your grandmother is very concerned about you. Now, tell me what's going on."

"As you can see, I'm not sick," Kallie said. "In fact, I've never felt better. Earlier, when I'd talked to my grandmother I was a little stressed about school and all because I have several mid-term exams coming up. I guess she took it the wrong way. But I'm fine, really."

"Your grandmother mentioned something about déjà vu sensations."

Kallie rolled her eyes and inhaled. "I had a couple of episodes of it. But, it's fine now. Like I said, I was worried about mid-terms before, but now I'm not."

Swag leaned toward her. "The sensations have gone away?"

She didn't want to lie to a reverend. But she also didn't want her grandmother to continue worrying. Mentally, she sent up a quick prayer of contrition. "I hadn't experienced any for a while. Plus, I talked to a school counselor and he agreed that they were most likely stress related."

Swag leaned back again. "Well then, that is good news. I'll be sure to call your grandmother and let her know. I told her that I'd call her after I saw you at Bible study."

"Bible study?"

"Yes, we have it on Wednesdays, noon and 7 p.m. We have a lot of college kids attend the noonday session. Can I expect you at that one?"

"I don't know. Wednesdays are pretty hectic for me."

Swag glanced at his watch. "Well, there's always the seven o'clock one. I don't know how late your grandmother stays up. I'd told her I'd call her after Bible study."

His veiled threat worked. "Okay," she said. The last thing she needed was for the pastor to call her grandmother back and tell her that Kallie had never before stepped foot in his church. "I'll be there at noon."

Swag smiled. "That's great. Then, I'll see you Wednesday."

"Yeah, Wednesday," Kallie mumbled. She escorted him to the door and stood watching as he drove away in his Volvo. Her grandmother was definitely a piece of work.

REMEMBERERS

*   *   *

By late Tuesday afternoon, Kallie had experienced three déjà vu sensations. The first two times hadn't been too disconcerting for her, as both had occurred at familiar places with her going about her usual routines. There was nothing weird about brushing her teeth in the morning or ordering her favorite sub at the campus cafe, so those two sensations had meshed almost seamlessly with her same ole—making her feel more like being in a rut than being caught in some kind of time warp. But her day's third bout of déjà vu, occurring during her General Psychology class, was unnerving.

Her psychology professor, William Jones, was sixty-something with a full head of cotton-white hair. He stood at the front of the class droning on and on about a topic which he lately seemed to be wildly obsessed with. "Man wants to be God," he was saying. "Or at the very least, he wants to do what only God so far has shown the capability of doing, and that's to make life." He paused, looking about the room as he often did during his lectures, daring one of his students to challenge his assertion. After several moments, it was obvious no one was willing to challenge him on this one. Jones started to continue, but then one of his students, a freckle-faced lad sitting in the second row, hesitantly raised his hand.

Jones nodded in the lad's direction. "Mr. Johns, you wish to object?"

"Uh," Johns said. "I don't know. Just...well how can you speak for all men? I don't want to make life. At least not like that," he added quickly with a light chuckle.

"Maybe, you're not a man," a male classmate sitting behind him said, playfully hitting him on the shoulder.

"More man than you," Johns retorted.

Jones smiled. "Settle down, gentlemen. Excellent question, Mr. Johns. You're rejecting my premise on the grounds that it may have been too narrowly centered, correct?"

Johns flushed red. "I...I, uh, guess I am."

"Good," Jones said. "I see your point. What man represents all men?"

"Right," Johns agreed enthusiastically.

"Okay," Jones said. "Now I could go all biblical on you and say that the actions of one man, Adam, essentially affected all humanity. But seeing how Adam at the time was the only man alive, I'll leave that discussion for another time. Instead, let me just say that man in my statement represents the consensus thought, whether consciously or unconsciously formed of all men. I admit it's not scientifically based. But I believe it's as sound as a young person's 'they.' As in, 'they' are always keeping us down. Or, is that 'the man' is always keeping us down?" He chuckled. "I always get 'they' and 'the man' mixed up. Anyway, man, the man, they, and the politician's 'the American people' are simply terms used to connote the assumed collective thoughts or desires of the believed majority."

There was silence for a few seconds, and then a red-haired girl sitting in the front row asked, "So when a politician says the 'American people', he's not saying he's speaking for everyone but almost everyone, since there is no singular 'American people,' but rather a nation of many, vastly different individuals."

"Yes, I believe so," Jones said.

"But how can they or you make that claim?" the red-haired girl asked.

Jones looked over the class and posed the question, "On what basis do you believe a politician feels comfortable speaking for the American people as a collective majority?"

"Polls," someone said from the back of the room.

"Elections," someone else offered. "Majority rules. If you win elections, you get to say that you speak for all the people. It's our system, our rule of law."

"It's not exactly law," another student challenged.

"Well, it's certainly tradition," someone else shot back.

Jones smiled, regarding the class with a smug look. "These are all great observations and thoughts. But the truth is, it doesn't matter on what authority the phrase 'American people' or the term 'man' is used. The hearer of such terms will either agree or disagree with whatever the person using the term is purporting. Outside of a few people occasionally questioning who they are, no one seriously challenges the use of the terms. And eventually, there will only be the original assertion which will be either accepted, rejected, ignored, or discussed. It will be out there for the public to digest one way or the other, which is often the intent anyway."

The red-haired girl frowned. "So you're just making a baseless claim?"

"My claim is not exactly baseless. It's one I sincerely believe I have the evidence to support, although not scientifically."

"Well, show us the evidence," the redhead said.

"With pleasure," Jones said. He looked around at the class. "What do popular movies such as The Terminator, The Matrix, I, Robot, and 2001: A Space Odyssey, to name a few, have in common with each other?"

"They've all made the actors and producers boatloads of money," Johns said to a chorus of amens.

"So true, Mr. Johns," Jones said. "But what else do they have in common?"

It was when the professor's question hung in the air that Kallie experienced her day's third unnerving feeling of sameness. When one of her classmates answered, "They all feature machines run amok," Kallie silently mouthed his response alongside him, matching him syllable for syllable.

"Exactly," Jones exclaimed. "But not just machines, manmade machines!"

"But what does that prove?" The redhead and Kallie said in unison, before looking at each other and saying, "Jinx."

"Uncanny," The redhead said to Kallie, which Kallie could have said as well, but decided not to, preferring to get off the verbal tic for tack.

Jones regarded them both curiously for a moment. "Some people say that fiction is man's truth."

"Another baseless claim," the redhead said.

"Perhaps," Jones said. "Still, man creating machines that ultimately become living, breathing entities is a theme that shows up repeatedly in literary and theatrical works."

"And that's the basis of your original claim?" The redhead said incredulously. "God," she said in complete unison with Kallie, "Man's ego knows no bounds."

Jones regarded the redhead curiously. "My ego, Miss Wilson, or man's ego in general?"

"I would say both," the red-haired Miss Wilson said. "Yours because you're assuming that, based on the creations of a few individuals, you've somehow figured out man's greatest desire. Man's in general, because what can I say, the statement's simply true. Man's ego is freaking boundless." The class erupted in laughter.

*   *   *

Her sleep that night was ragged and fitful. Twice she snapped awake, pulled from a dream that made no more sense in wakefulness than it had in the realm of unconsciousness. In the dream, she stood naked in an explosion of light. The light was in rainbow colors and it seemed to have come out of nowhere, bringing with it a myriad of indistinguishable sounds that she could somehow taste, feel, and smell. She stood in the center of it as it washed all over her. It was like she'd become one with some kind of formless entity. Then all of a sudden, she found herself standing in a field, surrounded by white snakes. Her mother was there, clinging to her arm as if Kallie could somehow navigate her through the snakes and out of the field. However, each time she started to lead her mother out, she awoke before taking the first step.

The next morning, she sat up on the edge of the bed, pushing the weird dream away. Still in yesterday's clothes, she craved a long hot shower and food. She hadn't eaten anything since yesterday's sub sandwich. The desire to be clean and fed comforted her. These were basic human needs and wants, which meant that despite feeling otherworldly during the last twenty-four hours because of the déjà vu sensations, she was in fact worldly, still very much human. She looked at the alarm clock on the nightstand. It was 6:30 a.m. Sometime during the night, she'd made a conscious decision not to go to her eight o'clock history class. She couldn't go. After Monday's pencil-dropping incident and yesterday's triple sensations, she wasn't in the mood to be around people. Besides, she had the creepy feeling that she'd already been to that morning's history class. Going again would amount to unnecessary redundancy.

As the hot water steamed over her, she considered the evolution of her sensations. Initially, they'd been similar to the ones she'd gotten sporadically as a child, just a short burst of weird familiarity, an odd 'been there, done that' sensation, usually lasting less than a minute. Back then, she'd even considered the sensations kind of cool. At least they'd never freaked her out like the recent ones. And she could not recall ever having more than one in a month. Sometimes there'd even been years between sensations. But the current ones, except for the past weekend's brief respite from them, were coming almost daily. Yesterday, there'd been three occurrences; she'd never had more than one in a single day before. And now this morning her sensations felt anticipatory. She could almost visualize the history class. She could see her classmates' faces. She knew what they'd wear. It felt sort of like she was...was that even possible? Could she have become psychic?

She dried off and then wrapped the towel around herself, walking back to her room. She recalled the movie Phenomenon where the main character played by John Travolta had suddenly become a genius. He'd learned later that his newfound intelligence had been caused by a brain tumor that would eventually claim his life. She was less fearful now that tumors or such were the reason behind her sensations. Dr. Frost and the others had given her a measureable amount of hope that the cause of the sensations wasn't something fatalistic. Kallie's assuaged fears were based in part on that glimmer of hope as well as her gut feeling. She was getting increasingly convinced that she was getting a gift. Of what, she wasn't exactly sure. But to her, yesterday's sensation trifecta, along with this morning's psychic-like one, seemed to support the gift notion. Whether Friday's MRI would bear that out, of course, remained to be seen.

She dressed quickly and walked downstairs to the kitchen. Since she wasn't going to class, she had enough time to eat something other than toast. It felt like a ham and cheese omelet type of morning. Maybe, she thought hopefully, the aroma would stir Maggie to life and she'd come down to join her for breakfast, giving Kallie a chance to try to convince her housemate to accompany her to New Vibe's noonday Bible study.

CHAPTER EIGHT

"Absolutely not," Maggie said. She pulled a gray sweat suit from the dresser drawer and threw the two pieces on her bed beside Kallie.

"But why not?" Kallie asked. She nonchalantly spread Maggie's sweat pants across the bed and placed the matching sweatshirt above it, smoothing out the wrinkles of both with her hand. Maggie could not be accused of having varied taste in clothes. Her wardrobe consisted mainly of sweat suits, frumpy jeans, and oversized sweatshirts and T-shirts. Kallie estimated that her roommate had about fourteen sweat suits in an assortment of colors.

Maggie grabbed a towel off the back of a chair and pulled on a shower cap. "Because I don't want to."

"But I cooked you breakfast," Kallie protested.

"And I thanked you."

Kallie held up the sweatshirt. "I'll iron this for you."

Maggie headed for the door. "And have people thinking I suddenly care about how I look? No thanks."

"Please!"

"Stop begging. It's unbecoming."

Kallie followed her down the hallway. "The service only lasts an hour."

"Exactly."

"Exactly what?" Kallie asked.

"Exactly, meaning you'd only be there an hour anyway. You can make it through that. It's not like you're going on a blind date or something."

"I know. But that pastor is kind of creepy."

"Why don't you ask one of the other girls?"

"Now you're just being cruel," Kallie said. Maggie knew both Shelly and Cynthia hated her. The feelings were mutual.

"Wish I could help you."

"No you don't." Kallie said. "Because if you did, then you would."

Maggie smiled. "You know, you're probably right." She closed the bathroom door in Kallie's face.

Kallie trudged back downstairs to the living room. She couldn't be upset with Maggie. She'd known it would be a longshot getting Maggie to go with her, especially if Maggie didn't want to go. That girl never did anything that she didn't want to do if she didn't have to do it. It was a major reason why Kallie liked her so much in the first place. Maggie was her own woman who put herself first. But she was also a good friend. If she'd suspected Kallie faced danger at the church, she most certainly would have gone with her.

But having an uncomfortable feeling wasn't necessarily an indication of impending danger. Besides, New Vibe was a church. She'd be going to a church in the middle of town, in the middle of the day. It was a church, for goodness sake. Why was it making her so uncomfortable? Well, for one thing, she answered herself, the other night the pastor had come by the house dressed like the grim reaper. And he'd done so after having received one phone call from a woman he hadn't even known. And she couldn't forget that she'd seen some of her college mates who attended the church. To her, they all looked sort of wacked out and mind controlled. There was something mildly strange about young people being that high on religion. Didn't they have enough to worry about and do without having to deal with the halleluiah brigade?

You're being silly, she chided herself. The reverend had already explained to her why he'd dressed that way. Besides, didn't she consider herself a free spirit who could dress anyway she liked, regardless of what other people thought? Wasn't that what Maggie did? And she'd praised Maggie for it. And as for the pastor coming to see her after he'd received that call from her grandmother, she should be thanking him, not condemning him for it. Lord only knew who her grandmother would have gotten to come over if the reverend hadn't agreed to do it. And as for her college mates—what student didn't look wacked out, especially during midterms? Of course she was being silly. There wasn't anything to fear about New Vibe Community Church. Still, she conceded as she sat down in the recliner in the living room that she'd feel a lot better if she had someone go with her. She checked her watch. It was seven minutes after eleven. She'd leave for the church in about thirty minutes.

Hearing a knock at the door, she went to it, pressing her eye against the peephole. "Who is it?"

"Seth Winters," said the voice on the other side of the door.

She peered at him through the peephole, her heart thumping so hard she thought she could hear it. *It was actually Seth Winters. Why was he here and how had he known where she lived?* She'd felt an attraction towards him since the first time she saw him while registering for classes. Before she'd found out his name, she'd simply referred to him as "the boy." She grabbed the doorknob with a suddenly clammy hand. She opened the door hesitantly, somehow feeling as if she was opening the door to her possible future. At the sight of her, Seth's eyes widened. The electricity was palpable. "Seth Winters," she repeated.

"Uh, hi Kallie," he stumbled. "I wasn't expecting you to answer the door. I saw that you weren't in class today. I thought maybe you were sick or something."

She was at a loss for words. He knew her name and noticed that she hadn't been in class that morning. Obviously he'd also paid attention when Professor Sampson had called roll, since the two of them hadn't been formally introduced. She stood motionless for a moment as her voice stayed on hiatus and her mind temporarily blanked out.

His face reddened. "I didn't mean to just drop in on you. But after Monday's class, I thought, uh...well, anyway I don't live that far from here; actually just a couple of streets over. I've driven behind you a couple of times. I guess you never noticed." Despite the coolness of the morning, small droplets of sweat formed across his forehead.

Her voice returned, and then it was as if an unseen force pulled her back from the door, inviting him inside. "I guess I'm not that observant," she said as he stepped into the foyer, closing the door behind him.

"I'd wanted to stop by sooner," he said.

"Why didn't you?" Kallie asked, surprising herself with her sudden boldness.

"I don't know. I guess I didn't want to frighten you."

"Why would that have frightened me?"

His face flushed a deeper red. "I don't know. I guess it shouldn't have." He looked away for a moment as if afraid he'd put his foot in his mouth. Then, "Um, listen. I, um, I know on Monday, something was, um, bothering you. And when you missed class today, I, um, I just wanted to make sure you were okay."

Kallie wasn't completely naive. She'd seen this stumbling around routine from boys before. Funny how she'd no inkling until now that 'the boy' had been the least bit interested in her. He was handsome, seemed of above average intelligence, and dressed nicely. But that was as far as she'd gotten in her thinking on the subject. Boys, even 'the boy', hadn't exactly been foremost in her mind since she'd returned to school. She hadn't sworn off boys for the books like Maggie had, but her nonchalance toward them had the effect of doing the same thing. Of course, living off campus hadn't helped matters either. Muting potential romances was one of the drawbacks. Other than going to her classes and to the cafe for a sub sandwich about three times a week, she hadn't spent much time on campus, which didn't really give boys or 'the boy' a chance to say much more than hello, particularly if the said boy was the shy type. Monday's conversation with Josh had been the first meaningful conversation she'd had with a member of the opposite sex since she arrived back on campus. And she had to admit that talking to someone with a deeper voice than Maggie's had felt nice. "I'm okay," she said. "It was nice of you to check on me, especially since you don't really know me."

Seth smiled sheepishly. "I know. That's my fault. I should have introduced myself sooner."

"Well, I guess I could have done so as well," Kallie admitted. She looked at her watch. It was getting closer to noon. "I wish we could talk longer," she said and meant it, "but I do have somewhere I need to be."

Seth smiled awkwardly. "Oh, I'm sorry, of course. Like I said I just wanted to check on you." He turned to reopen the door.

Watching him turn, she was suddenly struck by a bolt of inspiration. "Wait a minute, Seth. What're you doing at noon today?"

* * *

The interior of New Vibe Community Church lived up to what its steepled, white-cement exterior had promised. New Vibe was a traditional, old fashioned church. It looked no different from any other church she'd ever attended. It had stained, variegated glass windows, plush green carpet, and two rows of fifteen aisle-parted pews. On the backs of the pews were racks containing Bibles and hymnals, and small wood pockets which held note pads and tithing envelopes. Up front, a pulpit flanked by two tall potted plants and backed by a choir stand stood prominently on a flower-adorned altar.

As she and Seth took seats near the front of the church, Kallie felt more than a little silly. Here she was dragging poor ole Seth to a church in the middle of the day because she'd thought...what exactly? That she was going to be attacked by a bunch of robe wearing Hare Krishna lookalikes? Or maybe, she'd believed that the church's pastor with his rapper's last name and colorful personality would swoop down from on high, preaching a fire and brimstone sermon while his transfixed flock, singing, shouting, and Bible thumping, encircled and taunted her. But now, as she sat there engulfed by the sweet smell of old wood mixed with a faint scent of flowers, she realized that her worrisome thoughts had been a tad foolish. A church was a church. And despite sensing that New Vibe still lacked a certain something (just what that something was, she wasn't exactly sure), she told herself that it was still just a church.

There were only about ten other people here, including two that she thought she recognized from campus. Everyone sat quietly, either reading their Bibles or casually looking around and waiting for Pastor Swag. Kallie looked at Seth. If he was freaked out by her offer to attend church with her, he didn't show it. He met her eyes and smiled. She smiled back, and then they both faced front again and waited with the others for the pastor.

Five minutes later, Swag entered through a side door. He was dressed casually, with khaki pants and a black button down shirt with a clerical collar. Carrying a Bible, he stepped onto the altar and went straight to the pulpit. "Good afternoon," he said.

And then it happened.

The déjà vu sensation struck her with a fierceness she hadn't felt previously. She felt constricted, as if she'd been squeezed into a glass bottle. She was a part of the surroundings; in fact, immersed in them. Yet, somehow she was consciously separated from them at the same time. She turned to Seth. He was still looking intently at Swag as the pastor spoke. She looked around at the others. They were all looking at Swag, paying no attention to her. She could see their pending movements. And for the first time, she felt like she could do so not because she was somehow becoming psychic, but because she'd lived through this scene previously! She'd seen it all before.

She looked up front, locking eyes with Swag, and simultaneously the two of them said, "We're going to continue our study of Revelations today. If you would please turn to..." Kallie abruptly stopped, roughly grabbing Seth by the arm. "Let's go. I need to get out of here!"

They'd taken Seth's car to the church. Now, he drove them to a nearby sandwich shop. Once inside the shop, he found a back corner table, away from the windows. The shop didn't have wait staff. Food was ordered and paid for at one end of the counter, and then picked up at its other end.

She'd told him that she wasn't hungry; but he ordered her today's special anyway. It included what he considered the shop's best sandwich, the Reuben. He told her that she could take hers home to eat later; since for most college students hunger pangs often struck fiercely after midnight.

For his part, Seth didn't ask her what the matter was or why she'd all of sudden left a service she'd invited him to after the pastor had barely uttered a word. She appreciated him not making a big deal about it. She didn't really know him well enough to begin blabbering secrets to him. Not that what was happening to her was a secret. She didn't really know what was happening to her and probably wouldn't know until Friday's MRI test. Finally she said, "Thanks again for the sandwich and for coming with me today. I guess this was a heck of a first..." she paused. She didn't know exactly how to classify what they were on; since technically, it wasn't a date. She'd never asked a boy out before and honestly hadn't thought about it one way or the other. She supposed she was modern enough to do so, if the situation called for it and she was so inclined. But this outing hadn't been spurred by any romantic inclinations on her part. She'd wanted someone to go with her to Reverend Swag's church. Seth's showing up at her house had been a matter of convenience. Albeit a fortuitous one, she might add.

Sensing her awkwardness, he said, "I don't know. My father would be happy about my first outing with a girl being a trip to church."

Outing, she thought, smiling inwardly. That was the same term she'd just used to describe it. "He would? Why?"

Seth bit off a piece of potato chip. "He's a reverend." He stuffed the rest of the chip into his mouth.

Kallie sipped her soda. That's just great, she thought. She wondered what his dad would think when Seth described the 'outing' to him. "A preacher's boy? So that makes you wild and rebellious?"

"Nah, I think that only applies to a preacher's daughter."

They both laughed. And pretty soon they were laughing and joking like old friends about other things as well, everything from old television shows that they both liked, to recollections of some of their childhoods' most embarrassing moments. She found him unpretentious, easy to talk to, and incredibly gorgeous. After a while, she was ready for that Reuben, and afterwards, agreed with him that it was indeed a very good sandwich. When they'd finally decided to leave the shop a couple of hours later, she'd forgotten all about New Vibe Community Church and déjà vu.

CHAPTER NINE

Bennett was due a week of vacation and he decided to use it to visit his sister in Charlotte. He hadn't seen Helen and her family in over a year and he looked forward to the visit. He'd maybe do some fishing with his brother-in-law, Mark, and he could always count on his nephew, MJ, having the latest Madden videogame. And if the stars lined up right, his niece, Veronica, would be home for the weekend from college, giving him the opportunity to see the whole Ross clan under one roof and hear the welcoming and once familiar sound of family chatter. Yes, that was what he wanted to hear, needed to hear—the sounds of family. The numbing high he'd gained from his elixir-like hectic work schedule had finally worn off and was no longer helping him forget Elise and his girls. Besides, he no longer wanted to forget. He was now willing to embrace his memories of them. Maybe now the memories wouldn't hurt as much.

The early evening sky was cloudless, starless, and ink-black. He circled the long winding driveway leading up to his sister's home. The house was about seven thousand square feet with a three-car garage. Mark was an executive with a computer software firm, and, evidently, the company paid him well. Helen had been a teacher by trade, but Bennett couldn't remember when she'd last worked. He was very happy that his sister had found Mark. He was a good looking man as well as a great husband, father, and provider, and according to Helen, he was also her soul mate. From Bennett's vantage point, the two of them seemed happy and they were genuinely good folk. If anyone deserved the best that life had to offer, he often thought it was his little sister

Helen. She'd been only three years old when their mother died, and he'd always felt she'd been cheated out of something. He prayed that she'd never again experience the pain of loss as he had.

He pulled within fifteen feet of the garage and killed the engine. As he opened his car door, he heard the mechanically smooth rumblings of the garage door starting its ascent. It eventually reached its zenith, uncovering the back of a late model BMW 7-series. In the next instant, he heard the BMW's motor crank, and then saw its backup lights flash on. The car proceeded to inch back before suddenly screeching to a jerky halt.

Bennett had gotten out of his car and was walking the remaining length of the driveway toward the garage.

Helen hopped out of her car. "Dennard, is that you?" She ran to him, throwing her arms around his neck. "Why didn't you call?"

He hugged his sister fiercely. "I wanted to surprise you."

"Well, it is a surprise. A wonderful, wonderful surprise!" She stayed in his embrace a while, as if to savor the warmth of a brother she saw far too little. The night air had gotten colder as the temperature continued dropping. But neither sibling seemed to notice or care. After a few moments, Helen pulled back from the embrace. "I better call and cancel my meeting."

"No, no," Bennett said. "Don't go cancelling your plans. I can visit Mark and the children while you're at your meeting."

"Children? What children?"

"MJ and Veronica."

Helen smiled. "My, you have been away a while."

"It's only been a year."

"Try two years and even then I don't think either of them would have appreciated being called children."

Bennett laughed. "Well, let's not tell them. I imagine Veronica's away at college, but MJ's home, right?"

"No one's home," Helen said. "Since Veronica graduated from college, she rarely comes home. MJ's with friends on a weekend ski trip and Mark's out of town on business."

"Graduated from college?" he repeated.

"Yes," Helen said. "Last May, you don't remember?"

He lightly tapped his forehead. "Yeah, of course I remember. It just slipped my mind. She got my card, didn't she?"

"Yes, she got it and she sent you a thank you note. But she'd rather had you there."

Bennett frowned. The thank you letter was probably in the growing pile of mail in his house in Landover. He'd made a mental note to go through it the next time he made it home. He'd assumed most of it was just shred-ready junk mail anyway. All his bills were paid online and personal mail like thank you notes were rare events indeed. "I wish I could have been there. But I'll make the next one. She's getting her master's in psychology, right?" He was pleased with himself for remembering.

"Yes, she wants to combine it with her undergrad double majors in psychology and criminal justice. I think she eventually wants to follow in your footsteps."

He beamed. "ICE, really?"

"I don't know if it'll be that particular agency; but I got a feeling she's thinking federal in some capacity."

"That's great," Bennett said, before suddenly recalling what she'd just said about Mark and MJ not being home. "A weekend ski trip? But it's only Wednesday."

"MJ's school has back to back teacher workdays and the football team has an open date. It's like a high school fall break. So, he and his friends took off for the mountains."

Bennett looked gloomily up at the house. "You mean to tell me no one's in this big house?"

"Not at the moment. But that should be good news for you. It will give you a chance to have a little peace and quiet. I know you've been running ragged with that job of yours.

My meeting should only take a couple of hours. When I get back, we can catch up." She hugged him again and then walked back to her car. "You still remember the alarm code?"

"Yeah," he mumbled. "Your initials divided by two plus seven."

She smiled appreciatively and got back into her car, backing it up slowly before stopping beside him. The car window slid down. "The spare key is where it's always been. I haven't changed much inside, so you should be able to find what you need. Oh, Mark bought a new seventy-inch flat screen for his man hut."

"You mean cave," Bennett corrected.

"Whatever," she said. "It's just a playpen for grown men if you ask me." She laughed and continued backing up the car. Very quickly, she was gone, leaving Bennett standing alone in the driveway and suddenly aware of how cold it'd gotten.

The man-cave was located in the basement on the other side of a home gym. He walked through the gym, past a free weights bench and a treadmill, and arrived at the cave's entrance. The sign on the door read:

No admittance: Age 25 & under

Please remove your shoes

The sign included a picture of a cartoon man sitting on a recliner with his feet kicked up and his toes wiggling. Bennett smiled and removed his shoes, placing them near the door. He went inside and his feet immediately sank into lush carpet the color of green grass. He flipped on a light switch and looked around in amazement. The room never ceased to impress. It looked as if it'd been carved out the side of a stone mountain. The walls appeared made of rock. He could hear something akin to water running down a brook. In the center of the room was an L-shaped leather couch with two leather recliners as endpoints. To his right was the bar area, which he knew was stocked with various beers and liquors and a hoard of junk food. And at the front of the room was Mark's latest crown jewel.

The remote was in the pocket of one of the recliners. He sat down, kicking up the footrest. He turned on the TV and marveled at the pure hugeness of it. He flipped through the channels, trying to relax. But it wasn't long before the memories of his family, spurred on by the emptiness of the house and undeterred by the testosterone-inducing man-cave with its flashy theater-sized big screen TV, quickly overwhelmed him. He'd only kidded himself. He was not ready to face the memories. His week off work had not been his idea anyway. His supervisor had insisted, no, had ordered that he take the week off. It was also to include almost daily confabs with a therapist, but Bennett had been able to ward off that aspect of it with his promise to spend time with his sister's family.

"Just as long as you're not holed up somewhere alone and drinking," his supervisor had said.

The fears concerning Bennett drinking alcohol during his week off had been unwarranted. He no longer touched the stuff. Sure, he'd drunk a lot shortly after the plane crash that had snatched his wife and daughters away from him. But he'd just as soon quit. The initial high of the alcohol had been good. It was the aftermath of drunkenness that he couldn't deal with. Reality was made much worse after the realization that insobriety had lied. Nothing was okay. Nothing was going to be all right. At least it wouldn't be for a while. He couldn't wait for 'a while' with alcohol, especially since alcohol usually brought along its own set of problems.

He'd tried therapy, too. And just like alcohol, it'd initially been good. The therapist had encouraged him to talk about his feelings. What losing his family had meant to him. At first, he'd thought it was a stupid request. What had she thought losing his family felt like? As if he'd won the freaking lottery? He'd lost a beautiful wife, his soul mate. After only five years together, she was gone and so were his two daughters, Kelsey and Melanie, who at only four and three years old, had their lives unceremoniously snuffed out. It was devastating, almost indescribable. But eventually he had described it. And amazingly, putting words to the ache in his heart and the unexpected void in his life had been, well...therapeutic. He talked, and he talked, and he talked. And talking for a while had been good. But eventually talking had given way to frustration, because no amount of talking could ever answer the simple question of *why*.

The physical cause of the crash had soon been determined. It had been due to pilot error. After hitting significant turbulence, the first pilot had overused the rudder, losing control of the plane and crashing it into the Appalachian Mountains. Everyone on the plane, including Bennett's wife and daughters, perished. But in the three years since that fateful day, Bennett had yet to get a satisfying answer to the other 'why.' Why had his wife and daughters been on that plane in the first place?

He knew the surface answer to the question. Elise's mother had fallen ill, and so Elise and the girls were flying to Nashville to stay with her for a while. But the answer to the deeper 'why,' the one below the surface, still proved elusive.

He could still see the woman's face. She was a black woman and appeared to be in her mid-forties. Tears streamed down her face, smudging her makeup. Bennett had just escorted Elise and the girls to the metal detectors at the airport. After his family had gone through the scanners, he waved bye to them one more time before turning to leave. That was when he heard the commotion coming from another detector. The woman had already made it through when she'd suddenly grabbed her bag and screamed, "I'm not getting on. Something bad is gonna happen."

It was five years after 9/11 and everyone was still on edge and very much sensitive about terrorists, particularly when it came to planes. Though Bennett had been off duty, he went with the TSA agents as they escorted the woman to an interrogation room. The woman's name was Brenna Jackson. She answered their questions forthrightly. No, she didn't know anything about any terrorists attacking the plane. No, she herself most definitely wasn't a terrorist. But yes, something was going to happen to the plane. No, she couldn't be more specific. All she knew was that she was not to get on that plane to Nashville.

Forty minutes later, Brenna Jackson was still in TSA custody when the plane went down, forever changing Bennett's life. For the next two months, Jackson would undergo tremendous scrutiny. But the NSTB's investigation into the crash was conclusive—pilot error. Brenna Jackson, it seemed, had simply had a premonition that had ended up saving her life.

But why hadn't he had that premonition? Why hadn't he or Elise for that matter, had an inkling that the plane was doomed? The question ate at him. The therapist tried to get him to move on, to focus on something else. But he couldn't. He couldn't shake the fact that Brenna Jackson had somehow known that the plane was going down. She'd known! But how? He interviewed her a few additional times, but her answers remained the same. She didn't know how she'd known. She'd just known.

"I had a feeling. No," she corrected herself, "it was more than a feeling. It was like a deep force was around the plane. The closer I got to it, the more I felt it. After I went through the metal detectors, it was almost like me and the plane were opposite sides of a magnet. I tell you, I couldn't have gotten on that thing even if I'd wanted to."

He'd felt no such force and he'd had no ominous feeling. Of course, he wasn't the one going to ride the plane. Elise was. And he'd never know if Elise had felt something and had chosen to ignore it or hadn't felt anything at all. He asked Brenna if she'd felt anything the night before the plane crash and she said that she couldn't remember if she had or not. But if she had, it was clearly not as strong a feeling as the one she'd had at the airport.

Bennett got up and walked over to the bar area. He scrounged around, eventually finding a can of mixed nuts. He took the nuts back to the recliner, pouring himself a handful along the way. He flipped through the channels again and landed on one showing NFL highlights.

After the 2001 terror attacks, the president and congress vowed that such horrific acts would never happen again on American soil and thus had enacted the Uniting and Strengthening America by Providing Appropriate Tools Required to Intercept and Obstruct Terrorism Act of 2001 better known as, the Patriot Act. Most people only paid attention to the controversial aspects of the act, including its mandating roving wiretaps, the indefinite detentions of immigrants, and the authorization given to the FBI to search a person's email, phone, and financial records without a court order. But what the act also did was to put everything on the table to help root out terrorists before they could carry out their extreme acts of violence. Everything included the potential use of psychics.

During his investigations following the attacks, Bennett had discovered that there were other "Brenna Jacksons." Dozens of people had premonitions warning them to not get on the planes or go into work on that fateful day in September. Dozens of people's lives were saved by some uncanny force. Some even claimed to have had visions of the planes flying into the buildings. Initially, neither Bennett nor the government had given these claims much credence. But after his family had died in the crash that Brenna Jackson had successfully avoided, he spearheaded the effort to use paranormal activity in terrorism prevention. Psychics and premonitions were real. He was as certain of that as he was in his belief that whoever had killed Phillip Beamer had inside knowledge of Beamer's planned attack.

Bennett had considered all possible motives for Beamer's murder and nothing made logical sense. Although Beamer was on the government's radar, there wasn't an expectation that he'd commit a terrorist act anytime soon. Of course, the dead man's computer files indicated they'd been dead wrong in that assumption. Still, it didn't negate the fact that Beamer had not been considered an immediate threat. And even if he had, it was unlikely the government would have authorized the taking of an American's life on home soil, suspected terrorist or not.

There existed a possibility that Beamer's own organization had taken him out. But Beamer had kept a meticulous journal. According to it, everything was proceeding according to plan. There didn't seem to be a practical reason for a terrorist group to eliminate one of its own days before he was to commit its bidding.

A random killing had also been discussed. But even that appeared unlikely considering that killings just didn't occur in Buckleton, random or otherwise. No, the likely scenario surrounding Beamer's death was the one that was hardest for a rational person to believe. Someone with psychic-like ability had either killed Beamer or had had him killed. Outside of Beamer's terror group, only a psychic could have known what he'd been up to.

Bennett poured a few more nuts into his mouth. As he chewed, he wondered where Father McCarthy fit into all of this. He thought again about the cryptic message, 'McCarthy Knows,' which was on the back of the priest's card found amongst Beamer's belongings. Bennett didn't know the extent of the priest's knowledge, but he would venture a guess that it was a lot more than the priest had let on. But why would a Catholic priest hold back from the US government what, if anything he knew about a possible terrorist attack?

It was yet another question that he couldn't fathom the answer to. But he was going to have to start finding answers soon, because he was also certain of a couple of other things—another terrorist attack on American soil was inevitable. And the country would use any means necessary in order to thwart it, including the use of Catholic priests and psychics.

CHAPTER TEN

Piedmont Imaging Center was located in the North Dale Shopping Plaza in Charlotte, about an hour's car drive from campus. Josh had explained to Kallie that the center offered the university free usage of its facilities in exchange for a small financial stake in any potential future profits the program might garner stemming from its brain and behavior research. The plaza was anchored at one end by a Target and on the opposite end by a Michaels. Piedmont Imaging was dead center, snuggled between a shoe boutique and a store specializing in the resale of used clothes. Josh parked his Taurus next to a cart-return bin and then the three of them— he, Kallie, and Veronica Ross—hustled out of the car and went inside. A pretty receptionist smiled pleasantly at them as they waltzed past her and through a door leading to the backrooms where the MRI scanner was located.

Josh set Kallie up in a little side room where she was shown a fifteen-minute video about MRI and fMRI. Although she'd gone with her mother a couple of years ago when her mother had had her MRI scan, Kallie hadn't known that MRI stood for magnetic resonance imaging or that fMRI stood for functional magnetic resonance imaging. In fact, before the video she hadn't known there was even such a thing as fMRI. After the video was over, Veronica came into the room and had her fill out a questionnaire similar to the one that had been discussed on the video. The series of questions were to determine if she had any issues, such as prior surgery, ear abrasions, or metal in or on her body that would affect her being inside the scanner. It didn't take her long to check off the long list of 'no' boxes.

After she finished the questionnaire, Josh led her into another room. This one was adjacent to the room where the scanner was located. It was a tight little room with a glass window, through which the scanner was clearly visible. "The images will be captured here," Josh said, pointing to two computer monitors on a table.

"Oh cool," Kallie mumbled. She watched as Veronica sat down in front of one of the monitors, and then Kallie followed Josh into the adjoining room.

"I trust that this big boy needs no introduction," Josh said. He stood next to the MRI scanner. The machine looked like a big, plastic spool of thread. "This is going to be just like the video, except, of course, for one exception which I'll explain in just a minute. You're going to lie on this table, and we'll put this coil over your head." The coil looked like a storm trooper helmet, except that this one came with a mirror attached. He explained that the mirror was not for her to look at herself, but instead, while she was inside the scanner, she'd be able to see anyone standing at the end of the table. Next, he pointed to a plastic ball that was connected to the scanner by a short, white cable. "If you want to stop the test for any reason, just squeeze that. It's called a panic-ball." After Kallie nodded her understanding, he continued. "The coil also has a microphone and earphones attached. You'll be able to talk to and hear us." He waited for a heartbeat. Then he resumed, "After you're all set up on the table, it'll retract into the scanner. Once the imaging begins, it's going to be loud. Some people equate it to a jackhammer digging into the road. But as the video explained, it's just the magnetic field doing its thing. But unlike in the video, we will not be doing a fMRI scan today." According to the video, a fMRI scan was basically an extension of a MRI scan. Except in the case of a fMRI, she'd be given a call button to select her response to a series of questions or choices, which would enable the scanner to detect what area of her brain was responsible for different activities or thought patterns. "Instead, we're going to do a 'resting state' scan."

"A resting state scan?" Kallie repeated.

"Yes. In a resting state scan, you simply lie there. We won't try to artificially stimulate your brain in any way. We do these types of scans occasionally in order to get base images of the brain at rest, so to speak. But in your case, as evidenced by the constant sensations you've been experiencing, the brain may not be in a resting mood, which is one of the reasons why we consider you a gift to our project. Before, we've had to artificially induce déjà vu like sensations in our test subjects. But since you've been experiencing them on a regular basis, we're hoping to capture images of naturally occurring déjà vu sensations."

"How long will this take?" Kallie asked anxiously.

"It's hard to say," Josh admitted. "Ordinarily, an fMRI scan would be about forty-five minutes. But in this case, the resting state scan could be a couple of minutes or a few hours."

"You're going to wait until I have a sensation?"

"Or until our time runs out. We have the scanner booked for five hours," Veronica chimed in from the other room, her voice filtering in through the head-coil which Josh still held in his hands.

Instinctively, Kallie looked at her wrist before remembering she'd removed all traces of metal from her person, which had included her watch.

"It's eleven-twenty-five," Veronica said from the other room, her voice again filtering in through the helmet-coil.

Kallie looked toward the glass window and mouthed a thank you. She then turned back to Josh. She hadn't planned on the scan taking five hours. It would mean missing her afternoon classes. Before this week, she'd had perfect attendance in all her classes. She wondered briefly about where she could get today's missed class notes and then silently sent up a prayer of thanks that she didn't have any tests today, at least none planned. However, so far none of her professors had shown a penchant for surprise quizzes, although one never knew when the quiz-tide was subject to change. Regardless, she wanted to know what was going on inside her head. Whether it was good news or bad news, she needed to find out something today. "Okay, we'd better get started then."

"Good," Josh said. "Let's get you set up on the table." Before he left the room, he gave her some final helpful tidbits and a reminder that she should remain completely still during the scan.

The scanner was louder than she'd anticipated. But it didn't sound like a jackhammer. To her, it sounded more like the electronic whining sound you heard when you accidentally called a fax line. It was that sound on major blast. She remembered that after her mother's MRI her mother had told her that classical music had played through her earphones during the scan. It had been Mozart's Symphony No. 40 in G minor. The same music Kallie's mother had played for Kallie as a toddler to help her to go to sleep. Kallie still found classical music relaxing and longed to hear some at the moment. But Josh had told her that they didn't want stimulation of any sort and that included music.

After about forty minutes or so in the scanner, she began to get used to the loud sounds and even discovered a rhythm within them. She found herself becoming relaxed, and despite the noise, sleepy. Due to the extreme brightness of the scanner, she'd closed her eyes from the moment the table had retracted into it, and now that she'd mentally conquered the noise, sleep beckoned.

Josh's voice filtered in through the head-coil. "You're doing great. How do you feel?"

"Fine," she answered. "But I'm getting sleepy."

"Try to stay awake," Veronica said. "We'll do a dream-study at another time."

"I'll try my best," Kallie said. "But this is extremely boring."

"I know, kiddo," Josh said. "Just hang in there a little while longer."

After another hour, the pull of sleep was overpowering. In an effort to ward it off, she instinctively and quickly opened her eyes. It was as if she stared directly into the sun. She blinked her eyes rapidly in an effort to recoup from the temporary flash blindness. After several seconds, her eyes still felt a little irritated, so she closed them again. But when she did so, a vision as bright and swift as a lightning bolt flashed into her mind's eye. She saw an explosion, a powerful one, of a building. There was shattered glass and body parts everywhere, entangled together like a bloody plate of mixed vegetables. She could hear sirens and horrified screams filling the air simultaneously. It was complete carnage. And she could see it all as clearly as if she was currently watching a television program in high definition.

"Are you getting this?" It was Josh's voice coming through the head-coil. And then Kallie let out a loud wail as she repeatedly squeezed the panic-ball.

*　　*　　*

McCarthy found Johnny Swag in the sanctuary, kneeling at the altar. McCarthy moved quietly down the aisle and took a seat on the first pew.

Sensing someone's presence, Swag turned around and immediately spotted his mentor. "Father McCarthy!" he said, and sprang to his feet. "Why didn't you tell me yesterday you were coming into town?"

"I wanted to surprise you," McCarthy said. "Although with your remembering ability, I didn't think it would be possible."

The two of them shook hands and embraced. "Well, you succeeded in it. I didn't see it coming."

Swag led him through a door at the back of the sanctuary to the pastoral chambers. "May I offer you a drink," he said after they'd entered the chambers and McCarthy was seated on the brown leather couch positioned perpendicular to the large, oak-top desk.

"Scotch and water with a little ice if you have it," McCarthy said.

"Sure thing," Swag said. He prepared the drink and brought it over to him. "So what brings you out this way? Business or pleasure?"

McCarthy sipped his drink. "A little of both I suppose, but mostly business."

"Oh," Swag said. "Anything I can help you with?"

"Actually, yes, there is."

Swag sat down beside him on the couch. "All right. What's up?"

McCarthy took another sip from his drink and then placed the glass down on a side table. He faced Swag. "You know I've always been impressed with you. I sponsored your membership into the Alliance. And they've been equally impressed, perhaps more so."

Swag shifted testily. "With all due respect, how about dispensing with the preliminaries? What's on your mind?"

"The Rogue," McCarthy said. "The other Rememberers are certain he's here in the States. Somewhere in North Carolina, I'm told. He's changed his name obviously. But he's here. Yet your reports make no mention of him. I've been talking with you weekly and you haven't said a word. Why?"

"I think I'll fix myself a drink," Swag said. "Care for another one?"

"No, I'm fine, thanks."

Swag stood and walked to the back of the chambers to the wall-mounted liquor cabinet. As he prepared his drink, he smiled broadly at McCarthy. "My father was a Baptist preacher. For Baptists, drinking of any sort is usually frowned upon. My father never kept any of the stuff around. And his congregation thought that he was the salt of the earth. Few of them knew that he was a drunkard and a womanizer. I keep this liquor cabinet out in the open. I want everyone to know that I am who they believe me to be." He took a long sip from his drink and rejoined McCarthy on the couch. You were a basketball player, right Father?"

"I was."

"And from what I understand, you were quite good."

"I was fair, I suppose."

"There's no need for modesty," Swag said. "Four conference championships in a row. Three time consensus All-American. A shot at playing professionally. I'd say that was more than fair."

"What's the point?" McCarthy said impatiently.

"Exactly," Swag said. "What was the point? Including high school, you played, what, eight years of competitive ball? If you'd decided to play professionally and had a solid career, you'd probably played what, another ten years or so? And every year it would be the same. You knew exactly how the season would end. Oh, the last team standing may have changed, but ultimately you knew how it was going to end. A team would be crowned champion. The other teams would be disappointed. One or two of them would vow that next year they would be the ones standing on the champion's podium. And the next year, maybe the previous champion repeated or maybe a new champion was crowned. But regardless, the same scenario played out. One team blissfully happy, all the others bitterly disappointed. And every year, it's the same thing—over and over and over again."

"What does this have to do with the Rogue?"

"Have you stopped and asked yourself why he left?"

"He was disillusioned."

Swag smirked. "Of course he was disillusioned. But why?"

"I don't see how that matters."

"It matters because once you know why he left, you'll realize that this has nothing to do with stopping terrorist plots and saving lives, no matter how noble a cause that is."

"All right then," McCarthy said. "You tell me. Why was the Rogue disillusioned?"

"For the same reason you decided to no longer play basketball. He wanted more. You see, as a Rememberer he had the ability to see how this thing called life played out. And he had no desire to see how many championships he could win in a row. Or how many times he could lead the league in scoring or how many majors he could collect in a lifetime. Ultimately, he wanted off the merry-go-around."

"I don't understand," McCarthy said.

"The reason I can't find the Rogue is because he's changed the game. He's figured out a way to open demonic portals."

*   *   *

"You knew about this?" McCarthy asked Boland. He was following behind the bishop in Boland's greenhouse.

"I did," Boland said, stopping to water a plant.

"Then why wasn't I told?"

Boland ignored the question. The answer was obvious.

"But you told me to rein him in. How am I to be an effective mentor if he knows more than I do?"

Boland sighed. "Most effective leaders aren't skilled specialists in any particular area. They often have less knowledge on certain subjects than the people reporting to them. Leaders simply lead."

McCarthy didn't respond to that. Instead, they were silent as they continued walking down the aisle while Boland watered his plants. When they reached the end of the row, McCarthy said, "I'm concerned about Swag. What if he suffers from the same disillusionment as the Rogue? With what he knows about A.I..."

Boland held up the watering can, silencing him. "Swag is only a man. Just like the Rogue. Had we known about the Rogue we might have saved him. We'll monitor Swag."

"And you think that'll be enough?"

Boland smiled. "Well, it's that and prayer."

CHAPTER ELEVEN

Bennett slept until noon on Saturday, the latest he'd stayed in bed since before he lost his family. During those days he'd also kept crazy Sunday to Sunday hours, making it near impossible for him and Elise to simultaneously share the same bed for any significant amount of time. He'd always believed that most women probably wouldn't have put up with their husbands' hectic workload, particularly if there wasn't a huge pot of gold at the end of the rainbow. And though ICE was noble and worthwhile and the flavor of the month following the 9/11 terror attacks, it wasn't a path to early retirement riches. Few government jobs were. But he'd also understood that Elise hadn't been like most women. She'd known that his job was demanding and she'd also understood that not only was he good at it, but he loved it. So despite the fact that whatever family time he carved out was mostly doled out amongst his two daughters, she never once put any pressure on him to look for greener pastures, or at the very least, a pasture with more family-friendly hours. In fact, whenever he got the occasional weekend off and would literally pass out from sheer exhaustion the minute he got home, she'd never once awakened him, not that night, and not the next morning, even though he was usually woefully behind on his honey-do list. She'd preferred for him to get up as she'd repeated often, "When the very last ounce of sleep has left your body on its own accord."

Bennett sat up in bed, casting a scornful glare at the alarm clock. He'd had no intentions of sleeping this late into the day. "Thanks Helen," he muttered. She'd made it perfectly clear to him that his stay in her home would indeed be a vacation for him, which she'd determined meant, "No clock staring. No time keeping." And in the two days since he'd been here, she made good on her promise to try to get him to relax and enjoy 'having no work to do.' The two of them had stayed up each night until the wee hours, talking and laughing about old times and eating whatever suited their fancy. And despite himself, he'd begun to feel the first pangs of relaxation. Yet each morning, in an unconscious defiant gesture, he continued to rise with the roosters as if he'd had somewhere to go and something to do once he got there. But this morning it was apparent that his sister's skills in keeping him up, gabbing the nights away had eventually worn down his wall of resistance. And as he stood up to head to the bathroom, he realized that he wasn't the least bit upset about it. The sad truth was that he'd been on self-imposed uptime so long that he'd forgotten what to do with downtime. He'd forgotten how to relax. "Thanks Helen," he said again.

After he washed up, he went downstairs where he heard the surprising and pleasant sound of voices coming from the kitchen. Inside the kitchen, he was immediately drawn to the back of the head of the person sitting at the kitchen table. His sister stood at the stove, talking animatedly with her hands. She stopped midsentence when she spotted him standing in the entrance. "Good morning sleepyhead, or should I say good afternoon?" she said cheerfully.

"No thanks to you," he said. He was still staring intently at the back of the head at the table when it suddenly turned toward him, revealing his niece. A smile erupted across his face. "Veronica, I thought that was you."

She stood and glided laughingly into his embrace. "Why so formal? Whatever happened to Roni?"

"Oh, now you have amnesia. I think it was your fourteenth or fifteenth birthday when you forbid me to ever again call you Roni."

"That was then. This is now. I'd love for you to call me Roni again." She kissed him on the cheek before returning to her chair.

"Consider it done," he said. He sat across from her at the table.

"Oh, those wondrous teenage years," Helen said, and then turned back to the stove where she was scrambling eggs. He could also see a big bubbling pot of grits on the stove. The sweet aroma of bacon permeated throughout the kitchen. The sights, sounds, and smells of breakfast made his stomach growl.

"It sure smells good in here," Bennett said as he watched a slice of bacon disappear into his niece's mouth.

"Your plate's coming right up," Helen said.

"Good, good," he said. "Breakfast at lunchtime, you gotta love it." To Veronica he said, "What time did you get in?"

"About an hour ago. I was actually in town for a little while yesterday. But I had to go back to campus."

Bennett said, "You drove all the way back to campus?"

"It's just an hour's drive," Veronica said.

Helen placed a plate of food in front of him. He said grace quickly and then shoved a piece of bacon into his mouth. Between chomps he asked, "Why didn't you stop by here first? Didn't your mother tell you I was here?"

"She did. But I wanted to surprise you this morning. I thought you of all people would enjoy that."

"Touché," he said, winking at Helen. "So, what were you in town for?"

"We took one of our test subjects for a MRI scan over at Piedmont Imaging in North Dale."

"MRI scan?" Bennett said.

"Yeah, it's part of a class project," Veronica said.

Helen slid cups of coffee in front of him and Veronica, and then joined them at the table with her own cup. "I've always been fascinated by the brain."

Bennett scooped up a forkful of eggs. "It's full of mysteries, that's for sure."

Veronica sipped her coffee, and then said, "That's why MRI imaging is so valuable in mapping the brain. We're trying to solve some of the mysteries."

Bennett said. "Have you found out anything interesting?"

"Well, I'm biased," Veronica said. "I believe everything about the brain is interesting. But my group's main research area is memory. We're currently working on a project to see how déjà vu sensations relate to it."

"Déjà vu?" Bennett said.

"Yeah," Veronica said. "You know the 'been there, done that' feeling you get, although you haven't actually 'been there' or 'done that.'"

"It's been years since I've had one of those sensations," Helen said. "As a child I used to get them every once and a while."

"I think I had a couple of sensations before, too. But, it's been years ago," Bennett said.

Veronica said, "Our research seems to indicate that it's just a false memory experience anyway."

"False memory experience?" Bennett said. "What's that?"

"Basically, it's when a person has a strong recollection of something that didn't actually happen."

"How do you know that something hadn't actually happened and you just can't remember it completely?" Helen asked.

"I'll answer that by asking you a question. Have you ever been to the moon?"

"Now that's a silly question," Helen said. "You know I haven't been to the moon."

"Of course," Veronica said. "But what if you won a contest which included a trip to the moon and once you got up there, a strong feeling of déjà vu came over you whereby you could swear you've been there before. But of course, you know that couldn't have been possible because moon trips are expensive and not readily available to civilians anyway. Besides, you'd only won the one moon trip contest."

Bennett said, "You have a lot of cases of people thinking they've been to the moon?"

"No, Uncle Den. That was just an extreme example of how we know that a memory's false. People have recollected things that just weren't possible."

Bennett bit off a piece of toast. "What causes that?"

"Although we're not entirely sure, the growing consensus is that there seems to be a disconnection between a person's long term and short term memories. Short term memory helps a person get through their day to day. You remember where you parked your car. You remember where you work, where you live. Long term memories you don't necessarily need on a daily basis, but your brain stores them for when you do need them. You remember what year you graduated high school or college or you can remember a scene from your favorite episode of Andy Griffith. We believe déjà vu takes a current situation and tries to tie it to an old memory that just isn't there, thereby creating that sensation."

"I see," Helen said. "If you're able to connect a current feeling of familiarity to an old memory of something that actually occurred, you wouldn't have the sensation in the first place."

"Exactly," Veronica said. "We make those types of connections every day. We see something familiar and we say that reminds me of such and such. Sometimes, we're able to make that connection almost immediately. And even when we can't initially make the connection, our brain lets us know that there is indeed a connection to be made and it'll eventually be found. When the brain knows that there is no connection to be found because the searched for memory doesn't exist, it responds with the déjà vu sensation."

"So, a brain mystery is solved," Bennett said.

"Well, not quite," Veronica said. "Everyone doesn't buy the false memory theory."

"No?" Bennett said. "What're they saying causes it."

"Some scientists are exploring links between déjà vu and mental disorders like schizophrenia and anxiety. And of course, there are some theories that say it's related to past lives and reincarnations."

"Mmm," Bennett said. "I can see that."

"You believe in past lives, Uncle Den?"

"I'm not saying that. But, I remember when I felt déjà vu. It definitely felt as if I had lived that experience before. It sure as heck didn't feel like a false memory. It felt very much real to me."

"It did for me, too," Helen said.

"So what do you think, Roni? Any chance the sensations are related to reincarnation?" Bennett asked.

"Funny you should ask that. My take on that is the same as my professor, Dr. Frost's. My rational side tells me that it's highly unlikely. And probably could never be proven anyway. But the psychologist in me tells me that the apparent nonexistence of something doesn't mean that it isn't a real possibility. I guess that's why I was so excited about our déjà vu project. A part of me is seriously hoping to find a case which proves reincarnation or something. But so far, all our test subjects seem to support the false memory theory. Although for a time yesterday, I wasn't so sure."

"Why? What happened yesterday?" Bennett asked.

"Our test subject had been experiencing daily déjà vu sensations which we had considered a godsend because we've had to recreate the sensations in our other subjects before we could study it. But yesterday, we were finally getting the chance to study a naturally occurring one."

Bennett finished the last of his eggs. "How were you going to do that?"

"With the MRI scan. Since her sensations were happening daily, we figured we'd hook her up and just wait for one."

"Did it work?" Bennett asked.

"It took almost two hours; but it worked better than we'd imagined it would. Not only did she have a déjà vu sensation, but she also threw in a vision for good measure."

"A vision?" Bennett said. "What kind of vision?"

"She saw a terrorist attack, at least that's how she described it. She saw a big building explosion."

Bennett straightened up in his chair and leaned toward Veronica. "She said it was a terrorist attack?"

"Take it easy, bro," Helen said.

"Yeah, relax, Uncle Den," Veronica said. "She wasn't having a psychic moment. What we were able to see in the MRI images was that she was having an epileptic seizure."

"An epileptic seizure?" Helen repeated.

"Yes, we'd already known that epileptic seizures occur in the same temporal lobe area of the brain as the déjà vu sensations. In the past, some patients having a seizure would describe also having déjà vu-like sensations. So in the end, what we saw in her brain images wasn't really surprising. But it was still a bit of a disappointment. I was kind of hoping...I don't know. I guess I was hoping for a different reason for her sensations."

"I'm sure she was, too. It was probably devastating news for her to learn that she has epilepsy," Helen said.

"Well, we can't officially make that diagnosis. But she was able to call her family doctor and make an appointment to see him today, which was good, especially since today's Saturday. But, I believe she'll be okay."

Bennett drained the last of his coffee. "Tell me a little more about her vision."

CHAPTER TWELVE

On Sunday morning, before she'd left for church, Kallie's grandmother had taken the unnecessary liberty of pulling back the curtains in Kallie's room. Now a generous dose of sunlight sprayed evenly into the room, washing over Kallie and forcing her to pull the covers up over her head to block out the light. For a moment, she just lay there, listening to the sounds of the house. *That was the thing about an old house,* she thought. It never seemed to shut up. Its boards always creaked and moaned. Its pipes were forever humming whether water traversed through them or not. Even the slightest of winds would constantly whisper through windows that never seemed to shut completely.

She was thankful that her grandmother hadn't insisted that she attend church with her this morning. It was a minor miracle, particularly since Kallie wasn't in the mood for any hymn-singing, Bible-reading, witness-testifying, or whatever else the church usually grouped with the accompanying sermon, which mostly fell on deaf ears anyway. And she was especially not in the mood to be around a bunch of holier-than-thou people sending glorious shouts of praise upwardly on Sundays, after having no doubt spent most of the week breaking no fewer than half of the Ten Commandments. But she hadn't felt like driving back to campus this morning either. Although if her grandmother had lain down her usual Sunday church law, Kallie would have surely hit Hwy 74 with reckless abandon to get back to school, if for no other reason than to spite the old woman. But this morning her grandmother had mended her stringent church law, which meant either she was finally letting Kallie make her own choices about religion or, sadly, she was simply getting too old to fight. Kallie hoped it was the former. She loved her grandmother and hated disappointing her. But her church bored Kallie to tears.

As Kallie lay in her bed, she thought about yesterday's doctor visit. She'd been fortunate to be able to see Dr. Roberts so quickly. He was one of the few area doctors still committed to a six day workweek. After the MRI incident on Friday, Josh had asked for her doctor's name and number. After she'd given him the information, Josh made the call for her. He had even described to Dr. Roberts what was visible on the MRI scan. Afterwards, Dr. Roberts had insisted she come in ASAP and to bring the MRI images along with her. On Saturday, after studying the images, Dr. Roberts confirmed what Josh and Veronica's non-medically trained eyes had already determined...epilepsy.

Officially, Dr. Roberts had described what she'd had on Friday as a simple partial seizure. He'd added that meant the seizure was localized. In her case, localization was in the temporal lobe area of the brain and was most likely the cause of her déjà vu sensations. He explained that the sense of déjà vu was a common symptom of seizures in that region of the brain, though he could offer no concrete reason behind her sudden outburst of seizures. He'd said that there were various potential causes. In some cases, heredity played a part, although he doubted that was the reason behind hers. There was also a possibility of brain injury, but the MRI scan showed no evidence of such an injury, and she herself had no recollection of having sustained one. Those two facts lessened the chance that brain injury was the culprit behind the seizures. "We don't always know the cause," Roberts finally admitted. "Besides, right now I believe our main focus should be on treatment."

He'd outlined the various treatments she could undergo. And he'd assured her that by no means were the seizures or epilepsy life threatening or even life inhibiting. She should and would be able to live as full a life as she'd wanted. His words had comforted her despite the fact that she hadn't believed a word of what he'd said or what the images apparently had shown.

What she'd felt the past few weeks hadn't felt like seizures. Even if what she had could technically be called seizures or epilepsy, she felt there was more to it than that. She wanted to say something to Dr. Roberts about how she felt, but she hadn't known exactly how to frame her thoughts. She'd known the doctor her whole life and next to her mother and grandmother, he had been the only other person to have seen her naked. But telling Dr. Roberts that she not only didn't believe his diagnosis, but had also in fact believed she'd somehow become psychic, was a baring—one of the soul—that she wasn't ready to commit to. It sounded nutty even to her.

Besides, the good doctor would have probably assumed that she was just in a state of denial anyway. Earlier in the semester, she did her psychology research paper on grief and loss. She learned that there were different stages to the acceptance of grief and loss. Denial was the first one. And honestly, if she'd thought for a moment that she actually had epilepsy, there would be no doubt that she'd be in denial. But this wasn't denial. The vision she'd had while in the MRI scanner felt real. And she couldn't forget about the incidents in Professor Jones' class and New Vibe Church. She'd known what was going to happen both times before those things had actually happened. No, this wasn't denial. This was an increasing certainty that what she was experiencing wasn't déjà vu, nor was it related to epilepsy or seizures. This was something else entirely. But what it was exactly, she hadn't the faintest idea.

*   *   *

Spearman Road was five turns off of Hwy 74. It was a lonely, isolated dirt road, stretching about a mile and a half long. There were only two houses on the road, one at the start of the road, and one at its end. Both of the dilapidated houses were no more than glorified sheds standing only by the grace of God. Madame Isabel's house, the larger of the two, was at the end of the road.

It had been five years since Kallie's first and only visit to the house. But she was able to find it again easily. She could never forget the way to the place where her mother's death had been foreseen. Her mother had believed in psychics and had taken fourteen-year-old Kallie with her to see Madame Isabel, who, according to Kallie's mother, was the most popular psychic in Robeson County.

Kallie hadn't known much about psychics; but she sensed that Madame Isabel was different. The old woman had claimed that she could only feel the futures of certain people. But she never knew who those people were until they were sitting directly in front of her. She offered no money back if fortunes didn't come to pass. But she wouldn't accept money in the first place if she didn't feel the person's future as they sat before her. Kallie had never before heard the term "feel" in relation to someone's future. Most people had been turned away because Madame Isabel could not feel their futures. Janie Hunt had not been turned away.

Her mother had sat across from Madame Isabel at the kitchen table. Kallie had sat in a raggedy old wicker chair that had been set off by itself in a corner of the kitchen. An apple pie recently pulled from the oven had been placed on the nearby windowsill to cool. The pleasing aroma of warmed apples and pie crust filled the kitchen, masking the news Janie Hunt was about to receive. There'd never been anything deathly about apple pie.

On the drive to Madame Isabel's house, Janie Hunt had told Kallie that Madame Isabel was only ten years older than herself, which would have made Madame Isabel forty years old at the time. But the woman sitting across from her mother looked closer to retirement age. Her hair was a white dusty-gray. Her face was lined and drawn as if she'd suffered from insomnia. She wore a pink housedress that had frayed edges. Dingy-white house slippers donned her feet, the heels of which looked ashy and coarse.

Madame Isabel shuffled a deck of cards while staring intently at Janie. She pulled three cards from the deck, placing them down side by side on the table in front of her mother. "Are you sure you want to continue?" she asked.

Janie nodded her head, mouthing an almost silent, "Yes."

Madame Isabel turned over the first card. From where Kallie was sitting, she couldn't make out exactly what was on the card, but she could tell these weren't ordinary playing cards. She'd caught a glimpse of the cards as Madame Isabel shuffled them. They looked to have images of animals or something on their faces. Whatever the image on the first card was, it brought no reaction from Madame Isabel who'd simply glanced at it before placing it face down on the table. She moved to the next card, again looking at it with a blank stare before placing it face down on the table. She did the same thing with the third and final card. After all three cards were placed face down in front of her mother, Madame Isabel looked at her mother again, giving her one last opportunity to leave before finding out what the cards would reveal. Janie nodded her head slightly, indicating she was ready to know. Slowly, Madame Isabel proceeded to turn the cards over. After all three cards were face up, both Janie and Madame Isabel stared into each other's eyes briefly, before Janie looked away long enough to tell Kallie to leave the room and wait for her out on the front porch.

Kallie started to protest, but the look on Janie's face convinced her that she oughtn't. Reluctantly, she stood up and moved delicately past the table. On her way out to the front porch, she glimpsed the three cards on the table. They were all pictures of animals. But the pictures of a bird, fish, and frog had offered no clue as to what Madame Isabel would say as soon as Kallie was outside earshot.

Kallie stood now on the very porch she'd been exiled to five years ago. From the outside, Madame Isabel's house hadn't changed much. The exterior was off-white, old wood badly in need of a paint job. On one side of the porch, a beat up looking Chevy pickup was parked in the dirt driveway. On the other side was a tomato garden, nearly half the size of a surprisingly large front yard and unmolested by the mess of colorful leaves strewn about by the great oak standing watch in the center of the yard. *I didn't know tomatoes harvested this late in the year,* she thought absently. Taking a deep breath, she knocked on the front door.

Madame Isabel opened the door after the second rap of knocks without beforehand inquiring who was at the door. Odd, it seemed to Kallie, because there was no peephole and she didn't notice anyone peeking out through either of the front windows at her. Yet, Madame Isabel stood before her seemingly unsurprised, and, in fact, expectant.

"Come in, child," Madame Isabel said and stepped aside, allowing Kallie to enter. The older woman moved as if she'd aged tenfold since Kallie had last seen her. Kallie hoped to God that she herself wouldn't look so haggard when she turned forty-five. Madame Isabel acted as if every part of her body had an ailment. It looked like she was wearing the same housecoat and slippers she'd worn five years before. She led Kallie into the kitchen and indicated the same chair that Janie Hunt had sat in before. Kallie sat down and Madame Isabel sat down, as she had done in the past instance, in the chair directly across from her. "You act as if you've been expecting me," Kallie said. "Do you know why I'm here?"

Madame Isabel didn't immediately answer. She studied Kallie for a moment, looking at her as if she was a long lost relative. She closed her eyes briefly and then opened them again. This time, she smiled at Kallie. "Yes child. I know why you're here."

Kallie looked solemnly into Madame Isabel's eyes. Vibrant brown pupils sat in clear white sclera. She took a deeper look at the woman's face. There was definitely tiredness in it, but no more than would be present on the face of any person whose sleep had suddenly been interrupted. The haggardness on the woman's face was only surface deep and she might actually be considered attractive with a little makeup and care. She swallowed. "You told my mother that she was dying?"

Madame Isabel didn't blink. "Supposedly when had I done that?"

"It was five years ago. I was here with her."

"Did you hear me tell your mother she was dying?"

"No," Kallie admitted. "She made me go sit on the front porch before you'd said anything. But twenty minutes later when she came out, she took me to get ice cream. My mother used to think ice cream was the ultimate painkiller. She took me to get ice cream before telling me about my father. She took me to get ice cream when my dog ran away, and again when my grandfather died. My mother was never the same after we'd visited here. So, that afternoon's ice cream trip could've only meant one thing. And that one thing had finally happened last year."

"I'm sorry to hear about your mother."

"You don't remember me, do you?"

Madame Isabel ignored the question. "I never told your mother that she was dying. She'd already been diagnosed with cancer when she came here. She never asked me if she was going to die or if she could beat the disease. She was resigned to her fate."

Kallie frowned. "I don't understand. Then why did she come here?"

"You really don't know?"

"No," Kallie sighed.

Madame Isabel reached across the table and took Kallie's hands into her own. "She came here about you."

Kallie pulled back, bringing her hands in. "Me? What about me?"

"When your mother found out the cancer would eventually take her life, her main concern became your wellbeing. She'd known about you since your birth."

"What about me?"

"You have ability," Madame Isabel said in measured tones. "A very unique ability."

"I don't understand," Kallie said.

Madame Isabel pushed back from the table and stood up. "Follow me."

Kallie hesitated, but then slowly got up and followed Madame Isabel down a hallway. She was led into a backroom where Madame Isabel removed a quilted throw rug from the center of the room, revealing a basement door. Kallie followed her down into the basement where they were greeted by a tall, muscled man with a thick gray beard. "This is my husband, Jack," Madame Isabel said.

Jack looked at Kallie curiously and then anxiously glanced behind her and up the stairs. "It's okay," Madame Isabel said to him. "You can leave us now."

Jack's face softened. He looked back at Kallie, offering her a half smile before climbing the stairs.

"My husband's a little overprotective," Madame Isabel offered.

"He doesn't talk much?" Kallie said.

"Only when he has something to say," Madame Isabel said.

The basement felt dank and a little drafty. Kallie shuddered, wondering what she was about to find out. Madame Isabel pointed to a chair pushed under a small card table. Kallie sat down in the chair, looking anxiously at Madame Isabel.

Madame Isabel sat opposite of Kallie at the table. "You are a very special young lady."

"Really?" Kallie said.

"Yes," Madame Isabel continued. "Very special."

"Like mentally challenged special?"

"No, it's nothing like that. Much of it I can't tell you now. Consciously you're not ready to receive it. But what I can tell you is that it's related to your déjà vu sensations."

Startled, Kallie asked, "How do you know about those?"

"I have a gift similar to yours, albeit on a much smaller scale."

"Did you say gift? What kind of gift?"

Madame Isabel reached over to her left and retrieved a thick book from a stand lined against the wall. She placed the book on the table between them and looked intently at Kallie. "It's the gift of remembering."

CHAPTER THIRTEEN

The next morning Kallie overslept, awakening with only enough time to rush-brush her teeth, take a quick wash up of the vitals, and to throw on the same clothes she'd worn the day before. Luckily, on her way to campus, she hit the traffic flow just right, making it through every traffic light without once having to stop. She was able to get to Professor Sampson's class just before he closed the door.

She'd spent the rest of Sunday afternoon at Madame Isabel's house and didn't start the drive back to Bengate until well past eight o'clock. When she'd gotten back to her room, she'd immediately powered up her computer and typed in the search term, *eternal return*. She'd found a wealth of information on the subject and had stayed up most of the night reading through it all. Whether she believed any of it or not was another matter.

She ghost-sat through the rest of the day's classes, taking notes she doubted she'd be able to fully decipher later. She'd been too occupied with what Madame Isabel had told her and what she herself had discovered on the internet to concentrate on any of the lectures. By late afternoon, she was mentally exhausted. As she approached her car, she vaguely recalled talking to Seth after their morning class. But she couldn't for the life of her remember what it had been about. All she wanted to do now was get home and sleep a couple of hours, and then continue her research on eternal return.

"Kallie!" Someone shouted her name from behind her just as she retrieved her car keys from her purse. She turned around and saw Josh waving and jogging toward her.

"I thought that was you," he said as he approached her. He was breathing a little heavier than a twenty-foot jog should've required. "Is everything okay?" he asked between breaths.

"I'm fine," she said. "But you don't seem to be."

"Yeah, I really should cut back."

"Smoking?"

"Nah, sitting around." He took a deep breath. "Ah, that feels good. What did your doctor say?"

"He confirmed the seizures. But he's confident it's something we can handle."

"That's great. Will you still be able to participate on the project?"

"I hadn't thought about it. Would you guys still want me to? I mean, with my déjà vu supposedly being related to seizures and all?"

"The project's not just about déjà vu," Josh said. "You still have a brain and we're still essentially studying the brain."

"Well yeah, I guess I still do have a brain. We'll see," she said. She offered him a friendly smile before turning back to her car.

"Uh," Josh said. "I was kinda hoping I could buy you a sandwich or something. We usually buy our test subjects lunch and we were going to get you dinner the other day, but of course that didn't work out with your, uh..."

She looked over her shoulder. "Yeah, the seizure, right. Look, it's really sweet of you, Josh, but it's totally unnecessary. Besides, I'm really tired, maybe some other time."

"Yeah, sure," he said with strained cheerfulness.

She turned back to her car and then paused before turning back to him. "On second thought, I could eat a sandwich."

Josh smiled. "Did I sound that pathetic?"

Staving off sleep and conveniently forgetting the tightly sealed leftovers she'd brought back from home yesterday, she said, "Not at all. I just remembered that as a poor college kid I ought not to turn down too many opportunities for a free meal."

Josh laughed. "I know that's right."

They drove their individual cars, her Honda following behind his Taurus. *Figures,* Kallie thought ten minutes later as he pulled into Quiggy's. It was the same sandwich shop that she and Seth had eaten at last week. Evidently, the place was 'the spot' amongst Bengate students. A fact Kallie might have known had she not dropped out of school during her first semester last year or had had some semblance of a social life this year.

As she walked up to the counter to order, she remembered how good the Reuben had been and considered ordering it again. But today's special sounded absolutely divine. It was a Club Croissant—smoked turkey, shaved ham, crisp bacon strips, melted provolone, with lettuce, tomatoes, and red onion all stuffed into a flaky croissant. It came with a drink and a choice of either chips or fries. Both she and Josh ordered the special with fries. For her drink, she went with the sweet tea, while Josh ordered a Coke. She found a table by the window as Josh paid for the food and then brought it over.

Their conversation was just as pleasant and seamless today as it had been last week. Josh really was a great conversationalist and an even better listener. Obviously sensing that she didn't want to discuss epilepsy or seizures, he astutely stayed clear of those topics.

She took another bite of her sandwich and then finally asked him, "Why did you major in religion?"

Josh stuffed a fry into his mouth. "What you're really asking is what I plan to do with the degree?"

Kallie giggled. "Well, yeah. Sorry, I didn't mean to laugh. I guess I really shouldn't since I haven't even decided on a major yet."

"Nah, it's a fair question. I know when they hear that I have a religion degree most people think I'm some type of Christian freak or am vying to one day be pope or something. But the truth is I'm not even what you'd consider as fundamentally religious."

"Fundamentally religious?" she repeated. "That's not a phrase you hear every day."

"What I mean by that is that I'm not an ultraconservative, right wing Bible-thumper. In fact, I don't belong to any church. I haven't even been baptized. So obviously I don't have any designs on becoming a preacher or the pope."

A corner of her lips curved upward, forming a half smile. "I'll ask again, why study religion?"

"It's not obvious?"

"No, I'm afraid it's not," she answered curtly.

He furrowed his brow and bopped himself on the forehead playfully. "Funny, I thought it would be. Well, I studied religion and psychology because of my fascination with people. I'm curious about why people think the way they do. Why they believe in what they believe in or don't believe in. I don't think there's any better way to learn about people than by learning about their religion."

"Interesting," she said. "But wouldn't that only let you learn about some people? I mean, not everyone is religious. Some people don't even believe in God."

Josh sipped his soda. "You see. That's a misconception right there. Religion isn't really about God. At least it's not just about God. Religion is what a people believe in. Everyone believes in something, even if that something is to not to believe in anything, including a higher power. While some people may believe in God, others may only believe in nature." He pointed to a saltshaker on the table. "Some people might worship that. Their God might not be an omniscient presence from the heavens. It may be nature, science, an inanimate object, or nothing at all. To me, religion is not just belief in whatever. It's also non-belief in whatever. In other words, I feel that some people may religiously choose to disbelieve. And that to me is their religion."

"I kinda get your point," she said.

"Good," he said smiling. "I'd hate to have to get out the charts."

They ate in silence for a while and then she asked, "What do you know about eternal return?"

He chewed slowly, studying her for a moment. "As in the universe will recur?"

"Yeah," she said. "Do you think that's possible?"

"It's the prevalent belief in most Indian religions, such as Hinduism and Buddhism. But none of the Abrahamic religions believes in a recurring universe. For them, it's one universe, one lifetime, one timeline."

"But what about you? Do you believe it could happen?"

"I don't know. I suppose it could. It makes as much sense as any religious belief."

Kallie glanced around the sandwich shop. It was getting close to dinnertime and the place was starting to fill up. "It sounds like a crazy thought to me. And it sure doesn't square with the Bible."

"I wouldn't necessarily say that," Josh said.

"Listen, my grandmother dragged me to enough Bible studies in my day, and I can assure you that there's nothing in it about recurring time. I'm sure Pastor Martin would've mentioned it at least once. He could've kept some people awake with that bit of information."

"Do you know Revelation 22:13?"

She chuckled. "It's funny you would ask if I knew that particular verse. One time, I had to memorize it for Sunday school." She straightened up in her chair and in a pronounced voice said, "I am the Alpha and the Omega, the First and the

Last, the Beginning and the End." She smiled. "That's the New International Version translation, thank you very much."

Josh smiled. "I'm impressed."

"Well, don't be. I can remember a lot of verses, but only because I was made to. I'm not Mother Teresa."

"Okay," he said. "I'm not exactly sure how to take that. But anyway, what does the first, the last and the beginning, and the end connote?"

She thought for a few minutes, but couldn't quite grasp what he was referring to. "I don't know," she said finally.

"Think about it."

"I have and I give up," she said irritably.

"Time," Josh said. "The first, the last, the beginning, and the end represent time. And how can time or anything be first and last simultaneously or both the beginning and the end unless it's joined together, like a circle. Think about a wall clock. Midnight becomes noon becomes midnight becomes noon. The world is round. The planets revolve around the sun. Take Halley's Comet. It comes into view from earth every seventy-five to seventy-six years. What do you think it's doing? Touching the end of a line and coming back? No, it's on a circular path. Everything in God's creation is circular. He announces himself, Alpha and Omega. That's a circular concept. Based on it alone, I would argue that even biblically speaking, time is circular, not linear."

She slowly nodded her head. "That makes some sense I guess. But surely that verse couldn't possibly mean that."

"It could have at one time," he said.

"I don't understand."

He looked at her curiously for a moment as if trying to decide if she was prepared for what he was about to say. "Remember that the Bible's words were often interpreted and sometimes manipulated by very knowledgeable and powerful men. And sometimes those men didn't trust laypeople with everything that they themselves had known."

"Are you saying that there were Christians who believed in eternal return?"

"What I'm saying is...." He paused midsentence when he noticed the young man standing outside the shop, looking through the window at them. "Do you know him?" he asked Kallie.

Kallie turned and looked out the window. When she saw Seth standing there she suddenly remembered their conversation after class this morning. They'd agreed to a date for this evening at Quiggy's. Man, what this must look like to him, she thought. She smiled awkwardly and waved him inside. She turned back to Josh. "I'm sorry. But I was actually supposed to be here with him now."

"You broke a date to be with me?" Josh said jokingly. "And brought me to the very spot you were supposed to meet. I'm flattered."

"Hah, ha," she said. "You chose the spot. Would you mind terribly if he joined us?"

"I won't if he won't," Josh said.

A moment later, Seth stood at their table. "Sorry I'm late." He eyed Josh suspiciously. "I'm real sorry."

"Excuse me?" Kallie said.

"Our date," Seth said strongly. "I'm a half-hour late. I called your cell phone to tell you I would be, but it kept going to voicemail."

"I must've left it in the car. There's no need to apologize. I sort of forgot we made the date." She nodded toward Josh. "Seth, this is Josh. He's a grad student in the Psychology department. Josh, Seth." Reluctantly, Seth offered his hand and the two of them shook hands like little boys made to do so for not playing nice. "Join us," she said.

"That's okay," Seth said, eying the almost-gone sandwiches and just-about-finished drinks. "It looks like you two are about done anyway."

"Go ahead and order something," Kallie said.

Seth looked away for a brief moment as if trying to decide how big a deal to make the situation. "Okay," he said sheepishly. "I'll go order something." He turned stiffly and walked toward the counter.

"Nice meeting you," Josh said to Seth's back. To which Seth threw up his hand without bothering to turn around.

After Seth had gotten out of earshot, Josh said, "Listen, I know this is awkward. So, I'm going to bail."

"You don't mind?" Kallie said.

"Well, I do, sort of. But like you said, you two already had a date planned, and I do appreciate you spending part of it with me." He stood to leave. "But I would like to finish our conversation."

"So would I," Kallie said.

"I'll see you at tomorrow's project session?"

"Sure thing," Kallie said.

After Josh left, Seth returned to the table, carrying a food tray. "Sorry he had to leave," he said in feigned disappointment.

"Yes, he had some other place to be." She nodded toward his food. "You should have gotten that to go."

CHAPTER FOURTEEN

Father McCarthy's rented Impala fell in smoothly behind the red Mustang as it left the sandwich shop trailing behind the Hunt girl's Honda. In the past week, McCarthy had racked up hundreds of miles. After learning from Swag about demonic openings, he'd traveled to Rock Hill, South Carolina, to the home of Bishop Boland for confirmation. After that, he traveled back to Bengate. He'd wanted to speak again with Swag in person before making the trip back to Philadelphia. He'd wanted to make sure the two of them were still on the same page and there weren't any hard feelings between them. Swag seemed genuinely thankful for the priest's attempt at conciliation and as a show of his commitment to their working relationship; Swag shared with McCarthy his discovery of Kallie Hunt.

After finding out about the potential Rememberer, McCarthy spent the weekend finding out everything he could about the girl. He ended up tailing her from Bengate to Charlotte, back to Bengate, and then to Lumberton, with a stop in Maxton squeezed in on the way back to Bengate. Though the stop in Maxton to the home of a 'yellow pages' psychic was a bit curious, McCarthy's surveillance and background check of the girl hadn't found anything otherwise troubling about her.

Swag seemed to have genuine confidence in the girl. It was a confidence that McCarthy had yet to fully grasp or understand. He hated being in the position of relying solely on Swag's word on the girl, especially in light of his growing concerns about Swag. Admittedly, the young preacher's ability, as was the ability of each of the Rememberers, was invaluable to A.I. But in recognizing that value, McCarthy believed that A.I. ran the risk of corrupting Swag. His inclusion in the organization combined with his remembering ability afforded the young preacher with knowledge that McCarthy felt few, if any men were mentally equipped to handle. And now with demonic openings being included in the equation...he tried pushing the thought away. But if absolute power corrupted absolutely, what then was the result of having absolute truth?

Despite conventional scientific wisdom, there was such a thing as having too much knowledge. There was danger in it. That, too, was a truth. A truth the Creator recognized as soon as Eve and Adam partook of the forbidden fruit. At the dawn of existence, man hadn't been ready for absolute truth, and in many ways, despite the passage of thousands of years, little had changed. Man was still not quite ready. He was too prone to cockiness. Absolute truth was corrupting. It had corrupted Satan. It had led to the original Fall of Man. And man, drawn from dust and breathed into existence by the Creator, was still feeling the effects of the original corruption and was still prone to it. And Swag, being only a man, was just as prone. Even now, he exhibited signs of youthful 'bigheadedness,' or what McCarthy called 'the big-man-on-campus syndrome,' where many young and gifted athletes, after having smoke blown up their butts by parents, coaches, teachers, peers, neighbors, fellow citizens, and in some cases, the national media, acted as if they were larger than life, behaving like the preschooler who believed that the world actually revolved around him. It was human nature, and it sometimes required the harshness of life, i.e. career-ending injury, financial ruin, drug dependency, etc., to intervene before it could be corrected. Though in rare cases, the harshness never fully surfaced in the offender's youth, which more often than not led to the creation of a bitter, delusional senior citizen, who believed the laws of aging and death didn't apply to him.

Despite his misgivings about A.I.'s "smoke up the butt' attitude toward Swag, McCarthy understood the reason behind it. Within the organization, there was a considerable fascination with the Reverend Johnny Swag. Swag was both an Initiate and a Rememberer, only the second such combination in the organization's history. The first one, Herman Alexander, had been one of the founding fathers of the Alliance of Initiates. It had been Alexander's pitch perfect recollection of a previous life cycle that had motivated the formation of the original Initiates out of the body of the URO, as he'd been able to confirm what some of the Founding Fathers of URO had believed all along—that time, as well as life, was circular. Alexander's ability was viewed as a god-sent gift and it soon enabled Initiates to learn the truth about everything from the Creation, to Jesus, and to the End-Times. Although the degree of Swag's ability wasn't known, some in A.I. believed that the young protestant preacher was cosmically connected to Herman Alexander, which exuded hope within the organization that an even deeper knowledge of existence was well within its grasp.

The Mustang gunned through a yellow traffic signal in order to keep up with the girl's Honda. McCarthy's rented Impala screeched to a stop as the light changed abruptly to red. But it was no matter; from the direction they were headed, McCarthy knew where they'd end up. He drummed his fingers on the steering wheel, waiting patiently for the light to change. If the girl was who Swag believed her to be, A.I. would want to gain custody of her immediately. By observing her the past few days, McCarthy had already done some of the ground work. She had no apparent ties to any terrorist organizations. And although she was only nineteen, a typical rebellious age, she appeared only to be a clean cut college student. He would have to further evaluate the house she'd visited in Maxton, but he anticipated no surprises if Kallie Hunt was indeed a Rememberer.

When the light changed to green, McCarthy eased off the brake and stepped on the accelerator, robotically steering the Impala toward the Hunt girl's home. Swag had told him about the girl's vision on Friday at Piedmont Imaging. That seemed confirmation enough of her ability. But even if it wasn't, McCarthy still wanted to ensure that she'd become an asset for A.I. and no others. He could not take the chance on waiting. He would confront her tonight.

*   *   *

Bennett couldn't believe his eyes. There was Father Frank McCarthy parking a rented Chevrolet a few houses down from Kallie Hunt's house. A moment earlier, when the car had crept past him as he sat in his government-issued Ford sedan, Bennett had thought that his mind was playing tricks on him, offering a not so subtle suggestion that he'd been a fool to drive all the way from Charlotte to the house of a young girl that he didn't know to ask her about a vision she'd had. A vision that his niece theorized had not been a vision at all, only a weird dream. But as he looked through his binoculars at the anxious expression of McCarthy, his initial gut feeling was validated.

He looked back across the street at the house where moments earlier he'd seen a young woman and man enter after having parked their cars—her Honda Civic in the driveway of the house and his Ford Mustang at the curb in front of it. Bennett had pulled Kallie's address from the ICE database, which had listings for every registered college student in America, but her entry hadn't included her picture, so he had no idea what she looked like. He'd been about to exit his car to go up to the house to ask the young couple if they knew Kallie when McCarthy had driven by. Now, he decided to wait to see what McCarthy planned to do. He looked at his dash clock. It was seven-thirty. He reclined his seat, settling himself in. He had a sinking feeling that it was going to be a long night.

*　　*　　*

"So what's up with this Josh character?" Seth asked as soon as Kallie returned to the living room after having gone upstairs to change clothes. He was sitting on the loveseat in the living room.

Kallie sat down beside him. "Why? Are you jealous?"

"I don't think I have a right to be jealous. But I'd like to know."

"I don't think having a right is a requirement of being jealous. I think it occurs naturally. You're either naturally jealous of someone or you're not."

"Okay, I'm jealous," Seth said. "Does he mean anything to you?"

"Of course he means something to me. He's human, isn't he?"

"You know what I mean. Were you two on a date?"

She looked at him crossly. "I had a date with you. What kind of girl do you take me for?"

"Well, he was sitting at your table. And it looked like you were enjoying a meal together. In a lot of cultures, a shared meal has some overtones."

"Is that right? Care to enlighten me on these other cultures?"

Seth forced a smiled. "Okay, you got me. I don't know anything about other cultures. Is he interested in you? Or you in him?"

"Oh, choosing the direct question approach now!"

"It's usually the only way to get direct answers." He tilted his head toward her. "That is, unless of course, people elect to elude and evade."

She touched his knee lightly. "Listen, I've only known Josh a little longer than I've known you. He's really sweet and I consider him a friend. And he's in charge of the psychology project I told you about."

Seth smiled awkwardly. "Oh, okay." He paused. "Wait a sec, is that a friend before lovers type of thing?"

She giggled. "Wouldn't you like to know?"

He laughed. "I sure would."

She playfully flicked his hair away from his face. "I'm thinking about setting him up with Maggie."

"Your housemate?"

"Yeah, don't you think they'll make a cute couple?"

"Probably, but I think we'd make a better one."

"You and Josh?" she teased, "I hadn't considered that."

"Very funny," he said. "I'm talking about you and me."

She smiled again. "Slow it down, lover boy."

He looked into her eyes. "I will if you'll slow it down with me." This time he wasn't laughing.

For the next two hours or so, they talked, laughed, and simply enjoyed each other's company. She found out that his favorite fruit was an apple and that his favorite color was light blue. She told him that she always cried when watching the Wizard of Oz. The idea of a girl being lost and separated from her family, even cinematically, was frightening to her. While they talked, two of her housemates with visitors of their own had entered and left the house twice without either Kallie or Seth noticing or caring. They were lost in each other. It was Maggie who was finally able to break through their shared trance when she stood in the doorway of the living room, announcing that Kallie had another visitor.

The man was a priest as indicated by his clerical collar. Kallie glanced at her wristwatch. It was 10:05 p.m. She looked back at the priest and determined that she'd never seen him before, nor had she any earthly idea why'd he come to see her, particularly at this hour. Swag's image floated briefly in her head, making her wonder why she suddenly seemed to be attracting clergymen.

He clutched the handle of a briefcase with both hands, looking anxious. "Kallie Hunt?"

"Yes, I'm Kallie."

"Hello Kallie, My name's Father Frank McCarthy. I'm very sorry to call upon you at this hour." His gaze shifted from her over to Seth, who suddenly walked up, planting himself behind her. McCarthy looked back at Kallie. "Is there somewhere we could talk, alone?"

"Kallie, do you know him?" Seth asked.

"No, I don't," she said.

"Mister, what is this about?" Seth asked.

"Father McCarthy," McCarthy said sternly.

Seth cast a quick cautious eye at the briefcase in McCarthy's clutches. "Well Father, I'm sorry. But she doesn't know you. It's kinda late, don't you think?"

"Yes son, it is kind of late. And this is important." He faced Kallie again. "Can we talk alone?"

"I'm sorry, Father. But I'd feel much safer with Seth with me. Could you just state your business?"

Father McCarthy looked at Seth again and then back at Kallie. After a few seconds, the realization apparently hit that this was as good as it was going to get. "Okay," he said finally. "It's about the visions, Kallie. I'm here about the visions you've been having."

* * *

It had been just past midnight when McCarthy had finally exited Kallie Hunt's residence, capping almost five and half hours spent at the girl's house. For some reason, the priest had waited nearly two and a half hours outside the house before he'd approached it. During his two hours inside the house, Bennett had run the tags on both the Honda Civic and the Ford Mustang. The Honda was registered to Kallie Leigh Hunt. The Ford was in the name of Seth Winters. Bennett wasn't certain if the young man he'd seen entering the house with the woman was Seth Winters, but he felt certain that the young woman was indeed Kallie Hunt. The young man had left the house a full hour before McCarthy had. He'd slammed the door to the Mustang before gunning its engine to life and roaring off down the street, causing a few heads to look out the windows of some of the other houses.

After McCarthy left the house, Bennett followed him to Charlotte where the priest had checked into the Royal Inn & Suites near Douglas International Airport. Bennett spent the rest of the night inside his car, watching the priest's door. It hadn't opened again until four in the morning when the priest checked out. Bennett then followed him to the airport where he watched McCarthy return the rental vehicle and then catch a 5 a.m. US Airways flight back to Philadelphia. During the night, Bennett had half a mind to bust into McCarthy's room, yank him to his feet, and recite to him all the ways in which the Father's actions since yesterday had invited suspicion. He wanted to remind the good father about his business card with its cryptic message scrawled in blood being found on the body of a dead terrorist. Bennett wanted to see the expression on McCarthy's face when he told him that he knew about the terrorist vision the Hunt girl had on Friday. Bennett wanted to tell McCarthy how he didn't believe in coincidences. And even if he didn't entirely understand what was going on, he knew that the priest was somehow involved. But ultimately Bennett's wiser, logical head had prevailed; busting in the priest's door for an impromptu interrogation wouldn't have been the most prudent way for Bennett to find out what was going on. Such action on his part could later be deemed harassment, or worse, as felonious assault on an elder. He remembered his previous visit with McCarthy. The priest was obviously well versed in the art of admitting nothing and denying everything.

Besides, the truth was, suspicious or not, ultimately the priest's actions thus far had only constituted a big fat so what. Officially, he wasn't even a person of interest in the murder of Beamer, and as for Kallie Hunt, Bennett himself wasn't exactly sure what she'd envisioned and even if he was, he still wouldn't be able to stage a case around it. Even Bennett's niece's current stance was that Kallie Hunt had most likely fallen asleep inside the MRI scanner and had only been dreaming. But using his own common sense, Bennett knew that McCarthy wouldn't have suddenly flown to North Carolina because of a teenaged girl's dream. There was a reason the priest had deemed the girl important enough to warrant his presence. Bennett wondered if that reason had anything to do with the briefcase he'd seen McCarthy take into the girl's house. Slowly, he eased the Ford away from the airport, merging in with the outflowing traffic. He would go back to his sister's house for a shower and a quick change of clothes before heading back to Bengate where he would attempt to find out the reason behind McCarthy's sudden interest in the state of North Carolina.

CHAPTER FIFTEEN

Just as she'd expected to find him, Josh was in front of a computer monitor in the psychology lab. Another virtual reality simulation was on the screen. This one was modeled after a mall setting. After Kallie walked over to him, he removed the goggles and placed them down delicately on the table beside the keyboard. He looked up at her. "You don't look so good," he said.

"No longer blinded by my beauty, huh?" Kallie said.

"It's not that. You look as if you didn't sleep a wink last night."

"That's because I didn't."

"What, you got into an argument with what's his face?"

"I did," Kallie said, glancing around the room nervously. There were three other students in the lab. "But that's not why I couldn't sleep. Can we go somewhere and talk?"

Josh looked at his watch, causing Kallie to reflexively look at hers. It was 5:30 p.m. "Sure," he said. "The session doesn't start for another hour."

He took her to an empty lecture hall on the same floor. Rows of seats cascaded toward a blackboard backed lectern which itself stood front and center of a minutely heightened stage. They sat in two adjacent seats at the back of the hall. It took her several moments to collect her thoughts. Finally, after taking a deep breath, she said, "I was visited by a Catholic priest last night." She paused to let that tidbit sink in. But if Josh thought there was anything strange about a Catholic priest's evening visit to the home of a sometimes

Baptist girl, he didn't let on. Instead, he sat expressionless, waiting for her to continue. She rested against the back of the seat, closing her eyes for a moment. When she reopened them, she looked straight ahead at nothing in particular. "He told me that my déjà vu sensations didn't have anything to do with epilepsy. And that the vision that I had in the MRI scanner was prophetic. There would be a terrorist attack somewhere in America in the near future." She paused again, and then turned her head toward Josh, this time looking him directly in the eyes. "He said I was remembering something that was going to happen and that it's all related to eternal return."

Josh's eyes widened slightly. "You look as if you believe him."

"Ordinarily, I probably wouldn't have. But he was the second person in three days to talk to me about 'remembering' and 'eternal return.'" She told him about the weekend visit to Madame Isabel's and also about how she herself hadn't believed the epilepsy/seizure diagnosis in the first place. After she finished, Josh settled back into his seat. "Madame Isabel sounds like an interesting character."

"Yeah, she is," Kallie said. "And she seemed to know a lot about me. She said my mother brought me to her shortly after I was born. Apparently I'm special, but she wouldn't elaborate. She also said that she remembered my visit from the last life cycle."

"She's a Rememberer, too?"

"According to her, although she said she's a lower degree. She believes there're only about four or five fully capable Rememberers in the world, with maybe only one or two of those having ninth-degree ability, which she said is the highest level."

"Fully capable?"

"She said everyone has some remembering capabilities and that most déjà vu sensations are related to the ability. But only a small number of people ever develop it fully. She believes I'm going to be fully capable soon, eventually developing ninth-degree ability."

"Going to be?"

"She said that the remembering ability is like a muscle that has to be developed. She said that once my ability is fully developed, I'll accomplish great things."

"Like what?"

"She didn't say. Apparently my consciousness isn't ready to handle it all yet. She likened it to a baby being weaned off the breast. Only with me, it's the opposite. I have to be weaned onto the knowledge of what I'm to become."

"Interesting," Josh said. "So that's why you were asking about eternal return the other day."

"Yeah, Madame Isabel sounded convincing, but I'd never heard about eternal return. When I got back home, I researched the topic on the internet. And while at Quiggy's, I remembered that you were a religion major. I thought you might know something about it as well. After Father McCarthy's visit, I went through the Bible to see if there were any references to eternal return similar to the one from Revelations that you'd pointed out."

"I'm doubtful you'll discern much from the Bible," Josh said.

"Why?"

"Remember what I said yesterday about knowledgeable men maybe manipulating or even misinterpreting the Bible?"

"Yes."

"So, searching the Bible for evidence of eternal return could be like searching for a needle in a haystack. Even if you were able to find something that may allude to it, you might not be able to get the full correct meaning of it. It's likely that you won't even know what it is you're looking at, or even understand or notice the available clues anyway. It takes years of reading and studying the Bible to fully get it. Some religious people believe even then you have to be in the spirit to really grasp the fullness of the Bible. What did your internet search turn up?"

She regarded him curiously, briefly wondering if any of what he'd just said was only a religion major's defense of his intellectual territory. "Just a lot of general stuff."

"There's more stuff there; you just have to know where and how to look for it."

"So you know something about it?"

He hesitated. "Listen, this is a dangerous area to wade into."

"What do you mean?"

"We're talking about matters of the occult. Demons. Darkness."

"Are you serious?"

"Very. Eternal return is part of the forbidden knowledge. It's related to the Knowledge of Good and Evil."

"Are you saying like Adam and Eve?"

"I am. It wasn't knowledge that the Creator wanted man to have, at least not yet. But once the apple was bitten, the knowledge was ultimately released."

"Released to whom? I don't have it. I imagine most people don't either."

"Most of the information was resealed and kept away from mankind. Throughout time, what little that leaked out was often ridiculed as being mythical or of the devil. People were encouraged to shun it and not to seek it. But some people refused to listen to the Church and learned as much of the forbidden knowledge as they could. Thus, they were said by the Church to be devil worshippers. Originally, occult simply meant knowledge of the hidden. The word comes from the Latin word, occultus, which means clandestine or hidden. But the church was so successful in linking it with Satan that Satanism became the word's overriding association."

"If what you're saying is true, then why would Father McCarthy come to me? Why tell me what he told me?"

"I don't know. Is this Father who he claims to be?"

"I looked him up on the internet as well. He's definitely a Catholic priest."

"Okay, assuming he is who he says he is, and he is representing the Catholic Church, then there's got to be some major reason why they're confiding in you about eternal return."

"Well, it's no doubt related to my remembering ability and this potential major terrorist act."

"Possibly. But since when did the Church get into rooting out terrorists? And why not simply contact the authorities?"

"Contacting the authorities is exactly what Father McCarthy warned me not to do."

"Warned you?"

After Father McCarthy made his declaration about her visions, she'd asked Seth to wait for her in the living room and then she had the priest follow her into the kitchen. McCarthy sat opposite her at the table, placing his briefcase down by his feet. It took him only an hour to completely blow her mind with his spiel on remembering, eternal return, and terrorist acts. He'd also said that Reverend Johnny Swag would be instrumental in helping her to refine the ability, enabling her to identify the next terrorist attack in plenty enough time to prevent it.

"This all sounds kind of creepy," she'd said.

"It can be," Father McCarthy said. "But Swag can help you. He's been trained in developing the remembering ability. I understand he's very good at what he does."

"So, when or if I'm able to remember the exact details of the impending attack, I'll take that information to the authorities?"

"No," Father McCarthy said strongly. "That's what you mustn't do." He picked up the briefcase, placing it on the table between them. Seth came into the kitchen at that precise moment.

Father McCarthy froze, eying Seth suspiciously.

Kallie stood up and quickly ushered Seth out of the kitchen. "Please wait for me in the living room."

"What's going on Kallie? Who is this man?"

"You've heard who he is."

"I mean who is he to you?"

She stopped in her tracks, right in front of the entrance to the living room. "What are you asking me?"

"I think you know what I'm asking you," Seth fumed.

She could feel her heart rate speeding up. Her eyelids pinched together until they were nearly closed. She was looking at him, but was barely able to make him out. Her words strained out slowly. "Just who do you think you are?"

"You know who I am. I'm Seth Winters," he said facetiously. "The date you've rudely kept waiting in the living room." And with that, nearly two hours of carefully laid groundwork evaporated.

Her pinched eyelids suddenly reversed themselves and she stared at him with wide-eyed intensity as if seeing him for the first time. "You're also a jerk! You don't own me, Seth Winters. Not tonight, not ever."

"I know I don't own you. I'm only concerned about you."

"You can keep your concerns to yourself," she said.

"You're acting ridiculous. You shouldn't let strange men into your house."

She smiled wickedly before marching over to the front door, yanking it open. "You're exactly right. Good night, Seth Winters."

Seth looked at her as if she was beyond words, and then as if to punctuate the point, he left the house without saying another thing.

When she returned to the kitchen, Father McCarthy had opened the briefcase. "Sorry about the young man," he said.

Kallie wiped a tear away. "It's nothing." She nodded at the opened briefcase. "What's this?"

"It's proof as to why you should proceed with caution before going to the authorities." He removed the photographs from the briefcase and then closed it, placing it back on the floor next to his chair. With subdued flair, he lined the four 8x10 black and white stills side by side on the table, upturning them toward her.

She instantly recognized one of a plane flying into the World Trade Center. It was from the 9/11 terrorist attacks. Two of the other photographs also showed terrorist attacks. One was of the original World Trade Center attack in 1993 and the other one showed an explosion aboard a ship. She thought about her high school research paper, which ironically had been about terrorist attacks on US soil. She stared hard at the 93 WTC terrorist attack photo, a chill surging through her. The feeling was similar to the eeriness she'd felt when watching the black and white footage of President Kennedy at the Dallas Airport on that fateful November day, moments before he entered the last motorcade he'd ever be in—alive. It was strange watching a man who at that moment had no idea that he'd be dead in less than an hour.

The World Trade Center had survived the 93 attack, but eight years later, the outcome would be decidedly different. Her eyes moved hastily to the picture of the ship explosion. Recognizing the theme of the photoset now, she knew the ship was none other than the USS Cole. The ship had been attacked by terrorists in 1998. She began to feel uneasy and looked quickly to the next photograph. This one was not of a past terrorist act and she felt a soupcon of relief. The federal building captured in the photograph sat boldly undamaged underneath a clear blue sky with beams of sunlight haloed around its roof. She picked up the photograph, staring at it for a long moment, before looking curiously at Father McCarthy.

"That's the Strom Thurmond Federal Building in Columbia, South Carolina," Father McCarthy said. "If it hadn't been for one Phillip Beamer, that building would've been destroyed and about two hundred innocent people killed."

She was familiar with the name. Phillip Beamer had been in the news recently. "The suspected terrorist?"

"He was not a terrorist. He was a Rememberer, just like you."

She was speechless.

"Until the authorities had him killed," McCarthy continued.

"Killed?" she finally managed, barely able to say the word.

McCarthy stabbed the 9/11 photograph with his index finger. "We live in the most powerful and technologically advanced country in the world. How could nineteen foreigners carrying only box cutters commandeer our planes?" He moved his finger to the World Trade Center bombing photograph, stabbing it with equal fervor. "Records show that the authorities had an informant who told them of the planned World Trade Center bombing in plenty of enough time for them to have prevented it. Yet, they chose not to."

"Why would they choose not to stop an attack?"

"It's a good question," McCarthy said. "But I'm afraid it's one that I do not have the answer to. I simply do not know. Nor do I know why they decided to stop the attack on the Thurmond building, but had Beamer killed anyway. It doesn't make sense. But it's that uncertainty of what they might or might not do as to why we believe it's dangerous to alert the authorities about what we know. We're not looking for credit or publicity. We just want to save lives."

"Who're we?" Josh asked when she'd finished.

"What are you talking about?"

"You said that Father McCarthy said that *we're* not looking for publicity. *We* only want to save lives. Who are *we*?"

"I don't know," Kallie said. "I didn't ask him." She studied his face for a moment. "You don't believe him?"

Josh didn't answer her question. Instead enquired further, "You really believe the government killed this Phillip Beamer character because he'd tried to prevent a terrorist act?"

"I don't know. But Phillip Beamer is dead, and from what I can tell, the government has been slow to release details concerning his death. In any event, I'm not talking about some obscure AM radio personality sprouting nonsensical conspiracy theories here. Frank McCarthy is a Catholic priest."

"Nut jobs can come from all walks of life," Josh said.

"Really, you too?" Kallie said.

"I'm sorry," Josh said, "but this is a lot to digest."

"I know. That's why I'm telling you. I trust you. But I need you to take this seriously. I need you to take *me* seriously."

"Fair enough," Josh said. "How did McCarthy find you?"

"From Reverend Swag," she said. She told him about her grandmother calling Swag after Kallie had told her that she was a member of Swag's church.

"And Swag's the one who's going to help you remember."

"Yeah."

"Well, that's something."

"Do you know Reverend Swag?" she asked.

"Sort of, he's kinda famous in these parts. He was known as little Johnny Swaggert, the boy preacher. His father had him in the pulpit preaching by the age of six. He was all fire and brimstone. People used to come from miles around to hear that little dude shout the word. They say he knew the Bible backwards, forwards, and sideways."

"It sounds like there's more to this story. What happened?"

"His father happened," Josh said. "His father purported himself to be a man of the cloth, as well. He took his son all around the county saying that both he and his son were the chosen prophets of God. But Willie James Swaggert really was only a shyster who pimped out his only son and bilked people out of their money. He was later convicted of fraud, embezzlement, and just being an all-around asshole. Little Johnny Swaggert spent the last of his teen years bouncing around foster homes. But eventually, he got himself together, came back here, got a degree from Bengate, and went back to preaching. I think that surprised a few people. There were those that thought that maybe his experiences with his father would've jaded him, hardened his heart, and made him cynical towards religion. But redemption is the word they bandy about now for the most part when they talk about him. I've been to his church a few times. He's not a bad preacher. He's baptized quite a few Bengate College people. I think Professor Sampson joined his church a couple of years ago."

"Really? Professor Sampson doesn't strike me as the religious type."

"Yeah, well," he paused.

"What about his mother?"

"I don't know if Professor Sampson's mother is even alive."

"Not Professor Sampson's mother, silly, Reverend Swag's."

"Oh, I don't know. I think she's dead. But don't quote me on that. Anyway, when was the last time you experienced a déjà vu sensation?"

"This morning. I'm not as freaked out about them now, especially since I've learned about the probable cause."

He regarded her understandingly. "Still, I suggest you follow up with your doctor, if for no other reason than to play it safe. Okay?"

"Okay," she said. After pausing a moment, she said, "You never answered my question. You don't believe Father McCarthy, do you?"

"No, I don't, but I don't disbelieve him either. Let's just leave it at I'll have to research it some more." He checked his watch. "We better head back. It's about time for the session to start."

She nodded her head. "Thank you."

"For what?"

"For not calling me a nut."

He smiled. "You're too beautiful to be a nut."

As they walked back toward the lab, she said, "Oh, by the way, Professor Sampson's mother is still alive."

"World of wonders," Josh said. He looked as if he was going to ask how she knew, but then decided not to.

CHAPTER SIXTEEN

Kallie stopped short of following Josh into the lab. She stood frozen just before the room's entrance, marveling at the sight of the other students. Most of the chairs in the room were occupied by a warm body. This was the first time she'd seen any of the other project participants and all of them seemed happy to be here. An excited first-day-of-school like chatter filled the room. Though Kallie hadn't made many friends at college, she still scanned the room, hoping to find a familiar face. But she didn't see anyone she even remotely knew. She slunk to her seat, suddenly feeling like the new kid at school.

Josh went to the front of the room, taking his seat at the front table next to three of his colleagues—Cedric, Evan, and Marcus. The four of them sat facing the class. Only Veronica was absent, and judging by the way the four of them kept checking their watches and looking at each other, the group's lone woman's tardiness had the ironic consequence of being unexpectedly expected. Their shared conspiratorial looks screamed, "Ain't it just like a woman." Wisely, all of them had the good sense not to utter a word of public criticism. Especially since more than half of the project participants were of the fairer sex. However, after ten more minutes and still no Veronica, Josh obviously crossed his patience threshold. With a quivering lower lip, he commenced the session.

"May I have your attention," Josh began, raising his voice above the din. A few seconds passed before the chatter tapered down and eyes focused on him. "Thank you," he continued. "Each of you has been selected to continue forward in our Déjà vu /Memory Study. By now, you've all completed the one-on-one interview session, the individual memory activity, and have gone through the MRI scanner. We're now ready to proceed with the group memory exercise. In this exercise, each of you will enter the same virtual reality simulation as the other members of the group. None of you will be able to control where you go or what to explore. We're going to guide you through the simulation. We want to ensure that all of you will be exposed to the same thing at the same time, although we can't control what you decide to focus on while in the simulation. What's observed while in the simulation will be entirely up to the individual. The purpose of this portion of the study is to see what effect, if any, group memory has on individual memory, or to determine if there is such a thing as group memory, and by way of extension, group déjà vu. We plan..." he paused, evidently distracted by the person who'd just come into the lab and stood at the door. Kallie followed Josh's eyes to the door. It was Dr. Frost standing there, and judging by the anxious expression on her face, coming back to the lab hadn't been on her agenda.

"Excuse me," Dr. Frost said. "Cedric, I'll need for you to take over the presentation. Josh, I need to see you and Kallie Hunt." Without waiting for a response, Frost turned on her heels with military precision and went back out into the hallway. Kallie shared a quick 'WTF look' with Josh before they mutually and nonverbally decided that whatever it was that Frost wanted with them wasn't going to wait. They both scrambled toward the door. As she stepped into the hallway, Kallie felt a childlike apprehension brewing inside her as she heard Cedric's awkward attempts to pick up where Josh had abruptly left off.

Dr. Frost stood in the hallway with Veronica and a middle-aged man whom Kallie had never seen before. Veronica, looking as anxious as the professor, smiled awkwardly at Kallie and Josh. The man, handsome and casually dressed in blue Dockers and a yellow button-down shirt, looked putout, as if he were being forced to bear witness to something that had nothing to do with him.

"Follow me," Frost said to the improbable foursome. She led them down the hall to a conference room. Inside the room, Frost went to the head of the conference table. Veronica and the man sat in the first two chairs to her right. Kallie and Josh sat opposite of them on the other side of the table. After everyone had settled into their seats, Frost looked at Kallie and Josh, and then nodded at the man. "This is Special Agent Dennard Bennett."

"He's my uncle," Veronica blurted out.

Frost shot Veronica a quick piercing look. "Yes," she continued with a trace of irritation. "In addition to being Miss Ross' uncle, Agent Bennett is also with the Department of Immigration and Customs Enforcement, aka ICE."

Though she looked intently at Dr. Frost, Kallie could feel Bennett's eyes on her, studying her. Images of terrorist attacks and the name Phillip Beamer crossed her mind suddenly, sending chills down her spine.

Frost pulled a sheet of paper from the folder she'd laid on the table. After putting on reading glasses, she read from the sheet. "The privacy rule of The Health Insurance Portability and Accountability Act or HIPPA is intended to protect the privacy of individually identifiable health information," she paused and glared for a long moment at Veronica. And then, after apparently being satisfied that Veronica had accurately deciphered the meaning of her not so subtle glare, she continued. "Section 164.502 of the Federal Register's Department of Health and Human Services final ruling on Standards for Privacy of individually identifiable health information states that: Protected Health Information includes individually identifiable information in any form, including information that is transmitted orally, or in written or electronic form." She put the sheet back into the folder.

"Now, we've gone over HIPPA extensively before. And I've continually stressed our responsibilities in protecting the privacy of our research subjects. It's not just a moral obligation, but we have legal responsibility, as well."

Bennett shifted noticeably, but he didn't say anything. Frost merely looked at him for a moment before continuing. "With that being said, the United States government is permitted to access any information, private or otherwise, that it deems necessary to protect the nation's national security interests. In other words, the Patriot Act trumps the privacy rule." She turned to Veronica. "Although your actions were inexcusable and you needlessly and negligently exposed one of our research subject's private information, you've apparently been saved on a technicality."

"I never mentioned her name. I only described the vision to my mother and uncle," Veronica said defensively.

"It doesn't matter. Privacy means privacy. You never know who's listening to you or what someone may or may not deem important. In this case, your uncle's with ICE. But what if he hadn't been? What if he'd been an enemy combatant? What if he'd been someone who could've used that information against her? The situation could've been a whole lot worse." She stared at Veronica for what seemed to be ages, but in reality was only thirty seconds, before swiveling her head between Josh and Veronica. "I want the group in this conference room tomorrow afternoon at 5:30 p.m. We need to further clarify your understanding of HIPPA. The privacy of our research subjects is paramount and must be taken seriously. Is that understood?"

Both Josh and Veronica nodded affirmatively.

"Good, you two can go back to the lab now."

After the two of them left the room, Frost turned to Kallie. "In case you haven't figured out what this is about, ICE has an interest in your vision. Apparently, it has a whole division dedicated to the paranormal. Do you feel up to talking with him?"

"Do I have a choice?" Kallie muttered.

"Yes, you have a choice. But I believe it's best to get this over with as quickly and painlessly as possible."

"I agree," Bennett interjected.

Kallie looked from Dr. Frost to the agent. Though she was apprehensive and had no idea what the agent wanted to know, she agreed it was best to end this now. Surely, she could evoke some rights or something. But ultimately, she understood that if the government felt she had information critical to the nation's security, they would stop at nothing to get that information. "Okay, I'll talk to him."

"All right then," Frost said, turning to Bennett. "She's all yours."

Frost left the room, leaving the two of them alone at the conference table.

"Your Dr. Frost is a no nonsense woman," Bennett said.

Kallie wasn't sure how to respond to that. Kallie wasn't in the psychology department or any of Dr. Frost's classes, so the woman wasn't exactly 'Kallie's Dr. Frost.' But his take on Dr. Frost certainly fit Kallie's initial impression of her. In Kallie's only interaction with her, Dr. Frost had presented herself as a direct-approach woman of few words. But Kallie sensed that Agent Bennett wasn't looking for concurrence on his assessment of the psychology professor. He was attempting to break the ice with Kallie. Ice that he obviously and correctly guessed she didn't want broken. She didn't want to talk with him about anything, not about Frost, not about the weather, and certainly not about her vision. So she stared straight ahead, looking at nothing in particular and saying nothing at all.

"Listen," Bennett said. "I want to apologize on behalf of my niece. It wasn't her intention to compromise your privacy. She only told me about a girl who'd had a strange vision. Initially, she didn't mention your name because she had no idea that ICE would have any interest in it. The truth is, not many people are aware that the Department has a whole division devoted to the paranormal—the unusual or strange activity, mysterious sightings. Truth is, we have a broad reach. Not only will we investigate anything we believe could be a threat to the country, but we will also utilize any and every source to aid in that investigation." He paused, observing her reaction to what he'd said. But there was no reaction. She simply sat there, stone-faced, staring blankly ahead. After a few moments, he said, "Tell me about your vision."

She remained silent and refused to look at him. What would he do to her after she'd told him about the vision? Would she then be deemed a threat to national security? Would she be placed under constant surveillance? Or possibly killed?

"The vision, Kallie," Bennett urged.

The silence eventually grew too awkward for her. She got the impression that he could sit there for hours and it wouldn't bother him. Finally she said, "It was only a dream. I must have fallen asleep inside the scanner."

"Well then, tell me about your dream."

Kallie faced him. "I don't really remember much about it. There was a building explosion. People were running everywhere. That's about all I can remember."

"Try to recall something else. A place, a person, a time, anything," Bennett said.

Kallie shook her head. "I'm sorry. I can't."

Bennett looked at her fixedly, drumming the table with his fingers. "I'm not the bad guy, Kallie. I admit I was unartful with the privacy thing and I apologize for that. That's one of the areas we struggle with every day, keeping our citizens safe while respecting their right to be left alone. It's not easy. But to be honest, when it comes to keeping our country safe, I don't see a gray area. It's black and white. Either we do what is necessary to keep people safe or people die. It's that simple."

Kallie remained silent.

Bennett stood up and paced the floor. "Don't you even care? I know college kids can be self-absorbed. But eventually you've got to care about something other than yourselves."

Kallie glared at him. "People died on 9/11."

Bennett stopped pacing. "What?"

She looked at him pointedly. "People died on 9/11. You had the chance to prevent it and didn't."

Bennett sat back down at the table. "You don't honestly believe that, do you?"

"I have no problem believing the truth."

"I don't know where you've gotten your information. But that's not truth. If we'd known about 9/11...."

"You'd have done what?" she asked, cutting him off. "What would you have done? What could you have done?"

"Listen," Bennett said calmly, "you can't believe that righteous propaganda. You think your government would allow such a tragedy to be committed? Were there some people asleep at the wheel, ignoring some obvious warnings? That's possible. But there's no way your government would have knowingly allowed 9/11 to happen. No way. Your government protects its citizens."

"What about Phillip Beamer?" she asked and regretted it almost immediately.

Bennett's nose twitched. "Phillip Beamer, what about him?"

"Nothing," she said quietly.

"What do you know about Phillip Beamer?"

"What if he wasn't a terrorist? What if he'd tried to warn the government about terrorism and he was killed for his trouble?"

"Is that what you think? Is that the crap the conspiracy theorists are pushing these days?"

"I don't read conspiracy theories," she said.

Bennett pushed back from the table and stood up again. He walked over to her side of the table and sat in the chair next to her. "Is that what Father McCarthy told you?"

"What?" Kallie said. "How do you know about Father McCarthy?" Then, realization slapped her hard across the face. "Have you been spying on me?"

Bennett didn't answer any of her questions. "Beamer was a terrorist. But we had nothing to do with his death. He was killed by someone who knew who he was and what he'd planned to do. That's why I'm here talking to you. If you can tell me...."

But Kallie wasn't listening. She pushed away from the table. "Do you follow me everywhere I go? Is my home bugged? My car? Oh my God!" Her hand cupped her mouth. She suddenly felt creepy. And dirty.

Bennett pressed on. "Was it McCarthy who told you about Beamer?"

Kallie couldn't hear him. All she could think about was hidden cameras and strategically placed listening devices.

"McCarthy lied to you," Bennett said. "Do you understand me, Kallie? McCarthy lied to you. We didn't kill Phillip Beamer."

But he'd already lost her. She couldn't hear a word he said. She only wanted to get out of the room as fast as she could. She'd reluctantly accepted that a priest and fortuneteller apparently knew more about her own life than she did. But this revelation that her government was secretly spying on her was simply too much to bear. She felt as if she was being pulled from multiple directions and it frightened her. It seemed her life was no longer her own, if it ever was.

CHAPTER SEVENTEEN

Thursday, October 15.

Lieutenant Gary Conner stood in front of his four direct reports. "We have only two weeks until D-day gentlemen." He paused, letting his words hang in the air for added affect. A former marine sergeant who'd completed five tours in the Gulf wars, Conner had the annoying habit of always peppering his spiel with militaristic references. He was a tall man with a puffed out chest and a sucked in gut that looked as if it'd been surgically spawned.

Of course the lieutenant had no way of knowing how true his words were, Principe thought. Conner was only referring to October 29 as the day a presidential candidate would visit United Corporate Bank Center. The shift commander didn't know that on that very day UBC would, in fact, explode just like the coast of Normandy had on the historic day Conner was hyperbolically referring to.

"We will be ready," Conner continued. "We will treat Senator Frank as if he were the president. We've coordinated with his security team. Every moment of the senator's stay in our magnificent building, including his potty time, will be carefully choreographed."

Senator Joseph Frank was the Junior Senator from Massachusetts, currently serving the third year of his first six year term. He'd won the seat after a special election held after the sitting senator died following a massive heart attack. At thirty-eight years of age, Frank was young, handsome, and charismatic. In today's political climate, window-dressing and the ability to assuage a nation's fears of an apocalyptic financial meltdown were all that was needed for a viable shot at the nation's highest office. After graduating at the top of his class with a Finance degree from Harvard, Frank earned his MBA from Yale before embarking on a successful run up Wall Street where he managed to grow a substantial personal portfolio, write a how-to financial book, and avoid the scandalous pitfalls that had enveloped so many of his colleagues. He'd earned a reputation for being hardworking, forthright, and smart—in short, he was just the man the country needed at this point in time, or so his handlers proclaimed. And if after next year's primary season he were to successfully secure his party's nomination for the presidency, it would be an historic accomplishment on several levels, as not only would the unmarried senator be the nation's youngest presidential candidate ever on a major party ticket, he'd also be its first Jewish candidate.

"He's got a dump scheduled two weeks out?" This was from Officer Joey Locke, the dour-faced muscle bound specimen standing to Principe's right.

"If he needs to take one, it'll be on the agenda," Conner said without skipping a beat. "Gentlemen, this is a serious matter and we will treat it seriously. I don't care what anyone's political leanings are. I don't care if you think the Constitution is the Holy Grail or something you wipe your butt with. What I do care about is this building and the safety of Joseph Frank when he's in this building. Is that understood?"

A unified, "Yes sir."

"Good," Conner said. "I trust you've all read and absorbed Monday's email which included our list of objectives leading up to D-Day. First and second shifts are completing the new employee profiles and rundowns of expected media personnel. On third shift, we're responsible for the floor by floor search, which we'll..."

"Search for what, sir?" Locke asked.

Conner glared at him. "Anything out of the ordinary, something out of place, suspicious packages, or to be clearer son, bombs."

Locke smirked. "Bombs? Are you freaking kidding? Nobody can sneak a Twinkie in this building without us knowing about it. How in the world will anyone be able to get a bomb in here?"

Principe could see Conner's jaw line tighten as it became painfully obvious that Locke hadn't bothered to read the email, a good portion of which had been dedicated to suspicious package detection. Conner, who considered himself a bomb expert, had included full colored pictures of the different ways bombs could be camouflaged. The email had also included the security team's bomb response and procedures. Conner had detailed everything down to the tiniest nuance. And apparently, Locke hadn't so much as blinked at it.

With his lower jaw twitching uncontrollably, Conner said, "Perhaps son, there's some other line of work you'd like to pursue? Maybe something a little less meticulous, like scooping up dog crap off the sidewalk."

"No sir," Locke said sheepishly. "I was just saying..."

"Don't just say, son," Conner barked. "Just listen, and then just do."

"Yes sir," Locke said.

"And read your freaking email," Conner added through clenched teeth.

*   *   *

On Thursday afternoon, despite simmering misgivings about Father McCarthy born out of her unplanned meeting with the

ICE agent, Kallie honored her promise to the priest and kept her appointment to see Reverend Johnny Swag at his church. Dressed college-casual in blue jeans and a Duke University sweatshirt with its image of the university's mascot plastered boldly across his chest, Swag led her to a room at the back of the church. He didn't look as intimidating today as he had when he'd first come to her house wearing a black funereal suit. "This is New Vibe's computer room," he said proudly after flipping on the light.

Kallie followed him into the room, which didn't look like a computer room at all. At least not like any of the ones at Bengate. Here, rows of tables crowded against each other, making the room look busy despite the fact that it was quiet and Kallie and Swag were the only living souls in the room. In addition, there were only two computers in the so-called computer room, each sitting atop tables that were situated at opposite ends of the room. Old-fashioned typewriters sat atop each of the other tables in the room. "It sort of looks like a newsroom from the seventies," Kallie said, remembering an old movie she'd once seen.

"You get the idea," Swag said. He pointed her in the direction of the computer on the left side of the room. "Go ahead and turn it on," Swag said after she'd sat down in front of the computer. When the log-in screen appeared, she turned toward him. "Just enter 'Remember1' as the user ID and password. Capital R, numerical one, no spaces."

She followed his instructions and soon the computer desktop was visible. Swag checked his watch and then leaned over her to use the mouse to drag the cursor to the Skype icon. She caught a hint of his cologne and felt herself blushing. He smelled nice and manly. If he didn't own a creepy black suit or could recite scripture verbatim, Swag could easily be considered hunk-material. After a few moments and more keystrokes from Swag, Father McCarthy's headshot appeared onscreen.

"I'll leave you two alone," Swag said to her, and then he left the room.

"Kallie, it's good to see you again. Technology's a great thing, isn't it?" Father McCarthy asked rhetorically. Initially, the audio was a slight step behind the video, reminiscent of one of those poorly translated Japanese martial art movies. It was a little disorienting to her, more so a few seconds later when she saw the sudden change in his facial expression an instant before he said, "Is something troubling you? You looked pensive."

Surprised and somewhat taken aback by his astuteness, Kallie found herself at a sudden loss for words. After she'd found out that the government had been spying on her, her emotions had ping-ponged between anger and fear. How dare the government spy on her! Where exactly did they get off doing that to an American citizen? Especially one who'd been doing nothing other than minding her own business? But before she'd been able to fully consider her anger-fueled questions, fear had set in, bringing questions of its own. Since they were spying on her, what would that ultimately mean for her? Did they honestly consider her a threat to national security? Was what happened to Phillip Beamer going to happen to her?

Naturally, her anger and fear had waned in the two days since though it was still an unsettling feeling knowing someone had purposely watched her every move. She wasn't a naive girl. She knew that law enforcement officials oftentimes placed criminals under surveillance, sometimes recording the very information that would be used later to file charges against those very criminals. She got that. But she was no criminal. Then again, Bennett hadn't necessarily been acting on behalf of the US government. Nor could what he'd done be technically called spying. He'd merely decided to visit a girl who his own niece had told him had had a weird vision, one involving an act of terror. It was a plausible and innocent explanation. But what Kallie didn't get was why the agent had deemed her vision so important in the first place? Even if it was true that the government had an agency dedicated to investigating the paranormal, it wouldn't explain why Agent Bennett felt the need to go skulking outside the house of a teenaged college student.

As she'd considered these questions in the quietness of her bedroom, she realized she'd gotten so ticked off by Bennett's spying revelation that she'd completely ignored the agent's implication concerning Father McCarthy. Now, as she looked solemnly at the Father's face on the computer monitor, she again considered the agent's allegation. What if McCarthy had lied to her about Phillip Beamer? What if Bennett had been telling the truth? But why would McCarthy lie to her? It just didn't make sense.

She studied McCarthy's face on the monitor. He had the sweet face of an old man seemingly incapable of lying. He reminded her of her own grandfather. She used to spend a lot of time with her grandfather before he died when she was eight years old. Continuing to look at McCarthy's face on the monitor, she recalled a time when she and her grandfather had been out walking. It had been a few months before his unexpected death. They'd come to a stop at the edge of the woods about a mile from their house.

"What's the matter, grandpa?" she'd asked, looking up at her grandfather. A late afternoon sun slipped through the branches of the trees, highlighting him, making it appear as if he was glowing. The smell of honeysuckle, a staple of springtime in Lumberton, permeated throughout the air, pleasantly tickling her nose.

Her grandfather smiled down at her. "How do you know something's the matter?"

"You always get quiet when you're thinking about something. Momma says it's because you're working out a problem in your head. We've been walking for a while now, grandpa, and you haven't talked about anything. You didn't even mention how big and red grandmother's tomatoes have gotten. And you always say something about those. What problem are you working on, grandpa?"

He patted her on the head. "You are a very bright and observant young lady. There is something bothering me."

"Tell me, grandpa. Maybe I can help you figure it out."

"And I bet you can at that," he said. Looking around, he pointed to a spot under a white oak tree. "Let's go sit over there."

"Okay, grandpa," she said.

When they both had sat down, her grandpa said, "You remember our dog, King?"

"Yes, grandpa, he ran away when I was three. You said he wanted to go live with his real family in Fairmont. I still miss him. I used to wait up for him, thinking he would come back to live with us. But he never did. I guess he loved his other family more than us."

"No, that's not true at all." Her grandfather cleared his throat. "The thing is, King didn't run away, sweetheart. You see, we'd had King for many years before you were born. In dog years, he was very old and one morning, he simply died due to old age. Your mom, grandmother, and I didn't know how to tell you. We didn't feel you'd understand about life and death. So we made up the story about King running off to be with his family. We'd thought that King's dying would be too painful for you. But the reality was that we'd simply replaced one hurt with another one. We lied to you and for that, I'm sorry."

"Is something troubling you, Kallie?" Father McCarthy asked again.

She tucked away the memory of her grandfather. "No." She stared intently at McCarthy's image. The memory of her grandfather had shown her that even a lie with the best of intentions was still a lie. It had become apparent to her that either Bennett or McCarthy, or perhaps both of them, had lied to her. She needed to know which one.

"Are you sure?" McCarthy asked.

Kallie slowly shook her head. "Not exactly. I was visited by an agent from ICE."

On the monitor, McCarthy leaned toward her. "Dennard Bennett?"

"You know him?"

"Yes," McCarthy answered. "He visited me a few weeks ago. What did he want?"

"He wanted to know about my vision."

"What did you tell him?"

"I told him that it had only been a dream, and I couldn't recall the specific details of it."

"Good," McCarthy said warmly. "That's very good."

"There's something else," Kallie said. "Agent Bennett said that you lied about Phillip Beamer. He said that the government didn't have anything to do with his death."

McCarthy rolled his eyes. "I'm not surprised." He paused, his forehead crinkling. "What else did he tell you?"

"Nothing. I didn't give him a chance to."

McCarthy looked unconvinced. "Did he give you any indication that he knew about your ability?"

"No," Kallie said strongly, feeling as though she was being interrogated. "I'm not even sure what my ability is. How could I possibly know what he was indicating?"

McCarthy's face softened. "I understand," he said soothingly. "I know this whole experience is unsettling for you, to say the least. And you're probably trying to figure out who to trust. I can't make that decision for you. I can only tell you what I know. And then you'll have to decide whether or not to believe me."

Kallie closed her eyes. He was right. He couldn't make the decision for her. She would have to decide whom to trust and believe. From the first time she'd met him, she'd sensed that Father McCarthy had a calming way about him, just as her grandfather had. She opened her eyes. "If eternal return is real, why keep it a secret? Why not announce it to the world."

McCarthy smiled. "That's a good question and one that Reverend Swag will get into in major detail in a few moments. But for now, just imagine a world where everyone knew there was no ending, but you simply repeated the process over again. What do you think the criminal or evil element would do with that knowledge? How would people who are currently suffering in one capacity or another react?"

"I don't know," Kallie said. "I guess it could become a chaotic world."

"Yes, Kallie," Father McCarthy said. "That's exactly what it would become. It would be total chaos. Despite what atheists may claim, the threat of damnation remains our biggest deterrent to abhorrent behavior in the world. Unfettered human nature cannot be trusted. The church has long understood this. Now, I understand that conspiracy theorists have long held that the Church has kept secrets. And maybe in some instances in the past that's been to the world's detriment. But in this case, it's for the world's continued wellbeing. Can you understand that?"

"I think so."

"Agent Bennett and the US government may have valid reasons for their actions. They may feel that the national security of the country is superior to everything. But the Church has responsibility not to just one country, but to all humanity. Can you understand that?"

"I do," she answered meekly.

"Good, now are you ready to get started?"

"I am."

"Good. And now I'll leave you in the very capable hands of Reverend Swag. I'm positive that he can answer your questions. And if there's something he can't answer, he'll direct it to me later, and I'll see if I can answer it for you."

"Thank you, Father," she said.

At that moment, Swag came back into the room and went over to the monitor. "Are we ready?" Swag asked Father McCarthy.

"I believe we are," McCarthy said. "Keep me abreast of her progress."

"I will," Swag said. He logged out of Skype and then turned off the monitor. "Let's move to another table," he said to Kallie.

"Okay," she said and followed him to a table on the other side of the room. There was a computer on this table as well, but it was an older model, unlike the one she'd just Skyped on which had a flat screen monitor. The computer on this table was big and bulky-looking.

"Yes, it still works," Swag said, noticing how she was staring at the ancient thing.

She smiled. "What's with all the old stuff? Are you a hoarder?"

Swag laughed. "Not really. All of this stuff still works. And trust me, there's a method to this apparent madness. Have a seat." He directed her to the chair at the table in front of the computer. After she sat down, he walked over to the back wall and retrieved an easel and pad, setting them up in front of the table where Kallie was seated. Using a red color marker, he drew a huge circle on the pad. Above that he wrote the words, 'Circle of Time.' Then, he drew rectangles at alternating points on the circle. Underneath the circle, he drew a single straight line with an arrow point at one end. "This represents time," he said, pointing to the circle." Then, he pointed to the line. "This, contrary to general opinion, does not."

"You're saying that time is not heading infinitely in one direction, but rather circles back onto itself," she said.

"Exactly."

How do you know this?" she asked.

"The Alliance of Initiates."

"The Alliance of Initiates?" she repeated.

"Yes, you've heard of the United Religions Organizations?"

She scrunched her face. "I believe so."

"Well, A.I. was formed out of URO sometime after the discovery of people born with the unique ability to remember. Rememberers have been around since at least the second time cycle. No one knows how or why certain people are born with the ability, nor is it known how many people throughout history have had the ability. At least I'm not privy to that information. Currently, including you, there are four known Rememberers."

Kallie thought briefly about Madame Isabel and wondered if his figure included her. But she didn't want to ask in case it didn't. It was obvious Madame Isabel preferred operating underground. "These people that have the ability, the confirmed ones, are they okay? I mean are they dying or are they mentally ill in some way?"

Swag smiled. "No, they're not dying and they're not mentally ill. They're normal people who just so happen to be born with a gift. There's nothing mentally wrong with them, you or me."

"You have the ability, as well?"

"Yes, I have this unique and special gift," he said.

"But it doesn't feel like a gift."

"That's because you don't understand it."

"And you can help me do that?"

"That's why you're here. But you will have to trust me. Can you do that?"

"I believe I can," she said.

"Good. But I believe that in order for you to do that we need to address the elephant in the room."

She looked at him curiously, but didn't say anything.

"What have you heard about me?"

"Heard?" she repeated, knowing full well what he was referring to. "I really haven't heard anything."

He just looked at her.

She looked off for a brief moment, and then faced him squarely. "Okay, I know you started preaching at the age of six. And I know your father went to prison. I don't know if he's still there or even alive. I don't know if your mother is alive. I heard you bounced around in foster homes for a bit. But then you picked yourself up by your own bootstraps." She said the last part feigning a deep voice and puffing out her chest playfully.

He smiled. "Sounds like it would make a good Lifetime movie. Is that all?"

Isn't that enough? She thought but didn't say. "Is any of it true?"

"All of it. My father was sentenced to thirty years. But he only served six of them. He suffered a massive heart attack while in prison and died. I never knew my mother. She died shortly after giving birth to me."

Kallie felt tears welling in her eyes. "I'm sorry."

"Oh, don't be. Sometimes you never miss what you never had. And as far as my father is concerned, I've accepted what was and I don't dwell on it."

"You sound like a real together dude."

A half-smile creased his lips. "I don't know about that. But I've accepted what life has thrown at me. Do you have any more questions?"

"Yes, just one. When did you first discover your ability to remember?"

"I think I always knew, even back when I was preaching as a little boy. I think I even saw what was going to happen to my dad. I had a vision of him getting arrested. But at the time, I didn't think the vision was related to any kind of special ability. Even after he got arrested, I just convinced myself that I hadn't actually envisioned it, but rather I'd internally knew that he'd been doing wrong and would ultimately get arrested. Needless to say, I pushed the thoughts away. Then about five years ago, the ability became more pronounced and I found myself beginning to remember more and more. By that time, I'd taken over the ministry at New Vibe and had joined the United Religions Organization. Sometime afterwards, a member of A.I. learned about me and my ability. They initiated me into the group and then enlightened me on time cycles and eternal return. And as the saying goes, the rest was history."

"And you believe A.I. has told you the truth?"

"As they knew it. After my ability was fully developed, it no longer mattered, as I was basically able to confirm everything that they told me, and then some more. And you will, too, if you're ready to proceed. Are you?"

She nodded affirmatively.

"Good. Now your first step to understanding is disregarding your whole concept of time. Everything you know about it or think you know about it. Everything you've been taught about it or have ever assumed about it. You must forget it all. You will never understand eternal return through the lens of what you currently know or think you know about time. Is that understood?"

"Yes," she said softly.

He pointed again at the circle on the pad. "As I said before, this drawing represents time. In a moment, I'll show you a video that explains that further. But first, there is one other thing you need to know. Are you ready?"

"Yes,"

He took the red marker and underneath the title, Circle of Time, he wrote in big bold letters, the words:

God is Time. Time is God

After he finished, he put the marker down on the easel extension and then stood back. "Now," he said after a few moments, "let that phrase run in the background of your mind as you watch the video."

Reaching around her, he flipped on the computer. After the computer had fully stirred to life, he punched a few keys and moved the mouse across the desktop, stopping and clicking on a little icon of a globe with a thunderbolt slashing through it.

"The video runs about forty minutes," Swag said. He clicked on a speaker icon and adjusted the volume. "I'll see you on the other side." He stared at the monitor for a moment. And then, apparently satisfied that the video and audio were adequate, he left the room.

Kallie didn't know what to expect from watching the video. In fact, she didn't think watching a video on remembering or eternal return was even necessary. She'd already accepted what Madame Isabel and Father McCarthy had told her about her ability and what it had signified. She'd accepted it partly because it made the most sense to her, but mainly because she'd wanted to believe there was something special about her. What child didn't want to believe they were special in some way? Most likely every person that ever breathed air had thought themselves special at one time or another. Almost every child started out thinking that the world revolved around them, which of course eventually led to a crash and burn to reality when the potential harshness of life rendered that belief a cruel and utter joke, unless of course the child was born into the isolated world of the rich and famous or had otherwise indulgent circumstances.

Kallie hadn't thought the world revolved around her. Her mother, grandfather, and grandmother had tried to make sure she'd understood her place in God's kingdom. After the deaths of her mother and grandfather, her grandmother told her that despite God's taking away of the people she loved, He still loved her and Kallie was indeed special and unique. But then, so were all of God's creatures. Every person and thing was unique and special in their own way, and though God's ways could be mysterious, He still loved all his children. Her grandmother had tried to walk the thin line of explaining God's sometimes unexplainable actions. Kallie understood her grandmother's intentions. But they hadn't helped her to understand God's ways.

Kallie's eyes widened as she saw the Reverend Johnny Swag appear on the video. He was wearing a two-piece white suit with an open-collared silk blue shirt, reminiscent of the suit worn by John Travolta's character in the seventies' disco flick, Saturday Night Fever.

"You're probably wondering why I'm dressed like this," Swag said on the video. "Well, if you were alive during the seventies or are a big fan of the disco era, this get-up has sparked a memory."

The Bee Gees' 'Staying Alive' song began playing in the background and Swag did a quick two-step. Both the song and Swag's dancing stopped just as abruptly as they'd started. "I won't further embarrass myself," Swag continued. "Despite my obvious lack of dancing talent, I'm willing to bet that those of you that are familiar with disco were suddenly taken back to another place and time. For some of you, the Bee Gees song did the trick, taking you back and retrieving perhaps a forgotten moment." He winged his arms out. "That's what this suit is about. That's what the room you're now sitting in is about. All these old things, the old computer monitor you're watching, the newsroom setup of the room, all of these things are memory triggers. It's part of what we do here. It's all aimed at helping you to unearth and nurture your God-given ability to remember. We'll primarily use a technique called 'priming,' which is the form of human memory concerned with the perceptual identification of words and objects. It's like when you saw me in this suit and heard the Bee Gees song, you immediately thought disco and the seventies. I essentially primed your memory. Are you ready for the session? Sure you are. That's why you're here. That's why you're watching this video. So sit back and enjoy the rest of the video. And when it's finished, it will be time to get to work. Okay?"

Totally immersed in what Swag's screen version was saying, Kallie nodded affirmatively. Momentarily, she broke her trance and looked around the room at the old desks, chairs, and typewriters. Suddenly the room made sense to her. Time triggers. Just looking at the old things made her search her mind. Snippets of memories flickered on and off, partial images of old movies and television shows she'd seen, bits of old songs she'd heard. She could feel her mind churning, trying to make the connection between these things and a previous reality. Anxious to start her session with Swag, she could hardly contain her growing excitement as she watched the remainder of the video.

As the video's ending credits rolled, Swag returned to the room. "How do you feel?"

"Great," Kallie said. "The video is helping me put it all into prospective. I am curious about something though."

"What's that?"

"The seventies time-trigger, how would that work on me? I wasn't around for the disco era."

"That's why you have to forget your concept of time." He went to the drawing of the circle on the pad and placed his finger on a point of the circle. "Remember when I said that A.I. didn't have to tell me about the truth because I remembered it?"

"Yes."

"You didn't think about that when I said it? How could I remember something that I wasn't around for? Consider the book of Genesis. In the beginning, God created the heavens and the earth. Who was around to know that? If man had yet to be created, how could he record the history of creation?"

"I guess I never thought about it," Kallie said.

"Don't feel bad, no one ever thinks about it. But the reason man learned about creation, about Adam and Eve, was because of Rememberers. When your ability is fully formed, not only will you be able to know what happened after your point of existence on this circle, you'll be able to remember what has occurred at every point on this circle, before your existence came about and afterwards." He eyed her with a knowing grin as he traced his finger along the circle drawn on the pad.

*   *   *

Later that same night, Swag was back at his home when he received McCarthy's call.

"How did it go?" McCarthy asked anxiously.

"Better than expected," Swag answered. "Her memory is like a dam ready to burst."

"Then, she'll soon be able to help you locate the Rogue," McCarthy said with eagerness in his voice.

"The Rogue," Swag said as if he'd suddenly forgotten about him. "Sure, finding him will be no problem. No problem at all."

CHAPTER EIGHTEEN

Veronica lived in one of the off campus apartments the university owned and kept in reserve for its graduate students. It was a fairly good-sized, two bedroom apartment. She had meticulously decorated every inch of it with things she'd managed to snag either from flea markets, consignment shops, or amongst the discarded items of her fellow college-mates who'd wished to save on moving expenses or had simply been too lazy to properly dispose of the stuff themselves.

"Nice place you have here, Roni," Bennett said after taking the offered seat on a black, plushy couch. "Kinda shatters the myth of the struggling college student."

"Thanks," Veronica said, sitting across from him in a straight-back armchair. "But it's no myth. My parents footed the bill for the undergraduate degrees. But I'm on my own for anything beyond that, not to mention my health insurance. So, I don't have much money and probably won't have until a few years after I graduate. But believe it or not, I've spent less than five hundred dollars for everything you see in here."

Bennett whistled, looking around the room in amazement. "Wow! The place looks like you spent a mint."

"You just have to know where to find the deals," she said, smiling. After a moment, she asked if he'd like something to drink. He politely declined.

"I just stopped by to apologize again about the other day," he said. "I didn't mean to get you into any trouble with your school. I had another talk with your professor, Dr. Frost. She's a pistol, but I believe she understands the situation."

"I appreciate you doing that, but really it wasn't necessary."

"Anyway, I wanted to do it."

She eyed him carefully. "What's on your mind, Uncle Den?"

"Why you ask?"

"I know you didn't drive back here just to apologize for the umpteenth time and to tell me you had another talk with Dr. Frost. You could've just called."

Bennett chuckled. "I might have known you'd see through that ruse. Law enforcement is in your blood. You're right. There's something on my mind. It's Kallie Hunt. I believe she's holding something back."

"Holding what back?"

"I don't know."

"You think she's a terrorist?"

"No, I don't think that. But she knows something. Something that could possibly save lives in the future."

"Related to terrorism?"

"I believe so," Bennett said.

Veronica shook her head slowly. "I don't know about that, Uncle Den. She's just a college kid from a small town. What would she know about terrorism, other than what she sees on TV or reads in the paper?"

"You're missing the point," Bennett said. "I'm not interested in her dissertation on terrorism. It's possible that she might not even know what she knows."

Veronica's head tilted slightly to the side. "You're referring to her déjà vu sensations?"

"Yes," Bennett said, staunchly.

"You honestly think there's something to the vision she had the other day?"

Bennett shrugged his shoulders. "I honestly do." He paused. "Look, it could be nothing. But, then again, it could be something. I have to be sure."

"What's really going on Uncle Den? I got a feeling that you're the one who's holding something back."

Bennett sat up on the sofa, leaning toward his niece. "You're right. Quid pro quo. I'm going to confide in you, and I'm going to need you to keep this information to yourself. It's a national security matter."

"It should be able to go without saying. But you can trust me."

Bennett nodded his head. "I know I can. But as a rule, I never let anything go without saying it." He paused a moment. "Kallie Hunt received a visit the other day from a person who's an unofficial person of interest in Phillip Beamer's murder."

"Beamer, the suspected terrorist?"

"Beamer, who was known to have been planning an actual terrorist attack."

"But how would such a person know Kallie?"

"I don't know. But that's what I need to find out. Will you help me?"

Without hesitation she said, "Sure, I will."

After her uncle left her apartment, Veronica walked across the complex to Josh's apartment. He opened the door after the third rap of knocks. His eyebrows pinched upward when he opened the door and saw her standing there. "Veronica. What a pleasant surprise."

"I'm glad you still think so. I'm sorry for just dropping by. May I come in?"

He answered by stepping back, allowing her inside. Although his apartment's floor plan was similar to hers, his was sparsely furnished. The living room contained only a loveseat and a flat screen television. She followed him to the kitchen nook where a laptop sat atop the table. He slid into the chair in front of it.

"Who's that?" she asked, looking over his shoulder at the laptop screen.

"It's just a screenshot of Kali, the goddess of time, fighting demons."

"A videogame?"

"It's something like that." He closed the laptop and indicated the chair across from him at the table. After she took the offered seat, he said, "So what's up?"

"I felt bad about earlier and I wanted to come by and apologize personally. I didn't want you to think that I'd purposely do something to jeopardize the project or have your integrity impugned."

"It's water under the bridge," Josh said. "I've forgotten about it and moved on."

Veronica smiled. "I'm glad. I hope Kallie feels the same way?"

"I can't speak for her. But I don't think she's the type to hold grudges."

Veronica looked relieved. "I hope not. I feel really awful about what happened. Do you think we could all go bowling or dancing or something, Kallie included? You know, to show there're no hard feelings."

"That sounds like a good idea. I know the group wouldn't mind. But you'll have to ask Kallie."

Veronica bit her lower lip. "I was kinda hoping that maybe you could suggest it. She might still be a little sore at me."

"I doubt that."

"See, you know her better than I do."

He smiled. "Okay, if you want. I'll suggest it the next time I see her."

A look of relief washed over her face. "Would you? That would be great. Thank you."

"It's no biggie."

* * *

Through Kallie's bedroom window, Kallie and Maggie watched Seth pace the sidewalk in front of their house for thirty minutes. It had been Maggie who had spotted him first and she had run into Kallie's bedroom to tell her. "How long has he been out there?" Kallie had asked.

"I don't know," Maggie said. "I just happened to look out the front window and there he was. You want me to go and ask him what he wants?"

"No," Kallie said. "If that's how he wants to spend his Saturday morning, then let him."

"Are you still mad at him?"

"No, I'm not mad."

"I should say not. You're in love with him."

"Now why would you say something like that?"

"It's because I'm not blind. I've seen the way you've jumped the past couple of days every time the doorbell rang. You were hoping it was he. I've also seen you double and triple check the ringer on your cell phone. You keep looking at it as if trying to will it to ring and for it to be him on the other end. Even now, I can see you blushing because you know I'm telling the truth." She paused and looked back out the window. "And I'll tell you something else, too. Any boy that comes around at eight o'clock on a Saturday morning is either in love as well or is just plain weird."

It was another twenty minutes before Seth finally decided to ring the doorbell. Kallie had thought about sending Maggie down to answer the door, but then decided she wasn't going to play games. She went to the door and opened it without bothering to ask who it was.

"You saw me out here, huh?" Seth said after she'd opened the door.

"You were pretty hard to miss," Kallie said. "Come in."

He followed her into the living room. He sat down on one end of the couch while she sat on the opposite end of it. The loveseat where they sat together the other night, though just a few inches away, seemed as far away as another time dimension. For a while neither spoke. The silence was tense but not awkward. Each wanted to be here. Each had a lot to say, but neither wanted to be the first one to say it. Seth, it was silently agreed, drew the short straw. "Listen," he began, pacing himself, "I'm sorry. I acted like a crazed fool the other night."

Kallie exhaled a little. "I wouldn't say crazed, maybe a little jerkish." She smiled, trying to take the edge off the word.

Seth was all in now, the words flowing easily. "I know and I'm sorry. You think maybe we could start over again?"

I don't know Seth, she thought. How do I know you won't be one of those crazy, jealous, and abusive boyfriends? Someone who will try to cut me off from the outside world, belittle me, take away my self-confidence? She'd heard about guys like that and how some girls found themselves in abusive situations simply because they'd moved too fast. But she somehow knew Seth wasn't like that. There was something sweet and innocent about him. For some reason she felt strangely connected to him. I really like you, Seth Winters. She thought those things, but of course said none of them. It would be too soon. Even if he'd felt the same way, she'd likely send him running for the hills with any talk of love and connection. "I would like that."

He offered his hand to shake on the agreement to start over. It was clear by the tightness of his stare that he wanted to seal the deal with something stronger. She wanted to as well, catching a quick glimpse of his thin slightly moistened off-pink lips. But the lady in her won the day. Her grandmother, mother, and grandfather—may they rest in peace—would have been proud of her self-restraint. "I know you can take care of yourself," he was saying, "and I promise you that I won't overstep my bounds again. I can't promise that I won't always be concerned about you, or try to look out for you. But I will respect your wishes, whatever they may be. I'm not a crazed, jealous jerk. I know it'll probably take some time for you to see that. But if you give me the chance, you'll see."

"Okay," she said and clasped his hand. "I'm going to trust you. But understand this—I'm not like those naive girls from the Lifetime movies. I don't have low self-esteem. I don't feel I need you for validation. There will not be an endless carousel of bad behavior followed by my forgiving you and accepting you back. I'm fair; but I'm not stupid. Act like that again and there will be no next time."

"Understood," he said.

The handshake led to them spending the rest of the weekend together, including an impromptu "meet the families" excursion to their respective hometowns. For Kallie, it was a welcomed respite, a chance to get some time away from books, terror threats, and time cycles.

To their amazement, Bengate was practically the same distance from both their hometowns though in opposite directions. And since Lumberton and Florence, South Carolina, were only separated by about a one hundred and twenty mile stretch of I-95, they could make the trip in one big looping circle.

They decided to head east to Lumberton first, mainly because the trip would most likely require an overnight stay, and separate rooms or not, her grandmother wasn't about to let an unmarried couple sleep under her roof. Kallie smiled uneasily at the thought. She and Seth weren't a couple. Officially, they weren't anything at this point, not even declared friends. And it was that non-defined aspect of their relationship that further convinced her that an overnight stay at her grandmother's house wasn't a wise idea. The questions would be unrelenting. Her grandmother wouldn't understand that Kallie wasn't sure where this thing with Seth was headed. She only knew that she liked being with him and for her, right now, that was all that mattered.

To Kallie's surprise, her grandmother didn't ask one question about her relationship with Seth. In fact, her grandmother had seemed genuinely happy that Kallie seemed genuinely happy. Her grandmother saved all her questions for Seth, perhaps thinking that she could drill Kallie next week. She asked Seth a fair amount of questions about his family and upbringing. Kallie noticed a decided change in her grandmother's body language when Seth mentioned that his father was a Baptist preacher.

"A preacher's son," her grandmother said, nodding her head slightly. "Are you planning to follow your father's footsteps into the ministry?"

"I haven't decided yet," Seth said. "Bengate has a great divinity school; but I'm still weighing my options. I have until the end of next semester to make up my mind. I'm praying about it."

Her grandmother nodded her head a little more fervently this time. "In all things consult the master." And then she looked at Kallie and winked.

Kallie didn't know what to make of her grandmother's wink. Was she winking because Seth was consulting the master or had she winked because she wanted Kallie to consult the master? Perhaps her grandmother would expound on the wink next week when she and Kallie had their weekly confab, or perhaps her grandmother wouldn't mention it at all. Ultimately, Kallie decided she didn't care what the wink meant, if it meant anything. The few hours the three of them shared that afternoon was the best time she'd had as part of a trio since her mother's death.

Seth held the door of the Mustang open, waiting patiently as Kallie and her grandmother said their goodbyes. "I'll call you when we get to Florence," Kallie said. She kissed her grandmother on the cheek and then slid into the passenger seat of the Mustang. Seth closed the door, and then handed her grandmother a slip of paper on his way to the driver's side. "That's my home number," he said. "You can call anytime."

Ten minutes later, as he steered the Mustang onto the ramp to get on the interstate, Seth, as if he'd been analyzing the playback of the afternoon, said, "That went well."

Kallie looked over at him and smiled. "It did, didn't it? I think my grandmother likes you."

"I like her," Seth said. "Almost as much as I like her granddaughter."

"Do you think your parents will like me?"

"They're gonna love you. I think it's in our family bylaws or something. We have to love whatever person either of us drags to the house."

Kallie laughed and then settled back into her seat, gazing casually out the window. Trees adorned with the multicolored leaves of fall swished rapidly in and out of her line of vision as the Mustang sped steadily down I-95. For the briefest of moments, she thought about her mother, a dimple of sadness creasing her happy thoughts. She wondered if her mother had ever been as happy as she felt right now. And she also wondered, though not for the first time, if her biological father had been her mother's one true love. It was sad if he had been, particularly since her parents' relationship had obviously ended badly. Her mother had never discussed the circumstances of her breakup with Kallie's father, but it was the rare relationship that ended on amicable terms. All Kallie's mother ever told her was that Kallie had been born out of an act of love and not the result of a one-night stand or fling. But if they'd truly loved each other, then why couldn't they've made the relationship work? For most lovers, a relationship not ending in forever-after bliss was one that ended badly.

Of course, there was a possibility that Kallie's father hadn't been her mother's one true love. But that thought brought Kallie no comfort. In fact, it felt like a punch to the gut, because that would have meant that her mother had never experienced true love. Her mother had never spoken of any man other than Kallie's father and her mother had never dated anyone in Kallie's lifetime. As that realization struck, Kallie turned her head once more and looked at Seth.

Sensing her eyes on him, Seth turned his gaze briefly from the road.

"Do you believe in love at first sight?" she asked.

He smiled and faced forward again. "Are you saying that you fell in love with me the first time you saw me?"

"No silly. I'm not saying that. I just want to know your thoughts on the subject."

"My thoughts on the subject?" he repeated.

"Yes, your thoughts."

"Yes, I do. Of course, I don't think it happens as often as some people may think. But yes, I do believe it's possible."

"Me too," she said and smiled.

They became quiet, seemingly sharing the same thought. Then Seth turned back to her. "What're you thinking about?"

"Nothing," she said softly. But it was a lie. She was thinking about him. She'd never felt this way about anyone before. Perhaps it was too soon to emphatically claim her feelings to be love. But there was a warm sensation in her heart, one that she hoped would never leave. *Be kind, sweet, and gentle always Seth Winters,* she said silently to herself. She faced forward again and rolled down her window slightly, letting the coolness of the fall evening flow into the car. She was a big enough girl to realize that nothing in life was promised, not even love. You simply had to enjoy it whenever you got it, for however long you had it.

She'd fallen asleep before they'd entered the city of Florence proper, awakening just as the Mustang was noisily making its way down a long, gravel-topped driveway. She opened her eyes reluctantly. She'd been having a pleasant dream, one involving flowers and countryside-roaming on a bright and sunny summer day. Hazily, she looked out the window. The Winters' House was a fairly large frame and cobblestone-fronted structure. "And they moved to Beverly," she grinned, "Hills that is."

"Oh, you got jokes," Seth said. "It's not that big. Besides, we don't own it. It's a parsonage. It belongs to the church."

"To the church? It's bigger than my grandmother's church."

"Ha, ha, cute," Seth said. "Let's go meet my folks."

And just then, as if its inhabitants had been eagerly awaiting their arrival, the house's front double doors swung open, producing a short, pleasant-faced woman sporting a wide, friendly, high-charged smile. She was followed closely by a tall, distinguished-looking, gray-haired man whose smile was just as friendly as the woman's, though with a little less voltage.

CHAPTER NINTEEN

The Winters family seemed loving and close-knit; just as Kallie had always imagined a family that had both original parents living in the same household would be. There were four Winters kids. Seth and his older sister, Stephanie (a rising senior at Notre Dame), had already flown the coop, leaving only the two youngest siblings, fourteen year old fraternal twins, Cam and Ron, still living at home. Kallie watched Mrs. Winters dote on the two and Seth as if she'd thought the three would be off to war at any given moment. Seeing Mrs. Winters obsess over her boys made Kallie remember the summer before she'd first left for college. Her own mother had cried and laughed interchangeably just about every day that summer. She'd been very proud about her only daughter going to college; but she'd been sad at the same time because her daughter going to college had also meant she'd be leaving home. "It's my sweet and sour moment," Kallie's mother had said at the time. "My baby's all grown up now. It's the day parents pray for and dread at the same time."

"What are you studying at college?" Reverend Winters asked Kallie.

The television was playing noiselessly in the background as the four of them, the Reverend, Mrs. Winters, Seth, and Kallie, sat fat, happy, and content in the family room. The reverend had fried fish and french-fries, and made big bowls of coleslaw and potato salad, sufficiently impressing Kallie with his kitchen skills. After eating all they could hold, the twins had excused themselves with promises not to stay up too late playing videogames.

"I'm just taking the basic stuff now, English, biology, and philosophy—stuff like that. I haven't decided on a major yet. But I don't have to decide until next year anyway."

"Ah, philosophy," the reverend said. "How are you doing in that course?"

"It's probably my favorite," Kallie said.

"I see," the reverend said. "And tell me, where do you fall on the God question?"

"What do you mean?" Kallie asked.

"Retreat Kallie," Seth said. "Dad's setting you up."

"Asking her where she stands on the God question is not setting her up, young man," Reverend Winters said.

Mrs. Winters stood up. "I know where this is headed. I'm going upstairs and lay my clothes out for tomorrow." To Kallie she added, "Be careful dear, or you're liable to end up in tomorrow's sermon."

Kallie glanced helplessly at Seth and then looked to his father. She certainly wasn't prepared to get into a philosophical discussion with a minister about the existence of God. But although having just told her to retreat, Seth now seemed just as anxious as his father was to hear her response. Both of them watched her carefully, waiting for her to say something. "Okay," she said, "let me clarify. Are you asking what I think about the existence of God or what I think about philosophy's contrasting views on God's existence?"

"Great question," Reverend Winters said. "But I don't think the answers to both are mutually exclusive. As you probably know, philosophers have tackled the God question for as long as they've been able to think. Some philosophers, like Descartes, Kant, and Leibniz, believed that God's existence could be rationally proven. While other philosophers, namely Feuerbach and Nietzsche, used philosophy to challenge the notion of God's existence. But in my humble opinion, I think one uses philosophy to back up or support what one already believes."

"So what you're saying," Seth began, "is that philosophy doesn't prove God's existence one way or the other. If you believed in God before you studied philosophy, you most likely would believe in him afterwards, and vice-versa."

"Precisely," his father said.

"It's kind of a roundabout way to find out if I believe in God, isn't it?" Kallie asked.

Reverend Winters smiled. "Roundabout only if that were my goal. But, to be honest, I was only making polite conversation."

Kallie laughed. "So that's what passes for polite conversation around here?"

Both Seth and his father laughed and said in unison, "I'm afraid so."

"Okay, Reverend Winters, I have a question for you."

"I'm all ears."

"What are your thoughts on time-cycles?"

The reverend's eyebrows furrowed. "Time-cycles?"

"Yes," Kallie said. "Some religions and philosophers believe that time is not linear, but rather circular. And that we've already completed at least one time-cycle."

"I see," Reverend Winters said. "I don't believe in time-cycles. There's no question that time is linear."

"How can you be sure?" Kallie asked. "How do you know that once time gets to an end it won't simply circle back around?"

The reverend smiled. "I love the inner workings of an inquisitive youthful mind. I know because of the Bible, God's word."

"You're saying that there's no mention of time-cycles anywhere in the Bible?" Kallie said.

"That's correct," the reverend said confidently.

"What about where it quotes God as saying he's the Alpha and the Omega, the beginning and the end?" Kallie asked.

Seth's face became contorted and he was about to say something, but decided against it, deferring instead to his father.

"Revelation 22:13," the reverend said. "What does that verse have to do with time-cycles?"

"How can God be the first and the last or the beginning and the end? Doesn't that prove that the time points of beginning and end meet each other, indicating a circle?"

"I don't follow," the reverend said.

"I don't either," Seth said.

She wished Josh was here to explain it to them. Last week when he'd explained his take on the verse to her, it had made logical sense. "What I'm saying is that first and last, beginning and end are time-points, points on the line of time. Just like this moment that we're having now is a point in time. So, there's a beginning point and an ending point. And if God is both the first and the last, the beginning and the end, at the same time, that means the points are meeting. The only way they can meet is if those points have circled toward each other." She could feel little beads of sweat popping up on her forehead as both father and son stared at her, unsure of what to make of her theory.

Reverend Winters looked uneasily at his son, and then turned back to face Kallie. "Well, I would disagree with your premise," the reverend said. "I wouldn't say that first and last or beginning and end are representations of time-points, at least not in the sense you're referring to. The quote is merely God's declaration to us that He and only He was at the start of existence. And that He and only He will be at the end of existence."

There was an awkward silence for a moment, which was broken when Seth blurted out, "But what about eternal life?"

The reverend frowned. "What about it?"

"You said that God will be here at the end of existence. But God so saved the world that he gave his only begotten son and whosoever believes in him, will not perish, but have

184

everlasting life. Eternal life. Wouldn't that mean that there would be no end of existence or no ending point? Which could make both of you right, beginning and end could merge seamlessly into each other."

His father smiled again. "John 3:16. That was the first Bible verse you learned. The verse, of course, is God's promise to us should we believe his son to be our savior. The verse Kallie referred to simply means there is no end to God. It speaks of his eternal being. It's not speaking of time-cycles. And no, Son, it doesn't mean God is playing on a loop like some broken tape recorder."

"But what if God himself was time?" Kallie asked.

The reverend simply looked at her, and then shook his head slowly as if pitying her naiveté. "What are they teaching you at school?"

"I didn't learn this at school. I got it off the internet. It's a theory that God is time. The very act of existence is God. Isn't time the very measurement or proof of existence? Isn't it feasible that God and Time are one and the same?"

"Let me be clear," the reverend said, speaking deliberately. "Time is a human concept. Whoever said God is time was merely trying to box God into a concept, a human one. God exists beyond that. God exists beyond man's comprehension of time."

Kallie understood what the reverend was saying. Yes, God existed beyond man's concept of time. But it was clear that Reverend Winters hadn't understood her. Time was a human concept when you thought about it in terms of twenty-four hour days, seven days of the week, or twelve months of the year. But the God is Time concept as explained to her by Reverend Swag wasn't putting God in the concept of hours, or days, or months, or years. It was putting God in the concept of existence. Before God, there was nothing. And then there was God, a being, an existence. There was no time in nothing. Time was a something, an existence. Time only started when there was something. God formed from nothing into something. God and Time came into being something at the same time, essentially making God and Time, one and the same. She understood completely, but there was no way she'd be able to make the reverend understand it. Besides it was getting too late in the evening to even try. "I see," she said meekly and then yawned.

"Good," the reverend said, confident he'd won the debate. "Now, it looks like you two could use a little rest. Kallie, I trust you'll be comfortable in Stephanie's room."

"I'm sure," Kallie agreed.

"Good. I also trust that you both brought something appropriate to wear to church in the morning."

"Yes, sir," Seth said.

After the reverend left the room, Seth turned to Kallie, "I've never seen anyone debate like that with my father. You more than held your own. I think that God is time theory threw him for a loop. Did you really get that from the internet?"

"For the most part," Kallie said. She took his hand and looked into his eyes. "I appreciate you trying to help me out. I hope your father doesn't think I'm some kind of heathen."

"You don't have to worry about that. My father believes what he believes. He'll prove most of it with the Bible. And wherever the Bible is insufficient in explanations, he'll fill in the blanks with his faith. Right now, I guarantee you he's upstairs praying for understanding of the debate you and he just had. And we'll probably hear parts of it in his sermon tomorrow."

"You think so, huh?" she said.

"I do."

She kissed him. Just pulled his head into hers and kissed him. She didn't know why she'd decided on that moment in time. But she'd wanted to kiss him from the first moment she'd truly looked at him when he'd first come to her house a couple of weeks ago. But this moment somehow seemed right for their first kiss.

"God," he said when the kiss finally ended. "I've wanted
to do that for the longest time."

"Then why didn't you?"

"I'm a coward; I guess."

"Nah, you're not a coward. You might be too much of a
gentleman maybe, but you're not a coward." She kissed him
lightly on the lips again. "So your father will talk about this
tomorrow?"

"I'm almost positive."

Seth was right. Reverend Winters did incorporate parts of his
discussion with Kallie in his Sunday sermon. In a wide-
ranging oration that covered everything from the demons of
alcohol, premarital sex, drugs, and violence, to the need for
everyone to repent of their sins and follow Jesus, he gave an
impassioned plea for his congregation to not try and box God
into their human concept. "Our minds cannot truly
comprehend the awesomeness of God. We know about the
creation of the world in seven days. We know of the miracles
and blessings, the gift of his son to us. But we're simply
unable to truly grasp God." He tapped his head. "This brain
of ours is inadequate in allowing us to do so. So I say, stop
trying, stop thinking of God in our human terms. He is a
billion times, a quadrillion times more awesome than
anything we can humanly imagine. Just know that God is real
and that he sent his only begotten son to us, a son that will
take away the burden of our sins and protect us from our
demons. Can I hear amen?"

He heard several, as well as dozens of halleluiahs amidst a
thunderous applause.

*   *   *

Fat, reddish-orange, and dangling majestically from the vine, the indeterminates were nearly ready for harvest. Madame Isabel, on her knees in her garden plucking out the last of the weeds, was very pleased at this current batch of tomatoes. She'd feared an early frost would come and destroy her late season crop, but nature had been most kind this year. The fall weather had proved as nourishing as that of the spring.

Lost in thought and a prayer of gratitude for nature's mercy, she hadn't initially heard the footsteps trampling through her garden, coming towards her. When she finally heard them, two questions were birthed at once—why hadn't she heard her husband's truck pull into the driveway and why was he now moving so clumsily through her garden. When she realized the obvious answer to both questions, the footsteps had suddenly stopped behind her and she could hear their owner's breath vociferously entering the air in the now silence. Like a governor's call after the lever had already been pulled, the recollection had come just a tad late. "You'll fail again," she said without bothering to turn around, "just like before."

"All things won't be as before," he said calmly.

"She'll find out about you. She always does."

"Always is such a strong word. Things change."

She braced her body. "The more things change..."

"The more they stay the same," he said, finishing her sentence before bringing the knife down swiftly and harshly across her neck, nearly severing it from her body.

*   *   *

After Josh Levy set the car's cruise control on sixty-eight mph, he willed himself to keep the vehicle straight and his eyes opened. He most certainly didn't want to crash. He was on highway 74, heading to the little town of Maxton. Luckily, Sunday morning traffic on the highway was light. Otherwise, he could've hit a vehicle the couple of times he'd nodded off and drifted into the other lane. He hadn't slept and he'd had very little to eat or drink since Thursday. He couldn't remember ever getting so engrossed in his research. But time-cycles had proven very intriguing, very intriguing indeed.

He'd found out about Madame Isabel from a chat room. He was able to find her address on the internet and he determined that she was the same Madame Isabel that Kallie had told him about. Kallie had described her as some kind of psychic. But boy, was she more than that, much more! He looked at the odometer. The needle held steady at sixty-eight mph. He considered setting the cruise a little higher. But he quickly dismissed that thought. Though he was anxious to see Madame Isabel and connect the dots of his research, he didn't want to risk crashing his car and not getting there at all. Looking back at the road, he settled back into his seat and concentrated on just staying awake. Like an apparition, the old road song Ninety-nine Bottles of Beer on the Wall rose up in his mind and, without realizing it, he started singing. "Ninety-nine bottles of beer on the wall, ninety-nine bottles of beer. If one of them should happen to fall, then there'd be ninety-eight bottles of beer on the wall..."

CHAPTER TWENTY

The following Saturday afternoon's session with Reverend Johnny Swag was Kallie's fourth one of the week, and she was finally beginning to see the fruits of his "priming" technique. She could now make out parts of a face. She was lying down on the couch in Swag's office. Swag was sitting near her head in a brown leather rollback chair.

"Keep your eyes closed," Swag said. "Relax and clear your mind of everything but that face."

Kallie squeezed her eyes closed tighter.

Swag patted her arm, admonishing her gently. "Don't press. It'll come. But you have to relax every part of your body, including your eyes."

"Okay," Kallie said, and almost immediately, her arms and shoulders slumped imperceptibly and her eyelids stopped twitching.

"Good," Swag said. "Now tell me what you see."

She breathed in deeply. "Black eyes, flat nose, dark skin. But not dark like an African-American, more like extremely tanned. His facial expression is sad, but determined. It's in his eyes. He believes in what he's doing. He feels duty-bound."

"Can you smell anything? Any kind of scent?"

At first she thought it was a weird question. How could she smell an image? But then, her nose started twitching. She could, in fact, smell something. It was a kind of cleanliness, a lemon freshness mixed with aerosol. "I smell disinfectant, like in a hospital or a clean public bathroom."

"That's good," Swag said. "Your senses are coming alive. Continue to relax. Let it come to you."

"Okay."

"Now pull back from the face."

"Okay."

"Where are you?"

"It's a room. I see a mirror. I see his face in the mirror. He's looking at himself."

"That's good. Now, I want you to listen. Tell me what you hear."

She sat still, straining her ears. But, she could hear nothing. And after a while, the mirror and the face in it started to fade. "It's leaving me!" she said in a near panic. "Everything's going away."

He touched her arm gently. "Stay calm. It's all right. That's enough for now. Open your eyes."

She opened her eyes and sat up on the couch. She rubbed her forehead with the palms of her hands, trying to reorient herself with the present. "What happened? Everything started disappearing."

Swag slid from his rolling chair and came to her on the couch. "It's normal."

"Really?"

"Yes. You're almost there."

"It sure doesn't feel like it. Everything's kinda jumbled up. I can't tell my current memories from the previous life-cycle memories."

"It'll come. You don't have as far to go as you think. Developing your ability to remember is not like learning a martial art where you have to spend years learning your craft. The priming technique is more like prying open a locked door. Now that the door is cracked, it won't be long before the memories push through, flooding your mind. When that happens, you'll be able to separate them. Believe me."

"You make it sound as if it could happen any day now."

Swag smiled. "That's because it could. But don't worry. I'll be here to help you navigate through it." He shifted and patted her knee delicately. "Now how does a piping hot pizza sound? I'm talking pepperoni, sausage, cheese, and green peppers. I know a place that has the best pizza in these parts. It'll help take your mind off memories."

"That sounds great, but I'll have to take a rain check."

A corner of his mouth rose up slightly, a minor show of disappointment that she didn't notice. "Already have plans?" he asked.

"Sort of. I have a friend who wants to take me to a movie and some other friends who want me to go dancing with them. I haven't decided which to do yet."

"I see. Is the friend male or female?"

"Why you ask?"

"Why can't the whole group go either to a movie or dancing? Either they're friends of yours who don't get along or the movie-friend is a boy?"

She smiled. "That's very perceptive of you." She remembered Seth, Josh, and Quiggy's, and then nixed the idea of having the two of them back together so soon. "My movie-friend is a male, but I don't think he's very much into dancing."

"Okay," Swag said, "it was just a thought." He paused. "I wasn't aware you were dating. Is it serious?"

She regarded him for a moment, not sure why he was asking or even interested in her love life. As if reading her mind, he added, "I know it's none of my business. But I have a lot of young people in my congregation, and I've gotten my fair share of calls on matters of the heart, usually from a young lady after some young Romeo has broken hers."

It hadn't crossed her mind that Seth could break her heart, and now that it had, she inexplicably felt a sudden tinge of vulnerability and fear. "No one likes dealing with a broken heart," she said remotely.

"Have you ever had your heart broken?"

"No. But I've never been in love before either."

"Are you in love now?"

She looked at him and started to say something, but hesitated.

"If you feel it's too personal a question, you don't have to answer."

"No, it's not that. I don't mind answering." And she really didn't. She didn't know if it was the ivory-white clerical collar around Swag's neck or what. But she felt extremely comfortable talking to him. "I don't know if I'd clarify it as love. I'd say that I'm in strong like with somebody."

"You're in strong like. That's an interesting way to put it," Swag said. He held his hand out to her. "Let me see your hand."

She looked at him curiously for a moment before tentatively giving him her hand.

He took her hand, turning it palm up. "I'm going to read your palm."

"Read my palm? I didn't think Rememberers had to do such things."

"Of course we don't have to do it," he said smiling, "but palm reading is a very useful skill to have." Squeezing her hand gently, he studied her palm for a moment, before slowly tracing his finger along the lines of it. "Ah, I do see love in your future."

"You do?" she said, a feeling of excitement rising. "Is it Seth?"

He was still studying her palm intently. "Who's Seth?"

"The boy I'm in strong like with."

Swag looked up briefly. "I can't say for certain if it's Seth," he said before looking back at her palm. "I do see a man, a strong one. I see someone who's very knowledgeable in the ways of the world. He's someone who's capable of opening your eyes to all its possibilities. Is this Seth such a person?" He spoke slowly, deliberately. His words felt soft, almost sensual to her ears. He looked up, staring into her eyes.

Her breath caught in her throat. "I...I don't know if he is."

"You should know before you fall in love with him."

It suddenly felt very warm in the room. She pulled her hand back. "I've got to go. I have a million things to do before I meet my friends tonight."

"So you've decided to go dancing."

Feeling flushed, she said, "Dancing. Yeah, I'm going dancing."

*   *   *

"So, what's this guy's name?" Maggie asked.

They were in Kallie's car, driving down the interstate, heading to the club that was located just outside Charlotte.

Kallie took her eyes off the road momentarily to glare at her housemate. "I've told you a million times already. His name's Josh."

"Josh," Maggie said in a near whisper as she stared out the car window. Kallie could tell that she was trying to picture what Josh looked like. For all her talk about just being at Bengate for an education and not to man hunt, Kallie knew that Maggie was still a vibrant young woman, and for most women, in fact most people, the desire for human companionship always beckoned at some point. It was no different for Maggie. Kallie hadn't had to twist her arm to get her to come with her to the club. And the old girl had even cleaned up rather nicely. She was wearing a cute blue dress that fit her form perfectly. Kallie hadn't thought Maggie owned anything but sweats and oversized shirts. She'd said exactly that to Maggie earlier when they'd both been getting dressed for the evening. Maggie had simply responded, "I have other things for other occasions."

"You mean special occasions," Kallie had said.

"Just other occasions," Maggie had replied and finished dressing without saying anything more, letting the words hang ghostlike in the air.

"You say he's a grad student," Maggie said now, still staring out the car window. "Why would he want to meet an underclassman? Is he some kind of freak or something?"

"Maggie, you're incorrigible. No, he's not a freak. I've told you. He and his friends spend most of their time with their noses in books, so they're a little, how would you say, socially challenged."

"Oh right, you mean nerds. They're nerds. She's setting me up with a nerd."

"No, they're not nerds, at least not classically. You won't see any pocket protectors tonight or anything like that."

"Does he wear glasses?"

"I've never seen him in any," Kallie said. "Now would you just relax? It's not like it's a blind-blind date. I know him. We're meeting them at the club. Other people will be there. So, there's no pressure. I'm just putting two of my friends in close proximity to each other. I'm going to introduce you. You'll talk, maybe dance, and then we'll just let nature do what nature does."

"Okay, one final question. If he's such a great guy, why didn't you keep him for yourself?"

"Friend zone," Kallie said without hesitating. There was no need for any additional explanation. Besides, no girl could adequately explain why some guys landed in friend zone. But once trapped in the sometimes dreaded place, it was extremely rare for someone to escape it, sometimes to the chagrin of the girl, the guy, or both.

Maggie accepted that response and the two of them rode in silence, hearing only the sounds of the other vehicles flowing along with them on the interstate, carrying souls with plans of their own for the night, to points near and far.

After a while, Maggie turned to her. "Is Seth upset about you choosing your fat friend and the nerds over him?"

"I'm going to ignore your caddish references," she said and paused. Then, "A little I suppose, especially since I've hardly seen him this week. But he's going to go to church with me tomorrow."

"Man, you guys spend an awful lot of time in church. You'd think Seth would get the hint and run screaming in the other direction."

Kallie glanced at her. "What hint?"

"That you're preparing him for a walk down the altar."

"Girl, please. I'm not trying to get married anytime soon. Besides, going to church was his idea, not mine."

Maggie laughed. "Then, maybe you're the one who should be getting the hint."

The Tom-Tom Club was created out of the remains of a forty thousand square foot former distribution warehouse. It was located in the middle of a vast field in Chesterfield, SC, less than an hour's drive from Bengate's campus. Co-owned by Thomas Valley and Tomas Martinez, two thirty-something year old UNC MBA graduates, the club was the latest and greatest attraction for college kids in the Charlotte metro area. Rumor was that despite the fact that their first names were variations of Tom; the owners hadn't named the place after themselves. Instead, it was said that the name was an ode to the eighties duo of the same name. Thomas Valley was supposedly enthralled by the duo's song Genius of Love, especially the lyrics, 'There's no beginning and there is no end. Time isn't present in that dimension.'

Neither owner would confirm or deny the allegation. But the Tom-Tom Club, which also included an onsite restaurant, frequently employed an erratic schedule particularly on weekends, student breaks, and during the summer months. During these times, the club's hours fluctuated. It sometimes opened at noon and closed at midnight. Sometimes it opened at midnight, closing at noon. Other times, it opened at four in the afternoon, closing at four in the morning, and vice-versa. To ensure a steady crowd whenever it opened, the club offered free admission, half-off dinner entrees, and the occasional, surprise celebrity (P-Diddy, who'd once sampled the Tom-Tom Club's song on a Mariah Carey track, showed up one time at 4 a.m. and partied until nine that morning.) to the first so many patrons. The opening times were never announced in advance, so in order to be amongst the first inside, students had to drive to the club an hour or so before a possible opening time, thus keeping the club's parking lot constantly buzzing with activity. This had the added effect of making it seem as if the club was open infinitely.

By 10 p.m., the Tom-Tom Club's parking lot was filled to capacity and the long, narrow two-lane road leading up to it was lined with vehicles seemingly for miles away in either direction. Kallie parked her Honda behind a white Tahoe. As she and Maggie started to open their respective car doors, Kallie's cell phone chimed, momentarily freezing the two girls in place. Kallie pulled the phone out of her purse. The caller ID screen read *Josh*.

She brought the phone up to her ear. "What's up?"

"Where are you?" Josh asked.

"I just parked the car down the road. I didn't know it was going to be this packed."

"I don't know why not. I told you it would be. When you get here, don't wait in line. Go straight to the front and tell them that your name is on the list."

"Maggie's, too?"

"Who's Maggie?"

"My friend."

"No, it's Steve what's his name."

Kallie's throat tightened. "His name's Seth and I told you he wasn't coming."

Josh laughed. "Calm down, Tiger. I was only kidding. You're listed as Kallie Hunt plus one."

"Ha, ha," Kallie said. "We'll see you inside." She pressed END and put the cell phone back into her purse. She looked over at Maggie. "Let's go. We're on the list."

There was a sharp coolness in the air. The temperature had dropped thirty degrees from today's high of seventy. Kallie and Maggie fell in behind a sweet-smelling hoard of young people moving lockstep between the line of cars and the edge of the field.

Maggie's lower lip quivered from a mixture of cold and nervousness. "How do nerds get names on the list of a popular club?"

With wisps of her breath clearly visible in the cold, moonlit night, Kallie answered rather simply, "They know one of the Toms."

CHAPTER TWENTY-ONE

The Psych Club, as Kallie now referred to them, looked at home, laughing and joking like close family members at a barbeque. The five of them were squeezed around a little square table and two empty chairs, seemingly oblivious to the lively dancing and talkative mass of bodies around them. Seeing them enjoying themselves, Kallie almost felt as if she was intruding, especially since it didn't appear as if any of the other project members were here, and as far as she knew, weren't even invited. She had a good mind to turn around and go home, despite the promises she'd made to Maggie of a good time and the chance to meet the potential love of her life. But before she could even seriously consider that thought, Josh spotted them standing at the entrance and waved them over.

"It's about time," a bespectacled Josh said after they arrived at the group's table.

"How long have you guys been here?" Kallie asked.

"About two hours," Marcus said. He nodded toward Veronica. "Even she was on time."

Veronica playfully slapped him on the wrist. "Shut up, Marcus."

"Who's your friend?" Cedric asked, eying Maggie from head to toe.

Kallie introduced everyone, and then she and Maggie sat down in the two empty chairs. After everyone had settled down, Kallie pointed at Josh's glasses. "I didn't know you wore those."

"I wear contacts most of the time. But my eyes got irritated looking at a computer screen so much the last few days."

"But you're always looking at a computer screen," Evan said.

Josh looked at him. "And your point is...?"

Evan shrugged his shoulders. "No point, I was just saying."

Prince's '1999' suddenly blasted from the surround sound speakers.

Veronica stood up and pulled Evan to his feet. "I feel like dancing."

Cedric held his hand out to Maggie. "Care to flip the light fantastic?"

Maggie smiled and placed her hand in his. "Don't mind if I do."

Josh grabbed Kallie's hand and pulled her to her feet. "I'm sure this will piss off what's his face."

"Behave," Kallie said as she allowed herself to be led to the dance floor.

"I see where this is going," Marcus said. He bounced to his feet and quickly spotted a pretty girl sitting alone at a nearby table. He nodded toward the dance floor. She smiled her acceptance and the two of them fell in behind the others.

After twelve minutes and a collage of dance music from the eighties, nineties, and the early twenty-first century, and just before the DJ slowed everything down with a medley of romance music from the same musical eras, the group, with the exception of Marcus who stayed on the floor looking into his dance partner's eyes while Jackson and McCarthy crooned 'The Girl Is Mine' over the speaker system, returned to the table.

"How do you guys know the Toms?" Maggie asked.

"I went to high school with Thomas Valley," Evan said. "He was two years ahead of me and a jock."

"A jock? Now why would a jock hang around with a little squirt like you?" Veronica teased.

"He was a closet nerd and we were in FBLA together," Evan said.

"Future Business Leaders of America," Maggie said excitedly. "I was in that, too."

With a puppy dog look and a devilish grin, Cedric said, "You could lead me anywhere."

Maggie smiled at him. "Is that a line?"

"That depends," Cedric said.

"On what?" Maggie asked.

"If it's working or not," Cedric said.

Maggie didn't reply, but her smile and flushed cheeks spoke volumes.

Kallie looked at Cedric in amazement and wondered when he'd become so smooth. She turned to Josh and frowned. "Josh," she said through partially clenched teeth.

Josh looked at her. And for a moment his face looked dazed, as if he hadn't any idea who she was or where he was. "Yeah," he finally managed to say.

"You're zoning out," Kallie said. "Is something bothering you?"

"Actually, there is. Can we go somewhere and talk?"

They went to a part of the corridor that had been sectioned off from the main dance area and led to the restrooms. There weren't any speakers in this part of the club, making the music sound muffled, as if coming from underwater. There were a few other people in the corridor, mostly couples evidently wanting to talk without having to shout over the blaring music.

After finding an opening on the wall next to an exit door, Josh stared at Kallie for a long moment before saying anything. He had a weird expression on his face.

"What's up?" she asked hesitantly, afraid of what she assumed he'd wanted to talk about. It was the last thing she needed or wanted. She was still unsure of what, if anything, to make of the incident in Swag's office earlier today. It seemed as if her love life, so dormant less than a month ago, was on the cusp of complications.

"Have you heard from Madame Isabel?" he asked.

"No, why?"

"I went to see her this weekend. She's gone missing."

"What do you mean she's gone missing?"

He didn't answer her question. "How much do you know about her?"

"Only what I've told you. But what do you mean by missing?"

"Exactly that. On Sunday I went to see her. Her husband came to the door, looking devastated. Before I could open my mouth, he practically screamed at me, *'Where is my wife?'* Then he started rambling on and on about how he'd only been gone a little while running errands, leaving her working in her garden, and when he got back she was nowhere to be found. He didn't know where she could have gone. And since they only owned the one truck, he didn't believe she could have gotten far."

"Wow!" Kallie said softly.

Josh continued, "Nothing was out of the ordinary in the house. All her belongings were still there. There was no sign of a struggle. It was as if she'd disappeared into the thin air. Her husband was so distraught I had to drive him to the police department to file the missing person report."

"He didn't have to wait forty-eight hours?"

"No, that's only a television myth."

"What did the police do?"

"After the report was filed, they took us back to the house. They searched it and the surrounding area. After a couple of hours and no trace of Madame Isabel, they took the husband and me back to the station and interviewed us."

"They interviewed you? Why?"

"They wanted to know how I knew Madame Isabel, except they didn't call her that. Her real name is Bella Mae

Raiden. They also wanted to know how I happened to show up on the very day she goes missing."

Her eyes squinted slightly. "Why were you there?"

"Eternal return," he said. "I told you that I needed to research it further. Well, that research led me to Madame Isabel. Of course, I didn't tell the police that. I told them that I'd wanted my palm read and heard on the internet that she was the best in the business. That was partially true. While researching eternal return I eventually found myself in a chat room where I learned a lot of interesting things about Madame Isabel."

"Like what?"

His head tilted back a little, looking curiously at her over the bridge of his nose as if either he was unsure of how much to tell her, or how much she really wanted to know.

"Madame Isabel was a high priestess."

"Like in a church?"

"Not exactly. I don't think she's affiliated formally with a particular church or religion. I guess you could say that she's into Christian mysticism. Supposedly, she'd written a book that she claimed had been dictated to her by spirits or angels. She called it, *The Book of Origins*. But I was unable to locate anyone who has actually seen the book."

"You sound skeptical," Kallie said.

"I'm always skeptical."

"Yet, you went to see her. So, a part of you evidently is hopeful that the book exists."

He eyed her carefully but didn't say anything. She sensed that he had more to say but evidently had decided not to. She wasn't going to push it. Initially, she'd thought this little confab would include him professing his feelings for her despite whatever was going on between her and Seth. Feeling some relief that that hadn't been the case, she wasn't about to trade one complication for another. Whether Madame Isabel was a priestess or not was of no immediate concern to her. For the moment, she had enough religious figures in her life.

His gaze was suddenly averted away from her and to the area behind her. She turned her head and saw Maggie and Veronica coming towards them. *Powder room time,* she thought, realizing that the restrooms were located at the end of this corridor.

"I'm sorry about your friend," Josh said. "I know you wanted me and her to hit it off."

She turned back to face him. "Actually I just wanted her to meet somebody," she lied. "I guess Cedric qualifies as a 'somebody.'"

He laughed. "Almost always."

She smiled momentarily before her thoughts involuntarily turned back to Madame Isabel. "What do you think happened to her?"

"Madame Isabel? I don't know," Josh said.

"If she was this high priestess, maybe she went off for solitude. She might have gone off to add to that book of origins that you were talking about." It was a possibility albeit an unlikely one. Kallie had met Madame Isabel's husband. She was certain that he'd be aware of any of his wife's planned moments of solitude, especially any of a measurable length of time.

"I thought about that," Josh said. "And hopefully that's the case. But, I guess we'll just have to wait and see." After Maggie and Veronica approached, he tipped an imaginary hat. "Ladies."

"Gentleman," Veronica and Maggie said in unison and watched him as he walked past them, heading back to their table.

Maggie rubbed her two index fingers together, mimicking a childhood ritual. "Josh and Kallie sitting in a tree. Josh and Kallie, K-I-S-S...."

Kallie cut her off. "Rather juvenile, don't you think?"

Maggie laughed. "Yeah, but it's still very funny."

The trio entered the restroom and Maggie immediately commandeered the only unoccupied stall, forcing Kallie and

Veronica to share the remaining open space in front of the wall-length mirror. Since she wasn't wearing any makeup, Kallie feigned making minor adjustments to her facial appearance. She was actually watching through the mirror for a stall to open up behind her.

Veronica reapplied her lipstick and then looked at Kallie's reflection in the mirror. "You're very pretty."

"Uh, thank you," Kallie said. "So are you."

"Thank you," Veronica said and then hesitated. "Listen, I hope you don't harbor any ill feelings towards me about the whole privacy thing."

Meeting Veronica's gaze from her reflection in the mirror, Kallie said, "No, I don't."

Veronica smiled. "Good. I know my uncle can be overzealous at times. But he's harmless, unless of course you're a terrorist. But seriously, he really is easy to talk to."

Kallie looked at her fixedly. "Did your uncle put you up to this?"

Veronica's face turned a noticeable shade of red, almost matching the color of her lipstick. "Put me up to what?"

"Come off it, Veronica," Kallie said strongly. "I figured your uncle wouldn't give up so easily. He was pretty insistent the last time. Did he put you up to this?"

Momentarily caught off guard by Kallie's steely glare and sharp tone, it took a moment for Veronica to regain her composure. "No, he did not," she finally managed to say. "I'm genuinely sorry about what happened."

After staring into the other girl's eyes for what seemed like forever, Kallie's expression and tone softened. "Look, I'm sorry for that and I don't blame you for what happened. I know your uncle probably put you in an awkward situation." She stuck out her hand. "Friends."

Veronica smiled and took her hand. "Friends."

Just then, Maggie's stall-door opened and Kallie quickly turned on her heels and darted past her into the stall. "Beat cha."

Veronica laughed, but a blonde-haired girl who'd also been waiting patiently for a toilet to open up stared shock-faced at the closed stall door and looked as if she could spit nails through it, right into the body of its most recent occupant.

CHAPTER TWENTY-TWO

Sunday was women's day at New Vibe Community Church. It was an annual event that the church used to celebrate and honor its fairer sex, and in recognition of it and despite the fact that the color was out of season, most of the women wore white.

Swag stood at the altar, nodding his head agreeably as he looked upon his congregation. "Look at our beautiful women. Fashion experts call it a cardinal sin to wear white in October. But we don't adhere to what the so-called experts say here at New Vibe, do we? No, we buck tradition here. Yes, it's getting a little chilly outside. Yes, Labor Day is long gone, but white looks good on you. Turn to one of your neighbors and say, white looks good on you."

As Swag was talking, Kallie and Seth entered the sanctuary and took their seats on a middle pew. After Kallie sat down, the pretty twenty-something year old girl sitting next to her turned to her and repeated Swag's line, and then she and Kallie both smiled awkwardly. Kallie's dress was yellow.

Seth squeezed her hand and mouthed. "You look good in any color."

Kallie's eyes twinkled. "Thank you."

The sanctuary had been adorned with several kinds of flowers and smelled like a springtime garden. Orchids traced along the walls. Bouquets of white Casa Blanca lilies were situated at the ends of each pew. Up front, Swag, wearing a white suit himself, seemed to be standing in the middle of a gardenia garden.

Thirty minutes later, Swag began his sermon and it soon became very clear to Kallie why the church and the man were so popular. His voice was melodic, almost hypnotic. His sermon was something about the significance of the woman in God's kingdom and how she had the power and responsibility to uplift man. But to Kallie, it wasn't necessarily what he was saying. It was his voice. His tone was soothing and his delivery was so smooth that he could have just as well been talking about the benefits of having green grass.

For a moment, she could have sworn that Swag was staring into her eyes, talking directly to her. She felt a strange feeling swirling inside herself. She swallowed hard. Seth was sitting to her right, so she looked left. The girl sitting on her left was also watching Swag intently. Kallie looked around the sanctuary and saw that all the women were watching Swag intently. She felt foolish. No doubt every woman in the place was thinking that Swag was talking to her directly. They were hanging on his every word. Facing front again, she remembered the other night. Swag hadn't sounded much different from what he did now. Yet, she'd thought then that he'd tried to seduce her. Now she felt silly for having thought such a thing. Why would Swag want her romantically? He was helping her to remember, to develop her gift. He'd had a job to do. Besides, there were six years between them and he was a man of the cloth. More than that, he was a worldly man and she felt almost childlike in his presence. She turned and looked at Seth and suddenly realized why Seth had wanted to come here today. She'd spent so much time with Swag last week that Seth obviously wanted to see if something was developing between the two of them. It wasn't a thing to ask her about. It was something he'd needed to see for himself. But little did Seth know it was something that she'd needed to see for herself as well. Now she was satisfied that nothing

unusual had occurred the other night. She laid her hand atop
Seth's hands as they rested on his lap, squeezing them gently.

*   *   *

It happened toward the end of service during the call for new
souls to seek redemption and the Savior, and join the New
Vibe family. At first, Kallie felt unfazed by it. After all, at
this point the déjà vu sensations were no longer new and
unusual. She'd gotten used to them and rather expected them.
It was the intensity and scope of this latest one that finally
gave her pause. She looked helplessly at Seth. But he had his
eyes closed. She looked beyond him and all around her.
Everyone's eyes were closed. Of course, they were praying.
Swag had just said for everyone to bow their heads, close
their eyes, and pray to God to give anyone who may be on
the fence, the strength and courage to step forward into a new
life.

She felt herself being pulled away from her body and into
a tunnel of kaleidoscopic colors. Around and around she
went, spinning uncontrollably. She felt nauseous, as if she
was getting ready to throw up. She heaved. It was dry and
empty. Then mercifully, she was at the end of the tunnel and
the spinning stopped.

She was no longer sitting in a pew at New Vibe
Community Church. She was now standing in a building. She
saw large chrome-plated lettering on the wall behind and
above a huge U-curved desk. The letters spelled United
Corporate Bank Center. She was standing in the bank's
lobby. A bored security officer sat at the desk. He yawned
twice back-to-back as he indifferently watched the monitors
before him. Behind her, the night spilled in through revolving
glass doors.

A voice came from her right. "Look alive, Locke. Don't let Conner see you yawning. You're already on his S-list. Show time's in less than an hour."

Officer Locke stretched his face, shook his head, and readjusted his sitting position. "Yeah, yeah Roberts. Conner can eat one. And you can quote me."

"Have you seen Principe?" Roberts asked. "I don't want to try reaching him on the radio. In case Conner's listening."

"He's probably in a john somewhere," Locke said. "Radio reception's not as good in the stalls anyway."

"All right, I'm heading up to fifty to the media center."

Kallie saw Roberts enter an elevator. The clock above the elevator read 1:30. She looked behind her again, and through the glass doors she could tell it was definitely dark outside which meant the time was 1:30 a.m. She wondered what the voice had meant by 'show time.'

She started to wait for another elevator to take her to the fiftieth floor before realizing that she wasn't really here. She closed her eyes, thought fiftieth floor, and suddenly she was there, standing in front of the media center a few moments before Robert's elevator arrived.

There was a hoard of media representatives present. She saw folks from ABC, NBC, CBS, MSBC, FOX, and CNN, and some other alphabet-titled outfits, including foreign ones that she wasn't as familiar with. Walking amongst the media crowd, conspicuous by their ominous, dark-suited presence, were several earpiece-fitted men who had the air and attitude of secret service agents.

Wondering what in the world was going on, Kallie walked over and stood next to two reporters standing and talking near the crowded entrance of the bank's media center. She was able to catch enough of their conversation to learn that the media gathering was here awaiting the arrival of US senator and presidential frontrunner, Joseph Frank. Apparently, the news conference announcing a potential blockbuster US-Japan financial agreement was held at this hour in order to make the late-breaking afternoon news cycle in Japan and to gin up momentum for the opening of the financial market later this morning here in the states.

"It's rather presumptuous, don't you think?" she heard one of the reporters ask the other. "The arrogance and stupidity of youth. Leading in the polls in late October this year doesn't guarantee victory next November."

"Maybe not, but you got to admire his chutzpah, acting like the man before he's actually the man may still pay dividends," the second reporter remarked.

"Or it may bite him in his egotistical butt," the first reporter added. He nodded to the Fox reporters inside the room, sitting near the podium. "Those guys are ready to rip him to shreds."

"Either way, we've got a helluva story." They both laughed.

Kallie moved away from them and looked around. Apart from the oddness of the hour, this was a very routine event. But why was she drawn here? Then, she remembered the vision she'd had at the Piedmont Imaging Center. In the vision, a building had exploded. Could this be that building?

The answer came soon enough. She saw him. The dark-skinned, flat-nosed man she'd visualized during Swag's 'priming' technique. Swag had referred to him as the Rogue. The picture Swag had eventually shown her had matched the image in her mind's eye perfectly. She now knew that the man in the picture and in her mind was now going by the name Gerald Principe. She watched him leave the men's restroom dressed as a security officer. At first, she thought they'd locked eye to eye, before again realizing that she wasn't actually here, but was in fact having another vision. She followed him as he checked on explosives he'd placed throughout the building. This was the building from her vision. Principe was planning to blow up the UCB Center building!

"I know," she screamed.

"Yes, child," Swag was saying. "The spirit is moving."

Kallie opened her eyes. She was back in the here and now, and Seth was escorting her to the altar. The congregation was applauding. Bewildered, she asked, "What are you doing?"

Seth continued walking, holding her up. "There was an altar call and it looked like you'd gotten the Holy Ghost. You were shaking and mumbling incoherently. The pastor asked me to bring you to the altar."

Swag stepped down from the altar, and Kallie broke loose from Seth and approached him. "I've seen his face again," she said, practically screaming. "I know what he intends to do."

The congregation, thinking she'd had a religious epiphany, shouted and applauded wildly.

Swag gathered her into his arms and whispered softly in her ear, "Yes child, your eyes are opened. Now, tell me all that you've seen."

CHAPTER TWENTY-THREE

Wednesday, October 28

The Rogue was now going by the name of Gerald Principe and at three o'clock tomorrow morning, a little more than six hours from now, he was going to blow up the United Corporate Bank Center, killing lots of people. Due to the earliness of the hour, casualties would be limited, relatively speaking. But still, many people were going to die, including the Democratic nominee for president. The bank building was going to be destroyed and several adjacent buildings would sustain significant damage.

Kallie was in her bedroom, lying on her back, staring up at the ceiling. In her mind's eye, she'd seen it all unfold as clear as day. Swag had been correct. Two days ago, the memories of the past life cycle had finally pushed through, flooding her mind with terrible images and bringing with them two sleepless nights. She'd been able to think of nothing but blood and mayhem. Well, that wasn't entirely true. She'd had one other prevalent thought—none of it had to happen. She remembered enough of what had happened previously to prevent it from happening this time. She knew the perpetrator. She knew what he intended to do. She knew where in the building he'd placed the explosives. She'd only to call the authorities and spill her guts. But Swag had been emphatic—under no circumstances were the authorities to be alerted. For whatever it was worth and whatever it meant, A.I. would handle this.

That idea brought her little comfort. She kept thinking about Phillip Beamer. The late Phillip Beamer. According to Father McCarthy, Beamer had gotten himself killed by warning the government of a pending terrorist attack. But it was a charge that made little sense. Why would the government kill someone simply for warning it about a terrorist attack? Then again, why would Father McCarthy lie about the government having done so? She thought about the conversation she'd had with her grandfather when she was eight years old. Her folks had lied about the death of the family dog King because they hadn't thought Kallie would be able to handle the truth. Could Father McCarthy have his own noble reason for lying?

She closed her eyes and tried to discern the right from the wrong. But it was a useless exercise. Someone was lying; but it was impossible to tell who or why. Ultimately, she decided that right now it didn't matter. Opening her eyes, she sat up in bed. Whether the government or A.I. had killed Beamer, or one or the other entity was lying about it, was unimportant. Lives were at stake. Lives she could possibly save. She felt bad and a little foolish for suddenly doubting the Alliance of Initiates. After all, if it hadn't been for Father McCarthy and Reverend Swag, she wouldn't know what she now knew in the first place and the very lives she wanted to save would have been lost anyway, and, in fact, in the previous life cycle, had been lost already.

Still, she couldn't un-see what she'd seen or not-know what she now knew. Her laptop was lying next to her on the bed. She placed it on her lap and hit a key, bringing it out of sleep mode. Then, she opened a web browser and typed in a search term. She scanned the list of names and numbers before selecting one at random. She reached for her cell phone on the nightstand, feeling certain she was doing the right thing. Lives were in imminent danger. She wouldn't be able to live with herself if she didn't do all that she could in order to save them.

*   *   *

The voice was muffled, as if the caller had placed a cloth or something over the phone's mic. The cadence sounded stiff and unnatural. But the words were ominous and clear—the United Corporate Bank Center was going to be blown up. Captain Rob Granger had just retired to the bunkroom when the call came in on his department-issued cell phone. It was 11:05 p.m. When he'd initially seen RESTRICTED flash across the phone's caller ID screen, his first thought had been prank call. No one but his wife ever called his cell phone. After the city had listed individual firefighter cell phone numbers on its web page, a few of his colleagues had received the requisite bored teenager prank call. "I guess it's my turn," he said, frowning at his phone. But after taking the call and listening to the specifics of the threat, he became increasingly certain of two things. The caller was a female of an indeterminate age and this wasn't a prank.

*   *   *

The other thirteen security officers working the third shift had responded to Lt. Conner's code-black with a shrug of their shoulders and a "yeah right." They were already in heightened security-mode due to the presence in the building of the popular presidential candidate and his accompanying media hoard. Conner had already drilled them silly the past few weeks in anticipation of this day. The security officers had checked and rechecked every nuance of the building as well as every person entering it, making Conner's execution of the code-black, unnecessary overkill. But Principe, who'd been exiting the elevator when Conner's voice came, squeaking over his radio, shifted immediately into bomb response mode.

Code-black was the security team's bomb response plan and essentially Conner's baby. He'd spent several weeks devising the plan designed to be executed in a matter of minutes. Unlike his colleagues, Principe had spent much time with Conner over the past two years and he knew the man was not prone to hyperbole. The lieutenant would not have issued the code without a good reason for doing so. Besides, Principe had the added benefit of knowing that there were in fact bombs in the building. After all, he'd planted them.

"Radio check," Conner continued over the radio. "I need everyone's ten-twenty."

Principe snatched the radio from his belt clip. Bringing it up to his mouth, he pressed the push-to-talk button. "This is Principe. I'm on fifty-eight."

The beauty of the plan, according to Conner, was that each officer's assigned duty and responsibility would be determined by that officer's location and working task at the time the code-black was issued.

After the other officers had chimed in with their locations, Conner said, "I repeat, this is not a drill. We're in code-black. Everyone should act accordingly. Anyone unsure of what to do should report to the control room immediately. Conner out."

Since Principe had been on patrol near the sixtieth and top floor, his first responsibility would be to aid in the evacuation of the upper third of the building, making sure no employee straggled behind on any of the top floors. But he didn't expect anyone to be on the floors at this hour. These floors contained the executive offices. Although most of the bank's executives routinely worked twelve hour days, most were usually gone by nine o'clock.

Pausing at the elevator to consider whether to sweep this floor first or go on to the top floor, working his way down, Principe's thoughts suddenly turned to the reason for the code in the first place. Someone had evidently called in a bomb threat. His coworkers had most likely taken Conner's 'this is not a drill' statement with a grain of salt because it was extremely unlikely that someone could get a bomb into the building. But Principe knew better. Had someone discovered the bombs? Or had someone simply phoned in a hoax?

And then he knew. Of course, he said to himself. He moved quickly to the restrooms on this floor. Not only would a Rememberer know about the bombs, but also where he'd placed them. Running down the hallway, Principe checked his watch. It was 11:15. The gate wouldn't be in position for opening for almost another four hours. Now he was extremely thankful that he'd planted twelve bombs. He'd done so because he'd been overanxious. It wouldn't take that many to blow up the building. But he must've subconsciously known he'd need the other bombs. It would keep them busy. All he had to do now was move the bombs he'd planted on the fifty-eight and sixtieth floors to other resting places. And he knew exactly where. He burst through the restroom door, smiling devilishly. Soon, his demonic brethren would join him here on Earth.

CHAPTER TWENTY-FOUR

Thursday, October 29

The Harrison Tower was a block away from the United Corporate Bank Center building. Consisting of steel, concrete and mirrored glass, the structure stretched nearly seven hundred feet into the sky. It housed commercial offices, shops, a restaurant, museum, and tonight—a perfect and safe distance from which to observe the spectacular demise of the UBC Center.

At a quarter to one in the morning, Kallie and Swag bundled in their warmest winter wear, stood outside the side of the towering building. Though winter wasn't slated to start for almost another two months, the temperature had dropped thirty degrees from yesterday's high of fifty-nine. It was the first freeze of the fall season. She watched Swag punch numbers into a keypad, unlocking the door and shutting off the alarm system. She wondered only briefly how he'd come about obtaining the codes to do so, ultimately figuring it was related to either his remembering ability or the power and influence of A.I.

They entered the well-lit building, making sure to angle themselves away from cameras not seen, but surely there. Quietly he led her onto the elevator where he punched the call button taking them up to the roof. They kept their heads lowered. The elevator camera was buried somewhere in the ceiling. Swag hadn't spoken in over an hour, or more specifically, not since she'd told him about her call to the fire department. By that time he'd already gone over the plan to enter the Harrison Tower, so she couldn't be sure if his silence was due to him being upset over what she'd done or simply because presently he had more pressing matters to consider. Outwardly, other than not speaking, he hadn't shown any signs of being angry or upset. In fact, he seemed rather indifferent to the news, as if her calling in the bomb threat had made no difference one way or the other.

The elevator didn't actually open onto the roof, but to the floor below it. Once on the floor, they moved quickly to the stairwell. The stairs led to a large storage area at the end of which was a door that opened to the roof. Walking through the storage area, she could tell that someone had been in here recently, evidently rummaging through the building's Christmas decorations. A mixture of green and tinsel wreaths and fake Christmas trees were lying amongst long snaky holiday signage and boxes of ornaments. She smelled hints of frankincense intermingling with the static smells of the plastic foliage.

Outside, the thick cold was made nearly visible by a bulbous full harvest moon, which sat prominently near the western edge of the cloudless sky. The frosty air slapped furiously against Kallie's face, quickly distancing itself from the temporary warmth of the building. She followed Swag to a spot between two large rectangular air vents, and then sat down as he did, Indian-style.

"What now?" she asked.

"We wait."

She flipped up her coat collar. "On what?"

"You'll see," Swag said.

She brought her knees up to her chest, scrunching her head below the top of her coat. For the longest time, neither spoke. Eventually, she lifted her head and turned toward him. "I wanted to save lives."

"Excuse me," he said as if he hadn't heard her.

She straightened up, looking at him squarely. "I called in the bomb threat because I wanted to save lives. Innocent people need not die."

He stared off into the distance. "What's makes you think they would have?"

"Nothing, I guess. I just didn't want to take the chance."

He nodded his head indifferently.

She opened her mouth to speak, but paused at a sound coming from somewhere near the door they'd come through. Someone else was stepping out onto the roof.

Swag brought a single finger to his lips, silencing her. He got to his knees and crawled to the edge of the air vent. He peered around it and then turned back at her, silently mouthing, "It's time." He motioned for her to crawl next to him. She did so, slowly and quietly.

It was Gerald Principe. He walked to the edge of the roof facing the UCB Center and stepped onto the ledge. He held his hands up to the sky and began chanting.

"What's he doing?" Kallie asked.

Swag shushed her. "Wait here." He stood up and walked to the ledge. "It is as it was before," he said to Principe's back.

Principe turned around. "So it is. It was only at this moment that I saw."

"It's the strangeness of the ability," Swag said. "So you know who I am."

"I do," Principe said. "And does she?"

"Not fully," Swag said.

"What do you intend to do?" Principe asked.

"Rule," Swag answered. "With her."

"It's not possible," Principe said. "She can't be trusted. She'll deceive you as before."

"Not as before," Swag said.

"Can I join you?"

Swag inched closer to the ledge. "We'll see. But first open the gate."

Principe lowered his head compliantly and started chanting.

Kallie approached from behind, looking from one to the other. Speechless, she suddenly felt like an outsider, having heard the faintness of a conversation that made little sense to her. Then she heard something else, a thunderous roar from the heavens. She looked up. The sky, moon-bright and cloudless a few moments ago, had darkened tremendously as a gray fog had rolled in out of nowhere, covering up the moon. "Look," Kallie said, finding her voice and pointing toward the sky.

Swag looked up and a wicked smile crossed his face. Principe continued chanting.

"What's happening?" Kallie screamed.

Swag ignored her and looked intently at Principe who was now laughing mechanically and screaming a concoction of sounds that meshed noisily with the thunderous reverberation. Then he looked up at the heavens and began shouting in an unrecognizable language. He held up a cell phone and wildly pressed a couple of keys. Within seconds, a deafening grumble came from the direction of the UCB Center, rolling heavily over them. The Harrison Tower trembled. The three of them looked toward the UCB Center. The top of it had been blown into the ethers, shooting explosive fire in all directions. Even here, Kallie could feel the intensified heat pricking her skin as the light from the explosion reflected off the glass of the Harrison Tower, bouncing gorgeous shades of red and orange all around them.

Kallie's gaze went from the sky, which now seemed to be pulling away from itself, to the sight of Swag pushing Principe off the roof. Feeling weak-kneed, her body wavered backward and her eyes rolled to the back of her head, offering her only a glimpse of the strange creatures pouring from the sky's split.

She fainted dead away.

Swag stood unmoving. He was pleased.

CHAPTER TWENTY-FIVE

In 1980, the FBI created the first Joint Terrorism Task Force (JTTF) in New York City. Its primary purpose was to coordinate the efforts of the various levels of law enforcement (local, state, federal) in order to respond effectively to any terrorist attack within the United States. After the events of 9/11, the program was expanded to over 100 locations throughout the country, including all FBI field offices. In addition, the Bureau made a more concerted effort to create an atmosphere of information-sharing amongst law enforcement, thus eliminating 'turf wars' and fostering 'an all hands on deck' philosophy in which to defeat terror. This is how it came to be that a week after the UCB Center bombing, FBI Special Agent Robert Newhouse was in his office briefing ICE Special Agent Dennard Bennett on the Bureau's initial findings in its investigation of the most recent terrorist attack on American soil.

"So, you're not convinced that this security officer Principe acted alone?" Bennett asked.

Newhouse considered the question, as if wanting to parse his words. "We don't think he acted in conjunction with any of the other security officers. We believe that over the course of a few weeks, he smuggled in and set up twelve bombs. We haven't found any links with any terrorist organization and none of them is claiming responsibility."

Bennett sensed a 'but' coming and voiced it for Newhouse. "But..."

"About four hours before the bombs exploded, a call was placed to a local fireman's cell phone. The city had placed all firemen's work cell numbers on its web page. The fireman, by the name of Rob Granger, said the caller, whom he determined to be female, told him about the impending attack and where the bombs could be located in the building."

"But the information was incomplete. I mean there was still an explosion," Bennett said.

Newhouse leaned back in his chair. "Eight of the bombs were exactly where the caller said they would be. But the four remaining bombs were not."

"You think it was part of the plot, maybe setting up the first responders or the bomb squad?"

Newhouse rubbed his chin absently. "No, the four remaining bombs were on the fifty-eighth and sixtieth floors, exactly as the caller said they would be. Just not exactly where she'd said they'd be."

"So, what happened?"

"Principe." Newhouse said. "He was patrolling those floors when the fire department called building security to advise them of the bomb threat."

Bennett nodded his head knowingly. "He moved them."

"It appears so," Newhouse said.

"But...." Bennett stopped, unsure of how to frame his words.

"Exactly," Newhouse said, finishing Bennett's unformed thought. "Why would Principe move the bombs? How would he know that someone had called in with the bombs' locations? Who would know besides him?"

"He was working with someone," Bennett said unconvincingly. The remains of Principe's body had been found a block away from the bomb site. He could have gotten away clean, yet he stayed around to commit suicide. It didn't make rational sense. Of course, terrorism wasn't rational.

"There's something else," Newhouse said. He stood up and walked over to a flat screen monitor that had been rolled into his office on a cart. He flipped it on and pushed play on the accompanying DVD player. "This information has not been released. It's security video from the Harrison Tower."

Bennett turned around in his chair to see the video. On it, two people were seen entering the building and going directly to the elevators. A short time later, Principe, still wearing his security officer's uniform, entered the building and also went directly to the elevators. Newhouse pushed fast forward, stopping it about thirty minutes later in the video. The two initial individuals could be seen hurrying from the elevator and leaving the building. Of course, Principe's body, or what was left of it, was found later, splattered on the pavement in the back of the building.

Newhouse turned off the monitor. "We also have video of the two in the elevator. Both times, going up and coming back down. They kept their heads low. Careful to avoid the camera, evidently knowing it was located in the ceiling."

Bennett was momentarily speechless. Then he asked, "So, what are the theories? An assisted suicide bombing, punishment for a botched job, what?"

Newhouse returned to his chair. "We're exploring all possibilities. But one in particular is the reason why we've called you in. We understand that it's in your area of expertise." Reaching down, he opened a lower desk drawer and pulled out a stack of papers bound by a large paper clip. He tossed the stack on his desk toward Bennett. "These are from one of Principe's email accounts. It looks like Principe and Phillip Beamer had grown quite chummy."

Bennett picked up the stack and looked closely at the header on the first sheet. The email was dated two months before Beamer's murder. It was sent by Principe to Beamer at an email address that Bennett hadn't discovered during his investigation into Beamer's terrorist activities.

"We got lucky," Newhouse offered as if reading Bennett's mind. Sweeping a suspect's computer for all email and social media accounts was now considered elementary. Nowadays, a growing number of people kept multiple email accounts and had developed ingenious ways to keep them from others, namely spouses and law enforcement. Still, no investigator wanted any of his suspects to have an email account surface that the investigator hadn't learned about through his own investigatory efforts, and he definitely didn't want another investigator to be the one to discover it. "This particular email service provider is not widely known," Newhouse continued. "But it's popular with the criminal-minded, particularly pedophiles who are into file-sharing. Principe's email was still open on his computer desktop when we searched his apartment a few days after the bombing. If he'd been alive and known that we were on to him, he might've scrubbed his computer clean and we might not have ever found out about the email account. But judging by the way his apartment looked; we think Principe had every intention of returning to it."

Bennett nodded his head slightly, appreciative of Newhouse's professional gesture. It was apparent that the FBI was serious about promoting the spirit of cooperation between all law agencies in the war against terror. Not showing up a colleague went a long way in that regard. Bennett flipped through the rest of the stack and then felt his blood flow stop cold as he stared at an email message with the subject line: WARNING.

In the body of this particular email message was the name *Father Frank McCarthy.*

*　　*　　*

Four brave bomb response specialists had been killed and the corporate headquarters of one of the nation's leading financial institutions had been destroyed in an explosive concrete and steel beheading that had also significantly damaged several surrounding buildings. But in the days following the nation's second worst homegrown terrorist attack and its most devastating since 9/11, the mainstream media, frustrated by the government's unwillingness to compromise its investigation by feeding the media's incessant twenty-four hour hunger for information, decided to exacerbate the blame-game and finger-pointing. Republicans blamed Democrats and Democrats fervently pointed fingers at Republicans. While the average, sensible American only wanted answers to why the attack hadn't been prevented in the first place, and assurances that the necessary steps would be taken to ensure that another one wouldn't happen ever again in his lifetime or the lifetimes of his children or his children's children. Void of anything new and useful to report, the media gleefully played all sides against each other.

In Philadelphia, Father McCarthy, like most Americans, stayed glued to the television, waiting for any morsel of news concerning the attack. But unlike most Americans, McCarthy knew the real gist of why the attack had occurred. "How is she doing?" he asked, speaking into the phone receiver. He was in his office, having his fifth conversation in two weeks with Johnny Swag. When the young preacher didn't answer immediately, McCarthy wished this time he'd Skyped him instead. Misrepresentations were harder to pull off visually.

"Physically, she's fine. But mentally…" he paused again.

When it became clear that the pause would be interminable, McCarthy said, "I don't mean to second guess."

"Then don't," Swag said sharply.

McCarthy was undeterred. "I don't mean to second guess," he repeated strongly, "but the Alliance wanted the Rogue alive."

"He was too corrupted."

"It was not your decision to make."

"It was a decision that had to be made and only I was in the position to make it."

McCarthy looked off for a moment, dropping the phone from his ear. That was the Alliance's standpoint as well. It was clear that Swag had already spoken to them and received their blessing for his reckless act. It wouldn't be long before the young preacher would state the obvious—with the Alliance leadership's backing, he was untouchable. But he wasn't infallible. McCarthy brought the phone back to his ear. "Why didn't you prepare the girl?"

Swag groaned noticeably. "She was prepared. At least as much as she could've been." His words sounded distant, as if he was doing his own second guessing. "She had to see the demons for herself. Otherwise, she wouldn't have believed it. Even now, she's still a little unsure of exactly what she saw. The first week afterwards, she wanted to run away and bury her head in the sand, and she didn't want to have anything to do with me. And so I obliged her and stayed away."

"Didn't you consider that she could run and tell the authorities?"

"That wasn't likely to happen. You'd already crippled that possibility with your story about Beamer. She doesn't trust the authorities."

This time McCarthy groaned. He was still uncomfortable with the lie he'd told Kallie. But it was situations like this one that had justified it. If Kallie Hunt had gone screaming to the authorities about gate-openings and demons, she'd likely be locked up in a mental institution right now, not a useful outcome for herself or the Alliance. "Did she confide in her boyfriend?"

"No," Swag said confidently. "She came back to me as I'd anticipated. She knows that I'm the only one who can guide her through this."

"And you're certain that she's the one?"

Another pause, and then he said, "I'm certain within every fiber of my being."

The phone conversation ended with Swag's assurances that every demon released on harvest night would be rounded up and destroyed. The how of his bold commitment wasn't shared, but McCarthy didn't figure to understand it anyway. He was going to have to trust Swag, a difficult endeavor considering the young preacher was extremely reckless and a stick in McCarthy's craw. Swag had killed Beamer and now Principe with little concern about any potential blowback eventually flowing back to A.I. But the Alliance was blinded by Swag's remembering ability and acted as if he walked on water. To McCarthy, such blind loyalty to Swag was a dangerous scenario for someone with such a monstrous ego, and one he was increasingly beginning to suspect had all the traditional earmarks of a snake in the grass.

CHAPTER TWENTY-SIX

The weather was cold, gray, and wet. Conditions were typical
for the current November in the city of Brotherly Love. For
the first twelve days of the month, the sun avoided the city as
if it was a crab-infested whore. McCarthy spent the better
part of two hours in a drizzling rain, clanking a damp
basketball off the back part of the rim. Though he missed a
lot more than he made, he dutifully kept tossing the ball up at
the goal. It was painfully obvious that today, with the
weather and his off-shooting, wasn't a good one for
basketball. Back in late summer, he'd had a day where he
couldn't miss. That had obviously been an anomaly. He
regretted not having video of it. Now, he wasn't exactly sure
it had even happened, his memory of it quickly fading like
today's sunset. After clanking another shot, he spit a glob of
frustration onto the wet court. He couldn't make two jump
shots in a row even if his life depended upon it. Luckily no
life, especially his, depended on a bouncy round ball falling
successfully through a netted round metal cylinder. The fate
of the world wasn't dependent on his basketball prowess. But
basketball, whether he was making shots or not, helped him
to think. So despite the weather and the misses, he continued
dribble-splashing the ball off the wet concrete court and
eying a goal that now seemed as small as the eye of a needle.
As he did so, he thought of the fate of the world and the
many lives that were indeed in danger, all due to the situation
created by Swag's misguided blunder.

Swag had been indignant in defense of his plan to let the
Hunt girl glimpse the demonic forces that now threatened the

lives of countless others. "She wouldn't have believed me otherwise," Swag had said. And to that, McCarthy had thought, what had it mattered if she believed or not. It wouldn't have changed what was. Surely, Swag was smart enough to conceive that concept. If necessary, reality would have forced her to believe him sooner or later, but you didn't set a child on fire to convince her that fire burns. Sure, such a lesson when learned the hard way could be quickly grasped and would likely never be forgotten. But was burning off fingers and toes the smartest way to teach such a lesson? McCarthy thought not. In any event, the demonic portal should never have been allowed to open. Despite what Swag had claimed, McCarthy believed the young minister had been irresponsibly and needlessly careless.

But what was even more troubling to McCarthy was that neither Swag nor the Alliance seemed the least bit concerned about the ramifications of Swag's blunder. A demonic army had been unleashed upon the earth. It was an army that was undetected by the average human eye and hell-bent on the annihilation of mankind. Annihilation that no one would see coming. Throughout man's history, a sacred few had kept knowledge hidden from the masses. And as a result, an apocalyptic battle now loomed in which man was ill-prepared to fight because precious few souls knew anything about it.

McCarthy had petitioned unsuccessfully to the Alliance for some kind of education program, at least for the true-believers. But his request had been quickly denied. Although he agreed with their reasoning that such a program, however limited in scope, would be hard to implement effectively and could potentially only lead to widespread panic, he didn't agree that nothing but prayer should be done. He believed in prayer and had quadrupled his efforts in the days following the gate-opening, but he was extremely uncomfortable leaving the fate of mankind in the hands of an egotistical man-boy and a potentially naive teenaged girl.

Standing at the free throw line, he gripped the wet ball between his fingertips and looked pensively at the goal. Raindrops streamed down his face like tears. He looked towards the heavens. It was early evening and the sun had just about snatched up the last of its light and heat. He felt cold and alone. "Oh God, help us," he whispered into the showery air.

"How about that game of one-on-one?" a deep voice called from behind him.

McCarthy turned around and saw Special Agent Bennett standing at the gate. McCarthy remembered the ICE agent from his visit in late summer. This time Bennett was wearing dark sneakers and a light blue sweat suit, appropriate wear for playing basketball, if not cold, rainy weather. "I'm afraid I won't be able to provide you with much competition today," McCarthy said as the street light hovering over the court blinked on, eager to replace the sun's retreating light.

Bennett unlatched the gate and walked onto the court. "Oh, I don't know about that. As I understand it, you had a decent shot at playing pro ball."

"That was many moons ago," McCarthy said.

"Remember, I saw you here a couple of months ago. You still looked pretty good to me."

McCarthy tossed the ball to Bennett. "I couldn't miss that day."

Bennett took two dribbles before putting up a high-arching shot that swished cleanly through the net. "How about it, first to eleven?"

McCarthy retrieved the ball, shrugging his shoulders. "Sure, why not."

They played in silence. Even the rain stopped temporarily, as if God himself was interested in the game's outcome. McCarthy played a lot better than he thought he would, eventually finding the range with his jumper. However, Bennett played consistently well throughout the contest and eventually won it, 11 to 8. Afterwards, Bennett bent at the waist and, sucking in long gulps of hydrated air, said, "You're not going to ask why I came to see you on such a cold, rainy November day?"

McCarthy, also breathing heavily, wiped a mixture of rain and sweat off his forehead with the back of his hand. "I figured you'd get around to telling me eventually." He nodded toward the back of the church. "Let's go inside." He led Bennett into the church and back to his office where he offered the agent a dry towel and a bottle of water.

Bennett took the offered items, using the towel to dry his face and head. After draping the towel on the back of one of the chairs in front of McCarthy's desk, he took a long swig from the water bottle. Then, he looked squarely at McCarthy who'd already settled into his chair behind the desk. "Gerald Principe."

McCarthy showed no emotion. "Is that name supposed to mean something to me?"

Bennett sat down in the other chair in front of McCarthy's desk. "What do you know about him?"

"I suppose as much as the average American does, which is whatever the media has told us about him since the bombing."

"I think you know more, Father. I think you know a lot more."

"Now, why would you think that?"

Bennett stared intently at the priest, not even blinking. "For the same reason I thought you knew more about Phillip Beamer, because they both seemed to know so much more about you."

"I see," McCarthy said. He leaned back in his chair. "You know, Agent Bennett, as a priest, it's not uncommon that people would know me or things about me. Admittedly, I'm not George Clooney or some other Hollywood star. But I suppose I could be considered a public figure on some levels. In any event, I do regret that time and circumstances often prevent me from knowing intimately the many people that have taken the time and effort to know me."

"Father, I'm going to lay my cards on the table. This is what I know. Phillip Beamer was planning to bomb a federal building in Columbia, South Carolina. Gerald Principe bombed the UCB Center in Charlotte. Principe and Beamer were email buddies who seemed to think you were a threat to their terrorist activities. Both are now dead."

"I don't know what to tell you. I knew neither of them."

Bennett leaned in closer. "And then there's Kallie Hunt."

McCarthy didn't even flinch. "I'm sorry. Is she also a terrorist?"

"No, Father. She's not, at least not as far as I know. Who she is, is the young college student you were seen visiting a few weeks back in Bengate, North Carolina. She's the same Kallie Hunt who a few weeks back had a vision of a commercial building explosion, eerily similar to the actual bombing of the UCB Center."

"You're not saying..."

"Let me finish," Bennett interjected. "A young lady that I suspect was Kallie Hunt not only called in a bomb threat on the day of the UCB Center bombing, but also was seen entering the Harrison Tower with a gentleman who I believe was you. The same Harrison Tower from which Gerald Principe supposedly jumped to his death shortly after the UCB Center bombing. Are you going to tell me that these were mere coincidences, Father? Before you answer, understand, my one mission in life now is to get the truth."

McCarthy shifted in his chair. "And a noble mission it is. But there's something I need for you to understand, as well. When I first heard the voice of God calling me to the church, my initial emotion was fear. It wasn't the fear of God himself. I'd already had a healthy dose of that for as far back as I could remember. It was the fear of the responsibility of what he was calling me to do. He was bestowing upon me the role of shepherd to his sheep. If I were to fail in that role, I would be ultimately responsible for the damnation of the souls of many. It's an awesome responsibility, one which I dare not take lightly. I wish I could say that I've been perfect in my role. But alas, I'm only a man, born into a world of sin. I'm fallible. But what I can say is that every decision I've ever made has been made with the weight of many souls upon me. Suffice it to say, you will leave here today with only the knowledge you came here with. I understand you will do what you deem necessary in order to find your truth. And whatever that may be or wherever it leads you, I want you to know that I understand that you're only doing what you feel you have to do."

Bennett slumped back in his chair, seeming at a loss for what to say. For several moments they sat in silence, regarding each other with suspicion and respect. Then Bennett got up slowly, cast a long meditative look back at the priest, and then left his office.

CHAPTER TWENTY-SEVEN

To Charlotte's mayor, Bill Washington, the beheading of the city's largest building could actually be considered a blessing in disguise. Yes, he understood that four brave souls lost their lives, and yes, the UCB Center building might not be saved. And yes, three other buildings had also sustained life-threatening damages of their own. And finally, yes, the public's confidence had been severely shaken and fear had taken a strong root within the city. But God help him, he was a glass half-full type of guy. He was a maker of lemonade out of lemons. He was someone who never tossed away an apple because of advanced brownness or the occasional residential worm. There was always enough whiteness left in the apple to enjoy. You simply ate around the ugliness.

   And that's what Charlotte was facing now, a little ugliness. Some misguided wannabe terrorist had decided to try to rattle the fabric of humanity. But the late Gerald Principe had failed miserably in whatever quest he'd been on. Charlotteans, like their three-term mayor, were survivors, bouncers-back. *We may bend, but we shall not break*, Mayor Washington thought proudly before mentally harping back to 9/11 and the Big Apple's leader at that time. New York's mayor had shown fortitude in the midst of great upheaval. And whether purposefully or not, he'd also been able to parlay that tragic situation into unrivaled popularity, significant financial gain, and an even run at the White House. As he gazed out the window of his office, looking upon his wounded city, Washington felt a strong admiration for the man. The man hadn't let a horrific act of terrorism solely define him or his city. He'd taken that terrorist bull by the horns and whipped it into something useful.

Sure, Charlotte's mental foundation had been shaken, Washington thought. But physically, except for a four block area at its center, the city was virtually unchanged. The sun, as did the moon, still rose and set at its appointed time. A wise man once said, or maybe it was a verse somewhere in the Bible, that this too shall pass. Wherever it was written or whoever had said it, to Mayor Washington, no truer words could have been strung together. He believed wholeheartedly that this too shall pass. And he believed something else too— this particular event had marked the arrival of his ship. He'd made several national television appearances in the days and weeks following the attack. He'd said all the right things and displayed just the right kind of temperament. He was being called the quintessential crisis-manager. He'd shown himself to be foxhole worthy. The kind of man you'd want by your side at times of extreme danger. The people loved and trusted him. More than that, they needed him. They believed in him as their leader. Yes, this was indeed a blessing. Who knows, he thought as an insane laugh escaped his lips, maybe there was a White House in his future. President Washington. President William "Bill" Washington.

Yep, that sounded pretty good. Of course, he'd likely have to beat out the night's other big winner, Massachusetts Senator Joseph Frank. Last week, the junior senator, after having been rushed safely out of the UCB Center the week before, had risen significantly in the polls. It was a clear signal that the Democrats were winning public discourse on the fight against terrorism, be it foreign or domestic. But the pipsqueak and his Democratic cronies knew full well that tough talk on terrorism didn't equate to being tough on terrorism. Sure, they'd been able to pin the latest terrorist act on the current commander-in-chief, but it wouldn't be long before the wet-behind-the-ears politician said and did the wrong thing. And when he did, Washington intended to be there to twist the proverbial knife into Frank's sanctimonious back.

Charlotte, in its inaugural years, had once been dubbed "the City of Churches." A nickname it thoroughly enjoyed and had fully embraced through the years. There were over seven hundred places of worship within the city's borders, including everything from Catholic, to Presbyterian, to Baptist, and everything in between, including people who abhorred labels, preferring instead to simply worship their maker with simple, likeminded folk. It was a place where religion was bred openly and accepted by most as an essential and authoritative part of life. When preachers talked here, people usually listened. And what preachers talked about, almost uniformly, in the Sundays following the UCB Center bombing was the rising "ugliness" in people. They railed about how civil behavior and good manners were an endangered species. They complained about the random acts of violence, the short-tempers, and the unchecked fits of rage. Immoral behavior, they preached, was on a violently dangerous uptick, sending a general godlessness widespread over the city like a contagion.

Reverend E. B. Turner of First Baptist Church, the largest African-American church in the county, had personally witnessed a small fender bender turn into all out fisticuffs. He'd been traveling behind a silver Buick Century that had been closely following a Honda Odyssey. The Odyssey stopped short at a traffic light, which had shifted rather abruptly from yellow to red. The Buick had been unable to stop completely, causing it to lightly tap the Honda's rear bumper. This minor transgression enraged the driver of the Honda, a middle-aged mother of four, to no end. She stormed out of her vehicle and went stomping over to the Buick, banging on the driver side front door. It took the driver of the Buick, an old lady of about seventy years or so, exactly two seconds to emerge from her car, hopping mad and swinging punches. A patrol car happened upon the scene at that exact moment. But its presence only intensified the situation as the officer was immediately antagonistic toward both drivers, threatening to arrest them. Minutes later, a second officer arrived, but he wasn't much better than the first as he merely sat down on the hood of his car, laughing at the escalating spectacle. It was only after the arrival of a third patrolman that the tension started to compress. The officer, seemingly not surprised at the sight of two of his colleagues acting unprofessionally or two women tossing expletives and punches at each other over a minor traffic accident, soon got the situation under control and had almost done so without having to make any arrests. That was until the old lady tore into the first officer's arm like a pissed off rattler, literally losing her teeth in his muscled bicep.

And on and on it went throughout the city, with small incidents being blown incredibly out of proportion. And it didn't stop there. Priests discussed amongst themselves how a decrease in confessions had coincided with a significant increase in the number of people bearing witness to the transgressions of their loved ones and neighbors. People were being ratted out for excessive drinking, philandering, and all sorts of sins against God. One of Father Moynihan's parishioners had come in, confessing the sins of her eleven year old daughter who'd suddenly taken to actively trying to seduce her sixth grade teacher. The erstwhile innocent and sexually naive child had started acting like a harlot, the transformation having literally occurred overnight. One day she was shyly passing notes to her girlfriend, asking how to get cute Peter Townsend to notice her, and the next day she was hiking up her skirt, showing more leg and suddenly hot for teacher. Her mother, clearly clueless as to why or how this had happened, asked the priest plaintively if her daughter was possessed.

Father Moynihan had no immediate answers for her. Sometimes parents were the last to know about the ills of their children. As far as he knew, the child could have long been a young harlot in the making. Father Moynihan's head wasn't buried in the sand. He clearly understood that young didn't necessarily equate to innocence. He would have to interview the young girl, her parents, and the teacher before rendering his take on the situation. Still, he had to admit, something strange was in the air. Strange things were happening all over.

At Presbyterian United Church, Reverend Clifford Martin didn't need to conduct any interviews. He was ready to render his verdict to his congregation. "The demons that we've allowed to fester all these years have finally come home to roost," he thundered. "The demons of alcohol, of drugs, of premarital sex, of sparing the rod and spoiling the child, of not tithing, of not church attending, of lying, stealing, cheating, backbiting—it's all coming to a head right now, right before our very eyes. The battle for your very souls is being raged right now. Can I get a witness!"

His technical misunderstanding of the demons currently threatening the Charlotte metro area notwithstanding, Reverend Martin was actually on to something; although he'd no earthly idea how true his words really were. In fact, only a handful of people in the free world knew exactly what the citizens of Charlotte and ultimately the rest of mankind were up against. And two of those knowledgeable people were sitting in a booth in a diner in the small college town of Bengate some forty miles away.

CHAPTER TWENTY-EIGHT

A half-eaten chicken sandwich languished in front of Swag as he sat silently watching Kallie, who sat across from him in the booth, her own sandwich untouched in the middle of the table. She was reading from a book opened atop the table in front of her. It was the third time she read the passage, though this time she did so out loud, but softly. "The demons were continually drawn to her and ultimately their own demise. With unrelenting power, the goddess destroyed one after the other, crushing some with her bare hands, stomping many with her feet, and gnashing countless others with her teeth." She finished the passage and looked up at Swag; but she was unsure of what she should say or even think about the passage. Reading it three times had brought her no new revelations. Surely, Reverend Swag wasn't suggesting that she could crush, stomp, and gnash those creatures she'd seen fall from the sky. She wasn't a goddess. She was Kallie Hunt, college student, albeit one with a unique remembering ability. But unique ability notwithstanding, she was still only a college student and not yet qualified to land a job paying a decent living wage.

Swag stared deeply into her eyes. "You are she."

Kallie's eyebrows furrowed. "I'm who?"

"You are the reincarnation of the Goddess Kali (he pronounced it Kah Lee) and Eve, the first woman."

Kallie shook her head slowly. Okay, now he was truly mad. An insane man sat across from her. "I'm Kallie Hunt, college student. Just plain ole Kal..."

"The spelling and pronunciation of the name are a bit different. But the Goddess Kali and the college student Kallie Hunt are one and the same. Her spirit lives in you."

"I don't feel like a goddess. I feel like a college student. I can remember things, sure. But I'm not special otherwise. I'm just Kallie."

"All God's creatures are special," Swag said in a dead tone. "But your role here is different. You are who you are."

Her mind flooded with questions and she rushed them all at him. "But how would you know this? Why wouldn't I feel it? Why can't I remember it? What does...?"

He held up a hand, silencing her. "I know it's confusing. And I can't say I have all the answers. Why in this time-cycle I know and you don't is something I can't answer. All I can say is God moves in mysterious ways. Maybe he has a plan. Maybe there's just madness," his voice trailed off as he momentarily broke eye contact with her. When he faced her again, his expression was stoic, determined. "You saw the demons."

He was right. She had seen the demons. And he'd known that she would. And he'd known about her remembering ability. It seemed he knew more about her than she knew about herself. It seemed pointless debating him on whether or not she was a goddess. Still, she didn't feel like a goddess. She certainly didn't feel powerful enough to kill demons. She was no Buffy. In her mind's eye, she could still see them. Strange misshapen creatures that looked like variegated innards draped over jigsaw puzzle pieces. No, on this point, he had to be mistaken. Before that stance could fully plant itself, she asked herself, *What if he isn't mistaken?* She decided to play devil's advocate. "What if I was this Kali person? How could I defeat them? I don't even know where they are?"

He looked around at the other tables and spotted something on one of them. He went to retrieve it and then brought it back to their booth. It was a newspaper. He moved the book she was reading to the side and then unfolded the newspaper, spreading its front page before her. He pointed to a story beneath the fold. Its headline read: *Violent Crimes Surge in Weeks Following Attack.* Without giving her a chance to read the accompanying article, he opened the metro section on top of the front page. He indicated two articles: *Teacher charged with taking indecent liberties with 11 year old girl. Several Women Report Being Groped on Public Buses.* "Demons are spirits, evil, unclean spirits," he said.

"You're saying that the demons that fell out of the sky landed in the bodies of these people?"

"They didn't just land in people," Swag said. "Demons only need a body. Some may have landed in animals—dogs, cats, snakes, or any other living thing."

Kallie slumped back in her chair. "So, they could be anywhere."

"They can be and are," Swag said. He moved the book back in front of her and indicated the first sentence of the passage she'd already read three times.

She read the sentence out loud. "The demons were continually drawn to her and ultimately, to their own demise."

"They can sense your presence. They know that you can defeat them. They won't rest until you're destroyed. They'll come to you."

A lump formed in her throat. "They'll come to me?"

"Yes, they will eventually; but there is a way to speed up the process."

"I'm not sure I'd want to," she said absently.

Swag ignored the comment. "But we must hurry or they'll scatter away from this region."

"So, we get them to come to me. And then what?"

He picked up the remains of his sandwich and chomped off a huge piece of it. "You'll kill them all," he said chewing. He smiled roguishly, wiping a spot of ketchup from the right corner of his lips.

CHAPTER TWENTY-NINE

Friday, November 13

Professor Adam Sampson's home for the past eleven years
was a modestly sized ranch that sat left of center in a cul-de-
sac in a tree-crowded subdivision called Restive Willows.
The neighborhood was the virtual midpoint of the imaginary
line connecting Bengate's campus with Downtown Charlotte.
The homes were big enough for young, family-oriented
professionals, yet small enough for rising seniors who were
empty-nesters either by nature or choice and still had an
affinity for grass. The solidly priced houses had survived a
recent housing bubble and were routinely coveted by families
with household incomes running north of six figures, and
who didn't mind being lorded over by a homeowners
association known for issuing heavy-handed fines to any
resident even remotely affronting the neighborhood's
ambiance and appearance.

Sampson's home for the most part was exactly how one
would imagine a house with a single, meticulous occupant
and no children in its past or present to be. The walls and
carpet were unblemished. The solid oak furniture and
hardwood floors were unmarked and varnished to perfection.
The air was garden-fresh and floral-scented. The sweet,
flowery air, of course, wasn't exactly due to the lack of young
ones on the premises. Sampson, a professed green thumb

since adolescence, had squeezed plants and flowers into just about every inch of livable space. Tall ponytail palms lined either side of the foyer, leading to the living room where five-foot desert roses prominently guarded its four corners. There were several geraniums and golden barrel cactuses scattered throughout the place. And he'd placed snake and ghost plants on every windowsill. By his admission and design, his indoors could very easily pass for the outdoors.

He loved his plants and he took great care in nurturing them. Each day, he watered and fed them and talked incessantly to them. Sampson was a confirmed bachelor or, more precisely, a male old maid. And the plants were to him like cats were to some of his female counterparts. He thought his plants were significantly less of a bother than their feline contemporaries and, of course, plants had no need of litter boxes.

Standing over a potted ox tongue, Sampson finally heard the water dripping onto the floor. He looked down and saw that he'd overwatered the plant. Flowing water like a busted dam crept up the plant's pot and streamed down it sides. Dismayed, he put down the watering can and hurried into the kitchen to fetch a dry cloth.

After drying the floor beneath and around the plant, he assessed the damage. The dirt had muddied, but otherwise the plant was no worse for the wear. He added another layer of dirt to the pot, tamping it down with his hands. He placed the ox tongue back amongst the others and stood back. He wiped his hands on his apron and looked around the room at all his plants. Tonight, it was taking him longer than usual to water them. He labored in the act. He lingered for long spells over them, talking more to himself than to them. He overwatered some plants while skipping watering others altogether. His mind was not on them. His mind was on his body. He couldn't figure out what was happening to him. Why his body and mind were all of a sudden betraying him. In particular he thought, as he once again felt a growing erection stirred by the resurfaced mental image of the lovely coed who'd brushed against him earlier today, why now? Why after fifty-three years of life, had he, Adam Sampson, finally discovered girls? He mechanically picked up the watering can and then froze in place, casting a long lustful glare at one of the desert roses.

Growing up, it was widely assumed by everyone who knew him, including his father who himself was a self-proclaimed ladies' man, that Adam Sampson was gay-in-waiting. Wasn't it quite obvious? Any boy with a weird fascination with foliage and no interest whatsoever in girls had to be homosexual. It was probably written in a book somewhere. His father had originally held out hope that young Adam's disinterest in the fairer sex was due to some kind of prepubescent delay. Sometimes, it took boys a little longer to appreciate the opposite sex. Even the self-proclaimed ladies' man had one time preferred playing with dirt and frogs to girls. Yes, the boy's uncanny love of flowers was a bit disturbing. But hey, flowers would eventually help get the chicks. So there was even hope in that. But when Adam's teen years came and went without girls even remotely entering the equation, his father's gaydar began to detect the faint pings of homosexuality. And then when young Adam's college years followed the same course as his high school years, the pings became louder, bleeping off the freaking scanner! It was abundantly clear. Adam Sampson was not ever going to be into girls. It was time to face facts. No interest in girls meant an interest in boys. It was a simple equation.

Except that it wasn't.

A few years after college, Adam Sampson discovered something else on the road to his "outing." He had no interest in boys either! He had no interest in hanky-panky whatsoever, not with girls, boys, things, not even himself. It was only after graduating college as a twenty-two year old virgin with no plans or desire to rectify the apparently unacceptable social condition had he fully accepted the idea of no sex. But it took a little longer for him to finally put a name to his affliction. The term was asexual. And it wasn't an affliction at all. He wasn't sick. He was perfectly normal in his abnormality. There were others like him. They simply weren't sexually attracted to either males or females. He, like them, was an asexual! Not hetero, or homo, simply, a...sexual.

The first few years after his self-discovery were still quite lonely. He'd had no idea how much sex dominated most people's thought processes. And, of course, no one believed that he wasn't sexually attracted to anyone or anything. Most people still believed he was gay. But with the advent of the internet, he was finally able to chat with and meet others like him. Statistics put their percentage at about one percent of the population. Maybe a small number when compared to the number of straights and gays in the world, but it meant he wasn't alone. He connected with quite a few people who shared his lack of sexual desire and he eventually became part of a support group. They met monthly, discussing everything under the sun. Some had had sex and hadn't liked it. Others hadn't even bothered trying it. Things like the Sexual Revolution and AIDS scare had come and gone, and no one in Adam Sampson's little corner of the world had batted an eye. After talking for months with his newfound friends, he discovered something—none of them missed the joys and ills of sex.

But this past week all of that began to change for Adam Sampson. On Tuesday, he'd felt an awakening in his body that had been dormant since his birth. And since that day, his mind had been all about girls—cleavage, and thighs, and legs, and buttocks. Of short skirts and what lay hidden beneath them. Of what low hanging blouses and tight sweaters concealed. Of what lay nestled within form-fitting jeans and skintight pants. All day his mind rattled off things he'd like to do to this girl or that girl. On Wednesday in class, he'd finally gotten the gist of an old Eddie Murphy joke when he found out that at the ripe old age of fifty-three, he himself had no penis-control. Watching Ruth Coward, who sat at the front of his ten o'clock lecture, his body suddenly decided to acknowledge her taste in clothes. She'd been wearing one of those low-hanging blouses and just the thought of her supple breasts pushing against that silk fabric had brought his member to full attention. It had been an utterly embarrassing situation. He had to do the whole lecture camouflaged behind his desk.

Now, standing in his living room, still holding the watering can, and having a lustful fascination with the desert rose, he arrived at a new fact—something had happened to him. He didn't feel like himself. It felt as if his body had been invaded, putting him at war with himself. His recent thoughts weren't just of a sexual nature. Some of them were downright grotesque. He wanted to maim, mutilate, defile. He felt...unholy...unclean. The desert rose began to mock him, shape-shifting before his very eyes. First, it was Ruth Coward, and then it morphed into a little girl, and then to a little boy, and then ultimately it became a dog. And he wanted to do them all, and afterwards, defile and mutilate the corpses. The watering can dropped to the floor, hitting it with a splashy metallic ting. He stumbled backward, catching the glint of his car keys where he'd thrown them earlier on the coffee table.

He scuttled his dress-shoed feet across the hardwood leading into the dining room, leaving long double scuffed marks in their wake. He ended up against the blinds of the bay window, knocking two snake plants off the sill in the process. The potted plants fell to the floor in weighted thumps, cracking apart and scattering rich black dirt. He grabbed his privates, yanking fiercely; unable to shake the tantalizing image of the ever-changing desert rose from his mind. When relief finally came, spurting down his pant leg, he relaxed against the window, his breathing slowing in quick degrees. Outside, he could hear the shuffling about of fallen leaves on his lawn as if God himself walked across them, a witness to his transgression.

CHAPTER THIRTY

Twice the urge to stop and run inside a store to grope
something had nearly overpowered him. But Adam Sampson
resisted it fiercely, keeping his foot on the car's accelerator.
He had to get to New Vibe Community Church and Reverend
Swag. What resided inside him was demonic. He knew that
two and two was always four despite whatever Orwellian-
like ruminations implied.

But there was something else, too. It was midnight, the
witching hour and the wee moments of a Friday the
thirteenth. And *she* would be there. How he knew that was
lost to him as was why he needed to see her so badly in the
first place. He was being pulled to her. He needed to
savagely have his way with her. The thought hardened him,
making his member throb violently against his pants. He
started to free it, but resisted the urge. New Vibe was but a
block away.

He screeched to a halt in the church's parking lot. Leaving
the vehicle haphazardly angled, he stumbled out of it and
went wobbly to the church steps. The front double-doors
were unlocked. Surprisingly, there was no resistance. No
unseen force pushed him back. The door handles felt as cold
to the touch of his hands as the night air was upon the rest of
his uncovered skin. He entered unabated.

The sanctuary was partially dark. Bits of moonlight
managed to snake in through the variegated window panes.
Swag knelt at the altar amongst fake foliage and candles. He
was alone.

Sampson yelled. "Help me!"

There was an instant of silence. Then Swag, moving nary a muscle, said, "Stop fighting it. Give in to yourself."

Sampson moved closer to the altar. "You must help me, Reverend. Please! Help me!"

"Adsum," Swag said.

It was Latin. Strangely, despite the fact that he'd never studied the dead language, Sampson understood him perfectly well. "Adsum et tu dominus. *I'm here as well, master*," he replied, the dead words rose up from his belly of their own volition.

Swag stood up and turned around. His eyes were a fiery red and all of his fingernails were long. Harsh disbelief swept over Sampson. It couldn't be. Swag was one of...no, no. But as he watched Swag's bendy finger motioning him forth, he knew it was so.

Sampson had known Swag for over eight years and never before noticed the pastor's long fingernails. Then again, he'd had no inkling of this side of the young preacher either. Even as the wave of understanding swept over him, Sampson stared drop-jawed at Swag as he continued beckoning him hither; but Sampson didn't want to go and for a few moments willed himself still. Soon, however, his legs, as the dead words had before, started to move on their own accord. Then the demon once again exerted control of his tongue. "Cepi Corpus, *I have taken the body*." But Sampson strained against the forced movements. He wouldn't relinquish his body so easily. With much effort, he forced himself to his knees, crying out. "God, help me!"

Swag laughed harshly. "Fool! Esto quod es! *Be what you are*!"

"I'm Adam Sampson, professor of history!"

"Sampson is no more," Swag said. "It's over now. Fui quod es, eris quod sum. *I was once what you are; you will be what I am*. Et vadam ad eam. *Go to her*."

Sampson dug his knees deep into the green carpet. "No, I will not leave my body. You can't have it!" But the thing inside him forced him to his feet, and soon he was scraping across the carpet toward a room at the back of the sanctuary.

In the back room, Sampson discovered who 'she' was. She was asleep on a sofa. She wore blue jeans and a greenish-blue sweater that rose up just a little, exposing a little skin, making him think of Ruth Coward. But not even Ruth Coward could compare to Kallie Hunt who looked so beautiful and dangerous lying there, waiting for him. Memory of the death of a cancer-stricken mother and the accompanying near déjà vu-fueled mental breakdown of her daughter a day short of a year later was distant and foreign. All that remained was lust, a lust that was perhaps always there, simmering underbelly, masked by a pretended asexuality. He licked his tongue over his lips as savagely lustful emotions gripped him, controlling him more so than the demon within. He leapt the short distance to her, intending to finally have his way. To give into himself as Swag had so eloquently put it. Puckering his lips, he bent down. As he drew closer, her eyes opened.

Professor Adam Sampson was destined to be her first.

CHAPTER THIRTY-ONE

She was at the crossroads of wakefulness where dreams and reality crossed paths. Initially, she thought that she was on the dream side of the equation and merely aware that she was having a lucid dream. No Kallie, you're not birdlike. You can't fly. You were dreaming. Yes, Kallie, your mother and grandfather really are dead. No, you're not going on vacation with them. You were dreaming.

But this time, she wasn't dreaming. This time she really was awake and smack down in the midst of reality. This time she was on the reality side of things, the side where celebrities and mega-lottery winners were living the dream, and victims of tragic accidents and horrific acts of violence were living the nightmare. When she'd opened her eyes and saw the professor leering over her with vengeful lust in his eyes, she'd screamed—or wanted to. What had actually come out was only a quiet hissing sound. Yet, the demon within Sampson's body heard it perfectly well and responded to it like a dog would to a Galton's whistle. It leaped out of Sampson's body and landed right on top of her. And before she was even aware that she was doing it, Kallie was tearing into the shapeless entity with fierce abandon, clawing it with fingernails that had suddenly stretched out like vampire fangs and gnashing it with long fangs of her own. Incredibly and literally, she beat, bit, and ripped the demon-thing into nothingness. Sampson's body, once freed from the clutches of its uninvited guest, convulsed and then slumped to the floor beside the sofa, leaving its original proprietor dazed and confused.

Throughout it all, Swag, like a boxer's corner man, motivated and pushed her to reach deep inside her soul for something she hadn't known was there. "And it is written," he said, his voice melodious and hypnotic, his cadence-perfect, "With unrelenting power, the goddess destroyed one after the other, crushing some with her bare hands, stomping many with her feet, and gnashing countless others with her teeth." After a heartbeat's pause, clearly for effect, he added, "Let me guide you to your true self, Kali. You're a destroyer. Demons won't stand a chance. Nothing will."

After the defeat of Sampson's demon, Swag told Kallie that she was ready for the others. Then she and he took off in his Volvo, spending the remaining hours before dawn's break riding all over the metro area with Kallie's head leaning out the car window as she sent her ultrasonic squeal into the cold night air. Her message, heard only by the black hearted creatures that had fallen from the sky on the night of the UCB Center bombing, was simple and not unlike a school bully's "meet me after school at three o'clock down by old man Johnson's farm. I'm going to bloody your nose. By God I am." In her case, old man Johnson's farm (at Swag's suggestion) was a potter's field, which, coincidentally, was not too far from the Tom-Tom Club in Chesterfield. The time would be that very night before the stroke of twelve. As for the bloody nose, both sides understood that the stakes would be much higher. It would be existence or oblivion for one or the other.

* * *

Calling them out had seemed so ridiculously simple and for Kallie, had nearly strained credulity to its breaking point.

Yet, at a little past eleven o'clock, she, after having summoned the blood-seeking demons with her almost soundless pied piper like scream, stood in the middle of the potter's field, surrounded by gathering evil spirits. Their collective smell flared her nostrils. It was acrid like the pungent odor of old rubber set afire in a city dump. Their host-bodies had come by hook or by crook, some even stood before her in pajamas. There were third-shifters from various fields—firemen, policemen, hospital personnel, factory workers, night clubbers, and others, mixed in with Friday night homebodies. All were impervious to the reason for their nightmarish excursion to an unfamiliar area located far from their homes, previous destinations, and places of business. Their synchronized breathing intermittently formed massive exhalations in the nighttime coldness, floating to the heavens like smoke signals.

Ditching their modes of transportation on the side of the road, the demons, with a single purpose and mindset, headed to the field. In the days and weeks following the apocalyptic battle and the other troubling events of this Friday the thirteenth, including a two hundred car pileup on a desolate stretch of interstate miles from the city's border, none of the host-people would remember what had led them to the middle of nowhere, this isolated field filled with the buried bodies of the poor and unknown. And none of the city's other living souls, not common man, not anyone in authority, would be able to answer with any measurable confidence why the city of Charlotte's sudden rash of criminal and offensive behavior following the decapitation of its tallest building would suddenly decrease as quickly as it had recently increased.

For Kallie, who would know such answers, none of the questions held sway at the present moment. Earth's cleansing was at hand. A demon, residing in the body of a twelve-year-old pigtailed girl wearing a pink nightgown, drew first blood when it reached up and slashed grotesquely at Kallie's left cheek, perforating the skin, leaving a dotted line of blood. Absently, Kallie brought her hand up to her cheek, feeling the warm wetness of her own blood. She bought her fingers to her lips and kissed them, tasting her blood's metallic sweetness. Nodding and smiling at the demon-girl, Kallie opened her mouth and let loose the near soundless squeal that had invited the demons here and invoked Sampson's demon to its own demise. Now the demon inside the little girl leapt out of its host and lunged fiercely at her, as Sampson's had before.

The battle started.

Kallie's moves were fluid, matrix-like, and came in droves. She operated outside herself, practically floating above the host-bodies as they fell at her feet. Had she been an athlete she would've described it as "being in the zone." With hands, teeth, fingernails, and feet, she stomped, sliced, diced, and pureed. Demon spillage, in shades of dark reds and purples before eventually dematerializing, splashed everywhere, creating a red-purplish fog that temporarily tinted the florescent yellow of the half moon, making it appear as if a half-eaten apple had been set ablaze in the night sky. Swag watched the battle from the sideline, still and speechless. His pupils reflected the carnage like mirrored fiery, reddish-blue dots.

The battle raged for three hours. For the longest time, the demons' numbers didn't seem to waver, but neither did Kallie's energy or resolve. Each side found their second, third, and eventually fourth and fifth winds. But ultimately it, as do most battles, reached its bloody conclusion and a decision was rendered. There could be but one winner. And as the quiet rumbling created by hundreds of people suddenly awakening from a demonic stupor slowly gave rise to the panicky din of confusion and the collective facial expressions of "What the...," it was clear who that winner was.

Kallie stood tall over the mass of people whose bodies were suddenly their own once again. Then, without warning, she began to fall to the ground, finally giving in to thorough exhaustion and complete energy depletion. But Swag, who had moved to her side, was able to catch her as soon as her knees buckled.

"How do we get them home?" Kallie asked, falling into his embrace and looking around at the people, many of whom were obviously in a fugue state.

Swag lifted her up into his arms. "There're emergency personnel amongst the crowd. They'll figure it out. Right now, I'm getting you out of here."

She nodded agreeably and then closed her eyes, resting her head on his shoulder.

He'd parked the Volvo on the side of a dirt road located about a mile from the field on the other side of a wooded area. He carried her through copse all the way back to the car. When he finally reached it, he dug into his pants pocket for his car keys. Finding them, he popped open the door locks and loaded her sideways into the backseat.

She slid in easily, nestling herself into the black leather upholstery. She steepled her hands together, using them as a pillow under her head.

He leaned over her for a moment. "You did well. I'm proud of you." He leaned in further, sliding atop her and bringing his lips to hers. She opened her eyes just as he got there, and then fully met and reciprocated his kiss.

It was fifteen minutes to five o'clock in the morning when Swag finally made it back to the church. He found Adam Sampson in the same place and position he and Kallie had left him late last night, lying on his side on the floor beside the sofa. Swag kneeled down beside him, turned him over onto his back, and then shook him. Sampson, mumbling incoherently, attempted to roll back onto his side, but Swag held him in place. "No, no professor. It's now morning. Time for you to get up."

Sampson snorted and jerked involuntarily, looking like a man trying to regain his bearings after a long liquored night of revelry.

Swag stood up and pulled out his cell phone. He flipped through the list of contacts, selecting an underling. The call was answered immediately. "How long will it take you to get here?"

After he was given the answer, Swag said, "I'm going to need some help getting him into the car." He paused and listened. "No, the girl's not here. I took her home." He paused and listened again. "No worries, she's mine now."

They arrived at Sampson's house with about thirty minutes of darkness left to spare. It was early Saturday morning, just before the time a rooster would normally crow. The neighborhood was quiet and indifferent to most goings-on, particularly quiet unassuming ones. Swag parked Sampson's vehicle in the driveway and then he and a faithful servant, a hulking, bald sampling of pure obedience who'd followed behind Swag in his own Dodge Avenger, pulled the professor out of the car, taking him up the front steps and into his house. Swag had anticipated an alarm and had a readily prepared story should a police officer happen by. But no excuse would be needed. Though Sampson had an alarm, he'd apparently been into too much of a hurry on Friday night to set it. They entered the house without fanfare.

After they'd tucked Sampson into his bed, the professor opened his eyes. Understanding and remembrance fought for leverage, but his thoughts were muddled. He couldn't piece anything together. "What hap...happened?" he asked Swag.

"You've had a nasty fall," Swag said. He nodded to his servant. The servant left the room and a moment later, the front door could be heard opening and closing.

"Whe...where was I?"

"You were at church."

"Church?" None of it made any sense. Why had he been at church? Was today Wednesday or Sunday? He had no sense of time or place.

Swag stood over him, staring intently. "I wish there were some other way. I've always liked you Professor Sampson. You could have been a most faithful servant."

Faithful servant? What in God's name...and before the question could form completely, his mental dam broke. He tried to sit up, but he was still much too weak and Swag easily pushed him back down. "You're one of them! Let me up."

Swag smiled. "It's a shame that you've but two lives to give to the cause."

Sampson tried rising up against Swag's hand. But his effort was futile. He was barely able to move a muscle. And then, in his mind's eye, he saw her. "Kallie? What are you going to do with Kallie?"

"You needn't worry about Kali," Swag said evenly.

Though his body was still weak, Sampson's mind was sharpening rapidly. He caught the slight change in the pronunciation of the girl's name. "Kali?"

"Yes, Kali. She's a goddess and more powerful than you'll ever know."

Sharpening mind or not, this made no sense. Sampson, a professor of history, was very familiar with the Indian Goddess, Kali. She was a mortal enemy of demons.

Reading the confusion plastered across the professor's face, Swag said, "I'm sure you've heard the expression, 'if you can't beat them, you join them.'"

Sampson nodded his head hesitantly.

"Well," Swag said, with an air of arrogance that curled Sampson's blood. "It's not written in stone that you must join them. They can, after all, join you."

They were the last words Sampson would hear in this lifetime. Swag deftly removed the pillow from beneath the professor's head and calmly placed it over his face before firmly applying pressure.

CHAPTER THIRTY-TWO

She slept for three solid days. At some point she vaguely recalled Maggie opening her door, checking in on her, even bringing in a sandwich one time. But Kallie hadn't been hungry. She'd been tired. Dead tired.

Despite the gruesomeness of the events of Friday night and the wee hours of Saturday morning, her sleep was peaceful, and just, and filled with colorful and vivid dreams, most of which featured her mother. And in the odd way of dreams, some of them were remakes or variations of things she'd actually done with her mother, while others sprang from some region of her unconsciousness of their own volition, newly scripted and motivated to existence by only God knows what. But she welcomed them all just the same because it meant that for a little while at least, even if only in the realm of unconsciousness, her mother was with her again.

"You kissed him?" her mother asked. A bright sun's rays slipped through the cracks of the tree branches lording over the bike trail. The two of them were rollerblading down the trail. It was something she'd never had the chance to do with her mother when she was alive.

"Actually, he kissed me," Kallie corrected.

"But you kissed him back."

It was true. She'd kissed him back. She couldn't deny it. Even in a dream-induced conversation with her dead mother, she couldn't deny it. She'd kissed Reverend Johnny Swag. And most troubling of all, she'd liked it.

"What does it mean?" her mother asked her.

"I don't know."

Her mother skated a few feet ahead and then stopped, turning around to face her. Kallie skated up to her, stopping at arm's length. "I'll tell you what it means," her mother said. "It means you're young. It means you can kiss whoever you want."

"But why him?" Kallie asked.

"Why not him? Look, I'm not saying you should kiss every boy you see or that there won't come a time when you'll want to save all your kisses for one boy. What I'm saying is that it's no crime to kiss another boy. And you'll know when you're with the right one."

"Should I tell Seth?"

"Sorry, Kiddo. You're going to have to decide that one for yourself."

"But Mom!" Kallie exclaimed.

"Don't but me no buts, missy," her mother said. And suddenly, in the way of dreams, they were no longer skating on a bike trail. Now they were in a Five & Dime store and Kallie was now five years old, standing beside her mother and looking expectedly at a little doll. "You'll wait until your birthday."

"But mom," Kallie screamed again.

"If you keep that up, not even then," her mother said with a finality that shut little Kallie up in dreamland and brought big Kallie to the edge of wakefulness.

"But, but," Kallie mumbled as her eyes blinked open and she realized that she wasn't five years old. She sat up in her bed and slowly looked around her room, reorienting herself to the here and now.

There was a light tap at her bedroom door. She turned to it. It pushed open slightly and Maggie stuck her head into the room. "You awake yet?"

Kallie stretched and yawned. "Yeah, come on in."

Maggie came into the room, plopping down on the bed beside Kallie. "Man that must've been some party."

"Huh? What do you mean?"

"You've been out three days."

"What?" Kallie said. "What day is it?"

"Tuesday," Maggie said gleefully, obviously pleased to be the first to welcome her friend back to the land of the living. "I came in here a couple of times and stuck my finger under your nose to make sure you were still breathing. I even checked your temperature."

Kallie shifted uncomfortably.

"I put it in your mouth, silly. It was 98.6, perfectly normal. Other than the fact that you were sleeping like Rip Van Wrinkle, you were fine. So, I figured you must've been drinking like a fish and got yourself plastered. Either that or someone slipped you something. Still, if you hadn't awakened today, I was going to call a doctor or somebody."

"Thanks for caring, Maggie," Kallie said.

"No worries," Maggie said. "Now tell me about this party."

"Sorry to have to disappoint you. But I don't remember anything about it."

"It figures," Maggie said. "Well at least tell me who brought you home."

"What do you mean?"

"I didn't hear you come home Friday night and Saturday morning, here you were in bed; but your car wasn't here."

Kallie looked down at her clothes. She was wearing her light blue nightgown.

"I changed you into your nightgown on Saturday night when it became obvious that you weren't waking up anytime soon."

Kallie smiled weakly. "Thanks again."

Maggie nodded. "So, who brought you home?"

"I honestly don't remember," Kallie said.

"Well then, where's your car?"

Kallie looked off to the side, remembering. "I believe I left it parked at the church."

Maggie's jaw dropped. "The church! What, you got bunkered off communion wine?"

Kallie just looked at her.

"I know. I know," Maggie said. "You don't remember."

Kallie shook her head. "Sorry."

"It's okay as long as you're all right."

"I'm fine, really. Anyway, tell me what's happening with you and what's-his-face?"

"If you mean Cedric, we're doing just fine."

Kallie smiled. "We're?"

"Yes, we're," Maggie blushed. "Methinks he could be the one," she added in a Shakespearean accent.

Kallie playfully tapped her friend on the knee. "Well, whaddaya know. I'm so happy for you."

"I should thank you for introducing us."

"Although he wasn't the one I'd picked out for you."

"It doesn't really matter, does it?"

"No, I guess not, as long as you're happy."

"And I am," Maggie confirmed. They were silent for a moment. Then she asked, "Tell me what's going on with you and Seth? He came by here three times over the weekend. He said he tried calling you, but your phone goes straight to voicemail."

Kallie glanced over at the nightstand where her cell phone lay. "It probably does. I haven't charged it. The battery's likely dead."

"I know," Maggie said. "I told him that. But he didn't seem to believe me. I think he believes you're avoiding him for some reason. Is something wrong between the two of you?"

"No," Kallie said, "It's just that lately I've been extremely busy."

"Have you told him that?"

"No," Kallie said. "I'd have to see him to tell him." And she knew that there were a few other things she needed to tell him as well. It would be a difficult conversation. But one that

needed to happen. She didn't know if it would include the
part about her kissing Swag. That one might be too painful
for the both of them. But he needed to know about this
goddess/demon-killing business. They both needed to know
where he stood with it. The easiest thing would be for her to
keep everything to herself and just walk away. But Seth
meant something to her and she was certain that she meant
something to him. If their relationship was to end, then it
should end with all their cards placed face-up on the table.

"Well, you're going to get your chance to tell him now,"
Maggie said. She'd gone over and looked out of the window
after they'd both heard a car park alongside the curb out
front. "It's he."

She kept him waiting nearly twenty minutes. But she'd been
asleep for three days following an all-night demonic slugfest
and probably looked like whodunit and why. It was a small
price to pay. As she'd washed up, she worked out in her mind
what she would say to him. She'd decided that it was best to
just get it out there in one quick motion like ripping off the
Band-Aid of a partially healed scab. If you ripped it off quick
enough, the resulting pain would be lessened or nonexistent.
But when she finally came down the stairs and saw him
standing by the door, already looking defeated, she was
momentarily thrown off her game. She opened her mouth to
say something, though she had no idea what words would
emerge. But it quickly didn't matter because when he saw
her, he spoke first.

"Professor Sampson is dead."

CHAPTER THIRTY-THREE

As Seth drove her to New Vibe to retrieve her car, he filled her in on the discovery of the professor's body the previous night. "No one had heard from him all day Monday. He hadn't shown up for work and hadn't called in. Apparently he called his family every weekend and when they hadn't heard from him and found out he hadn't gone to work either, they requested that the police send someone to his house to check on him. They found him in his bed. They say he probably had a heart attack. But I think they're going to do an autopsy."

They were silent for a while, listening to the sounds of everyday traffic and people going about the business of their lives. Then Seth said, "I thought he looked a little out of it all last week, but I didn't think all that much about it. But on Friday, when I saw him heading to his car, he looked a little better. You know, happy that it's Friday sort of thing. I figured he probably just needed to rest. I had no idea that would be the last time I'd see him alive."

The last time she'd seen the professor alive he'd been leaning over her, grabbing at his pecker. Understandably, she didn't share that memory with Seth.

Seth pulled into the church's parking lot and alongside her Honda. She started to get out, but he gently touched her leg, stopping her. "Wait. What's going on?"

She continued staring out the window at her car, reluctant to face him. "What do you mean?"

"Something's happening between us. Something's different. You're distant."

Still staring out the car window, she shook her head slowly. "Nothing's changed, really. It's just... I'm busy. You're busy."

"We're too busy for each other?"

She turned and faced him. "Let's not do this now. With the professor and all, this is not the right time."

"I disagree. This is the perfect time. You're here. I'm here. I don't have to talk to your voicemail. I don't have to send messages through your friends."

"Is that what this is about? You're not getting enough time with me?"

He leaned back, throwing his hands up mockingly. "Aren't we mighty full of ourselves? I hate that this relationship is such a freaking burden on you and that your time is oh, so precious."

She turned back to the door again, grabbing hold of the door handle. "I don't have time for this."

"Yeah, I know. So why don't you go ahead and leave."

She paused and looked over her shoulder at him. "This is not working."

He poked his tongue on the inside of his jaw. "I know," he said wearingly.

"So, this is it," she said.

"Yeah," he agreed and looked away.

She got out of his car and walked quickly to hers.

She didn't look back.

*   *   *

Veronica wasn't expecting to see her uncle outside her door. But there he was, standing there after insistently ringing her doorbell for several minutes. She'd fallen asleep as soon as she'd gotten home. Evidently, her hectic school and part-time work schedule had finally caught up to her. Sleep had come

way too easily. Before the relentless ringing of the doorbell
had invaded her slumber, she'd been cast ashore on some
nameless island after a three-hour cruise was blown terribly
off course. This time there were only two survivors of the
mishap, she and the professor. And somehow, they'd both
managed to swim ashore to the uninhabited island that was
surprisingly well stocked with her favorite seafood and wine.
Lots of wine. It was just she and the professor and lots of sun
and wine. No Ginger, no Mary-Ann, no books, no goals, just
she and the professor with nothing between them but desire
and opportunity. Oh, this had better be good, she thought
bitterly as she glared through the peephole at her uncle. The
dream had been her first shot at a good time in months.

She snatched the door open, barely able to contain her
contempt.

Seeing the expression on her face and the haphazard way
her clothes draped her body, her uncle immediately launched
into apologies. "I'm sorry, Roni. You have company. I caught
you at a bad time."

It was insult added to injury, being busted for having a
good dream. "No, Uncle Den. Come in. I'm just dog-tired. I'd
just fallen asleep."

"Well, I'm sorry to have awakened you."

"Me too," she said and meant it.

"I wouldn't have barged over here unannounced if it
wasn't important. I need your help."

She regarded him warily. "Don't tell me it involves Kallie
Hunt again."

He shrugged his shoulders apologetically.

*   *   *

Josh sat alone at a table in the back left corner of the campus
library, a thick book open before him. It was seven o'clock,

Tuesday night. He was running on fumes and barely able to keep his eyes opened. In addition to his heavy graduate workload, heading Dr. Frost's memory project, and the two undergraduate religion classes he taught on Tuesdays and Thursdays, he'd been unable to tear himself away from his research on eternal return, life-cycles, and demons. He tried to convince himself that the extra research work would pay dividends for a possible topic for his next year's dissertation. But he'd already done significant legwork on his original topic, the one with the working title, "The Effects of Religion on the Financial Futures of Urban Youth".

His current research uncovered the tenebrous connection between eternal return, time-cycles, and demons. But one had to be meticulous in order to find it. He found relevant material related to each in various venues, including the Bible and other religious books, manifestoes written throughout history supposedly by religious nuts (which he found buried in the links of some obscure websites); surprisingly, even some gothic comics and horror B-movies contained very accurate data. It was as if different bodies of thought had each been given a piece of valuable information about time and origin and then were sent to their respective corners of existence, never for their trains of thought to meet. It was like an existential jigsaw puzzle.

He'd called Madame Isabel's business line several times the past couple of weeks. Initially, he got the same business greeting with her hours of operation. But eventually the greeting was removed and the phone just rang before eventually peeling off into the intermittent buzzing of a dead line. He knew from newspaper accounts that she was still missing. He'd hoped that her husband would pick up the phone anyway, although he knew they most likely had a private home line, which he, of course, didn't have the number to.

He'd been able to put the various pieces of the puzzle together and the developing picture was quite disturbing. Yet, the picture was incomplete. A piece of the puzzle was missing. He strongly feared the missing piece involved Madame Isabel's *Book of Origins*, and, quite possibly, his friend, Kallie.

*   *   *

At ten o'clock that same night, Johnny Swag finally answered his cell phone.

"Johnny, why haven't you called me?" An irritated Father McCarthy bellowed into the phone.

"These weekly calls are no longer conducive to me," Swag said calmly.

"Conducive! Now listen here, you...."

The line went dead.

So mad he could see red, McCarthy angrily hit the redial button. The call went straight to voicemail as it would the next few times he called, until McCarthy, pissed off and fed up, and clued to the reality that he was helpless to do anything about it at the moment, finally gave up and went storming off to bed.

*   *   *

"I'll get it," Kallie called out to her housemates. She'd left her room and was standing in the middle of the upstairs hallway. The doors to all the other bedrooms were closed, so it was likely that none of the others gave a rat's butt as to who was at the door anyway. She could hear Maggie talking on the phone, probably with Cedric. When the two of them weren't stepping on each other's shadow, they were going at it nonstop on the phone. *New love,* Kallie thought with a touch of jealousy, and bounded down the stairs.

She'd hoped it was Seth. They'd only been broken up since the morning, but she missed him terribly. She would apologize first and hope he wouldn't act manly and stubborn, as if he hadn't missed her as much as she missed him. She'd been wrong to get so upset with him in the first place. All he'd wanted was to be with her. He'd been patient. The past couple of weeks she'd been unfair to him and the relationship. Sure, she'd had her reasons, but he didn't know any of them. She'd told herself that she wouldn't allow them to break up without all their cards being placed face-up on the table. She owed him that. She owed their relationship that. And that was what she was going to tell him as soon as she opened the door.

"Who is it?" she asked when she reached the door, her heart thumping with anticipation and hope for reconciliation.

"It's me."

Kallie's heart dropped. The soft voice was not Seth's. She opened the door to find Veronica standing there. "May I come in?" Veronica asked, glancing around nervously.

"Sure," Kallie said, and stepped back, allowing her in. "What's wrong? You look as if you've seen a ghost."

"Can we talk?"

"Yeah sure," Kallie said. She led Veronica into the front room and flipped on a light. She went to the couch and sat down, indicating for Veronica to join her. "What's wrong?" Kallie asked again.

Veronica turned and faced her, folding one leg under her other. "You remember the vision you had at Piedmont Imaging?"

"Yeah," Kallie said uneasily. "What about it?"

"Homeland Security has subpoenaed Josh and my notes on that vision."

Kallie's eyes widened. "What?"

"And they believe that the vision was of the UCB Center bombing."

"That's ridiculous," Kallie said.

"Maybe," Veronica said. "But, on the night of the bombing, a girl called in to the fire department to warn them about it."

Kallie stood up.

Veronica said, "They've traced that call to your cell phone. They also have video of a person matching your physical dimensions walking with a man in the building where that terrorist guy supposedly jumped to his death."

Kallie backed slowly toward the entrance to the living room. "Why are you telling me this?"

"They want you to answer some questions, Kallie. They want you to go with them."

"You're saying I'm under arrest?"

Veronica stood up and walked toward Kallie. "No, you're not under arrest. I'm not law enforcement. It's like I said, they just want you to go with them and answer some questions. No scene, no big deal. But it's going to take a few days. So you should probably pack a change of clothes."

"Who are they?"

"Immigration and Customs Enforcement, they're a division of Homeland Security."

"But, I'm in school. I have classes."

Veronica reached her, softly touching her shoulder. "They'll take care of that. They'll work it out with your professors. And I'll tell your housemates that you're participating in another phrase of our memory project and will be back in a couple of days. No one has to know anything about this. And when it's over, you'll come back here and it'll be just like before."

Kallie heard someone stepping up behind her. She turned around and saw Veronica's uncle flanked by three or four other black-suited men. She turned back and faced Veronica. Veronica slowly nodded her head, and indicated upstairs. Then, she escorted Kallie upstairs and to her bedroom.

Kallie pulled her suitcase from beneath the bed and absently pulled things from her closet and drawers, throwing them into it. She had no idea what to pack. She had no idea where she was going or how long she would be there. All kinds of thoughts flooded her mind. Was she being kidnapped? Was this even legal? Did she need a lawyer? Then her thoughts turned to her family and friends, the living and the dead. She thought about her grandmother, Seth, her grandfather, her mother, and finally, for some reason, Professor Sampson. She would make this as painless as possible. She'd answer their questions and then she'd come back here. And things would be like they were before. She'd remember all the things that happened in a previous lifetime and in between classes and dates; she'd kill demons. She looked weakly at Veronica who stood in the doorway. "I should tell Maggie. She'll worry."

"No, write her a note," Veronica said. "Tell her to call me and that I'll explain everything."

A note, Kallie thought. Yeah, that was probably best. Tonight Maggie would have questions that Kallie wouldn't have answers to. She walked over to her desk and took out a sheet of paper from the middle drawer. The note was simple: *I'm participating in an onsite memory project for a few days, call Veronica if questions, 919-555-5555. Talk to you soon, Kallie.* She placed the note on her pillow. She entered the hallway, closed her bedroom door, and then followed Veronica to the stairs. She looked at Maggie's closed bedroom door and heard her friend's cackling voice, "Boy, you so crazy!"

CHAPTER THIRTY-FOUR

Swag equated what fulminated within him to joy although a part buried deep within his core knew that true joy was forever beyond his reach. But it was that deep-rooted knowledge that fueled his rage as it had his former self many eons ago. But the times, he thought with bitter-sweetness, were changing. He'd climbed down from the precipice of defeat and now stood on the cusp of complete victory. News of the dark one's demise had been greatly exaggerated and the revelations completely erroneous, utter falsehoods. Finally, man would see, angels would see, all God's creatures would see, that 'so sayeth the Lord' had been complete bullcrap. And all along, Lucifer, the wronged angel, had been right. And now Lucifer would reclaim his rightful place. It was all coming to pass. He'd sacrificed years for the coming victory. He'd uttered his own falsehoods, publically giving praise to one so undeserving. He'd walked amongst the true heathens. But in the end, his self-sacrifice would be worth it all. In the end, he would rule.

He stepped onto the altar, glaring at the choir stand. How his ears still burned from hearing the songs of praise and worship to the false deity, the real charlatan. How his skin now crawled at the thought of him having stood among them. How he himself had preached the Word of lies at this very pulpit. And all who had heard him had known that they were lies. In their hearts, they knew. Guest preachers had also stood in this very spot, echoing his fallacies as he had at their churches. Blaspheming preachers, who like him, had known the real truth, and in their actions had reiterated that they knew. They'd collected tons of tithes, not to give to the false deity who they'd known to be a fraud, but instead to spend lavishly on themselves. The glorification of self was his one true message. Swag picked up a potted plant and hurled it into the choir stand where it crashed against a middle pew, shattering its ceramic container, and splashing its black dirt on the pew and floor like dung. He laughed harshly and then kicked over the pulpit, sending the Bible atop it tumbling to the floor. He picked it up and ruthlessly tore out pages. "So sayeth the Lord! So sayeth the Lord!" he cried out furiously, letting the sacred pages flutter helplessly to the floor where he kicked them into a pile. He tossed the last of the Bible on top of its innards lying at his feet. Then he whipped out his member and peed where he stood.

For the next two hours, with his fermented rage violently swirling within him, he trashed God's house, oblivious to the fact, or simply not caring, that his very presence at New Vibe's helm the last year had already defiled the church. This was not holy ground. But in the end, it didn't matter. His desecration was symbolic. It was his spiritual cleansing. In the end, this was for him. And when it was completed, he dropped to his knees amidst the rubble. "I was falsely accused and wrongly removed from my rightful place of high honor. I was the most glorious and beautiful of all the angels, and You made promises to me that weren't kept. They've called me the great deceiver, but it's You who deceives. My time has come. So sayeth the Lord? No, so sayeth, me, Lucifer!"

Slowly, he rose to his feet, clearly aware that the job wasn't quite completed. He was at the finish line, but had yet to cross it. Again, the woman was the key. They'd taken her into custody. But she would be released soon, and he'd be there to receive her. Isabel, the late priestess, had said that Kali would stop him as she'd done before. But Kali would not rise up against him. She would not rise up against her husband. She would join him. She trusted him more than she trusted herself. The good Father McCarthy had helped to see to that. And now McCarthy's reward would be the opportunity to live and then ultimately to serve his new, true master.

In Swag's body, he felt himself growing aroused in anticipation of the consummation of his pending marriage. Soon, Kali would be his, and afterwards, she would take her rightful place beside him.

*　　*　　*

Kallie was being held at Fort Bragg. The base was only thirty minutes from her hometown of Lumberton. But no one from Lumberton knew she was there, not even her grandmother. Which made item number five on the list of her non-rights (You can have no visitors) seem like a waste of paper and ink and the breath of the intake processor who'd read the list to her in his uncaring, dronish baritone.

Her rights as a US citizen had been trumped in the name of national security. Miranda didn't exist. There was no one phone call. There was no right to an attorney. There would be no jury of her peers. There was no right to remain silent, and anything and everything, whether she'd said it or not, could and would be held against her. They could hold her indefinitely, and as if to prove that point, she'd been there for eight days before anyone had said an authoritative word to her.

Her accommodations, however, were fairly pleasant, three-starish. Her room contained twin beds, which she figured was mostly just designed psychological warfare. It was fairly obvious that she wasn't getting a roommate anytime soon. She would have no human contact. It hadn't been listed, but it most certainly had been implied and subsequently implemented. Most days she didn't even see the guards though she knew they were out there somewhere. A very noticeable camera had been positioned on the wall above the television. She suspected there were others. She knew they watched her every move.

For the first three days of her captivity, she'd cried nonstop. She hadn't signed up for this. She'd been a nineteen year old college student, bravely picking up the pieces after the unexpected sickness and death of her mother. She'd moved forward with her life. She hadn't blamed anyone for her situation, not even her absentee father who should have been there to take up the parental slack left by her mother's death. But she hadn't harbored any ill feelings toward him or anyone else. She didn't reside in the land of regrets, or hatred, or what-ifs. She'd moved on. And even after her mind had played its version of the rerun game and she thus found out that she was to be some kind of real life Buffy the Vampire Slayer, she hadn't wallowed in self-pity or doubt. She'd moved on. She simply accepted her destiny, mostly without question, and moved on.

She'd cried because her mother had died and wasn't there for her. She'd cried because she and Seth had broken up. She'd cried for her part in the breakup. She'd cried because she'd kissed a reverend. She cried at what that could possibly mean for her soul. She'd cried for the loss of Kallie, her carefree past self. She'd cried at not being able to tell her grandmother any of it. And finally, she'd cried for crying, for allowing sadness to build so much as to compel tears. But then suddenly, on the fourth day, it was over. The tears stopped. She'd cried out. Her heart hardened to acceptance. She sat on one of the twin beds, the one closest to the barred window, feeling numb, feeling as if nothing really mattered anymore. There was no need to move forward. Moving forward would eventually only circle back to here, how she felt right now. Her locale may change, but her emotions would be as they were now. It was pointless trying to control the outcome. Inevitability was in the driver's seat, the inevitable of the inevitable. Ultimately, what would be would be.

At the end of that fourth day, armed with her new outlook on life, her appetite returned. The food was somewhere between her grandmother's cooking and typical school cafeteria (though most days it lingered closer to the latter). She was allowed to watch television and listen to the radio. And for up to two hours a day, she was allowed outside. The recreation area was a closed, fenced-in area where a bevy of security cameras were hidden in plain sight, a constant reminder of the seizure of the one thing that truly mattered to her. The one thing they alone had the power to control or give back. Her freedom.

On day nine, she was taken to a small interrogation room where Veronica's uncle, Special Agent Dennard Bennett, was waiting for her. She hadn't seen him since the night she'd first arrived. The room was windowless and contained only a small card table and two chairs. The walls were a dull pastel. Bennett was sitting in one of the chairs at the table. A single bulb-light hung overhead.

"How have you been?" he asked after the accompanying guard had removed her handcuffs, seated her in the other chair, and then left them alone. He sounded like a cheerful psychiatrist from one of those late night psychotic movies. The one who would swear in the middle of the movie that he'd miraculously cured his patient of all mental ills, only to have said patient cut off the psychiatrist's head with a hacksaw and placed it in a shoe box before mailing it to the psychiatrist's wife who would get it at their home, opening it just as the movie's credits rolled.

"Fine," she said, rubbing her wrists. The handcuffs were also psychological-warfare. What threat did an unarmed college student pose? Her ability to kill demons notwithstanding, of course.

"I'm sorry about that," Bennett said, looking at her wrists. "It's just standard procedure."

"It's okay," she lied meekly.

"Otherwise, is your room all right? Are you comfortable?"

"Yes, thank you. Everything's fine. When can I go home?"

"Soon," he said in the same cheery voice. He smiled warmly. "I guess this will be our first full conversation since...."

"The science building at Bengate," she said anxiously. "It was six weeks and two days ago."

Bennett tilted his head slightly and grinned. "Impressive."

"I remember dates. It helps pass the time."

"I see."

"When will I be able to go home?"

Bennett leaned back in the chair. "Well, of course, that all depends on you."

He casually picked up the large manila folder that had been lying on the table in front of him. He opened it, taking out three photographs, and laid them right side up in front of her. "Take a look at these."

She studied the photographs. The first was of a pretty woman, probably in her late twenties or early thirties. The second picture was of two young girls, no more than four years old and looking remarkably similar to the woman in the first picture. The third picture was of an older lady, perhaps in her mid-to-late fifties. After viewing all three pictures, Kallie looked up and slightly shrugged her shoulders.

He tapped the picture of the younger woman. "My wife, Elise." Slowly he moved to the next picture, tapping it lightly as well. "My daughters, Kelsey and Melanie." He paused a moment. "The three of them were killed in a plane crash."

"I'm sorry," she said.

"Thank you," he said, and then they were both mutually silent for a moment, in honor of the dead. "It's been three years," he said suddenly. "Sometimes I can still feel it, raw and fresh as if it'd only happened yesterday and I can still stop them from getting on that plane." His voice was tense and Kallie could see one of his hands tighten into a fist, but after a moment, it loosened again and he laid it flat upon the table. "Most times, though," he continued, "I see it as it is. The plane goes down. Pilot error. My wife, our babies, snuggled and seat belted to their ultimate doom." He chuckled sickly and looked remorsefully at Kallie. She quickly averted her eyes, looking down at the third picture. Bennett followed her gaze, "Brenna Jackson," he said as if suddenly recalling a name that had been dangling anonymously for a while at the tip of his tongue.

"Who's she?" Kallie asked. She felt captivated by the picture. It was a color photograph; but it carried the haunting richness of an Andy Warhol black and white.

"Just a plain, everyday woman who'd had a ticket to the very plane that carried my family to their deaths. Ms. Jackson, however, had had a premonition, telling her not to board that plane. And she didn't. Today, Ms. Brenna Jackson lives in Camden, New Jersey, with a loving husband and three cats. She has three grandchildren living down south in Georgia. She sees them on a regular basis. She flies all the time and hadn't had a premonition warning her about planes before or since."

Kallie continued staring at the photograph. She didn't say anything.

Bennett reached into the envelope and pulled out two more photographs, which he laid to the right of the Brenna Jackson photograph.

Kallie looked at the two additions and for a brief moment, time stopped. The photographs were of her and Swag inside and exiting the elevator on the night of the UCB Center bombing.

"Is that you?" Bennett asked.

Kallie slowly nodded her head affirmatively.

"Who's the man?"

Kallie looked up, slowly shaking her head.

Bennett leaned toward her from across the table. She could smell hints of a breath mint. "Listen, Kallie. I know you didn't bomb the building. I doubt the person with you in the photograph bombed the building. I don't know what you're able to do. And even if I did know, I wouldn't likely understand it. Maybe you have the gift of premonition like Brenna Jackson. And maybe somebody's taken advantage of this gift. Maybe they believe that their cause is a noble one. And maybe you believe the same thing. They're terrorists, right? Gerald Principe, he was a terrorist and deserved to die. And maybe he's right. Maybe you're right. But neither of you can take the law into your own hands. Principe had to be tried in a court of law. Tell me who is in the photograph."

Kallie stared at him and then closed her eyes briefly. When she reopened them, she again shook her head. "What would you do? Would he get a trial? Or would you bring him here? Or take him to Guantanamo Bay?"

Bennett ignored all that. "This is your opportunity to go home, Kallie. Tell me who's in the photograph. Is it Father McCarthy?"

Kallie was silent.

"Your grandmother's probably worried sick about you. Or maybe there's a boyfriend back at college who's getting anxious. Your family and friends need for you to do the right thing. Who's in the photograph?"

Kallie felt nauseous. They'd taken her cell phone and hadn't allowed her to make any phone calls. Veronica had told her that she'd call her grandmother and explain things. But that was a week and a half ago. Kallie usually talked to her grandmother at least once a week. If Kallie didn't get a chance to talk to her this week, her grandmother would indeed worry herself sick. But Kallie wasn't going to talk about the other person in the photograph. There were greater concerns. She remained perfectly still, her steely eyes reiterating her resolve.

CHAPTER THIRTY-FIVE

Officer Neil Noll could say one thing about the young college kid who was sitting in the metal-back client chair in front of his desk. He was persistent. Likely didn't have much commonsense—most of those egghead-types didn't, you know. But he was persistent. A persistent kid he could deal with, for Officer Noll had the patience of Job. He had to in this job. What the town of Bengate lacked by way of the career criminal, it made up for in droves with the stupid one. Although stupid had taken a nasty turn recently, he thought sourly, recalling the recent vandalism of the church over on Elm Street. Some ignorant fools had completely trashed the place, smashing out windows, tearing up and pissing on the Bibles and hymnals. It was no doubt some bored college or high school kids behind it. It was those types of kids he didn't like dealing with, the malicious ones who had no regard for life or limb. Kids with that kind of disrespect were difficult to get a handle on. They were too close to the evil side of things.

This was the fourth time this week that the Josh Levy kid had been to the Bengate Police Department and God only knew why. Noll's response was not going to change. Kallie Hunt was not missing. She hadn't been kidnapped. Her name had been included on the government's detainee list, which it sent to all law enforcement agencies who'd taken the time to sign up to receive it. He'd told this to the Levy kid the previous three times he'd been here. Neil had used the same robotic voice he used to tell deadbeats that their cars hadn't actually been stolen; they'd been repossessed. Huge difference. Most of them would feign ignorance anyway, knowing full well that they'd missed payments.

The department usually received the list of pending repos across the telefax about a week out from month's end. Most times, the owner was about three or four months in arrears, unless of course he'd been financed with a previous repo showing on his credit report. In which case, his vehicle was subject for takeover if expected payment was no more than a minute short of timely arrival. Most financial institutions sent their repo info to the police department for fear of a conscientious law enforcement officer stopping the repo man from reclaiming its property from the breaker of the financial promise, thinking it was being stolen. The government shared their detainee list for generally the same reason. No need for local police to waste valuable man hours searching for a kidnapped victim or missing person who wasn't really kidnapped or missing.

"They can't hold her forever without charging her with something," the kid said smugly. "She's got rights. You've got to do something."

"And what do you 'pose I do, son?" Noll asked. It was a pat response, as well. There was nothing he could do. And even if there was, Noll wasn't sure how eager he'd be to do it. The Hunt girl was probably one of them Jane Fonda liberal types and had likely gone and gotten herself labeled an 'enemy combatant,' which was the government's polite way of saying we got you by the balls now, or in the girl's case— the bra straps, you traitorous son or daughter of a bitch. And if that was the case, the government could hold the girl until pigs flew or hell froze over. And either length of time would be just fine by Noll.

"Can you at least tell me where she's being held?"

Noll's answer was short and clipped. "No."

The kid sighed heavily. "If you're not going to help, then I'll take this to the media. Kallie's a citizen. They can't get away with this."

See, now that was exactly what Noll had meant. The boy didn't have commonsense. All the book smarts in the world didn't mean a hill of beans if they didn't have commonsense. By damn, it was just essential for everyday living. "Now look, son. You can go and do that. Go on and call that troubleshooting reporter, Debbie Riddie or Riddle, or something or other..."

"Riddell," the kid corrected him.

"Yeah, that's her, Debbie Riddell. You can call her, and then what? The government is still not going to release your friend until they're damn good and ready. Because from what I understand, the 2001 Authorization for Use of Military Force, AUMF, Public Law One-oh-seven-forty, not only gave the president the right to go kick Iraq's ass, it also gave him the ability to hold any traitorous citizen-terrorist for as long as he damn well pleased. So call old Debbie Riddell if you don't mind wasting your time. But know this. Right now, no one but you and the government knows your friend is in custody under terroristic suspicions. If those suspicions prove wrong, then your friend is released and sent home. She's out what, a few days, a couple of weeks, maybe even a month or so. And maybe she has a little mental wear and tear for her troubles, but eventually she'll be just fine. Eventually, she'll return to normalcy. No harm, no foul. But if you go blabbing to the media, then everyone will know about that suspicion of terrorism. And even if the government decides that they'd been wrong and send her home, the taint of terroristic suspicion will hang over her like a dark fog. It may even hang over you. And some people, regardless of what the government may say later, will still believe your friend's a traitor and a terrorist. Because why else would the government have held her so long?" Noll leaned back in his chair mighty pleased with himself. It was always good to show one of the egghead-types what a good batch of commonsense looked like. He could tell the kid felt a little defeated, but he was probably nonetheless thinking awfully hard on what Noll had just told him. He'd slumped back in the metal-back, his chin nearly resting on his chest.

"Okay," he finally said. "Maybe you're right."

"Of course, I am," Noll said, confidently. "My advice to you is to go on home and let the wheels of justice roll a bit. In the end, everything will work out the way it's s'posed to."

* * *

After leaving the office, Josh drove forty minutes down Hwy 74, heading toward Maxton. He was going to Madame Isabel's house although, as far as he knew, she was still missing and likely dead. But if ever he needed a psychic or fortuneteller, it was now. Where had they taken Kallie? Not that he had a plan to free her even if he did know where she was. Still, if he just knew where they were stashing her, then just maybe....

It was a foolish idea, he finally told himself. Psychic abilities weren't likely to have transferred from wife to husband. And there was little chance her husband would turn over Madame Isabel's *Book of Origins*, if it in fact existed, to a complete stranger. He drove ahead a couple of miles before U-turning at an opening in the highway and heading back to Bengate.

He arrived back at his apartment at five minutes after six. It seemed to be a hopeless situation. He hated to admit it, but officer Noll had been right. He couldn't contact the media. Kallie wasn't a terrorist and eventually the government would arrive at that same conclusion. And when they did, Kallie had every right to live her life as normally as possible and not under the taint of terroristic suspicion. But to be fair, living normally might not exactly be in Kallie's cards. There was something unique about her, something even beyond her remembering ability. He could sense it.

He powered up his computer and briefly considered going into one of the occult chat rooms. But he decided against it. There was still something he didn't know about Kallie and eternal return, but he knew that he'd gleaned all he could from the chat rooms and the internet. He stared blankly at the screen for a few moments before powering the computer back down.

He walked over to the loveseat, plopping himself down on it, his feet dangling off one end. It was not the most comfortable position, but he was tired and not thinking clearly. He only needed to catch a couple of z's and then he'd be able to tackle this thing with a full head of steam. There was a way to help Kallie. He just hadn't figured it out yet.

He'd just about drifted off when he heard someone knocking at his door. Reluctantly, he pulled himself away from sleep's edge and walked groggily over to the door. He leaned against it without bothering to look through the peephole. "Yeah?"

"It's Cedric."

Josh opened the door to find both Cedric and Veronica standing there. Rubbing his eyes with both fists, he nodded them inside.

"Dude, you look like you haven't slept in weeks," Cedric said.

"I feel like it, too," Josh said. He sat down at the kitchen-nook table, indicating for them to do likewise on the loveseat. "I won't be able to sleep until I find out where Kallie is. Bengate Police will only say that she's in the government's custody. But they won't tell me where."

"I know where she is," Veronica offered.

Josh's eyes widened as he looked at her, and then to Cedric who was nodding his head, confirming. "How do you know?"

"My uncle," Veronica said, dropping her head.

"Yeah, apparently Kallie had left Maggie a note saying that she was off to take part in an onsite memory project and if there were any questions she could call Veronica, which Maggie did the next day. Veronica confirmed the project and told her that it would only last a couple of days, but after Kallie hadn't come back after a week, Maggie got worried."

"Why wasn't I told about this?"

"I haven't seen you," Cedric said. "Our next group session isn't until next week. Maggie didn't find out you'd stopped by the house asking about Kallie until late last week. Her housemate's message had only said that Kallie's boyfriend had stopped by. Maggie assumed she was referring to Seth. Anyway, when Veronica didn't return any of her calls, she asked me what I knew about the memory project. Of course, I didn't know anything about it. So I went over to Veronica's apartment to find out."

But Josh had been looking at Veronica when he'd asked the question. Veronica stared intently at the floor beneath her feet. Finally, she looked up and met his eyes. "Look, I'm sorry, okay? My uncle told me he needed to ask her about the UCB Center bombing. He told me Kallie had information about it. That she was somehow involved. He showed me pictures. I thought she'd only be gone a couple of days."

"They can hold her indefinitely," Josh said, his nostrils flaring. "She can't call anybody. Her grandmother has probably worried herself to death."

"I'm sorry," Veronica said. Her eyes started to tear.

Josh waved a dismissive hand. "Never mind that now. Where is she?"

Veronica sniffled and wiped at her eyes with the back of her hands. "Fort Bragg."

CHAPTER THIRTY-SIX

At 8:50 the next morning, Josh stood outside the late Professor Sampson's history class. The class was temporarily being taught by Liz Suggs, one of Josh's former classmates. Josh hadn't seen her much since they'd both finished undergrad. He'd heard that she'd decided to go to law school, but had delayed it in order to work, hoping to save enough to take a huge bite off the tuition.

Seth was the next to last student to leave the room. Josh stepped away from the room's entrance, not wanting to draw Liz's attention. He knew she probably had another class to teach on the heels of this one and most likely wouldn't have time to chitchat, but he didn't want to take the chance. He'd love to catch up with her, but he wanted to hit the road as soon as possible. If he'd known where Seth lived or had had his number, they could have left for Fort Bragg either late last night or first thing this morning. But all he'd known was that Seth was in Kallie's MWF 8 o'clock class. He'd meant to get here before the class had started, but he'd overslept.

Seth, looking surprised when he saw Josh standing near the steps, mumbled a "Hello" and started to walk past him.

"Wait," Josh said. "Do you feel like a road trip?"

At a quarter to ten, they left Seth's apartment and hit highway 74, blowing past the Bengate Police Department's white-stone four room building just as a collared priest walked inside it. They'd decided to take Josh's Taurus. Seth's

Mustang was newer and faster, but offered little in the way of a backseat. Although they had no idea how they would accomplish it, they had no intentions of coming back to Bengate without Kallie.

Josh had packed several days' worth of clothes and encouraged Seth to do the same. While Seth packed, Josh told him all he knew about Kallie's current situation. He included his conversations with officer Noll, stressing the officer's warnings about involving the media, and ending with what Veronica and Cedric had told him last night. Josh and Seth agreed that Kallie's grandmother should be told what was going on. Seth had met the grandmother once before and knew how to get to her house, which was the main reason Josh had wanted Seth to ride with him in the first place. That, and the fact that he believed Kallie and Seth had broken up prematurely. He remembered how Kallie looked whenever she talked about Seth. Her face lit up. She'd been really into him. And now, despite Seth's attempts at nonchalance, Josh could see the same thing in Seth. He missed her. Josh suspected that part of the couple's problems may have had something to do with Kallie's remembering ability and Seth not knowing anything about it. If that was the case, he hoped that they could work through it. Regardless, he wasn't going to mention anything about Kallie's ability to Seth, as he didn't believe it was his place to do so.

They rode in silence for a while, lost in their individual thoughts. When they were about an hour outside Lumberton, Seth spoke, "Do you think she'll want to see me?"

"Yeah, I do," Josh said. He wanted to add more, but decided not to. Even that short statement was pure speculation. He hadn't spoken with Kallie to confirm it, but he genuinely believed it. And when he looked over at Seth who'd gotten quiet again, he saw a young man who genuinely wanted to believe it.

The highway sign stating that Maxton was only twelve miles away came up before Josh was ready for it. He knew they'd reach the town before Lumberton and that he would go to Madame Isabel's house once they did. He just hadn't figured out how he would explain the little deviation in plans to Seth without adding something about Kallie's remembering ability.

"What gives?" Seth asked after Josh turned off the main highway.

"Just got a quick stop to make," Josh said, kicking the proverbial can five minutes down the road.

The husband's old Chevy truck was parked desolately in the driveway. Josh parked the Taurus alongside the road in front of the house. Even from here, he could feel the sadness hanging over the house. He opened the car door to get out.

"Who lives here?" Seth asked.

Josh ignored the question. "Wait here."

It took ten minutes for Madame Isabel's husband to come to the door. Josh had started to leave despite the presence of the truck in the driveway and the sound of movement coming from inside the house. Maybe the old man didn't want to be bothered. But at that moment, the front door creaked open.

The man looked curiously at Josh for a long moment before an expression of recognition creased his face and he smiled faintly. As the man continued looking at Josh, it was only then that Josh realized that he didn't know Madame Isabel's husband's name. Josh and the husband were never formally introduced, having met under unusual circumstances. Her real name was Bella Mae Raiden. But Josh didn't know if Raiden was a maiden or married name.

"Hello, sir," Josh said. "I don't know if you remember me." The man looked much older now than he had before. Evidently he'd worried himself sick about his wife's disappearance. Even with his light smile, Josh could tell there'd been no good news concerning her whereabouts.

"I do remember you," the husband finally said. "She said you'd be back. And you are."

"Who said I'd be back?" Josh asked with rising excitement. Without thinking, he tried looking past the husband into the house. "Is Madame Isabel here?"

The husband stepped outside onto the front porch, looking past Josh and toward the Taurus. "But she said there'd be two of you. Where's the other one?"

CHAPTER THIRTY-SEVEN

"Dang if that preacher ain't called you right," Noll said. He leaned back in his chair, regarding Farther McCarthy from head to toe.

"What do you mean?" McCarthy asked.

"He'd said you'd come around here. A Catholic priest, wearing the clerical collar." He lightly brushed the back of his hand across his neck as he said this. "And by George, here you are in the flesh."

"When did he tell you this?"

"The other week shortly after it happened. He didn't seem too agitated about it all though. Took it all in stride. Me, I felt the devil himself at work in the place. The church, I mean. The things those kids did...."

"Kids?" McCarthy said.

"Sure it was kids," Noll said, his face contorting for emphasis. "Couldn't have been anyone but kids. Yeah, I know their parents would say that their young'uns weren't as bad as it appeared. Will say that maybe they'd been a little bored and had gotten a little carried away. But to me, if you go pissing on the Holy Book, then you're as bad as it appears, and worse!"

"Do you know who vandalized the church?"

"No sir, I hadn't got the slightest clue. But we've got other churches here in Bengate. And believe me, sure as I'm living and breathing, those little hell rats are going to do it again. The devil's in their blood, you see. They won't be able to help themselves. And when they do, you can best believe I'm going to nail their hides to the wall. Now that's a campaign promise you can make book on."

McCarthy simply nodded his head. "Did Reverend Swag tell you where he was going?"

"Nope, he didn't and I didn't rightly ask. But he'll be back soon."

"How do you know that?"

"One reason is that he told me that he would be. And secondly," Noll said, as he reached under his desk, pulling out a set of keys. He handed the keys to McCarthy. "He's expecting to meet with you. He said there's something he wants you to see in his chambers. He said it's on the computer. I guess it was a small miracle those hellacious devils didn't go trashing about in there."

McCarthy took the keys, looking at them suspiciously as he turned them over slowly in his hand.

"That big one opens the side door to the church," Noll said. "The others are to his chambers and what not. He said you'd be able to figure it out. I expect you'll be safe over there. The ones that did all that damage won't likely make a return trip over there anytime soon. The place is still a mess."

The church smelled awful. McCarthy was reminded of the time a few years back when one of his parishioners, a twenty-six year old husband and father, had lost both his wife and three year old son in a deadly vehicle crash. The family's Dodge Caravan was a mangled total loss. The insurance company, worried about storage fees and its own bottom line, had requested that the husband get over to the salvage yard ASAP to remove any personal effects from the vehicle so they could move the salvage to their own storage facility. Devastated by the loss and without family and friends in the area, the young man had asked McCarthy to accompany him to the tow yard. The young man hadn't known how much seeing the family vehicle in its current condition would affect him. There were only a few things left in the van, all of which were of sentimental value only, some pictures, CDs, and a few of the son's toys. Included amongst the items was a small sippy cup of milk that had spoiled. As soon as the young man opened the van door, the rancid odor of spoiled milk mixed with the scent of the young wife's dried blood on the dash panel had rushed out to McCarthy, who'd been standing a few feet back. How the young man had withstood the odorous onslaught, McCarthy would never know. But he himself had doubled over and vomited.

The smell inside the sanctuary was similar to that, but worse somehow, as if someone had thrown in some rotting fruit for good measure. McCarthy walked quickly to the pastor's chambers. The door to the chambers was closed, but not locked. McCarthy entered and discovered, to his pleasant surprise, that the odor didn't reach this far. He closed the door behind him.

The computer was atop Swag's desk. McCarthy sat at the desk and powered the computer on. As he waited for the computer to go through its paces, he glanced around the chambers. It was in pristine order. How nice of the vandals to have spared this room, he thought sarcastically. Scanning the room, his eyes came to a rest on the file cabinet and its metallic lock sitting in the far corner of the room. Suddenly he became aware of the keys in his hands, wondering absently if he'd have need of them.

The desktop came up without need of password entry. There was only one icon and it was aptly titled, VIDEO.

He clicked on it.

CHAPTER THIRTY-EIGHT

The husband's name was Jack Monroe. And he'd insisted that Josh go and get Seth from the car immediately. Seth, though a bit curious as to whose house it was and why they were there, hadn't wanted to get out of the car, only doing so when Josh told him that the reason they were there had something to do with Kallie.

But thirty minutes into Mr. Monroe's spiel, Seth began to shake his head in disbelief. There were no such things as time-cycles. You got one shot at this life thing, one shot. That was it. He looked over at Josh, who was literally sitting on the edge of the couch, hanging on every word this old nutcase was saying. When Mr. Monroe finished talking, he sat back and regarded them both as if he'd just dropped some serious knowledge on them. And if the look of fascination plastered across Josh's face was any indication, he'd bought what the old man was selling hook, line, and sinker.

Apparently pleased with himself, Mr. Monroe stood up. "Now, I'll go and get the book."

"You mean you have an actual copy?" Josh asked eagerly.

"Copy?" Mr. Monroe said, scrunching his face. "Heck no. I have the original manuscript." He left the room to retrieve it.

Seth thought Josh would pee himself. Josh slapped the couch excitedly and looked at him as if Christmas had come early. "You don't seriously think..." he stopped himself. Of course Josh seriously thought, which was why he was acting like a gushing schoolgirl in the first place.

"What's the problem?" Josh asked.

"You're seriously asking me that?"

"Yeah, I am."

"Kallie's holed up on some military base. We have no idea how we're going to get her out. Her grandmother's probably near death with worry. And here we are wasting time, listening to some old coot talking about his dead wife's visions. Now don't get me wrong. I'm sorry that she's gone. And I understand the old fella's probably lonely and missing her. But we shouldn't be encouraging him. Kallie is just Kallie. She's not this remembering thing the old guy's been talking about. Maybe people have premonitions. I'll grant you that. And no, I don't understand how those work either. But I know it's not because we've been here before. That's just not possible."

"Why are you being so close-minded about this?"

Seth rolled his eyes. "Just because I'm not willing to believe this impossible nonsense doesn't mean I'm being close-minded. I'll admit it'll probably make a nice psychological discussion one day. But not right now. We should be thinking about Kallie."

Josh stood up and pointed an accusatory finger at Seth. "You are being close-minded and this is about Kallie. And you'd better seriously consider how you really feel about her and decide for yourself if you want to continue on this journey. Because like it or not, she believed in this impossible nonsense."

Seth had to hand it to him. It was an impassioned plea. And Josh had to have his reasons for giving it. But Seth knew Kallie. She hadn't mentioned anything to him about this so-called remembering ability or time-cycles. And he suspected the reason why was because she ultimately knew it was complete nonsense. Sitting around with your philosophical friends, expounding on the ramblings of dead philosophers and adding your old two cents worth on the ways of the universe was one thing. Young people did it all the time. But there came a time for serious thinking, a time to look the facts of life dead in the face and accept them for what they were. There was one shot at life. One. But he didn't say any of this to Josh because he understood that it wasn't his mind that was closed. It was Josh's.

"Here it is," Mr. Monroe said, reentering the room. He was carrying a bound sheaf of papers. "The original *Book of Origins.*" He handed it to Josh as if holding out a newborn baby. "Be careful with it. Bella said the papers were alive. Sometimes things in the future changed and she would make adjustments. It was rare, but it happened. And whenever it did, she either added pages to the book or erased and rewrote. I never understood her process and didn't question it. She did the entire book in shorthand, all seven hundred and thirty pages." He paused, looking intently at Josh. "But you'll be able to understand it. It had been dictated to her in a dream by an angel."

Josh took the bound pages from him, holding them in his hands for a long minute, staring mesmerizingly at the cover.

Seth rolled his eyes again and looked away.

* * *

McCarthy felt compelled to view the video again. It was his third time. It was an action-packed fifteen-minute film. The first time he'd watched it, he wondered how Swag had gotten the time and money to make it. It was definitely professionally done with lavish special effects. It was like something made out in Hollywood. But on his second viewing, he realized the how of the video didn't matter. It was the what, the why, and the when. After the third time, McCarthy's mind became as clear as spotless glass and he realized that his initial concerns about Swag had been ill placed and unjustified. The young man was pure salt. The purest salt of the earth. McCarthy x'ed out of the video and then powered down the computer. He didn't need to view it again. It was now deeply embedded in his mind. Even now, he could still see Swag's piercing eyes and hear his melodious voice. And now he knew the truth, the real truth. It was no longer hidden. Lucifer had been wronged. The powerful film had depicted it so clearly. The fallen angel had been unjustly deceived and falsely accused. But this time, things were going to be made right. Wrongs would be corrected. McCarthy stood up and walked over to the filing cabinet. He felt a strong sense of purpose and pride. He would have a part in the correction process. Lucifer was entrusting him with the ceremony! Oh great day! He held up the keys in his hand. The middle one would unlock the filing cabinet. The book containing the marrying words was in the top drawer. He pulled it out and whatever had rested on top of it dropped near his feet. He reached down and picked it up. It was a little plastic baggie. Holding it in front of his face, he saw the pair of earplugs. Absently, he put the curious little package in his pants pocket and then returned to his seat at Swag's desk with the book of ceremonial rituals. Slowly, he pulled back the cover and turned pages. The words to the wedding ceremony of angels and demons were on page 620.

It would be his second wedding ceremony performed this month.

CHAPTER THIRTY-NINE

They arrived at Kallie's grandmother's house shortly before eight o'clock. Josh had let Seth drive from Madame Isabel's house since Seth had been to Kallie's childhood home once before and knew the way. Plus, it gave Josh a chance to read the *Book of Origins*. He'd read it in the near darkness of the car, using only the soft illumination from the reading light located in the blinder. Mr. Monroe said it was his wife's wish that Josh and Seth be given the manuscript. Josh knew that revelation bothered Seth. How could anyone know what he was going to do before he'd actually done it? Seth couldn't grasp the concept of remembering and refused to try, dismissing it as utter nonsense. But Josh knew that the thing that really turned Seth's head was the part about the demons. Josh admitted to himself that it had probably been too much for Seth to take in one sitting. Josh hadn't wanted Seth to hear any of it anyway since it involved Kallie. She should've been the one to tell Seth. But time and circumstance had prevented that. Besides, she would probably be the only one who could get Seth to believe any of it anyway.

When Mr. Monroe had insisted that their stop at his house had already been known and that he'd been anxiously awaiting their arrival, Seth sucked his teeth noisily. Seth told them that life, for the most part, was a series of spontaneous events strung together. There existed either things of pure chance or things resulting from careful preparation, like beautiful flowers sprouting from the planting of seeds. But otherwise, he said plaintively, "The only thing one could

truly predict about life was that it was truly unpredictable."
But Mr. Monroe had only smiled politely and continued on
with his story, telling them that he'd been like a child
listening to bedtime stories when his wife Bella talked of the
future, sometimes even asking her to repeat the story. Seth
folded his arms across his chest and stared at the ceiling.

Twice on the ride to Kallie's grandmother's house he'd
mumbled his disapproval of Josh's detour to Madame
Isabel's. Firstly, complaining about the time wasted listening
to that crap about eternal return and demons. The second
mumbling was about how it was too late for them to come
knocking at an elderly lady's door. "Ms. Hunt most likely
wouldn't even open it." Josh considered Seth's first point
highly debatable. But his second point was immediately
proved categorically wrong. The door opened before he
could rap it a second time.

The old woman stood in the doorway. She'd been crying.
Even in the combined dimmed illumination of the porch light
and half-moon, Josh could see her tears, stringing down her
face like shiny gray streaks of silver. "Oh Seth," she cried
out, reaching up and hugging him around the neck. "Is Kallie
with you? Tell me she's with you! Tell me she's all right."

Seth folded his head atop hers. "No ma'am." The words
sounded as if they were being piped in from the bowels of the
earth. "She's not with me."

Her knees buckled and then she collapsed into Seth's
arms. Josh helped him take her to the living room where they
laid her down gently on the sofa. Seth hurriedly left the
room, coming back almost immediately with a glass of water.

"Here, Ms. Hunt. Drink this," Seth said.

She lifted her head slightly and took a tiny sip from the
glass before waving it away. "What happened to my
grandbaby?"

Seth told her everything he knew, but purposefully and
perhaps smartly, left out the parts about Mr. Monroe,
remembering, and demons. However, Josh could see

realization trying to nip at Seth's core of disbelief during the telling of the government's involvement. A puzzled look had crossed his face when he tried to explain that part to Ms. Hunt. Josh could imagine the question Seth was asking himself. Why would the government believe that Kallie would know anything about a terrorist attack? Simply because she'd had a vision of some sort? Surely, the government was made up of smarter people than him. But just as the seed of doubt tried to surface, Seth just as quickly and stubbornly pushed it back down.

"What would the government want with my baby?" Ms. Hunt asked.

"We don't know exactly," Josh said, before realizing he hadn't been formally introduced. "I'm Josh Levy, by the way. I'm a friend of your granddaughter's."

Seth pleaded with his eyes for Josh not to say anything about demons or Kallie's so-called remembering ability. It wasn't necessary. Josh had no intention of delving into those waters with Ms. Hunt, figuring the woman presently had enough to wrap her head around.

"We're going to the base in the morning and demand that they let us see her," Seth said.

There was determination in his voice and it seemed to spark something in Ms. Hunt. She sat up on the sofa and reached for the glass of water that Seth had placed on the coffee table. A slight frown crossed her face for a moment at the slight condensation ring left on the table. She took a long gulp and swallowed noisily. She pulled a coaster from the stack next to the table's flower centerpiece and placed the glass on it. She looked at Seth. "I appreciate you willing to do that. I know how much Kallie means to you. But your demands won't mean a thing to the military. They only understand hierarchy, or chain of command. My late husband used to say that all the time. He was a veteran of the Second World War."

"So you're saying there's nothing we can do?" Seth said. He sounded defeated, a complete turnabout from the moment before.

"No," Ms. Hunt said. "You just have to follow the rules of hierarchy."

"But who should we call?" Josh chimed in. "The president?"

"Well, I don't know him personally," Ms. Hunt said, "but I do know someone. And he's very close to Kallie."

*   *   *

At ten o'clock that night, Kallie was finally taken back to her room. She'd been grilled for eight straight hours with Bennett hurling question after question at her. But after the first hour, it became apparent that all he'd really wanted to know was the name of the man in the photograph. Every question he asked eventually circled back to that one. It became monotonous. It was his personal version of congress' historically repetitious, "What do you know and when did you know it?" She surmised that he suspected it was Father Frank McCarthy's figure in the photograph, but was unable to prove it. After a while, even Bennett became bored with his charade and sent her back to her room, though with a promise to pursue the same line of questioning bright and early in the morning.

She couldn't wait.

*   *   *

Across town, Johnny Swag checked into a Motel 6. It was an older one. The exterior refinish of the place was a flaky white and blue, some of which had peeled off and now flickered in the wind like broken off, fake painted fingernails. The place's cement stairs looked worn, as if giants had spent centuries trampling up and down them. The interior of his room was only slightly better, although there was a large dark stain on the carpet in front of the television. He'd checked in at a quarter to eleven. And from the looks of the clientele checking in at the same time, Swag guessed that no one came to the motel for its ambiance, which was fine by him. He felt amongst his elements. Personal gratification was definitely the ticket. After he'd signed his name on the registration card, he made eye contact with a lady of the night and had thought what the hay. He had almost another full day to kill.

* * *

The Hunt house had four bedrooms, including the guest bedroom where Seth slept the night. Josh spent the majority of the night in the living room, his nose buried deep in the *Book of Origins*. But eventually sleep conquered him as well, and he succumbed to it from his spot on the sofa. During the night, Ms. Hunt brought out a quilt and laid it atop him.

The next morning, the three of them awoke at five o'clock sharp, neither needing the aid of an alarm nor a nudge from the others. Anxiety and anticipation of what the day would or would not bring yanked them all back to fearful wakefulness.

As soon as her feet touched floor, Ms. Hunt washed up in the bathroom and headed for the kitchen. Not long after, the house was filled with the sweet smells of scrambled eggs, percolating grits, fried bacon, and toasting bread. The scintillating scent tickled Josh's nose, reminding him of his own childhood home. Still, his appetite had been suppressed by his concern for Kallie and the task of what lay ahead of them. But he scoffed the breakfast down anyway for fear of offending Ms. Hunt. He could tell that seeing them both eat so heartily comforted her somehow, temporarily masking the fact that her granddaughter was thirty miles close, but under military lock and key, and the only hope for her immediate release was dependent upon the tender mercy and political ability of the girl's estranged father.

After he managed to swallow the last of his second plate of eggs, Josh pushed back from the table and placed the finally empty plate in the kitchen sink. He picked up the bottle of dish detergent and started to squirt some into the sink.

Ms. Hunt was still sitting at the table. When she saw what he was up to, her nostrils flared. "Drop that detergent where you stand. I'll take care of the dishes."

Josh turned to her. "I don't mind, really. It's not fair for you to cook us breakfast and then have to wash dishes."

Ms. Hunt softened a little, flaring only one nostril. "You're a well-mannered young man and I appreciate the offer. But I'll do my own dishes, thank you very much. Now, would you kindly back away from my sink?" Her eyes fixed sternly on his and the other nostril slowly began flexing again.

Seth stuffed the last of a bacon strip into his mouth. "Better do as she says, Josh. I've been down that road before. It ain't pretty."

Josh slowly backed away from the sink. Almost instantly, Seth and Ms. Hunt broke out in fierce laughter. Josh looked at them oddly for a moment. He smiled hesitantly and then started laughing right along with them. The three of them laughed as if they'd never heard anything so funny. They held their stomachs and sniffed back laughter-induced snot. When their laughter finally chuckled to a stop, Josh wiped a tear from his eye. He knew the reason behind the laughter. It had been strictly diversionary, a futile attempt at masking the improbable plot of the foolhardy. Their plan was a difficult one at best. Asking a sitting United States congressman to intervene in a Homeland Security matter related to national security was unwise. The congressman would likely laugh in their faces anyway, even if they were interceding on his daughter's behalf.

The goodbyes were short and sweet. And so was Ms. Hunt's request. "Bring my grandbaby home."

Seth kissed her on the cheek and said, "We will."

It was a bold promise and one he would undoubtedly do everything in his power to fulfill. But the odds were stacked against them. Josh, after once again turning over the control of the Taurus to Seth, wished he himself could muster a more positive attitude. But he was under no illusions. Getting Kallie freed was going to take a Herculean effort. He looked at Seth and then closed his eyes as Seth steered the Taurus onto the interstate, praying silently. After praying for traveling mercies for their trip down I-95, he stepped it up a notch and prayed that the gates of Fort Bragg would open and the powers-that-be would release Kallie without Seth and him having to do anything greater than simply showing up. If you're going to pray, he thought after opening his eyes, might as well swing for the fences. But barring the gift of the miraculous home run, he'd accept the softening of Kallie's father's heart and a subsequent increase in the congressman's political powers.

CHAPTER FORTY

There was no miraculous home run. They couldn't even get onto the base. A military checkpoint had been set up at the end of the road leading to it, blocking all civilian vehicles from entering. Seth and Josh didn't have the proper identification or any official reason to be there. The guard, without batting an eye, ordered Seth to back the Taurus up and U-turn it the hell away from there. His steely glare fixed on Seth as Ms. Hunt's had earlier fixed on Josh. But no laughter followed the guard's words.

Josh had figured it would be a long shot getting on base, but he'd wanted to at least try. It would've been great if they could have gotten Kallie released without having to involve her father. Even though her grandmother had initially described Kallie's father as someone that "was very close to Kallie," it was clear to Josh that the feeling wasn't reciprocated by Kallie. She talked about her mother all the time; but had barely mentioned a father.

Congress wasn't currently in session; meaning Representative Ander Cleaver of the 7th congressional district was back at his residence in Wilmington. Ms. Hunt had the address and phone number. She'd called several times, but had continually gotten voicemail. She didn't leave a message since she didn't know whose ears would hear it or who was responsible for returning the congressman's messages. They didn't have time to wait to give the congressman the heads up of their arrival. They would have to make a cold appearance at his house. It would take two hours to drive there.

Seth continuously tapped the car radio's scan button, trying to find a station to his liking. He finally decided on one playing a Katy Perry song. Josh went back to reading the *Book of Origins*. Forty minutes into the ride, the music began sounding monotonous, so a frustrated Seth turned the radio off. After thirty minutes of radio silence, Josh said, "Listen to this." He read from the *Book of Origins*. "Pride cometh before the fall with lust nipping closely at its heel. Lucifer was the most beautiful of all the angels. Even his speaking voice had been like the playing of a harp. After God, he was the most respected in all of Heaven. His place as God's trusted protector of the throne was eternally assured. But Lucifer wanted greater things. His desire was to occupy the throne itself. But God was eternal, an everlasting spirit. There would be no succession. Lucifer thus set his sights on what he considered a more reasonable, if less desired, expectation—a sharing of God's throne. But God had no intention of sharing his throne with a subject, no matter how beautiful or wise the subject was. God, the first being, created from nothing, yet the Creator of everything, was as compassionate as he was powerful. God, considering Lucifer's feelings and his standing amongst the other angels, wanted to help Lucifer to save face. Therefore, God created his son, the Savior, and then announced in a glorious heavenly ceremony that the Son and not Lucifer would ascend the throne. God believed that the Savior's ascendency to the throne would not be received as a negative reflection on Lucifer who would still maintain his place of leadership within Heaven's hierarchy. The Son follows the Father. It was the natural order of things.

"But Lucifer did not consider God's naming of the Son as his rightful partner and heir as a compassionate one. Lucifer felt he was still being ridiculed by the other angels. He felt slighted, and he considered God's act as the ultimate slap to Lucifer's face and he openly complained about it. Eventually, Lucifer decided to show his displeasure at God's decision by

becoming a pain in God's side. Initially, his acts of
disobedience were akin to those of a rebellious teenager. He
didn't completely disobey God's rules; he just bent them at
will, doing his ritualistic duties either late or out of God's
order. But even those small acts of disobedience were
noticeable amongst the angels who'd all always followed
God's rules to the exact letter." Josh paused for a second and
looked at Seth who seemed to be listening to the story. So he
continued reading. "The second in command of the angels
was Kali (he pronounced it as Kah-lee). She was also the
second most beautiful of the angels, though some had argued
that she was even more beautiful than Lucifer. Kali saw
Lucifer's acts of disobedience in a different light. He was the
bad boy."

"Wait a minute," Seth said, interrupting Josh's reading.
"You're not going to say that this Kali being had a bad boy
fetish?"

"Yes," Josh said, "a serious one." He started to read from
the book again.

"Wait a minute," Seth said. "Give me the cliff notes
version."

Josh closed the book and turned to Seth. "Well, the two of
them, Lucifer and Kali, began a relationship."

"Did they fall in love?" Seth asked, with obvious interest.

"No," Josh said. "I don't believe it was love. It was more
like lust."

"Lust? You mean they had sex in Heaven?"

"Not in the way you're thinking," Josh said. "You're
thinking of it in human terms. But sex for man was created
for procreation purposes. Angels do not procreate. There's no
need to."

"Oh," Seth said.

"Anyway," Josh continued, "Kali started becoming
derelict in her own duties. Eventually it was brought to God's
attention and he called her in, strongly reprimanding her. But

as any earthly father knows, telling a girl not to see a boy because he's bad for her often has the opposite effect."

Seth nodded his head knowingly. "She continued seeing him."

"Yeah," Josh said, "but Lucifer's little acts of disobedience soon turned to out and out revolution. Angels eventually had to choose sides."

"And which side did Kali choose?" Seth asked.

"Unfortunately," Josh said, "originally the wrong one. Lost in lust, she hadn't seen how dangerous her relationship with Lucifer had become. Lucifer led his troops into battle against God's angels and had them on the ropes. It wasn't until that point that Kali's eyes were finally opened. She rejoined God's angels and with her skills and leadership, Lucifer's army was finally defeated and he was ultimately ousted from Heaven."

"So she came to her senses in a nick of time?" Seth said.

"Yes and no," Josh said. "God was pleased with what she'd been able to do, but her act of disobedience could not go unpunished. She, too, was ousted from Heaven. But God, being the compassionate being He is, gave her another opportunity to prove herself. He sent her down to earth in the form of a woman."

"What woman?" Seth asked eagerly, though it seemed he already knew the answer.

"The first woman," Josh said. "Eve."

Seth shuffled noticeably, obviously knowing how the rest of the story ended. They rode in silence for a while, and then Seth asked, "I know you read that story to me for a reason. So what does it have to do with Kallie?"

"Everything," Josh said. "Kallie is Eve."

* * *

Shortly after one o'clock, Seth flowed behind a black BMW into the Porter Ridge Subdivision. "That was easy," he said. Porter Ridge was the most exclusive gated community in Wilmington, and the BMW's driver hadn't once looked behind him before entering. "They might as well snatch the gate off its hinges if the residents aren't going to be mindful of who's coming behind them." He paused a hiccup's moment before adding bitterly, "Of course they could get a couple of those grunts from Fort Bragg to man the fences."

He parked the Taurus halfway up the driveway. There were no other cars present, although they could've been parked inside the garage. The two of them got out of the car and with a strong sense of purpose, marched right up to the front steps.

Josh rang the doorbell and a moment later, a heavily accented female voice came over the speaker. "May I help you?"

"We're here to see Congressman Cleaver," Seth said.

There was a moment of silence and then the woman spoke again, "The congressman will be at his New Haven office location tomorrow morning around nine o'clock. You won't need an appointment. He'll meet with as many constituents as possible on a first come, first served basis."

"Listen," Seth said. "This is important. We need to see the congressman now."

"Unfortunately, the congressman doesn't see constituents at his residence."

Seth sighed. "It's extremely important."

"Sir, you have to leave, or I'll be forced to call the police."

Seth pounded his hand into his fist. "Do whatever you have to do, but we're not..."

Josh held up a finger, cutting him off. "We understand," he said softly into the speaker mic, "but before you call the police, could you please inform the congressman that we're here on behalf of his daughter, Kallie. She's in serious trouble."

They waited on the steps for several additional minutes. Then finally, the front door opened. A young Hispanic woman invited them inside and escorted them to the living room. She told them that the congressman was on a conference call and would see them as soon as the call was over. Josh sat down in an antique wingback, while Seth sat down on the couch. A few moments after the young woman left the room, Seth turned to Josh. "You don't seriously believe Eve has been reincarnated as Kallie, do you?"

"What? You don't believe in reincarnation?"

"Does anyone?" Seth asked sarcastically. "I mean other than probably Buddhists."

"Actually," Josh said, "there are some sects of Judaism that still believe in it, as well. Christians don't necessarily believe in it despite evidence of it in the Bible."

"Evidence, what evidence?"

"I don't suppose you read the Bible much," Josh said.

"I read it more than you think. My father's a Baptist minister and I'm minoring in religion. And no, I haven't decided if I'm going to follow in my father's footsteps."

"I wasn't going to ask."

"Sorry, most people do."

"Anyway, are you familiar with Balak?"

"Yes," Seth said. "He was the king of Moab who tried to hire Balaam to curse Israel."

Impressed, Josh smiled and nodded his head. "Right. The story's in the book of Numbers. If you recall, there's a speaking donkey involved in the story."

"A speaking donkey, so?" Seth said. And then there was realization. "Oh, speaking donkey, reincarnation. I get it."

"Yeah, it's amazing how Christians can read the verse and not even consider how a donkey would be speaking. I could show other examples, too…" his voice trailed off as he looked toward the entranceway to the living room.

At that moment, a baby was crying from somewhere upstairs. Josh stepped slowly in the direction of the wails and

suddenly felt a strange sense of déjà vu. This room, or was it
this very moment, seemed somehow familiar to him. "I've
been here before," he said quietly.

"Huh," Seth said.

"This house, this room, I feel like I've been here before."
Seth stared at him. "Déjà vu? You're kidding, right?"

"I'm not exactly sure," Josh said, and stood up, looking
anxiously about the room. It was a vague feeling; but
nonetheless it was there, simmering beneath the surface of
his memory; although he was certain he'd never been here
before. How could he have? He was standing in the middle of
the living room of a sitting United States congressman.
Yet...with a sense of increased knowing, he walked slowly
out of the living room and headed toward the stairs and the
baby's cries. At the bottom of the stairs, the cries were even
louder. Glancing tentatively behind him, he slowly started
up. The nursery would be on the left side of the upstairs
landing. He knew that as well as he knew about the ink-dot
birthmark on his right forearm. He stuck his head inside the
room, seeing the back of the young woman who'd earlier
escorted them into the house and the living room. She moved
in a slow rhythmical dance, holding the baby while singing
softly to it. Josh, hearing the soft gurgled sounds of the
baby's return to contentment, eased back out of the room.

The room beside the nursery was the master suite. A huge
four-poster squatted in the center of the room. To the left of
the bed were his and her walk-in closets. The sight of the
closets unleashed the full memory of this particular time and
place, and he realized that he'd in fact never been here before.
This was the actual room to the one he'd designed on the
computer to fit Kallie's description of the room she'd virtually
visited on the day he'd first met her. It was her father's room,
a room in a house that she'd never physically been in, at least
not yet in this lifetime. He walked over to the dresser drawer
and picked up the framed picture. It was of the congressman,
his wife, and their three kids. The picture was the companion

to the one an angered Kallie had mentally-simulated and sent virtually smashing to the floor.

"What are you doing in here?" An anxious tenor rushed into the room from behind him, almost causing him to drop the picture; but he managed to secure it in his grip just in time before gently placing it back on the dresser and turning to face the voice.

It was Congressman Cleaver.

"I asked you a question, son. What are you doing in this room?"

Caught off guard, Josh stammered. "We...well, I'm not sure I can explain it."

"I believe you'd better think of something pretty damn fast. But first, you need to remove yourself from my bedroom."

Josh stepped gingerly past the congressman into the hallway where he waited while the congressman gave the room a quick once over. Apparently unable to determine if anything was missing, he pointed Josh toward the stairs. Josh walked quickly to the stairs and down to the living room. Seth was in the same spot as before.

Congressman Cleaver followed him into the living room. "Now what were you doing in my bedroom?"

"What? Dude," Seth said. "Man, that is so, not cool."

"I know it looks crazy, sir. But, it's related to your daughter, Kallie. You see, that room, this house. Kallie had described it to me in explicit detail."

"Man, seriously," Seth said. "Have you totally lost your mind? Kallie has never been here. We seriously don't have time for this."

But the expression on Cleaver's face had softened. "Wait, let him finish."

A stunned Seth said, "I do not believe this."

Cleaver indicated for Josh to sit down on the couch beside Seth while he himself sat down in the brown leather wingback.

Josh sat down and started talking slowly. "You see, sir. We have this virtual imaging software, which we use in our memory projects. Your daughter, well, at least we've been told that she's your daughter..."

"Kallie Hunt is my daughter," the congressman said in a strong, unapologetic voice. "Now continue."

Josh leaned back against the couch and told him everything, leaving out nothing, and ending at the part when the Fort Bragg soldier told Seth to U-turn the Taurus the hell away from the base.

While Josh spoke, Cleaver sat stoically, barely moving a muscle. He hadn't even seemed to breathe. And now that the telling was over, he leaned back in the chair and nodded his head sluggishly. He looked like a man who'd been put through a battery of tests and had now heard the doctor's confirmation of what he'd suspected all along. It's cancer and it's terminal. "What now?" Cleaver asked after sucking in and releasing a wearied breath.

"What?" Seth said, "You believe him?"

"I do," Cleaver said simply. He was looking at Josh when he said it, and the two of them exchanged knowing nods. They'd both known because Madame Isabel had known and written about it in her *Book of Origins*. Josh had only finished reading the book's depiction of this first meeting between him and the congressman, shortly after he and Seth had crossed into Wilmington proper. The congressman had first known five years ago, when he'd been approached by the mother of his firstborn, telling him of the occasion when he'd be asked to help his daughter. It had been welcomed news, as he'd always wanted a relationship with his daughter. He'd always needed and wanted to be in his daughter's life. He was waiting patiently for the day when he'd finally be able to tell her how much he'd loved her mother and had wanted to marry her. But it had been she who'd refused. She'd believed that an interracial marriage would hinder Ander Cleaver's political future. A future he hadn't even considered at that point in his life. But one she'd insisted was in the cards for him. And for reasons of her own, it had been Janie Hunt's decision to keep Kallie's birth and paternal parentage from the world at large. "What now?" Cleaver asked again.

"Can you call someone who can get ICE to release her?" Josh asked.

"If I can't," Cleaver said, "then, I've wasted twelve years in congress." He left the room and came back a short time later, carrying a sealed envelope. "Tell the guard at the gate that you're there to pick up Kallie Hunt, and then give him this envelope. They will bring Kallie to you." He handed Josh the envelope.

Josh took the envelope, running his fingers on the raised congressional seal.

"I want to see her," Cleaver said. "Can you tell her that?"

"Yes, I'll tell her," Josh said.

Cleaver escorted them to the door. "Is there anything else I can do?"

"Nothing I can think of at the moment," Josh said. "But you might want to consider getting new furniture for that upstairs bedroom and maybe ditching that picture on the dresser."

CHAPTER FORTY-ONE

It was time.

Swag's Volvo idled at the same military checkpoint where four hours earlier Seth and Josh had been refused entry. Swag stood outside his car, chitchatting with the very guard who'd spoken directly to Seth. "Are you going to do at least twenty years? I heard that was the magic number for military men."

"It is for the air force and army," the soldier replied. "I think the other branches have to serve about thirty years. It's all about retirement pay."

"Is that a fact?" Swag said absently. He was no longer interested. He was staring intently at the approaching jeep. It was she.

The guard followed Swag's eyes, seeing the jeep coming as well. "This is outside procedure. You must have some major pull, sir."

"I must do at that." Swag said.

The jeep pulled up and the guard walked over to the driver's side and handed the driver the envelope. The driver opened it, pulling out the paper inside. After reading it, he looked at Swag with a quick head to toe observation, and then he folded the paper, returning it to the envelope which he then placed in his jacket pocket. He turned to the soldier sitting next to him in the passenger's seat and nodded affirmatively.

The soldier got out of the jeep and helped Kallie from the backseat, escorting her over to the checkpoint where Swag stood waiting. The girl, obviously tired and drained, stepped forward, nearly collapsing into Swag's arms.

*　*　*

"You sure she'll be released?" Seth asked. They were back in the Taurus. Again, Seth was behind the wheel.

"You heard the congressman," Josh said without looking up. He was reading the book again.

"Yeah, the congressman," Seth said glibly. "What do you make of him believing all that nonsense about Kallie?"

"I don't make anything of it, Seth. You're the only who has his head still buried in the sand."

"It just doesn't make sense to me."

Josh looked up. "What doesn't make sense?"

"I know you think I haven't been paying attention to any of this. But I've heard everything you've said about eternal return, demons, reincarnation, and all that jazz. What I don't understand is why Kallie can't remember any of it. Even if she somehow believes she's this Kali reincarnated, why doesn't she know what this Swag character knows?"

Josh smiled. "Finally, you're asking an intelligent question."

"Well, give me an intelligent answer."

"I will, but first do you accept the concept of reincarnation?"

"Yes, for purposes of your explanation, I will accept the idea of reincarnation."

"Good," Josh said. "For purposes of trying to enlighten you despite your pigheadedness I'll accept your lukewarm acceptance. I think she may suffer from dissociative amnesia."

"Guess I shouldn't have asked."

Josh shook his head. "I disagree. If you don't know, you'd better ask somebody. Ignorance is not bliss; it's dangerous."

"Okay, what is dissociative amnesia? And how does it apply to Kallie? And please dumb it down."

"All right, I'll nutshell it. But you should understand that this is my analysis. I'm not a licensed psychologist and Kallie or Kali is not my patient. But I have studied her from her participation in our memory project and I've seen her brain scan. And I'm working toward my doctorate in..."

"Okay, okay," Seth said impatiently. "I'm not going to sue you if your analysis is wrong. Just tell me what you think."

"All right," Josh said. "I've read to you before about how Kali had been ousted from Heaven for her part in Lucifer's rebellion."

The Taurus climbed to nearly eighty mph and started to shake violently. Seth eased up on the gas, steadying it.
"Yeah, yeah, she was sent back as the first woman, Eve."

"Yes, exactly. When Lucifer found out that Kali had been sent to Earth in the form of a woman, he went to her and was determined to seduce her once again. Kali/Eve was living in the Garden of Eden with Adam. Though Kali missed Heaven, she loved being on Earth. She loved being Eve and most of all, she loved Adam. But Lucifer brought out things in her that she initially couldn't control. She'd been attracted to his badness. He understood that and used it to his advantage. Once again, he was able to get her to disobey God, except this time she'd also deceived her one true love, Adam. And of course you know how that part ends. God punishes her a second time and He punishes Adam as well, banishing them both from the Garden. Kali was mentally crushed. She couldn't believe she'd allowed Lucifer to use her again. She hated that she'd allowed it to happen. She hated being a victim to his deception. She wanted a redo. She wanted to go back to the very beginning and make it not so. But of course she couldn't really do that. So, she unconsciously did the next best thing. She blocked it all from her mind, convincing herself that it hadn't actually happened. She erased everything from her memory, totally dissociating herself from her past."

"That's a hell of a theory," Seth said. "Pardon the pun."

"I know. But like I said, I'm not Kallie or Kali's psychologist. So it's not official."

"Maybe not," Seth said. "But I guess it makes as much sense as anything else." He paused. "And you believe Kali as Kallie is still dissociating?"

"I do. But what will it take for you to believe any of this?"

Seth didn't answer immediately. He stared straight ahead, his eyes fixed firmly on the road. "I don't know," he said after a few moments. "I just don't know."

It was seven o'clock when they arrived at the base. The same guard as before was on duty. He stood at the booth and regarded them with a look of thankful pity like the old woman who loved bringing news of bad tidings. He stepped out of the booth and leaned down, peering inside the Taurus. "State your business."

"We're here to pick up Kallie Hunt," Seth said. He handed the guard the sealed envelope.

The guard took the envelope and walked back to the booth. Moments later, he returned and it looked to Josh as if he was smiling. The guard handed the envelope back to Seth. "She's gone."

"What do you mean, she's gone?" Seth demanded.

"It means exactly what I've said. Someone has already picked her up. Now sir, you'll need to turn this vehicle around."

"Wait a minute," Seth demanded. "That's not possible. How is she gone?"

"Sir, I suggest you seek answers to your questions elsewhere. The young woman Kallie Hunt is no longer on this base. Now turn your vehicle around or it will be impounded and your stay here will be a little longer than you've anticipated."

The veins at Seth's temples pulsed wildly. Josh patted him gently on his shoulder. "Let's go. We'll find her."

CHAPTER FORTY-TWO

"Something's not right," Seth said. "She's got to be on that base. That's guy's freaking lying!" They were on I-95, heading back toward Lumberton. The Taurus's speed was only forty-five mph, the interstate minimum. Kallie's grandmother was expecting to see her grandbaby. They were in no rush to get to Ms. Hunt's house without Kallie in tow.

Josh's cell phone chimed. He answered it. After listening for a few moments, he said, "It had your congressional seal as well?" He received his answer. Then he said, "No sir, I have no idea...yes sir, I will....goodbye." He ended the call and looked over at Seth. "A man presented a sealed envelope just like the one the congressman had given us. The guards released Kallie to him."

"What?" Seth asked. "Who?"

"I have a good idea. But we have to get back to Bengate."

"What about Ms. Hunt?"

"If who I think has Kallie, then we don't have any time to waste."

Seth hit the gas, pushing the Taurus up to seventy. "You think it's this Swag character, don't you?"

"Yeah, I do."

"You've been reading that *Book of Origins* like it's a predictor of the future. It didn't say anything about this? We're spinning our wheels here while this Swag guy's been steps ahead of us."

"I believe Swag was originally a Rememberer who's now demon-possessed. Madame Isabel was or is a Rememberer, though I believe strongly, it's was. Anyway, she and Swag would have generally remembered the same events. But now that Swag's demon-possessed, the demon within him also saw the same events and can alter them to his liking. Unfortunately, seeing is faster than reading."

"He was able to beat us to the punch because he now controls the machine?" Seth said. "Well you'd better flip on that light and get back to reading that book."

"Oh, so now you believe?" Josh taunted.

"We don't have time for pettiness. Just read the book and find out where we need to go."

"It's not going to be as easy as that. The book is no longer going to do us any good. In case you haven't realized it, we've gone off script. In the previous life-cycle, the Swag-demon doesn't get Kallie at Fort Bragg. We do. Now, I'm afraid we're moving in uncharted territory."

They got into Bengate at 10:15 p.m. They drove to Josh's apartment where they both availed themselves of the facilities and Josh retrieved his forty-five handgun. The gun was licensed, but Josh had never had occasion to use it for anything other than target shooting.

"You know how to use that thing?" Seth asked.

"Very much so," Josh said.

"You don't look like the gun-toting type."

"Why, is it because I'm a liberal? Understand, most liberals aren't against guns. They're against fools with guns."

"Will you be able use that thing to shoot Swag if it came to that?"

Josh started to say something, but hesitated, and then said, "Let's hope it doesn't come to it. Now let's boogie over to New Vibe."

Bennett had just exited his vehicle, heading to his niece's apartment, when he saw Kallie's boyfriend Seth driving a Taurus into the apartment complex. Bennett had been away eating lunch when the word had come down to release Kallie

Hunt. No one had consulted him. He hadn't even been given
fair warning that she would be allowed to walk. But that's
how it was sometimes. Crap always flowed down hill. It was
the rule of government physics. He'd had no idea who'd
picked her up or where they'd taken her. He drove to Bengate
as fast as he could and went by her house; but she wasn't
there. He parked his car alongside the curb outside her house
and waited for a while to see if she'd show. She didn't and he
couldn't wait any longer. Her neighbors were getting restless
and it wouldn't have been long before one of them called the
police. The order releasing Kallie had included a "no
harassment" warning written expressly for him. And he didn't
need any higher up to know that he'd blatantly disobeyed a
freshly given directive. But Kallie Hunt had answers to some
serious questions. He was certain that she'd been just about
ready to provide those answers when someone in brass pulled
the rug out from under him.

He'd decided to ride over to his niece's apartment on the
off chance that Kallie Hunt's boyfriend would come cruising
into the complex with the kid from that memory project thing
that Kallie Hunt had participated in. Of course, in actuality, it
wasn't the off chance he'd hoped for or had even anticipated,
but a gift from the gods. He deftly pulled behind the Taurus
as it high-tailed it out of the complex parking lot, with
Kallie's two friends and a forty-five handgun in tow (he'd
seen Josh pull it from his waistband, carefully placing it on
the floorboard of the Taurus), and heading to only God knew
where.

*　　*　　*

It was her wedding day, or rather night.

She'd never dreamt she'd buy her wedding gown off the
rack. Heck, she hadn't even considered it as a possibility

when as a starry-eyed little girl she'd lain in her bed at night as most girls usually did at some point in time and dreamt of such things. But there she'd been earlier that day, after having been released from military custody, at a cozy shop called Gowns-N-Things in St. Paul. The small town was located about seventeen miles north of Lumberton. She selected her dress from amongst a circular collection of many dresses. All of the dresses looked mostly the same, changing only in size—small, medium, or large. A gown off the rack? There was something ungodly about it. Weren't measurements needed? Alterations? Fittings? Maybe gowns off the rack were the latest trend, she thought, the prices of weddings being what they were. Of course, none of it mattered now. She was getting married, tonight. It was all so fast, yet it seemed so wickedly right. The timing was perfect. And she had no doubt that Johnny Swag was the man for her. She felt so alive with tumultuous passion whenever she was near him. Her feelings of lust and wanting felt so bad that they felt so good. And to top it off, he knew her. He knew her better than she knew herself. She'd heard of couples who could finish each other's sentences. What would those sick couples say about a man who could start hers? Yes, she'd convinced herself, marrying Swag was the right thing to do. It was destined.

*　*　*

McCarthy spent the entire afternoon preparing the sanctuary, robotically going about his duties. The smell had been the hardest thing to tackle and he wasn't sure how successful he'd been in getting rid of it, as his nose had grown somewhat accustomed to the horrendous smell that had nearly floored him when he'd first entered the church. There wasn't anything he could do about the busted out window panes. But he'd swept up most of the pages torn from the Bibles and hymnals, vacuumed up a lot of the black dirt spilled from the knocked over pots and plants, and he'd gathered up most of the wood from the severely damaged pews, placing them off to the side in a pile. There were still a good amount of stray leaves and petals sprinkled here and there, but for the most part, the place looked better suited to host a wedding, particularly if one's goal was to get married in a ransacked greenhouse. After he'd done all he could think to do, he hurried back to Swag's pastoral chambers to change into his ceremonial attire.

CHAPTER FORTY-THREE

The old woman told her she looked beautiful and Kallie wanted to believe her. It was, after all, her wedding night, and she wanted to be beautiful. In fact, she needed to feel beautiful. She was in a room at the back of the church, the one the choir used to change into their robes. The old woman was a senior member of the church. Johnny had called in some members of the congregation to assist in the wedding ceremony and to serve as witnesses to the most glorious event.

The woman brushed Kallie's hair away from her eyes. "I do believe you're the most beautiful of all the brides I've ever seen. And I've seen a lot. I'm ninety-one years old."

"Thank you," Kallie said softly. "I only wish my mother and grandmother were here to see me."

"Are they passed on?" the woman asked.

"My mother has. But my grandmother doesn't even know I'm getting married. She should be here. I should call her."

The woman continued brushing her hair. "There isn't time now, child. And you shouldn't worry. This is your night. It's your wedding night."

"Yes," Kallie said, "it is."

*   *   *

They were fifteen minutes away from the church. Seth was gripping the steering wheel so hard that his veins bulged out the back of his hands. He looked anxiously over at Josh. "You're sure there's nothing in that book we can use?"

"No, I'm not sure. There could be something related to it. All I know is that the scene we're riding up on is not in the book. I don't even know what we're riding into."

"Are you even sure they're at the church?"

"No," Josh said and looked out the passenger side window. "I have no idea where they are. I'm going on gut now. So, just get there."

Meanwhile at the church, it was a strange sight to behold. Father Frank McCarthy in full priestly regalia, standing stiffly at the altar, with a thick book of ceremonial rituals open in his hands. Swag stood next to him, awaiting his bride to march down the aisle to him. About twenty or so other exiled spirits residing in the bodies of his former congregants would bear witness to the event, perhaps the most spectacular one of all existence, the marriage of fallen angels.

Kallie entered the sanctuary from the north entrance. Two sullen faced preteen girls paced in front of her, dropping dead white and red roses in her path. Loud screeching music blasted from the walls, sounding as if untalented adolescents were behind them playing musical instruments for the very first time.

McCarthy read from the ceremonial book. "What the Dark Father brings together let no being cut asunder."

The witnesses murmured in unison. "Yes, old dark one. Yes master, receive your bride."

McCarthy continued. "Let all here witness a promise finally fulfilled."

The witnesses chorused, "Yes, old dark one. Yes master, receive your bride."

McCarthy cleared his throat. "Two beings falsely cast out from Heaven will join together in Earthly bond, and then together claim their rightful thrones in Heaven."

"Yes, old dark one. Yes master, receive your bride."

* * *

The Taurus pulled into New Vibe's parking lot. Seth and Josh had just opened their respective doors when a blue sedan pulled in roughly behind the Taurus.

Bennett got out of the sedan. "Hold it right there, fellas, and tell me what's going on."

Seth said, "Listen, mister. I don't know what your problem is or what you want. But we're kind of in a hurry."

Bennett pulled out his identification. Then, looking at Josh, he said, "I need to know what you're planning to do with that gun."

Josh backed up cautiously. "Be careful, Seth. I know him, but he could be possessed."

"Holy crap," Seth said. "Swag is still a step ahead of us. What should we do?"

Bennett looked curiously from one to the other. "What are you two talking about? Who's Swag?"

Josh looked anxiously at the church. He didn't know what was supposed to happen, but he had a sense that time was running short. "Your boss, or should I say your master," Josh said.

Bennett followed Josh's gaze to the church, and then noticed the sign. "Reverend Johnny Swag. Wait a minute, you two are planning to kill a preacher?"

"He's no preacher," Seth said. "He's a demon."

"Seth!" Josh shouted.

"We don't have time to be out here lolly-gagging," Seth said. "Either shoot that son of a bitch or tell him what's going on."

"Yes, one of you had better tell me what's going on," Bennett said.

"Listen," Josh said. "We don't have a whole lot of time. Swag is demon-possessed and he picked up our friend today from Fort Bragg. He's dangerous and we don't know what he's planning to do with her. But whatever it is, it's going down right now while we're out here shooting the crap with you."

Bennett said, "Kallie Hunt's inside this church?"

"Yes!" Seth said. "Now can we go?"

"Yes," Bennett said, turning toward the church. "Let's go."

CHAPTER FORTY-FOUR

McCarthy cleared his throat again. "If there's any being here who objects to the joining of these two, speak now or forever..."

"I object!" Seth shouted. He'd run into the sanctuary. Josh was dead on his heels and Bennett was close behind him.

A collective hiss rose angrily from the congregation. Josh waved the forty-five wildly from side to side. Bennett grabbed the arm of the hand holding the gun. "What are you doing?"

Josh snatched back from him. "I don't know how effective this thing will be. But I suggest you get your hand off me and pull out yours. This ain't Kate and William's wedding. Look around!"

Bennett, still holding tight to Josh's arm, looked all around him. The place looked out of sorts. The windows were smashed. Pews were askew. Some were even damaged, a couple completely. Their remains piled in a heap against the wall. The place looked storm-ravaged. A hint of something foul-smelling bandied about the air. Then, after staring into the lifeless eyes of a few of the congregants sitting in the pews, he shuddered. "My God...."

McCarthy stopped reading and looked toward the objection.

"Continue," Swag commanded him.

McCarthy's body shifted nervously. He seemed at a loss as to what to do next.

"The book!" Swag shouted. "Finish reading the passage."

McCarthy cleared his throat once again and shuffled his shoulders as if trying to regain his composure. "If anyone..."

"You've read that," Swag said angrily. "Skip down to…" and he said, "now do you Kali..."

"Uh, yes, yes, of course," McCarthy said. He turned to Kali. "Do you, Kali, take Lucifer, to have and to hold for all of existence? To..."

"Kallie!" Seth shouted, interrupting McCarthy again. He ran toward the front of the church. One of the congregants, a rather large fellow, started to rise, obviously intending to impede Seth's trek to the altar. Josh spotted him and shot his gun into the air. It struck the ceiling, causing plaster to flutter down upon the congregation like dirty snow, startling the bruiser long enough for Seth to scoot past him.

After Seth called out to her, Kallie froze where she stood, her mouth agape.

She was facing away from him as he approached the altar. He spoke to her back. "I love you, Kallie."

When she finally turned around, it was as if Seth was seeing her for the very first time. She was standing there in her white wedding gown, pulsing with unimaginable energy. She was the most beautiful creature he'd ever laid eyes upon. And in that one instant, standing at the front of the defiled church, amongst heathens and dead flowers, knocked over potted plants and trees, in that one instant, in a place eerily symbolic of the Garden after the Fall of Man, his eyes were opened. "Eve." The name, one he hadn't uttered consciously in eons, rolled with pleasurable awareness off his lips.

Tears streamed down Kallie/Kali/Eve's face and her face glowed suddenly with her own renewed recognition. "Adam."

They ran to each other. Their two bodies and life forces collided and meshed, casting potent rainbow light throughout the church. The light curbed in front of McCarthy, slapping him violently across his face and knocking him against the front of the choir stand and ultimately back to his original senses. Within moments, he shook off his mind's fogginess and slowly regained a consciousness he hadn't had since his initial viewing of Swag's video.

All of this took place in a matter of seconds with Swag watching it all in utter disbelief and disgust. He'd waited an eternity for his revised moment and had been willing to give Kali her third chance at fulfillment. And she, after having betrayed him twice already—once in Heaven and then again in Eden—chose to betray him, yet a third time. She was the quintessential tease, refusing to go the distance. But this would be her last time deceiving him. Kali, he'd decided, would have to be destroyed.

Swag hissed at her. Kallie/Kali/Eve let go of Seth/Adam and turned around. "Lucifer," she said with absolute clarity. "This will be the last time you deceive me."

"Funny," Swag/Lucifer said. "I was just thinking the same thing."

He swiped at her face, drawing first blood.

She rubbed her cheek, wiping the blood with her fingers. She tasted it. She opened her mouth and let out the high-pitched scream that only demons could hear. The unclean spirits in the congregation, motionless during the recent fracas started trembling noisily as if they'd never heard anything so awful in all of their existence. Kallie, who'd quickly become an old hand at demonic destruction, leapt at Lucifer.

Lucifer stumbled back, his eyes flaming bright red with anger and hatred.

Kallie/Kali/Eve landed in front of him, stepping forward softly. "Johnny, are you in there? I can help you, but you must push him out. Can you hear me? You must push him out. "

Lucifer smiled. "Ah, it's the young preacher you seek? I can assure you that he's been a most kind host since London. But, I'm afraid he will no longer be joining us in this Earthly realm. But if it's any consolation to you, I can report that he went kindly into that good night, and didn't put up nearly half the struggle as your little fat Professor Sampson."

Kallie/Kali/Eve swung out, scraping her fingernails across Lucifer's face, drawing blood. "I've defeated you before and I will again." She opened her mouth, letting loose her high-pitched squeal.

Frowning, Lucifer/Swag pulled at his ears. He looked over toward the choir stand where Father McCarthy was just now getting back onto his feet. A bewildered and dazed McCarthy reached inside of his robe and pulled out the earplugs he'd found earlier in the filing cabinet. He studied the plugs for a moment and then looked curiously up at Lucifer. The dark one stared at the priest menacingly, still grabbing at Swag's human ears. The priest smiled knowingly, and then popped both plugs into his mouth, swallowing them.

Lucifer glanced around the room, shouting at his loyal subjects, who themselves were in varying amounts of distress. "Mutare corpora, ut in eis! *Change bodies and get her!*

The demons immediately left their current human hosts and leapt into the bodies of Josh, Seth/Adam, and Bennett. Instantly, the three of them turned toward Kallie, rushing toward her.

Kallie/Kali/Eve, seeing them coming at her, stopped her high-pitched squealing. "Fight them," she commanded. "It's your body, push them out. Tell them to leave. They're not welcome."

Bennett had no Earthly idea what was happening. One minute he was watching the weird unraveling of the strangest wedding he'd ever witnessed, and the next he'd felt some type of malevolent force enter into his body, controlling his very movements and desires, making him want to rape, maim, and plunder. But first, he was to have his way with Kallie Hunt. He'd felt an urging and was just about to act on it when Kallie Hunt's voice pushed through the heightening madness in his head. Bennett forced himself onto his knees and gripped his head with his hands. He was not a deviant psychopath! "Get out of me, damn you! You're not welcome."

Josh had known that demonic possession was possible. But he hadn't known the swiftness in which it could happen. The malevolent spirit entered his body with such rapidity that it had taken him by surprise, and before he'd realized what he was doing, he was moving toward Kallie, gun drawn, intending to empty the chamber into her body. But then, Kallie/Kali/Eve spoke to him. Her voice was symphonic, commanding. Josh threw the gun across the room and rooted his feet in the carpet where he stood.

Seth/Adam had only taken a step toward Kallie/Kali/Eve with the unclean spirit inside of him. He'd just gotten Eve back and there was no way in Heaven or Hell he'd lose her again. The power of love within him helped vanquish the invading evil spirit within moments of its arrival inside his body. But just as quickly as the weaker evil spirit had been evicted, a more powerful one took its place. And this one, empowered by a violent rage birthed before the creation of man, took root quickly and firmly, silencing Seth/Adam before he knew what hit him.

All the unclean spirits, including the ones expunged from Josh, Bennett, and Seth/Adam immediately gathered together, forming a big dark mass. The sound of their demonic collaboration sounded like nuclear thunder. Its appearance was that of a black, heavy rain-filled storm cloud. With maddening quickness, the demonic mass rushed toward Kallie/Kali/Eve with hurricane-wind like speed and force.

But Kallie/Kali/Eve was now emboldened and strengthened by the complete knowledge and full awareness of who and what she was. She destroyed the rudderless mass of evil in a matter of minutes. And when she finished off the last of it, she looked around the church for her existential nemesis. But the spirit of Lucifer had long since departed the former Reverend Johnny Swag, leaving the young minister's lifeless shell slumped at the altar.

Kallie/Kali/Eve heard footsteps fast approaching behind her. She turned and saw her beloved Seth/Adam coming quickly toward her. She ran into his embrace, kissing him passionately.

"Marry me," Seth/Adam said. "Right here, right now."

"We don't have a marriage license," she said and kissed him again.

"We can get one later," he said, "let's commit to each other now."

And that made perfect sense, she thought. Their love and commitment to each other was much stronger than any law or slip of paper could ever convey. "Yes," she said. "I'll marry you, right here, right now."

They both turned to Father McCarthy, who was still standing near the choir stand. He smiled at them. "So, we'll have a wedding after all. I believe I can conjure up the words."

They all gathered around the altar, the priest, the bride and groom, and the two human witnesses. Seth/Adam looked into his soon-to-be-wife's eyes. "With all my heart I love thee and will gladly take thee as my wife."

Kallie/Kali/Eve looked into her future husband's eyes. "I love thee as well. And I..." she paused. His once vibrant brown eyes looked dark and foreboding. "What movie always makes me cry?"

"What?" Seth/Adam asked.

"There's a movie that always makes me cry," she said. "What's the name of it?"

"What does it matter?" he asked. "I love you."

"And I love you. And I know that your favorite fruit is an apple and your favorite color is light blue. Don't you know what movie makes me cry?"

Father McCarthy smiled. "It may sound irrelevant, son. But marriage is not to be entered into lightly. If you don't know these answers, there's no harm in waiting until you truly know each other."

"But, I'm Adam," Seth/Adam said, nearly screaming. "Who knows you better than me?"

"Perhaps no one," Kallie/Kali/Eve said. "But what movie makes me cry?"

"I don't know, damn it!" Seth/Adam said and this time he was screaming. "I don't know!"

"Well, you should know," Kallie/Kali/Eve said. And she opened her mouth, letting loose her ultrasonic scream which only demons could detect. Seth/Adam's body convulsed rapidly and seconds later, Lucifer's demonic spirit was unceremoniously expelled from it. As soon as the last of it was free of Seth/Adam's body, Lucifer hissed wickedly at Kallie/Kali/Eve. His form was that of a giant snake and it stretched high above her, his forked tongue slapping down at her. Kallie glared up at him, readying herself to gnash him to bits. But he quickly came back down to her eye level, first as Johnny Swag, and then as a priest, next a child, a suburban mom, an elderly lady, each form lasting but a second, flashing before her like the broken tape of a movie reel. Suddenly the images slowed, until finally ending with one of the Christian Savior morphing into that of the classical Devil, complete with fiery red eyes and horns. And then he was gone. Kallie waved her arms out in front of her, not entirely sure if the Great Deceiver was truly gone. But it was just air in front of her. The others, save Seth/Adam who was still slumped at the altar, moved about the trashed church, looking for any signs of a demonic presence. But there were none. The demons and their leader had vanished into nothingness as if they hadn't ever existed at all.

With his body now demon-free, Seth/Adam rose to his feet and stumbled toward Kallie/Kali/Eve, collapsing at her feet. She kneeled down beside him. Wearily, he looked up into her eyes and said breathlessly, "The Wizard of Oz."

CHAPTER FORTY-FIVE

It wasn't until the spring of the following year that Bennett finally got around to flying back to Philadelphia to see Father McCarthy. Although no one could have ever accused him of being religious or even a somewhat semi-regular churchgoer, Bennett had made it a point throughout his adulthood to occasionally step foot inside a church at least once or twice every blue moon, if for no other reason than to pacify the ghost of his dead aunt, his mother's sister, who had raised him and Helen after their mother's death. In life, his aunt, for whatever reason, had always been very concerned about his church attendance. And for the most part, he'd always complied with her unspoken desires, communicated it seemed, even now from the afterworld. That was of course until the events of last fall. Since that time, he'd steered way clear of all places of worship.

"Hmm," McCarthy said after Bennett had confessed this to him. They were sitting on the bench at the end of the basketball court behind the parish. It was a beautiful late spring afternoon. They'd already played two games of one-on-one. Bennett won the first game and McCarthy took the second one. They decided to take a break before playing the rubber match. "That's very interesting. I'd just assumed your church attendance had increased. I mean you can no longer doubt...."

"No, I don't doubt," Bennett interjected. "But that's just it. What's the point in going to church? None of those preachers really know anything about what I witnessed. I was freaking possessed. I was raised a Lutheran. I don't even think we believe in possession. At least my church didn't preach about it. Oh, they've railed on and on about the demons of alcohol, and fornication, and all that jazz, but nothing about actual demonic possession. It seems to me that to them, Satan is only a concept. You know, a symbol of evil?"

McCarthy didn't say anything for a few moments. Then, quietly he added, "He's much more than that." He paused again. "But that's not the only reason to attend church. You should go for the fellowship. The communion with others in the glorification of the Creator, and, as you say, all that jazz."

"Yeah, maybe," Bennett said and didn't complete his thought. He waited a few moments before asking, "Will the next terrorist attack also be a demonic gate-opening?"

"Doubtful," McCarthy said. "But anything's possible. As I've told you, Principe was a Rememberer who'd become demonically possessed. That's how he found out about opening the demon portals in the first place. Most terrorists are simply that, terrorists. Initially, even A.I. hadn't known about the portals."

"Why didn't you tell me about this the first time I came to Philadelphia?"

"If I'd told you, would you have believed me?" McCarthy asked.

Bennett rubbed his chin and breathed in deeply. "No, I guess not."

McCarthy nodded knowingly.

After another few moments of silence, Bennett asked, "Do you think those two are really Adam and Eve?"

"Yes," McCarthy said without pausing to consider the question. "I really do."

They became quiet again, both enjoying the relative peacefulness of it. Yet and still, they knew evil lurked all around them. It was never vanquished completely. It was a reality they both understood all too well.

*   *   *

His head was lying on her lap. They were at the park, enmeshed in the essence of each other; the sound of gleeful playing youth surrounded them. She rubbed her fingers through his hair, enjoying the moment. She'd forgotten how soft his hair was. Then again, she'd forgotten everything. Seth had told her about Josh's disassociation theory, even admitting that he evidently had fallen victim to it as well sometime after their original banishment from the Garden. Whether the theory was true or not, she supposed didn't matter now. The two of them were together again.

"Why did he do it? Lucifer, I mean?" Seth asked. "Why would he show you how to destroy demons?"

"It's part of his deception. He knew I would eventually find out anyway. But he figured that by then he would be in control of my mind." She said this without a trace of bitterness, just simply as a matter of fact.

"But he watched you kill so many of his own," Seth said.

"That's just it. Lucifer doesn't care about others. He's about self. Always has been, always will be. People or beings will foolishly follow him, but he'll care about none of them. Only himself, that's all that matters to him."

They were silent for a while, and then she said finally, "I've never said I was sorry."

"About what?" Seth said.

"Everything," Kallie said, and it was as if just saying the words had lifted a heavy weight from her chest. "If not for me, you wouldn't have been banished forever from the Garden."

"I don't know," Seth said. "I was bound to screw it up sooner or later."

She laughed, playfully bopping him on the head. "Silly."

"Besides," he said, and he was serious, "I didn't have to bite the apple."

And it was true, he didn't have to. "Then why did you?" Kallie asked.

Seth looked up at the sky. It was a gorgeously clear blue. "For the one reason that I don't even think He'd considered. In fact, I know Lucifer didn't. I love you, Kallie. I always have. And I always will. We're cosmically connected. And there's nothing anyone, or any being can do about it."

"I love you too, Seth," she said. And then she leaned down and kissed him fully on the lips.

THE END

Other Works by C. Edward Baldwin

Fathers House (A Crime Fiction Novel, available now at Amazon and most places where paperbacks are sold-IndieBound)

Giovanni's Metamorphosis & the Road to Same Sex Marriage in America (A Kindle Single essay)

A Needful Change & Other Stories (A book of short stories)

From 1-3 to Champions (A non-fiction self help book, April 2015)

In 2016, be on the lookout for Book 2 in the Rememberers series, Killing God

Find C. Edward Baldwin:

FaceBook

Pinterest

LinkedIn

Twitter

Tumblr

Goodreads

I hope you enjoyed this novel as much as I enjoyed writing it.
Thank you!

CPSIA information can be obtained at www.ICGtesting.com
Printed in the USA
BVOW04s1031210415

396851BV00001B/1/P